I Got Love for A Philly Thug

-

A Standalone by Giselle Gates

Acknowledgement

If it wasn't for Rahmah Chaplin, I probably wouldn't have written this book, lol. Thank you so much for helping me and making me feel like I'm from Philly.

Thank you for purchasing, "I Got Love for A Philly Thug." Feel free to browse Amazon and the Lit Reading App for the rest of my catalog, I hope you enjoy and thank you for the support. Below is a list of my previous work and social media contact.

- Shawty Got A Gangsta In His Feelings 1-3
- Daughter of a Trap King 1-4
- I Love You For My Soul 1-3
- You Might Be My Plug For Love 1-4
- My Louisiana Thug 1-3
- The First 48: Money Making Meeka 1 -3
- He Was My Thuggish Valentine (A Novella)
- No Matter What, I Choose You 1 and 2 Finale
- Married to a New York Menace 1 and 2 Finale
- One Kiss For All My Troubles
- Ain't No Love In Hip Hop: Love vs Fame 1 and 2 Finale
- If The Hood Could Talk (An Urban Paranormal)
- Witches from the Eastside (An Urban Paranormal)
- The Good Girl Who Loved A Savage 1 and 2
- Girls Like Me Love Gangstas Like You 1 and 2 Finale

Social Media

- Facebook: Giselle Gates
- Instagram: @gisellegates_theauthor
- Snapchat: Authorki16
- Facebook Like Page: Authoress Giselle Gates
- Reading Group: Just Kickin' It With G.G.

"Damn, man, this shit wasn't supposed to turn out the way it did. She was everything, the woman of my dreams, my soulmate, but I didn't want to admit it, and most importantly, my best friend. I treated her like shit, and now I can't take any of it back. She was a good woman, but I didn't love, or treat her, like she was a good woman. Never in a million years I thought life would be like this without her. Damn." ~ *Clover Porter, aka, Spitta.*

Chapter 1 (May 5th, 2008)

I never really knew what love was while growing up. Shit, maybe because I never had a true example of it staring me in the face. With my pops being killed by a dirty cop, and a mom rarely home, because she was trying to make ends meet, I taught myself what love meant. My pops was too heavy in the streets to be at home showering us with love. Don't get me wrong, it was love in the house, but not the kind of love I watched on shows like the *Brandy Bunch.*

A lot of times, I questioned myself what the fuck love was, but now I know. Love is kind, love is pure, love is patient, and love is also something I took for granted for a long fuckin' time. To me, love is also Manhattan Mullen. Baby girl was pure like cocaine from Columbia, real rap! When I met her, I finally had a true example of love looking me dead in my eyes.

It all stared back in 2008, I was just a young bol, pedaling pills for my older brother Smoke. I was trying to make a name for myself in the trenches and drug game, plus, fuck as many bad bitches my dick would allow me to. Besides sleeping with everything that had a pulse, buying fast cars, and rocking designer clothes, I didn't see much in my future. Well, besides death, or the pen, that's the only shit I saw for myself. I didn't know what I wanted out of life until I spotted Manhattan walking out of the Wells Fargo Bank over on Walnut Street.

She wore an all-black Nike jogging two-piece suit, with black running shoes. I was so stunned by her smile and beauty, I let her get to the red light that fast. I swear, man, that girl made time freeze when she uttered that first word to your boy. Nearly wrecking my Camaro trying to dodge through traffic, I managed to stop her, but also stop traffic. Horns were honking like crazy and drivers were calling me everything, but a child of God. It's not like I cared though, I've been called worse by better people. I just had to get her attention and number by any means. If not, I would regret it for the rest of the day, fuck, probably the rest of the week.

Jumping out of my car looking fly as usual, Manhattan honked her horn, also cursing me out. She was so bougie that her cursing was corny and cute to me. Pronouncing the entire words and not shouting them out in broken English sounded weird as fuck.

"What the fuck are you doing? Are you serious right now, joe ass nigga?"

"I'm dead ass serious right now. Beautiful woman, can I have your name?" I asked her, while leaning against the window trying to grab her hand. Hat wasn't having that shit, and didn't waste any time sizing me up. Pulling away quickly, with a mug on her face, Hat replied, "nigga, no, I don't know you!"

"Girl, stop playing, I know you know me. Shit, you at least heard of me in these Philly streets," I licked my black lips, smirking. Removing the big brown sunglasses from her face, Manhattan said, "I've heard OF you, but I don't know you, Clover, is it?"

"Yea, Clover Porter, but my jawns call me Spitta. Can I have your name so I can stop holding up traffic?"

"I'm Manhattan, Manhattan Mullen, but my jawns call me Hat," she replied, flipping her long, brown bouncy hair, trying not to smirk. By the way her lips trembled, she struggled not to like a motherfucker.

"It's nice to meet you, Hat." After waiting for me to move, cars started to drive pass us, sticking me the middle finger. I could only laugh, talking to her was worth every middle finger flipped at me and curse word. It's not like I haven't been called a black motherfucker before. Hearing that was like music to my ears, yo.

"Damn, you're going to have the whole city pissed off, you drawlin' at nine in the morning," she laughed, flipping her hair again, exposing the entire beauty of her face. If you ask me to describe Manhattan …. I turned into a square quick, bro. She was breathtaking, with plump pink lips that she never embraced. I always told her to be secure about the things she saw as flaws. Though I saw them as something to praise on the daily. Her innocent behavior was precious to me, Manhattan could never do any wrong in my eyes. Now, some people didn't think she was all that, and as beautiful as I always described. Some defined Manhattan as plain, because her backside wasn't pumped with ass shots, she wore her real hair, and rarely covered her face with a touch of make-up. I loved her that way, Hat's clear skin was flawless, it was perfect to me.

"Fuck them joes, your conversation is worth it," I smiled.

"Oh, really?" She spoke sarcastically, making me raise my eyebrows with a big grin on my face.

"Very much so, but do you have a boyfriend? I don't want to have to beat up anybody for talking to their girlfriend."

"No, I don't, I've been single for a while now," she stated, looking in her side mirror at the traffic. With every curse that was thrown at us, Manhattan snickered a little bit more. I guess after hearing 'black ass bitch' a dozen times, it became funny to her.

"Damn, a girl like you shouldn't be single when a man like me is walking this earth," I smiled.

"Boy, you have a way with words," she rolled her eyes, placing the sunglasses onto her face. Slowly grabbing her hand, she didn't she pull away this time, I replied, "I'm just being honest, maybe I can change that one day."

"Why would you want to change that, Mr. Porter, I like being single."

"I bet after spending a few hours with me, that will change," I licked my lips again, stating. By the way Manhattan hesitated, but smiled at me, I already knew she was feeling a nigga big time, yo. It didn't matter how much she thought she could hid it, I could see the love in Manhattan's eyes already.

"I don't do good with bets, homeboy," she laughed.

"Shit, I'm glad to know that, but do you want to know something else?"

"What, Clover?"

"I think …… You should put my number in that phone, we should talk on a daily, I take you on a date every week, we fall in love, then we can live happily ever after."

"Bol, is that all the game you got?" She laughed.

"It's not game, Miss Manhattan. I would love to take you out to dinner and talk more, we can go wherever you want to."

"I don't know about all of that fall in love mess, but I'll give you my number," grabbing her phone from the passenger's side and handing it to me, I didn't waste a second programming my number into her phone. Once I was done, I handed it to her, saying, "now you're stuck with me for life." I laughed, but smacking her lips, Manhattan said, "once again, you're drawlin, but I like your style. You gotta lil' flavor to you," she laughed.

"Just a lil' bit stank," I laughed as well.

"Yea, just a lil' bit, but before we get ran over, I need to go. It was nice meeting you Mr. Porter, have a nice day," blowing me a kiss and laughing, Manhattan drove off in her red Mustang with the top back. Her hair blew in the wind like she was in a music video or something. I was left standing in the middle of Walnut Street, blushing, but hoping she would call me soon.

See, what Manhattan didn't know is that I've watching her for a lil' minute now. What else she didn't know is that I knew she was watching me too. She wasn't the type of shorty to approach a nigga like me, but I couldn't blame her. With the reputation I had ……. I probably wouldn't approach me either.

Finally hoping into my car speeding off, I grabbed my phone to see if Hat called yet. She didn't, I felt mad thirsty, but brushed it off turning my music up. On a day like this, the temperature was right, and it had me feeling good. All I needed was a bad bitch on my side, but none of these hoes could keep my attention after I caught a nut. It was still early in the day, you never know what will happen when the sun sets, and the street lights come on, on a Saturday night.

Ten minutes later, I pulled up to my brother, Smoke's, house in Chesnut Hill. Clerk Porter, one of the realist jawns I knew, a solid as nigga is what Philly labeled him. Clerk got the nickname Smoke when he was eighteen years old. Most people thought because he smoked a lot, but that wasn't the reason at all. Smoke was wild and didn't mind leaving your block full of gun smoke if he ever felt like you were drawlin or he felt disrespected.

"Yizzzoooo, Big Smoke," I said, jumping out my car dapping him down. Making sure I grabbed my phone, I laughed at myself. This girl really had me hooked already.

"What's the move, young boy?" Smoke didn't make eye contact with me as he sprayed tire cleaner on his tires. Smoke was sweating bricks, but he loved cleaning his cars. Even when his 1984 Oldsmobile Cutlass or Range Rover wasn't dirty, he was still baking in the sun to clean them. Smoke and I were close, I told him everything. He was loyal in the game, which is why everyone respected and looked up to him.

"Fuckin off as usual, I'm really waiting for Carter to call me. I gotta pick him up from the airport, yo."

"Bet, bet, I talked to Harlem earlier, he said his homie from Queens got stabbed today," Smoke shook his head, making sweat splash everywhere. I took a few steps back saying, "damn, I know exactly who you're talking about. Johnny could have stayed in Rikers Island for all that," I laughed.

"Niggas want a sob story when they get in the can, but they forget how they was jacking niggas in the streets. He better be lucky that nigga didn't slice his neck like a turkey for Thanksgiving," he chuckled.

"Real rap, but do you remember that lil' chick that told Kansas I was cute?"

"Yea, ain't her name Hattan," he questioned.

"No, nigga, it's Manhattan, but anyways, picture, I saw her on Walnut Street like twenty minutes ago. I stopped traffic to get shorty's number," I laughed.

"What?" Smoke dropped the blue sponge, laughing. Thinking about it and saying it aloud, I sounded like a damn fool for that stunt.

"Word to Mommy, we were all in the middle of the street talking like it was legal. I've been watching shorty for a Lil' minute though, never really had the right moment to make my move on her."
"So, you thought making your move in the middle of traffic was," Smoke asked, shaking his head. After letting sweat drip into his eyes, he finally used his tight wife-beater to wipe his drenched face. Smoke was one of those big swole niggas, who looked like he spent most of his life locked up in San Quentin State Prison. Smuts love that shit, gave them something to lust over.

"What'cho yella ass think? You know I had to make my presence. Even if she doesn't call me, she'll always think about the day Spitta held up traffic to talk to her," I laughed.

"Ard, Casanova, I hear you," he laughed, but grabbed the sponge to continue to clean his car. Before I could say anything, my phone began to ring in my pocket.

"Yoooooo," I placed the phone on speaker, waiting for the caller to say something. Before speaking, they cleared their throat saying, "uhh, is this, Clover?"

"Yea, but who is this?"

"It's Manhattan, the girl you stopped traffic for," she laughed a little.

"I didn't forget about you that fast, baby girl. It's no need for an introduction," I chuckled.

"Hey, I had to make sure you knew who I was, didn't want to get called the wrong name."

"Never that, but what's up with you, kinda surprised you called," I uttered, shuffling in my pockets for my pack of swisher sweets and bag of weed. Once I found it, I motioned for Smoke to roll me a fat sweet.

"Good, I needed a smoke break," he laughed, walking towards me to grab the stuff from my hands.

"Huh," she stated.

"My bad, that was my brother talking, but like I said, I'm surprised you call."

"To be honest, I wasn't going to call at you first," Manhattan answered.

"Why not and what made you call?"

"Let's be real, Clover Porter. Your name is ringing in the streets and it's not for saving kittens out of burning trees," Manhattan laughed.

"I know, I know, but I'm young and single. Maybe if I had a girl like you in my life all that would change," I smiled as if she could see me. Maybe if she could see the smile on my face, Manhattan would know how serious I was about getting to know her.

"You never know who that woman will be, because I'm not a girl," she giggled.

"You're right, you're all woman. Since you made this phone call, what's next with us?"

"What? We're going to finish this conversation. Maybe we can meet in a PUBLIC place for lunch today or tomorrow."

"Ard, but why did you say public like that," I asked.

"Because you might be crazy, yo," she laughed.

"You won't find out until you spend time with me. I promise, I won't bite you unless you want me to."
"Are you trying to turn me on," Manhattan giggled.

"Only if you want me to," I chuckled, shaking my head.

***

"Hooonnneeeyyyyyy, I'm home," Manhattan shouted, walking into her sister's house, heading straight for her room.

"I'm in the room, Lucy," she shouted back in an Italian accent. Walking into the room with her sunglasses and keys in her hand, Manhattan gave Marcy a quick hug.

"What's up with you, sis," Manhattan asked, while sitting on the end of her sister's bed.

"Girl, just got off, I'm fuckin tired, word to," kicking her black work shoes off, Marcy rubbed the back of her aching neck. She was sleepy as fuck, but rather stay up gossiping with Manhattan.

"I'm going to be the same way tomorrow, but that bag is more important than sleep."

"Hell yea, but where are you coming from," she asked.

"The bank, but guess who I ran into and stopped traffic for me," dropping her head, because Manhattan knew her answer would shock Marcy sister, she slightly chuckled.

"Who, Hat," Marcy inquired.

"Spitta."

"Spitta, Spitta who, I only know one Spitta," Marcy revealed.

"We're probably talking about the same Spitta, Clover Porter," she mumbled.

"Ugghh, what were you doing even talking to him or giving his ass the time of day?"

"What' cha mean, ugghh, I thought you and Clover were kind of coolish?"

"Girl, just because I'm fucking a few of his homies and young bols don't mean we're cool. Since I was fucking with Teddy way back, I couldn't stand his ass. I guess you won't let that lil' crush on him die down, but you need to. Nothing good will come out of fooling with Clover Porter."

"Why not, he seems like a pretty cool dude? I mean, he DID stop traffic to get my number," Hat cracked a smile, staring at the floor, but it quickly faded away when Marcy gave her a stale face. Placing her hands on her hips, Marcy shook her head laughing at her sister. She didn't mind making Manhattan feel like shit for liking him.

"Hat, I'm pretty sure that wasn't his first time doing that to get some random smut's attention. Anyways, Clover is full of himself, arrogant, a HOE, and so damn rude. Girl, I'm telling you now, stay farrrrr away him, you won't regret it. We got into it two weeks ago for him being all in my mix with Gary."

"What? What happened," she asked.

"Girl, I tried busting Gary's tires, but he come running out of TNT not minding his own damn business," pulling the short blonde wig off her, Marcy walked to her closet to place the wig on the shelf. Then she pulled the stocking cap off searching her closet for a few pieces of clothing.

"Why were you trying to bust his jawns," Hat laughed.

"Because he won't learn until I stab his ass, but back to Spitta. He started running his mouth saying I needed to move around because I was drawlin'. Hat, what the fuck I didn't tell his Lil' black ass. You know them niggas from north Philly don't have respect for women, so he called me all kinds of bitches and hoes. I'm telling you now, leave that garbage in the projects for them no lives bitches!"

"Damn, Marcy, I didn't say I wanted to marry the dude tomorrow."

"If you're not thinking about marriage, why bother wasting your time with anyone at this point," Marcy asked.

"Uummm, Marcy, you're thirty-five, not married, and fooling around with some young bols," Hat expressed.

"Unlike you, I never said I want to be in love, married, and with a bunch of kids running through my house. We all know that's your dreams, not mines!"

"Ohhh whatever, you said that, but I know you want love. If not, why are involved with so many people? You're looking for love and you don't even know it!"

"No, I'm looking for good dick and a great time, that's it," Marcy rolled her eyes in the direction of Manhattan as she removed the smelly clothes from her body. Standing there in her mismatch bra and panties, she tried her best to throw salt on my name. I guess she never heard the old saying, 'The heart wants, what the heart wants.'

"You act like it's a bad thing I want love, kids, and a marriage," Manhattan uttered.

"I never said that, but if you're fucking with Spitta, that won't be in your present or future. Like I said, stay far away from him, that's the best advice I'll ever give you in life. When you DO get married to someone, we're going to sit back and laugh at how you lowered your standards by talking to him for a second."

"Enough of that, where are you going," Manhattan questioned.

"I'm going bend a few blocks with Gary's ass," she laughed.

"Lord, Marcy, but hey, do your thang," Manhattan laughed, tossing her hands in the air.

"Your ex-boo asked about you," Marcy smiled, pulling her hair into a high ponytail.

"Who and I hope you're not talking about June," flaring her nose, but Manhattan also rolled her eyes hoping her sister wasn't talking about her ex-boyfriend.

June Falcon and Manhattan dated two years ago, a relationship that only lasted a year. June was from southwest Philly, a real square ass nigga.

"You know it and of course he asked about you," she blushed, but Manhattan sat there with a stale look on her face.

"I don't know why, that nigga made my life a living hell when we broke up. He has no reason to be dramatic like he was!"

"Girl, don't say that bol made your life a living hell," Marcy uttered.

"You don't re-call calling me non-stop, popping up to my house unannounced, and not taking NO for an answer, making my life a living hell???"

"No, that's called fighting for his relationship, that was sweet to me. June is an overall sweet guy, I sure do miss him being around. His clown ass kept me laughing," Marcy laughed.

"Well, if you miss his annoying ass that much, date him. I'm giving you my permission and my blessing, hunn."

"Girl, fuck you, I don't want your sloppy seconds."

"Okay, now we can end this conversation about June," Hat uttered.

"How about this, we end the entire jawn. It seems like you're in your feelings about Clover," Marcy smirked, pissing Manhattan off a little, but she brushed it off by laughing.

Chapter 2

"How was work today," I asked.

"Work was very good, actually, but I have to do it again tomorrow," Manhattan chuckled. Manhattan seemed a Lil' nervous, but I couldn't understand why. I was trying to win her heart, I should have been the one biting on my bottom lip and not making eye contact.

"That's good, that's good, I wanted to bring you lunch today."

"Aww, that would have been sweet, but why didn't you," she questioned me.

"I wasn't sure if another jawn would be doing the same thing. I didn't want to get my heart broken already," I laughed.

"Boy, whatever," Manhattan rolled her eyes, laughing.

Three days, Manhattan and I talked all day for three days, like we were in high school. The only thing I was missing was my mama in the background yelling at me for sneaking on the phone. Now, a nigga like me didn't like doing too much talking on the phone, but I didn't mind my phone being attached to my ear for her. We could talk for hours and still have a lot of shit to run it about.

"It's so damn hot today. Lord, I'mma need more than this water ice to cool me down," doing a Lil' dance with her water ice and Philly cheesesteak in her hands, I sat across from Manhattan smiling. With her hair pulled into a high bun showing off her rosy cheeks, her natural beauty held everyone's attention who walked by. During the summertime, most smuts were wearing booty shorts to show their asses off, but not Hat. Sitting in crowded ass Max's for our first date, she wore a black and white camisole with the matching jogging shorts. In this hot weather, she'd rather be comfortable than cute. Max's was full of people making me wish Manhattan would have chosen a calmer place for our first date.

"It is, I don't think I can get any darker," I laughed.

"I hope not," she joked.

"Can't everybody be transparent like your light skin ass," I laughed again.

"Ooohhhh, there we go with the pale jokes," she giggled, waving her middle finger at me. I wanted to be cheesy and kiss it, but I didn't want to seem like a cornball.

"Hey, you started, but I was thinking about something."

"About what," Manhattan asked, shoving a big bite of food into her mouth. One thing about Manhattan, I learned quickly was that she didn't mind gettin' her grub on in front of me. She wasn't one of those shy girls who didn't like to eat in front of men. If she was hungry, Hat was going chow down like nobody's business.

"We should catch a jawn later today. I have to handle some business once we leave here, but after that, I'm all yours. That's only if you want that, real rap."

"Boy, shut up, and what kind of business, Clover Porter," Manhattan side eyed me asking, but Hat already knew the answer to her dumb question.

"Stop playing, stank, you already know that answer. Like I was saying, we should catch a movie later tonight. I want to spend more time with you on your day off," I replied, taking a small bite of my sandwich. She had me so nervous that I could barely eat without feeling like she watched my every move.

"Okay, but what if I wanted to see that movie, *What Happens in Vegas*?"

"Then I guess I'll be laughing at Ashton Kutcher tonight," we laughed.

"Great answer, Clover Porter, you're smarter than people think you are," she winked her eye in a goofy way, making me laugh.

"You just loovveeee saying my name, huh?"

"Yep, I sure do, it has a nice ring to it. How many times do people ask you if Rich Porter is your cousin," Manhattan laughed clapping her hands. Her joke was corny, but it still made me laugh.

"I hear that dumb shit at LEAST three times a week, but I'm used to it now. I have no relations to that man, let me clear the air by saying that."

"Thanks, I can check that off my list of questions," pretending to have a piece of paper in front of her, Manhattan written an imaginary check on the table.

"I thought you would have wanted to go to a fancy restaurant like Panorama, Xix Nineteen, or Ambra. Not Max's, eating cheesesteak, sucking down water ice," I laughed, splurging my lemon water ice. A couple of jawns I smashed, walked by with dirty looks on their faces, but I didn't pay them hoes any attention. Neither did Hat, she was too busy enjoying her food and my company.

"Uuumm, no, no, and hell no, I hate Ambra. Vernick is my favorite restaurant, but it has nothing on Max's. It's something about getting a greasy ass sandwich from here makes my whole week better," she grinned.

"Vernick, huh? The woman has good taste in jawn. Our next date, I'm taking you there, I want to see you dressed up in a little black dress and a nice pair of heels. Can I get that, stank," I smiled, asking.

"Probably so, Clover Porter, IF we get to a second date."

"Trust me, we will," I uttered.

"I remember back in the day my dad used to take Marcy and I here every day. Then we would go to the Poppi Store for a water ice and hang out for hours. Sometimes I wish we could go back to those days."

"I can be your daddy and do those things," I smirked.

"Haha, that's funny, Clover, but you can buy me another water ice when we leave."

"You got that, but can you see yourself getting serious with a guy like me?"

"I don't know, I usually don't date the street type, but I can't judge you because of that."

"If you don't date the street type, what makes me different," I asked, dying to know.

"I don't know, Clover Porter, maybe it's the fact you actually listen when I talk. Everything isn't about you, and I like that, even though I don't want everything to be about me."

"What if this does turn into something serious, how would you feel about that?"
"As long as you love and treat me right, I wouldn't have a problem falling for a thug. I just hope you don't plan to stay in the streets all your life, baby boy."

"No, that's not my plan, I have plans, don't worry, ma."

"Okay, like what?" She asked, finishing the rest of her sandwich.

"I've been thinking about investing my money here and there. I'm going to buy a few houses and put them on the market for rent," I replied.

"Okay, okay, Mr. Porter, I knew you were smart. If you need help with that, let me know. I have an aunt who's a realtor," Manhattan answered.

"Word to?"

"Yeeeppppp, but what kind of hustler are you?"

"What," I laughed.

"I'm dead ass serious, what kind of hustler are you? Are you the kind that hustles out of his house, or the kind that's on the block?"

"Yo, both of those are an insult. I've been off the block a loonnngggg time ago, and the last place I hustled out of was my mom's house. We call that serving niggas where you sleep at, never a good thing to do."

"Why do you say that?"

"When these clowns know shit like that, they become cutthroat snakes. I've been shot, and shot at a few times. When a bullet almost took my mom out, it was a must shit changed. I was twenty when that happened, but it still feels like it just happened."

"Woowww, that's crazy."

"Some noodle bull from Strawberry Mansion, but he just disappeared after that," I stated.

"He disappeared, huh, just like that?" She asked, with a stale glare on her face.

"Yea, you hit it right on the money, haven't seen that nigga since," I tapped on the table, laughing.

"Okay, Clover Porter, enough of that."

"To answer your previous question, I'm a lazy hustler. I make moves and dough from my phone, word to. Sometimes I do drop off, but that's not often. That's what I have my young boys for, they'll die behind me, real rap. One thing you never have to worry about is me showing you that life, or even bringing it home. I leave that shit exactly where it belongs, in the fuckin' wind and streets."

"I like that, I think I'm liking you more."

"See, that's what happens when you take the time to get to know someone," I expressed, looking over my shoulder. I could feel my old hoe, Shonda from out north, mugging me. When her and Hat locked eyes, I knew I had some explaining to do.

"Clover Porter, why is that girl with the big booty staring so hard?"

"Huh?" I asked, sounding dumbfounded. Smacking her lips and locking eyes with Shonda again, Manhattan asked, "why is that girl staring at us, mostly you?"
"Oh, Shonda, I used to fuck with the noodle bull," I chuckled, but Manhattan didn't mind that shit funny at all.

"Noodle bull, huh? How long ago was it you and this thicker than a snicker noddle bull was fooling around?"

"Shiiidddd, about a month ago, but it wasn't bout nothing serious. With Shonda, you get what you can see, a fat ass, pretty face, and designer clothes. Shorty can't hold an intelligent conversation if her life depended on," I laughed, shaking my head. Besides Shonda's good pussy and stashing my work in her Gucci handbag, I didn't miss shit about that hoe. Always had her hand out, wanting something, most of the time she only got this long dick. On a good day, I might have popped her off with a few dollars to show her my appreciation.

"Hhmmm, okay, but it seems like she didn't do any healing in that month. Boolll, if looks could kill, my blood would be everywhere on the table. All on your cheesesteak and water ice," she laughed, accidentally snorting, but she wasn't shame of her goofy ways.

"I swear, Hat, I love your sense of humor. You don't find a good sense of humor in a lot of women," I uttered.

"Thanks, Clover Porter," Hat smiled.

"Damn, Spitta, you can't speak," with her soft hands stuffed in her tight Red Robin white jeans, she approached the small table. Her chubby belly was exposed a little, showing the tattoo of her son's name, Malik. Slightly sizing her up and down, I replied, "I didn't know I had to go out my way to speak."

"So, it's like that," she asked, mugging Manhattan, but being the woman, she was, Hat smiled back, saying, "hi, it's nice to meet you, pretty girl."

"Anyways, who is this bitch?"

"Bitch," Hat questioned snickering.

"Nah, Shonda, don't call Hat out her name, you fuckin' crazy. You know Kansas owes you an ass whipping anyways, don't make me make Kansas give it to you today," without saying anything, Shonda hauled ass, forgetting she ordered her food. Before you knew it, she pulled off in her Jeep disappearing.

"Clover, you didn't have to tell her all that," Manhattan mumbled.

"That's light work to what I should have said. I don't care who it is, I won't ever let anyone play on you."

"Ard, but why does Kansas owe her an ass whipping?"

"The last time I stayed at the bitch's house, I woke up with a couple of hundreds missing from my pockets," I chuckled.

"What, dead ass?"

"As serious as a freshman on her first day at Temple."

"Wwooowww, maybe she always does that to guys. That explains why she dresses so nice, shit, I can't even afford Gucci shoes." Hat shrugged her shoulders laughing and once again, she snorted grabbing a few people's attention. She didn't care that they were staring at her, Manhattan really thought that corny shit was funny.

"Maybe so, but forget her," I replied.

"Can I ask you something else, Clover, since we're asking questions?"

"Yea, yo," I said, taking a bite of my sandwich.

"Why do they call you Spitta? I don't really like that name," Manhattan giggled sucking on her water ice.

"Damn, that was harsh, but when I was little, I used to spit a lot when I spoke. At first, everyone called me Spitty, then it changed to Spitta. Now I'm stuck with this dumb ass nickname," I shook my head chuckling, but I always held Manhattan's hand tighter. I'm not sure if it was the cool weather, or the way the sun was setting, but the vibe was on a hundred. It made me want to be closer to Manhattan in any way possible.

"I'd rather call you Clover," she giggled, covering her mouth.

"You want to know something, Hat," I asked, taking another bite of my sandwich. Clearing her throat, Hat said, "what?"

"I've been watching you, since you were dating ole' boy."

"Ole' boy, who? June," she inquired, with a mouth full of food. Instead of replying, I nodded my head, saying, "yea, him, and I know you told my sister, Kansas, I was cute," I laughed.

"Uuumm, yea, I did, so what," Manhattan giggled, wiping her mouth with the napkin. Man, it's like everything she did made me fall harder for her. It was no hiding that I was a sucker in love for Manhattan Mullen.

"Why didn't you go for what you wanted," I snickered.

"I don't know, like I told you when we first met, you don't have the nicest rep."

"That's crazy how Philly is slandering my name," I laughed.

"Hey, you gotta be giving them a reason, but who am I to say that."

"If you don't mind me asking, why did y'all break-up," I questioned.

"June and I were just….. Together, if you know what I mean."

"What DOES that mean," I asked, chuckling.

"Well, he loved me, I liked him, but we weren't in love with each other. That's not a bad thing though, you can't force anyone to love you. He didn't want kids, but I want kids. He doesn't believe in marriage, but I do. We can't live in sin forever, I don't believe in that shit."

"If you didn't love him, or wasn't in love with him, why were you with him?"

"June and I come from the same kind of family, it's was only right we at least try to make it work. My family looovvveeddddd him and I thought eventually I would love him too."

"Hhmmpphh, that's interesting to hear, that tells me a lot about you."

"What do you mean," she asked.

"It means that's you put everyone before yourself. That's a good and bad thing, but in your case, I'll look at it as a good thing."

"Why in my case," She asked, with a serious look on her face.

"I don't know, Hat, I can see that you're different, I'm going always treat you differently. In my eyes, you're going to always be right."

"I wouldn't give you a reason to ever question, or think I was wrong, Clover Porter," looking at me under her eyes, Manhattan then ran her tongue across her white teeth, smiling.

"That's a bet, I hope it stays like that. I hope I don't have to max June out, dude is still loving on you."

"He'll be okay, but it's not him I'm worried about. It's my sister not minding her damn business is what I'm worried about. Before you know it, everyone in my family will know about you, thanks to her."

"To say you come from a good family, you and Marcy are totally different. If I didn't know you two, I would need proof y'all were sisters, yo," I laughed.

"Now Marcy is a different story. She became ratchet like that when she dropped out of Temple," Manhattan laughed.

"I'm pretty sure you told her about us, I can only imagine the shit she said about me," I replied.

"To be honest, she had a lot to say about you, but I can't judge you off what others have to say."

"Thank you, real rap, but I don't really like your sister. Shorty doesn't have a solid reason she doesn't like me."

Marcy Mullen, Manhattan's older, judgmental, and annoying ass, sister. I knew more about Marcy than I knew about Manhattan because Marcy was more of the hood chick type. Besides that, she fucked with a couple of my homies out in Harrison Projects and Germantown. I never understood why she had the nerve to be judgmental, when she fucked with joes who were worse than me.

We didn't get much because she didn't like me. The bitch only knew OF me, so what the fuck was Marcy judging me off?

"What happened between you and Marcy two weeks ago?"

"What'cha mean?"

"She told me y'all had an argument or something in the projects."
"Oh, that. Your crazy ass sister was outside the projects, trying to bust Gary's tire and windows on his new whip. I ran out there to stop her, we passed a few words, Marcy threw her red drink all over me, drawlin. Mind you, I had all white on, I mean from head to toe, stank. I can't lie, I called her out her name a few times, but I was pissed," I said.

"It's crazy how I was told half of that," she chuckled, shaking her head.

"What were you told?"

"Marcy told me that she tried busting his tires, but she didn't say anything about windows. Just how she didn't say anything about throwing a drink on you. Since we were kids, Marcy loved playing the victim role, and as a grown woman, she still does that."

"Marcy, better stay out my way, and in her lane. I won't disrespect her anymore, because she's your sister, but just make sure she doesn't tell me shit."

"Ard, Clover, damn!"

"Just making sure you feel what a nigga is saying," I answered.

"Anywyas, let's change the subject. You said you didn't have kids, but do you want kids, Clover," she asked.

"Hell yea, I want a bunch of mini Clovers running through my house," I laughed.

"A bunch, damn, slang that dick."

"Nah, it's not like that, I come from a big family and I love that."

"Aaawwww, that's super cute, I swear, I'm learning so much about Clover Porter," she smiled.

"Stick around longer, you'll learn more."

"I hear you, Clover Porter, I hear you," she said.

***

Driving to my mom's house, who only lived a few houses down from Smoke, Manhattan still had my attention. Call me a sucker, but she had a jawn in love already. Before going to my mom's house, I had to hit a few licks down Broad Street, fuck with a couple of my young bols in Glenwood, and give some attention to a few smuts I had no attention to ever call. Them bitches were just something to do while out hustling and to kill time.

For two hours, I trapped, making moves and I spent the whole time on the phone with Hat. It's like I couldn't get enough of her conversation, laughter, or voice. Shorty had my full attention, but I knew after she would put that pussy on me, I would sprung like T-Pain. See, I wasn't in any rush to fuck Manhattan, I wanted to make love to her body. It had to be deeper than getting my rock hard. Making love to her meant I was one step closer to her, it couldn't get any better than that, did?

"I really enjoyed myself with you today, Clover Porter."

"Same here, but more days like this are yet to come," I said.

"Ard, ard, I like that way that sounds, but did you make it to your mom's house yet," she questioned.

"Yea, I'm sitting in the driveway. When I get in there, I'm rattin' on you," I laughed.

"Why, what did I do?"

"I'm telling her you keep asking me if Rich Porter is my cousin," I laughed.

"Nnnooooooo, don't tell her that, she's going to hate my guts," Manhattan giggled.

"I'm just joking, baby girl, but let me walk in this jawn. I'll call you when I get a chance."

"Okay, but be careful out there," she uttered.

"That's all I know, bye," I said, disconnecting the call hoping out my car. At 4: 00 pm, the sun was baking my black ass and I was ready to step foot in my mom's house. I know her well so, the ac pumping like cold Alaska air.

Sliding my key into the doorknob, I entered the house saying, "Maaaa, where you at?"

"In the kitchen, Clover," she shouted back, as I closed the door. My mother, Augustine Porter, my best friend, and true ride or die. Unlike of my homies and their moms, we had a close relationship. I never really hid anything from her, it was kind of hard not telling Augustine the truth. Since I hopped off the porch, she had my back in the streets. A lot of people didn't feel that, but my mom didn't give a fuck about their feelings. Protecting and riding for her seed was the only thing Augustine cared about. My mama had a heart made of gold, sometimes, that was her downfall. If we would allow her to, Augustine would open her home to the homeless and treat them like her own kids. Too bad me and Smoke didn't play that shit, didn't need no random jawns thinking they ran the place.

Walking through the big living room, then entering the kitchen, I spotted my mom at the stove. Herbs and vegetables surrounded her, my mom loved to cook, she was in her zone.

"Hey, Ma."

"Clover, if didn't know any better, I would think you were pregnant. You're glowing like the sun, baby," dropping the big spoon on the stove laughing, my mom stared at me a little longer, giving me a tight hug as if she missed me.

"What," hugging her a Lil' tighter, then sitting at the kitchen table. The aroma filled the whole house, making me hungry again.

"I said you're glowing like a pregnant woman. Hhmm, maybe someone is pregnant, I hope so. I would love a grandchild before I die," she laughed.

"I don't have anyone pregnant, Ma, I'm just happy."

"Hey, as long as my baby is happy and healthy, I can't complain," she smiled, walking back to the stove. A few seconds later, Kansas and Smoke walked into the house, geeked up with low red eyes. The smell of weed slapped my mom's nostrils, making her turn around sizing Smoke and Kansas. If I didn't know any better, I would have thought they were her enemies instead of flesh and blood.

"Hey, Mommy," Kansas said, walking cheerfully to my mom. Then she gave her a kiss and hug, but my mom didn't show much affection back. Kansas started blowing at eighteen-years old and has been a walking chimney ever since. My mom hated that Kansas smoked so damn much, she always said Kansas too pretty for such a bad habit.

"Hey, Ma, is that gumbo I smell," Smoke kissed my mom on the lips with his eyes barely opened. The way he smirked waiting for my mom to reply only annoyed her even more. If she didn't love us so much, she probably would have kicked their asses out.

"What did I tell you two about coming in my house higher than a kite!?"

"Ma, be cool, ard, we smoke weed, not dope," Kansas giggled, leaning against Smoke who was already laughing.

"Chile, hush, it's all the same in my eyes," she replied.

"Tell that to a nigga that smokes weed, Ma, he'd be ready to kill you," Kansas replied laughing. Her laughter always annoyed my mom since Kansas was young.

Kansas Porter, my sister, who was older two years older than me, but acted like we were forty years apart. We were close, much closer than Smoke and I were. Don't get me wrong, Smoke and I were tight, but Kansas was easy going and much easier to vent to. Sometimes, Smoke was in his own world, dealing with his own shit that none of us knew about.

"Don't let it happen again," she snapped, pointing at them.

"Mommy, you tell us that every day and we don't listen," Kansas laughed.

"I mean it this time, but anyways. Where are y'all coming from, probably up to no-good," my mom chuckled, turning around to stir the pot again.

"Kan and I was chilling by the crib."

"I was on a date," I said, smiling.

"Spitta, fuckin' a girl and sending her on her way is not a date," Kansas laughed.

"Shut up, Kan, that's not what happened. With this girl, I'm not even sweatin' her about sex, real rap."

"A date, what kind of date, Clover," Augustine asked.

"A real date, Mom, not any of that funny shit Kan is talking about. I met this girl few days ago, her name is Manhattan Mullen," I said to my mom, smiling big. Kansas and Smoke's snickering and smiling had me shame, but I was blushing like a fool.

"Manhattan, like the city," she asked, making Smoke bust out into laughter. Smacking my lips, I looked over my right shoulder saying, "it wasn't that funny, noodle bull, but back to you, Ma. She's so damn perfect and beautiful, ask Kansas. Manhattan told Kan I was cute a while back."

"Yea, just like the city, Ma, but she's good people. Today was our first date, and guess where she wanted to go," I chuckled, dropping my head.

"Where, Clover?"

"Muthafuckin' Max's."

"What?" Everyone asked, looking like they were confused, but I was still laughing.

"On my life, I'm dead ass serious. She's kind of the stuck-up type, so I thought she would want to go to a fancy jawn, but nah."

"Well, that's good, at least you know she isn't like those money hungry girls who are always dying for your attention," my mom uttered.

"You're right about that. We enjoyed ourselves, besides the Lil' run-in with Shonda."

"Shonda who? Better not be the one you were fuckin' with a few weeks ago?"

"Yea, stealing Shonda. She approached the table drawlin' and had the nerve to call Hat a bitch. What I didn't want to tell that bitch, but I didn't want my baby Hat to see that side of me."

"What did I tell y'all about calling women bitches and hoes," my mom snapped softly, slamming her hand on the countertop. Instead of being scared, we all laughed. My mom was about five feet tall weighing a hundred and four pounds, she could never put fear in our hearts.

"Mommy, if it looks like a duck, and quacks like a duck, it's a damn duck," Kansas laughed.

"Let the church say amen," Smoke laughed.

"Tell me something about her," my mom uttered, making me smile. "Damn, I can tell you a lot about her, Ma, Hat' so damn amazing.

Hmmm, let me see where I should start off first. Well, you know her name is Manhattan Mullen."

"How can we forget it, you said it like a hundred times," Kansas laughed.

"Mind your business, Kan, she has a beautiful name. Ma, she's originally from south Philly, but lives in Old City. Manhattan is also a veterinarian, no kids, she doesn't smoke at all, barely drinks, and she basically a got girl."

"She sounds really nice, Clover, I hope I meet her," my mom smiled.

"Oh, trust me, you will," I smiled.

"Alright, enough about Manhattan, we gotta go, Ma. We'll be back later though, you know I'm not missing that gumbo," with a smile on his face, Smoke gave my mom a kiss on the cheek. Kansas did the same thing following behind Smoke. I waited until I heard the front door close to speak again, but my mom beat me to it.

"You know what's crazy, Clover? You remind me a lot of your father when we first met. I remember curving him so much, it became funny to the both of us," she laughed.

"What, real rap," I leaned against the fridge laughing. I love hearing stories about my mom and dad, their love was real. I know they never had to question each other about that.

"Yes, do you want to know what made me finally say fuck it and go on a date with him?"

"Yea," I chuckled. Stirring the pot a little, my mom then walked to the round kitchen table to take a sit across from me. With a smile on a face, she said, "It was about 9: 30 am on a Sunday morning. I was leaving my boyfriend's house, going to my house to get ready for work. I don't know where your father was or coming from, but he followed me aallllll the way down Broad Street. Cavin called my phone until I pulled over to talk to him. Your father wasn't stopping until he got me and he did, that's why our bond was so close. We were close from that day on. No one could ever take Cavin's place, that man was really my lucky charm," she laughed.

"Ma, I know I be in these streets baggin' everything with a heartbeat, but one day I want to find love like that," I laughed.

"I had to learn that you don't look for it, Clover, it'll find you."

"Yea, that makes sense. Tomorrow is the anniversary of daddy's death. How are you dealing, Ma, and don't lie to me? I'm not Kansas or Smoke, so you don't have to put on a front."

"The anniversary of his death is always hard, but each year I'm learning to deal with it better. Some days I do think about him all day and it hurts my soul that he isn't here with us. I would do anything to see that big smile, or hear that loud laughter through the house," she chuckled, rubbing her hands together staring at the kitchen table. That was my mom's way of fighting back her tears, she did it all the time.

"As much as you would a yell at daddy for laughing loud, I never thought you would miss that," I laughed.

"Trust me, baby, it's the smallest thing I miss. Like making him a cup of coffee in the morning or running his bath water when he was on his way home. One thing about your father is that he kept me busy and I loved it. One day, the pain of missing him will go away, I can't wait," she whispered.

"In due time, Ma, it'll all stop hurting, word to," reaching for my mom's head to give it a kiss. A tear rolled down her face, with laughter spilling from her mouth. I know it was hard for her, but we could never take that pain away from her. Seeing my mom cry showed me at an early age that money could never buy happiness. When you're hurting, you're just motherfucking hurt, yo."

"I know, baby, but I always thank God for you three. Your father lives through each one of his kids, that's my piece of Heaven on Earth. Well, my pieces of Heaven on Earth," she chuckled a little, wiping the tears from her eyes. Knowing my mom, she wanted to break down at the table, but she was trying her best to be strong. I knew the moment I walked out the house, Augustine would be all alone.

"Ard, but I was thinking I stay here tonight."

"What, really? You haven't stayed here in months," she questioned.

"I know, but I want to stay here today. Then tomorrow we can go to the graveyard to put some flowers."

"I like the sound of that, baby, thank you."

My father was killed when I was six years old, I never looked at a cop as someone who protected the community. To me, they were the opps, waiting for any opportunity to kill a black man. Seeing my father gunned down from my bedroom window will always make my stomach ached. The way his body hit the ground and made the loudest thump I ever heard still gives me nightmares.

When he was killed, it took a big toll on our family, especially my mom. She became depressed and got drunk just about every day of the week. My mom was a true drunk and we got teased about it a lot. In her eyes, she didn't need rehab, she just needed her husband back in her life. Smoke, Kansas, I, were too busy helping my mom sober up and trying to maintain a household, that we couldn't grieve about our father's death. It took a year for her to realize she was at rock bottom and it was time to get her life together. Since that day, my mom has been sober, I'm proud of her for that. Even when she wasn't sober, Augustine Porter was still my queen.

Chapter 3

Three days had gone by since we visited my dad's grave, and I can't lie, my head was all fucked up. It was hard seeing my sister and mom breakdown the way they did. Most of the time we were there, Smoke stood there not knowing what to do. A part of Smoke wanted to cry his heart out, while the other half had too much pride to do that. I wish I could have broken down, but I had to be strong for everyone. Being so strong for them, I found myself slowly becoming depressed. My dad and I were mad close and when he was killed, I felt like a part of me was killed also. My mom was a damn good mother, but she couldn't take my father's place, it's just some things a woman could never teach their son. Don't get me wrong, she did her best, but I had to show myself how to be a man. The only thing my mother could do is give me an example of what a woman is supposed to be. For that, she always had my respect, a hundred percent.

Seeing my father die took a toll on my childhood and everyone witnessed the drastic change in my demeanor and behavior. For a while, my mom made me seek professional help because of the nightmares I would have. I was so depressed as a child, and no one could fix it. Not even lying on someone's couch, expressing my feelings, could fix my depression.

Sitting on my large black couch in a pair of blue brief boxers and socks, I stared at the walls in silent. I also had my trap phone pressed against my ear, listening to my homie talk about nothing important. Cope was rambling about the same hoes he told me about last week, weak shit. I can't lie, I wasn't paying attention to much he had to say. Other things were on my mind, like my father. If I listened closely, I could still hear my daddy's laughter and that brought tears to my eyes. Shit like this was why I rarely visited his grave, it always put me in a fucked-up head space. What made matters worse, I could never tell my mom how I felt. It would only make her feel worse than what she already felt in her heart.

"Mmmaaannnnnnn, I had a three-some with these two smuts last night."

"What," I chuckled. Cope Hicks was my childhood best friend, who I met right around the time my father was killed. About three weeks ago, Cope converted to Islam, and that's all he talked about. He often tried to make me do the same, but that wasn't my cup of tea. Cope was also from north Philly and ran the same streets I did. If it wasn't for Cope, I don't know how I would have handled my father's death. Plenty of times I wanted to rock out, but he kept me with a cool head. Because of that, I always felt like I owed him my life. I remember crying, and taking long walks thinking about my dad, and Cope was there with me. He didn't ask any questions, he just let a nigga be in his bag to clear his head. I always told myself I would pay him back for all he did, which wasn't much in his eyes. The moment I got on in these streets, it was only right I put my nigga on. How the fuck could I eat good and my big homie was starving? Cope was a hungry hustler like me, who had an expensive taste for the finer things. He didn't mind dropping stacks in the strip club, or at the mall, because you couldn't take the bread with you to Heaven. Why not ball out while on earth?

"Mannnn, Spit, I don't even remember them broad's names. I think one was from Fairhill and the other one was from Yorktown."

"Nigga, keep fuckin' all them hoes and your dick gon' be in your pocket before you know it," I laughed.

"Look who's talking, just like that movie. I guess because you're faithful now, you ain't diving in pussy like you use to," Cope smirked.

"Fuck no, I'm chilling, bro, but what's up with you tonight?"

"You know me, fuckin' off like always, but what about you? I hope you ain't staying in the house, AGAIN!"

"Yea, probably so."

"Bro, you gotta shake that shit off, you know your pops wouldn't want you like this," Cope said.

"I know, I know, I just need a minute to get my head together," I answered.

"Ard, but I'm giving you the rest of the day to be depressed and shit. By tomorrow morning, I'm dragging you out that house to get some fresh air," he laughed.

"I believe you and that's a bet," I chuckled.

"Damn, my annoying as baby mama is calling. I'mma hit yo' line back."

"Bet," disconnecting the call, I closed the Razor phone dropping it on the couch. As I closed my eyes to fall asleep, a soft knock on the door made my eyes fully open.

"Knock, knock, is anyone homeeeeeeee," standing on the other side of the living room door, I knew it was Manhattan with a frown on her face. She had been blowing up my phone all day trying to talk to me. I mostly gave her short conversations and dry text messages. I didn't like ignoring my baby, but I couldn't shake these emotions off if I wanted to.

"Who is it," I shouted, walking to the door, peeping through the blinds and sheer white curtains. Manhattan's Mustang was parked in front of my house perfectly, like it belonged there. Seeing her beautiful bare face actually put a smile on my face, and for a moment, it's like my problems vanished. Not just missing my dad, all these other problems I had in the streets.

"Clover Porter," she spoke, with a little bass in her voice, Manhattan had to be upset with me. Hopefully, once I told her what was going on, Manhattan would feel where I'm coming from. Without replying, I opened the door, finding Manhattan standing there with a blank face. Rubbing my eyes, but also letting her inside, I said, "what's up, baby?"

Manhattan didn't reply, she closed the door, sitting on the couch with her arms crossed in front of her chest. Since she wore a red, short pencil skirt, her long legs were exposed, looking good as fuck. On top of that, her white button-down blouse revealed some of her breasts. Even with a bra and undershirt on, I could still see her big brown nipples were on hard.

"You look nice," I said, chuckling, but planting a kiss on her forehead while sitting next to her.

"Really, Clover Porter, freaking really?!"

"Bae, calm down, iight?" I said.

"You're talking all calm and shit, looking all good, but you had me worried about you."

"I'm sorry, Hat," I worded.

"What's up with you? Why do I feel like you're ignoring me," Manhattan questioned.

"I'm not, baby, lot of shit on my mind. That's why I've been distant and shit, I didn't want to take my problems out on you."

"What's wrong?" She asked, kissing me on the forehead, but also sitting closer to me on the couch. Manhattan was an affectionate person, it was only right she held my hands, staring me dead in the eyes.

"You know we visited the grave three days ago," I said.

"Yea, did something happen?"

"Shit be hard, since we went there, my mom has been depressed. She hasn't left the house yet, I don't know what to do about this."

"I don't understand what you're saying, Clover," she uttered.

"It's complicated, Hat, but one day, I'll tell you and it'll make sense."

"I think at 2:15 pm, on a Saturday, is the perfect time to tell me," holding my hands a little tighter, Manhattan stared deeper in my shallow eyes, attempting to figure out what the problem was.

"It's not that easy, baby, but I PROMISE, I'll tell you everything one day," I replied.

"Clover, why do I feel like you don't show much emotions?"

"That's because a nigga been in the streets too long. Show no love, love will get you killed," I chuckled.

"That's Lil' boy shit and I'm not in the streets, you know you can open up to me," she replied.

"I will, in due time, baby girl," planting a kiss on Manhattan's forehead, I could see it in her eyes that Manhattan wasn't done with this conversation. Eventually, I had to tell her something to make her stop questioning me.

"Clover, why haven't you told me how your father died? To think about it, you don't talk about him much. Why is that, yo?"

"Like I said, shit is hard."

"Baby, please talk to me and tell me something. I don't like seeing you like this," she begged.

I hated showing emotions in front of anyone, especially a woman, but I couldn't fight back my tears. For the first time, I wasn't shamed to cry in front of a woman. I knew Manhattan would never throw this in my face if we got into an argument. Shorty was trustworthy, plus, Hat already proved her loyalty to me.

"It was two weeks after my sixth birthday, when my father was killed. December 14th my dad was standing outside in the cold ass snow, hustling anything he could. At the time, we were living on Ogden Street, in north Philly. He was never one of the police's favorite people, so they always found a way to harass him."

"Was your dad selling drugs," she asked, wiping my tears away, but tears began to fill her eyes also.

"Nah, bootleg cd's, but they thought he was slanging heroin. Every time he stepped foot out of the house, my mom worried about him, but he always laughed it off. He told her she had no reason to worry, because he always minded his own damn business. About 9:30 that night, my dad was still outside hustling in the cold, when the cops rolled up on him. Before you know it, they were throwing him on the cop car and in the snow. By that point, my dad started losing it, and started to fight the cops off. Before you know it, this Lil' rookie Mexican cop pulled his gun out, shooting my dad twice in the chest.

I was staring out the window the entire time, something I can never erase from my brain," dropping my head into Manhattan's lap, she gasped loudly, holding me tightly. I sobbed like a Lil' bitch, but that's exactly what I felt like for sobbing in front of her.

"Oh my, God, Clover, I'm soo soo sorry. I- I -I didn't know you watched your father die. I can only imagine how that makes you feel, especially as a kid."

"I swear, Hat, you wouldn't understand the half of it. We all try our best to stay strong for my mom, but it still hurts. You would think after all these years the pain would fade away in thin air," I whispered.

"Every time we're hurting, we always wish that. Too bad life doesn't work like that, my baby, but I wish it did," she whispered back, kissing the back of my neck. Hat made chills run down my spine, but I loved the feeling.

"It's crazy how I tell my mom shit like this, knowing that I cry just as much as her," I said, wiping my eyes.

"Clover, I'm so sorry you're going through this. I can't bring your father back, but I will be here to help you through the healing process," she said, kissing me on the lips with her arms around my neck.

"Do you promise to always be here, no matter what?"

"I promise, I won't ever leave your side."

"I wonder what good deed I did to deserve you," I said, saying. Manhattan was blushing so much, she couldn't even utter a single word.

Chapter 4 (July 2008)

Standing on the step at my mom's house, I could sense Manhattan was nervous. If you asked me, I thought it was cute how she had the jitters. Then again, I thought everything she did was cute. You would think she was meeting the president, or the queen of England. Since she already knew Smoke and Kansas, Manhattan was really only meeting my mom. Manhattan had nothing to worry about, I already knew my family would love her like I did.

"I wish I would have worn jeans and a nice blouse. Your mom might think my dress is too short, then she's going to think I'm a hoe, and not like me," Manhattan exhaled, staring at her loose-fitted black sun dress. With a pair of low-top black Chuck Taylors on, her hair pulled into a high messy bun, and only wearing a little pink lip-gloss, Hat looked comfortable and easy on the eyes. Her attire was perfect for Sunday dinner, Manhattan had no reason to put on a club outfit to meet my people.

"Be cool, you look nice, you know I like when you show a Lil' leg," I laughed, but Hat didn't. I smacked my lips, shaking my head. She took today wayyyyy too serious, and it wasn't that deep. Even if my people didn't like her, that wouldn't mean shit to me. I was still fucking with shorty, because I had mad love for her already.

"What if your people don't like me, Clover," tugging on the bottom of her dress, Manhattan looked over her shoulder as if she was searching for something or someone. Wrapping my arm around her neck with a smile on my face, I then kissed her smooth cheek, making her giggle.

"Bae, be cool, ard, they will love you."

"Are you sure, like, for real," she inquired, with the sweetest look on her face. Manhattan was big on that family shit, I liked that. My family was close, but we weren't close like the Mullen's. I had cousins out in south Philly that I hadn't held a conversation with in years, but it didn't bother me. Shit, clearly it didn't bother them either, because they didn't try to reach out to a real nigga. Most of the time when Smoke and Kansas saw or 3rd cousins, they pass them bitches up like strangers. My mom hated that, but they were grown, she couldn't force Kansas and Smoke to do anything.

"I'm sure, baby, now, stop acting like you can't still a muthafucker's heart on sight," I laughed, opening the door. My mom was in the kitchen, cooking with gospel music blasting through the house. Walking to the radio, I decreased the volume saying, "Ma, we're here."

"Wow, nice house," Manhattan said, staring at the design and interior of the house. Smirking while closing the door, I replied, "let's just say Smoke and I take good care of my mom."

"What about Kansas?"

"We take care of her a lil' bit," I laughed. A few seconds later, my mom entered the living room saying, "Manhattan, it's finally nice to meet you," my mom smiled, giving Manhattan a hug. Hugging her back, Manhattan wasn't caught off guard by the amount of affection my mom gave her.

"It's nice to meet you as well, Clover talks about you all the time," Hat replied.

"Likewise, and I've heard a lot of great things about you. I didn't know they still made good girls like you anymore," my mom laughed.

"Ma, really?"

"What, Clover? I'm just saying, but anyways, make yourself comfortable. I was just about to put the cornbread in the oven," she uttered.

"Bet, what are you cooking?" I asked, while Hat and I sat on the couch. Seeing how comfortable she became, I was glad she wasn't nervous anymore.

"I'm cooking collard greens, baked chicken, cornbread, and a slab of short ribs on the side."

"Short ribs and greens, my favorite," Hat smiled, laughing.

"Good, I have enough to go around twice," my mom laughed, making her way back into the kitchen. Adjusting her dress a little, Manhattan began to walk through the house examining the pictures on the wall. When Manhattan noticed a baby picture of what I looked like, she gasped, turning in my direction.

"Baby Clover Porter?"

"Yeeeppppppp, in the fuckin' flesh," I laughed, standing to my feet, walking in her direction.

"Aawwwwww,you were so freaking cute, I would have pinched those chubby cheeks all day," giggling and grabbing my cheeks, I could tell Manhattan enjoyed this.

"Was? I still am, shorty," I replied.

"Nah, you're alright now," she joked.

"Yea, whatever."

"Is this you, your dad, Kansas, and Smoke, for Halloween?"

"Yea, this was the year he was killed, my dad was a big fan of Halloween," I replied.

"Oh, okay, I can see where you get your looks from and why your mom never moved on. Your daddy was one finnneeeeee man," she laughed.

"At least we know I'mma still be something serious," I laughed.

"Yea, yea, yea, Clover, but where is Smoke and Kansas?"

"Probably somewhere in the back of the house," I said.

"Back of the house, damn, how big is this place? and I see someone's favorite color is white."

"It's a five-bedroom home, three bathrooms, with a guestroom. Big nice backyard, just incase we give her a grandchild."

"Woowwww, I would love to see the entire place," she answered.

"Alright, I'll give you a little tour," as I grabbed Manhattan's hand, Smoke and Kansas walked into the living room, looking high as usual. Smoke nodded his head at Manhattan, while dapping me down. Then he said, "what up, lil' bro, what the lick read?"

"Cooling, big bro, coolin', but I gotta holla at you about something. Niggas in Spanish Harlem and the Bronx said that shit is jumping," hearing those words made Smoke rub his hands together.

"Word to, let's do that shit again, Carter got that shit on lock." Besides prescription drugs, Smoke and I pumped that heroin like it was going out of style or business. Fuck, it didn't matter who wanted to buy or smoke it, Clerk served their asses without thinking about it. A couple of niggas had light problem, because a nigga served their mom or aunties on the daily, but we just didn't give a fuck. Plenty of times my mom stumbled into the Poppi Store already, but I don't remember a time where the Chinxs didn't take her money. Besides, if it was the other way around, niggas wouldn't have hesitated serving my mom. On the strength of us, they probably would give her bad drugs.

"Hi, Kansas, hey, Clerk," Manhattan nervously said.

"What's up, Manhattan," Smoke said.

"Hey, girl," Kansas said.

"I see my Lil' bro finally let you out the house," Smoke laughed, but in a joking manner, Hat rolled her eyes.

"Nah, it's the other way around, I finally let him out the house," she laughed.

"You sound a Lil' pussy whipped, Clover," Kansas laughed, joking.

"I know your ass ain't talking, ole' boy have you in the house all damn day."

"Uuumm, ole' boy has a name, and it's Ryan," she rolled her eyes. I didn't really like Ryan and to be honest, I didn't have a reason to.

Well, besides the vibes I get from him and the rumors I hear about him being abusive to Kansas. I never seen it for myself, and Lord knows if I ever do, shit will be bad for Ryan. I never had a problem making a nigga disappear into thin air.

"Yea, whatever."

"Anyways, Manhattan, I remember you saying how cute Clover was. Now look at you two, all booed up," she laughed.

"Yea, he's my baby," she said, blushing, and kissing me on the lips. Kansas had a huge smile on her face. It's been at least five years since she seen me loving on a woman.

"Everyone, the food is ready, come in here," my mom shouted from the kitchen.

"I guess it's time to eat, y'all," Smoke said, rubbing his hands together while we walked into the kitchen. I could feel Hat hands getting sweaty as I held her hands. I didn't understand why she was nervous again. By the vibe I was getting, I could tell everyone was looking her.

"Good, because I'm starving, feels like my stomach is tap dancing in my back," Kansas rubbed her stomach, with her red eyes lower than low. Tapping her on the back, I whispered, "what the fuck y'all was blowin' like that?"

"Oowops, but I gotta leave this shit alone," Smoke said, laughing, knowing he was lying to us and himself. That nigga was a weed head and wouldn't stop smoking if you begged him to.

"Man, Clover, Smoke and I got so fucked up last night on two oowops. I felt like I was floating, just missing some damn moon boots," Kansas laughed. When Kansas walked into the kitchen, I swiftly grabbed Smoke by the arm, but I kept my eyes on Kansas. She stood next to my mom, annoying her by giving her a kiss on the cheek. I laughed a Lil' bit at the way my mom flared her nose to inhale the weed smell that lingered on her clothes and in her hair. My mom probably would have punched Kansas in the face if she could, but she loved her too much for that. It didn't matter how old Kansas was, she was always going to be a mama's girl.

"Let me rap to you for a sec, bro," I worded to Smoke. Just because Kansas was in the kitchen, didn't mean her nosy ass wasn't ear-hustling on our conversations. Kansas did that a lot, because she worried about us a lot. Smoke or I wasn't dead, so Kansas had no reason to worry herself.

"What's up, bro?

"I heard some shit about this Lil' noodle bull of a boyfriend that your sister goes with."

"Who, Ryan?" He questioned.

"Unless she got a new dude, yea, I'm talking about him," I whispered.

"What up, talk to me?"

"Uumm, Hat, go in the kitchen while I talk to my bro, I'll be there in a minute, baby," pulling Hat closer to me, I kissed her lips and squeezed her ass. She was a little embarrassed and couldn't even look Smoke in the eyes, but she still managed to say, "okay, baby." I waited until she was completely in the kitchen to pull Smoke down the hall and say, "I heard from a reliable source that things ain't a-1 with Ryan and Kansas."

"What?"

"Real rap, someone told me Kan ain't seen that nigga in three days. Why? Because he's in Harrison Projects laid up on coke. I'm more than sure this rumor about him beating her is true. Now I'm ready to beat Kansas' ass, then his. I don't put my hands on anybody's sister, so ain't no nigga gon' treat my sister like a fuckin punching bag."

"What the fuck we gon' do about this? because you know she won't tell us the truth. Matter of fact, how do we know for sure it's the truth," he questioned, kind of annoying the fuck out of me. Unless I knew it was legit gossip, I wouldn't tell Smoke anything.

"Like I said, this is a reliable source, Lil' bitch I was fucking days before I met Hat. She was at her people's house on Popular Street three days ago, when Ryan caught a flat tire."

"What the hell they were doing on Popular Street," Smoke asked, sounding curious.

"Check this out, bro, Ryan fuck with one of the girl's stepsisters. Ryan went there to drop the bitch some money, but he told Kansas he was bringing his sister some cigarettes. When he noticed he had a flat tire, Ryan started tripping and spazzed out on Kan."

"Maannnnnn, you got me heated right now, I should go in the kitchen and flip that fuckin' table over," Smoke closed his fist tightly, breathing heavily, looking over his shoulder. If Kansas would have walked out of the kitchen, no telling what Smoke would have said or done.

"How the fuck you think I felt hearing that shit? I couldn't flash out like I wanted to, but the next time I hear anything, I'm crashin'. I don't give a fuck who's in my way," I said. I wanted to speak loudly, however, I kept my voice low. Kansas probably was still ear-hustling in the kitchen.

"I love it when you talk like that, Lil' nigga, you know I'm right behind you."

"Fuck, I already know that," I chuckled. This was the kind of shit that made Smoke's dick hard.

"What's up with you and shorty though? You're looking real suckerish right now," Smoke laughed, crossing his arms on his chest and standing ten toes. I wasn't a mind reader, but I knew exactly what my brother was thinking.

"Word to, I'm in love with her," I grinned.

"What," he laughed, asking.

"Dead ass, she's good people."

"You're what," he asked again, still laughing.

"Damn, nigga, you can't hear, I'm in love already. Shorty have a good heart and she ain't nothing like what I usually get with," I said.

"The money hungry type, or the hoe type," Smoke chuckled, yawning.

"Both."

***

After getting to know Hat on every level possible, letting her meet my family, wining, and dining her, Manhattan finally agreed to be my woman. I can't lie, I was buck and happy to be with her. Hat made me work hard to be her man, but it was worth it. See, Manhattan was a different kind of woman, she didn't need me to spoil her with money, Hat did that on her own. What she wanted was time, loyalty, someone to protect her, and real love. Not that fake shit that only last for a few months. Hat wanted a lifetime partner and lover, I had to be that person, or the next man would do it with no problem. That was simple shit I didn't mind giving her. If I could give her the world I would.

On the 4th of July, I dedicated all my time to Hat. My phone was jumping with licks calling, but all week I was in the trenches hustling. I really didn't have time for Hat, and had to make it up to her. It was like our first holiday together, it meant a lot to me, and I knew it meant a lot to her sensitive ass.

Penn Landings was crowded with smuts everywhere, half dressed, niggas showing off their pockets full of money, and people with their families just looking to have a good time. With the weather being perfect, the sun shining just right, and clear skies, I couldn't ask for a better day. Seeing the different and blended families made me wonder how life would be when I had kids with

Hat. I couldn't wait to take them here and talk about how Mommy and Daddy met.

Walking near the water, holding hands with Hat was nice, but I saw the expressions on some of the people's face when we passed by. I guess they were surprised to see ole' Spitta tied down with a woman, and not posted up with a bunch of bitches. Maybe it was the type of woman I was cuffed to that really surprised them. I usually went for the big booty ghetto type, but this rip, that's not what I wanted. It's not like those kind of bitches got me anywhere in life, besides giving me fire pussy and head. Besides, I had enough attention on me, I didn't need my shorty bringing more heat my way.

Because of my rep, Manhattan decided we should keep our relationship quiet. After today, that shit would be out of the window. My phone vibrated non-stop in my pocket, but I already knew why. If it wasn't for drugs, it was nosy muthafuckers calling just to be in my business. It wasn't no one's business who I was with.

"I'm surprised that Kansas and Clerk aren't here acting like two ghetto fools. Those two act like they are the Double Mint Twins," Manhattan laughed.

"They actually came already, but they're coming back. It's only 5: 15 pm so I know they're somewhere getting high, like always," I laughed.

"That sounds about right, but what about Cope's crazy ass? He should be somewhere around here showing off a stack of money," she chuckled.

"Naw, ole' Cope don't do large crowds, he never did. He might pass through in his ride, but that's about it. If Cope start feeling paranoid, he'll get to bussin' that iron like it's nobody's business. Trust me, I've seen it happen too many times."

"What," Hat laughed a little.

"I'm serious, I want to enjoy myself today and not dodge bullets."

"Uummm, I'm going to need Cope's grown butt to learn how to deal with large crowds," she laughed.

"I always told him that, but he's stuck in his ways," I said.

"Just like you with going to church?"

"Yea, just like that, you hit it right on the money," I laughed, making Manhattan roll her eyes. Before family, it was God, Hat was also big on religion. She didn't miss Sunday services for anyone, OR anything. Even if God dropped from Heaven on an early Sunday morning, Manhattan still wasn't missing church for him.

"Clover, I don't understand, what's the big deal about going to church? It's only for two hours and a few days out of the month," she spoke softly, trying not to get upset with me. With a conversation like this, Manhattan was bound to piss herself off, because I wasn't saying anything to please her.

"Baby, you think with all the bad I've done, those church going people would want me there? As soon as I step foot in there, the whole jawn might go up in flames. People are going to recognize me and try to toss me out of there by my collar. So, before I disrespect anyone's grandma, I'll stay my ass home and watch the game."

"The house of the Lord is the one place we go to not be judge," she uttered.

"You say that, but people are still going there to judge folks. Besides, I don't have to go to church to show my love for the Lord. I drop to my knees every day and night to thank him," I shrugged my shoulders saying, I was ready for this conversation to end, but Hat still had a lot more to say.

"Look, Clover, I'm not going to beg you to come to church with me anymore. What I'm going to say is that we do go to church to show the Lord our love for Him. It is HIS house, yo, and we also go to get the word. Maybe if you had that floating in you, you wouldn't jump in your sleep so much." I let her hand go, and suddenly stopping, I looked Manhattan in the eyes saying, "what?"

"Oh, I guess you're a little hard of hearing like your brother. I SAID, if you had the word of the Lord floating through your black ass body, you wouldn't jump so much in your sleep," she answered.

"I don't know what you're talking about," I mumbled, trying to brush her off. Somehow, this conversation turned into something I didn't want it to.

"Every day this week, you were jumping in your sleep. At some point, you started talking to yourself and fighting off something. Baby, what the hell is wrong?" Slowly releasing Manhattan's hand, I exhaled loudly, turning away. Being the affectionate woman, she was, Manhattan softly grabbed my face, trying to make eye contact with me, but I didn't allow her to. It felt like every time Hat looked me in the eyes, she saw the real me and nothing, but the truth.

"On my mama, you be breaking me down like a brick," I chuckled. Putting my attention on the calm waters.

"What," she eventually adjusted my head, making eye contact with me.

"Nothing, but can we drop the subject and talk about this another day?"

"No, Clover, I prefer to talk about it now! That way we can get it out in the open and figure out what's the problem. Baby, I'm only doing this because I care about you. If I didn't care about you, I would rollover when you're jumping in your sleep, instead of praying over you." Breathing louder, I then held both of Hat's shoulder's, asking, "Why do you do that?"

"Do what, Clover?"

"Care about me so much."

"Because I got love for a north Philly thug, duh," laughing with her hand over her mouth, Manhattan stood on her tip toes planting a kiss on my forehead. It made me laugh and smile.

"I love the sound of that, but let's just say the jumping in my sleep is me fighting with my demons. Some days it feels like I'm winning, then some days it feels like I'm losing. Most days I'm def dancing with the devil, fuck, damn near doing salsa. Seeing the shit, I see in the street will have you jumping in your sleep and a lot more," I laughed.

"That's why the big c-word needs to be a part of your daily life and language. No, I'm not talking about cocaine, that's the only c-word you know!"

"I also know crack," I smirked, pissing Manhattan off.

"That wasn't funny."

"I'm just joking, baby girl," I answered, continuing to walk.

"Look, baby, I know you're not living right. At some point in your life, you have to. I'm not going to pressure or nag you, but I do worry about you sometimes."

"You don't have nothing to worry about, baby girl, I'm straight," I said, smiling, holding her hand tighter. I know it didn't matter what I said, Manhattan would still worry about me every time I wasn't in her presence.

"Okay, Clover."

"Since you're off work tomorrow, I had something in mind."

"Oh yea, what's that?"

"We should good a room for two days to kick back and chill. I wouldn't mind seeing that Lil' slim body in a swimsuit," I laughed.

"Clover, you see me in panties and bra very often," she laughed.

"True, but I just want to get a way for a quick minute. We both can clear our minds and I'll leave my trap phone behind. You'll have all my attention and time, ard?"

"That's a bet, I'm loving the sound of that, because I hate that little trap phone, ugh!"

"Woowwww, I'm glad to know that," I chuckled.

"I was thinking," Hat said, as she adjusted her sunglasses on her face. In her little red sundress and matching sandals, she looked amazing.

Before saying anything, I kissed her neck, replying, "what up, beautiful woman," I smiled, sounding corny as fuck, but I couldn't help it.

"How about we go to Vegas at the end of the month, just for a few days?"
"That's a bet, a few days out of the fuckin' state would do me good," I uttered.

"Good and don't be thinking about marrying me in Vegas. I know I'm fine and all, but that shit is cheesy," she giggled, flipping her hair. The warm sun bounced on her smooth skin making her glow as if she was pregnant.

"I thought about it, but you deserve better than that. On another note, what do you think about moving in together?" I asked, catching Manhattan off guard, and causing her to choke a little. After pounding on her back and chest a little, she finally gathered herself to say, "What?"

"I guess youse hard of hearing too, but I'll say it again. What do you think about us moving in together? I know we just started dating, but what's the wait?"

"The wait is that I need to make sure you're serious about this relationship," Manhattan implied.

"Of course I am, haven't I showed you that," I questioned.

"Yea, you have, but what if in a few months, you change your mind? My feelings are hella deep for you, Clover, but I like the way things are now. I hope you're not mad at me, are you?"

"No, baby, I'm not," I said, kissing her lips.

"Good to know that. Seriously though, what if youse really related to Rich Porter," Manhattan laughed, clapping her hands. Slightly tugging on her long hair, I replied, "shut up, Hat," I laughed.

"Just joking, but I can't wait until the fireworks show, that's the best part of the day," she laughed.

"Hat."

"Yes, Clover," She said, turning to me, looking me dead in the eyes, Hat made me nervous in a way. When she cracked a small smile, I did the same saying, "you're the best part of the day, fuck these fireworks."

"Aww, look at your hood ass being sweet," she giggled.

"Only for you, but you'll learn that soon, I hope."

"Seems like Kansas is a fan of us, I wonder why," Hat smirked.

"That's because Kansas knows when I'm truly happy. I ain't trying to stroke your ego or anything, but it's been a while since I been this happy."

"Oh, really," she smirked, like she didn't believe me.

"Yea, but I need to ask you something about my sister," I said.

"What about her," She asked.

"Have you noticed anything out of the ordinary?"

"Like what," Manhattan questioned.

"Shit, like her relationship, what I'm hearing in the streets I don't like," I replied.

"The few times we hung out, Ryan's name wasn't mentioned."

"Ard, but if you see, or even hear, some funny shit, let me know," I demanded.

"Yeessss, sir, I sure will, but what's the problem, or should I say issue?"

"It's not an issue, yet, but like I said, I don't like the shit I'm hearing," I answered.

"If you don't like it, why don't you ask her about it?"

"Kansas loves to be in me and Smoke's business, but hates us to be in hers. If I ask her about it, Kansas is going to deny everything, and swear I'm buggin'," I said.

"You do know what's done in the dark will come to the light?"

"Word, but I don't have time for that. I need to know of this shit is true or not," I laughed.

"That's why you should just ask her, but I'm not going to get into y'all business."

"Only if I ask you to, baby. How about we hook-up Cope and one of your co-workers?"

"What? Which one?"

"What's her name, Ryker, right, cute Lil' red bone?" I said.

"Yea, but I don't think Cope is really her type."

"Well, what is her type?"

"I don't know, but I know it's not anybody that looks like Drake," she giggled.

"Ayo, Spit, what up, homie," rushing to clutch my heat that was tucked under my white t-shirt, I turned around, finding my homie. He stood a few feet away from us with his arms opened and a big grin on his face. Manhattan sized him up and down, she could tell Tiny was a loose cannon. If you caught him on the wrong day, Tiny could be your worst nightmare. Straight from New York out of Spanish Harlem, shit, what the fuck did you think he would be?

"Oh, what up, T? Come here," I motioned to him.

"Clover, who is that," Manhattan asked.

"Be cool, bae, that's my homie from New York, Tiny."

"Tiny, for a big ass nigga, he should have the nickname." Tiny, but the government knew him as Supreme Gaines. Tiny was a seven-foot nigga weighing at least a solid two-hundred and fifty pounds. If I ever had a problem in his neck of the woods, I only had to make one phone call. Tiny can clear the business every time with no problem.

"Damn, big bro, your black ass could have told me you were coming to my city," I laughed, dapping him down once he was close to me.

"Bro, you're ten shades darker than my black ass, but you better check your phone. Nigga, I been calling you all damn day," he chuckled, making his big belly jiggle like keys.

"She's the reason I ain't answer my phone, Tiny, this is my lady, Manhattan."

"Okay, okay, nice to meet you, Miss Manhattan," Tiny smiled, shaking Manhattan's hand. In a dry tone, she replied, "nice to meet you also. Baby, excuse me for a minute, Macy is calling."

"Ard, take your time," as Manhattan opened her Razor phone, I kissed her lips and grabbed her ass. She walked away shaking her head and grinning.

"Hello?"

"Manhattan, where the fuck are you," Marcy asked.

"Girl, why the hell are you cursing at me like I'm one of your niggas?"

"Why am I getting phone calls that you're at Penn's Landing with Clover's ass," clearing her throat, but also trying to see if I was looking at her, Manhattan turned the other way.

"I don't know why, fuck. I'm a grown ass woman and I can go wherever please. I wanted to go to Penn's Landing with Clover Porter, and that's what I did. All this extra shit, you can keep to yourself. If I knew that's why you were calling, I would have never answered the damn call!"

"Giirrrrllllllllll, you sound so fuckin' stupid right now!! Are you living on the same planet as the rest of the people who are talking about Spitta?? He's going to hurt just like he's hurt every other girl!! That boy is damaged and is only damaging people he comes in path with!"

"Why do you always have to judge someone when you're NO BETTER THAN THE NEXT bol or smut? I don't know about these other women, but I see something in Clover. He needs help, and if I want to be the one to help him that's my business. Not yours or anyone else's business, ard?!"

"I wish I could record you, that way, you can hear how stupid you sound! Spitta has you so damn wide open," Marcy laughed.

"Look, Marcy, thanks for all your advice, but I'm good. I'm not sure how Clover treats other women, but he treats me good."

Even though I was occupied with my homie, I could still hear most of Manhattan's conversation with her sister. Sooner, than later, Marcy was going to respect my gangster and keep my fuckin name out of her mouth.

"I bet you aren't the first girl to say that, and you won't be the last. Once he's done with you, Clover is going to toss you to the side and forget you ever existed! Just watch, I've seen this shit happen plenty of times with him. Literally, walking over bitches he met, and fucked a few hours ago, leaving them heart broken. Is that what you want," Marcy shouted, asking.

"You have to be a damn fool to be heartbroken by a nigga you fucked on the first night. I'm pretty sure you can relate to this though," Manhattan laughed.

"It doesn't matter if you fucked the nigga on the first night or waited a year later. No one deserves to get fucked on like that and you know that."

"You know what, Marcy, I'm going to end this call and continue to enjoy my dad with my MAN. SOMETHING YOU DON'T GET TOO OFTEN, BYE!!"

Chapter 5

"Hat, I'mma call you back!"

"Wait, baby," she shouted.

"Manhattan, what," I shouted back through the receiver.

"Clover, please don't do anything stupid, you need to calm down," she begged crying, but I didn't want to hear that. Disconnecting the call to answer Smoke's call, this was the person I needed to talk to. In a situation like this, he was the last person to calm down. He was just as heated as me.

"Hello," I shouted, barely steering the wheel. My hands were occupied with the clip I was filling with bullets. It's like I didn't have a mind anymore, and nothing anyone said could calm me down. Knowing Smoke, he was in the exact mind-frame as me.

"I SWEAR, CLOVER, I'MMA KILL THAT NIGGA!! WITH MY FUCKIN' BARE HANDS, I'M GOING TO CHOKE HIM UNTIL HIS FUCKIN EYES POP OUT THE SOCKETS, Where the fuck is this nigga at, man," Smoke shouted so damn loud through the receiver, that I could feel his spit splashing through the phone. He had my ear ringing, but he had every right to be upset. About an hour ago, ago, Kansas called us crying in a way I never wanted to hear my sister, or any woman crying, for that matter. Once she calmed herself down and told us what happened, it's like Smoke and me lost our minds.

Not even a month after my old hoe told me what happened with Kansas and Ryan, I get a phone call from Kansas' neighbor, saying we needed to go there fast. Thank God my mom was visiting a friend in Pittsburg for three days. Something like this would have broken her heart for good.

"Mmmmaannnnnnn, find that nigga and kill him, end of discussion," I said, ending the call. Swerving, but almost losing control of the wheel, I drove through the neighbor's lawn. The green mailbox and blue trashcan was run over, but I didn't care. I spotted her neighbor, Star, running out of her house with a towel and first-aid kit in her hand. She looked scared and destroyed, but seemed a Lil' relieved when she saw me.

"Star, where the fuck is my sister, where is she?"

"She's in the house, Clover, her house. Oh my God, I thought she was dead. I swear, I thought Kansas was dead. She didn't want me to call the police or ambulance, Kansas only wanted you and Smoke to come here. I even went to your mom's house, but I don't think she's there," Star became emotional and weak, which made her drop the items and collapse to the wet grass. Quickly grabbing her, I held her in my arms saying, "Sshhh, sshhhh, sshhh, calm down, Star, everything is gon' be iight. My mom is in Pittsburg, but she doesn't need to know anything about this, ard?"

"Ard, I promise I won't say anything, but can you please check on Kansas," she cried out, pointing to the house. The living room door was opened with a big footprint on it and it was almost off the hinges. Looking at things from a distance had me heated, somebody had to give me real answers, asap!!!

"I will, but I need you to go in the house and get yourself together. Matter of fact, don't stay here tonight just in case that nigga come back tripping," as I reached into my left pocket to hand Star a hundred-dollar bill, she gasped at the sight of my gun.

"Clover, why do you have that," she questioned, tempted to reach out and touch it. Glancing at it laughing, I replied,

"The same reason a Christian carries a Bible, to protect myself. Now, take your things and you this money and leave soon."

"Okay, make sure Kansas calls me," she spoke softly. Star was a sweet and quiet girl, she reminded me a lot of Manhattan. To think about it, the only difference between the two was their choice in colleges and skin tone.

"I will, bye," running across the street and entering Kansas' dark house, I was ready to shoot up the place because of what my eyes were looking at. Broken glass covered the floor, furniture was flipped over, and blood stains splattered everywhere. I wasn't sure whose blood, but I didn't give a fuck. I wanted Ryan's blood on my hands by any means, real rap. This mess had his name written all over it. There was no way this could be Kansas' work. Don't get me wrong, she could turn into a lunatic fast, but she wasn't a fool to damage her own property. Kansas always took pride in the things we brought her and what she worked hard for.

Walking down the hall and entering Kansas's dim room, my heart raced. She sat on the floor, staring out of the window, sniffing, but also slowing patting her face to make the tears vanish away.

"Where the fuck Ryan at, Kansas?" Since my gun wasn't on safety, this bitch could bust at any moment. If Ryan appeared anywhere in this motherfucker, no telling what I would do. Instead of replying to my question, Kansas dropped her head, chuckling as loud as the pain granted her to. Since it was midnight, only a little light from her neighbors' backyard shined through her broken room window. I spotted Kansas' tears falling rapidly, with blood falling on her bare lap. She wanted to wipe the tears on her shoulder, but brushing it against anything would cause too much pain.

Kansas sat on the floor Indian style in only a bra and jogging shorts that revealed most of her ass. Even in the dim room I could see the bruises on her pained filled body. Some of the bruises were new, but a few were in the healing process. Majority of her legs and arms were covered with black and blue scars. The bruises looked painful and made my heart ache for my sister. Kansas was a beautiful and intelligent woman who didn't have to deal with this kind of bullshit. Kansas could literally, have ANY guy her heart desired, I've seen this shit happen with my own eyes. Real talk, doctors, lawyers, attorneys, and business owners, have begged to take Kansas on one date. I never understood why she would settle for goofy cats like Ryan, or even the nigga before that named Ace. Poor Ace, Smoke ran him away, but Kansas still doesn't know that. Ace had a problem with keeping his hands to himself and I wasn't talking about being abusive. A few times, I noticed some of my work disappearing while he was around. It took one good ass beaten from Smoke, while I stood there laughing, for Ace to disappear and never come back. He didn't call or text Kansas anymore, which broke her heart, but a nigga like that she didn't need in her mix. If he didn't have a problem stealing from us, I knew that clown wouldn't have a problem stealing from her. That's if he didn't already do it right under her nose. See, a nigga like Ace probably was never in love with Kansas. In his eyes, he saw a girl who was the sister of two of Philly's hottest niggas and I can bet my last dollar he saw that as his come-up. It's no secret Smoke and me spoil Kansas rotten, but she's no lazy bum. Kansas never had a problem going get her own money, but why should Kansas bust her ass when she has us? That's goofy shit if you ask me, but then again, who the fuck am I, yo?"

"Kansas, where is that clown?" I shouted through a closed mouth. Her lack of response pissed me off more.

"Do you see how beautiful the sky is at night, bro," Kansas sobbed a little, but tried to hide it by pressing her lips tightly together. Too bad her bottom lip was split open and only caused her to be in more pain.

"Kansas, where……. The….. Fuck is he?"

"I remember when we were younger, daddy and I used to sit on the steps just looking at the stars. If we didn't hear any gunshots or any fights break out, that was a good night. Sometimes, we would joke around and try to count how many stars were in the sky. Then, Daddy would name his favorite four stars Clover, Clerk, Augustine, and Kansas. I would ask him which star was his favorite, and Daddy would whisper in my ear, Kansas was his favorite. Then he would say I couldn't tell y'all because you and Smoke would cry," she laughed.

"Yea, I remember that, Daddy always tried his best to spend time with us. Even if it was something simple like sitting outside. We loved that shit though, you can't put a price on quality time."

"Man, I guess God doesn't make men like that anymore. I sure wish he did though, that way I could have a little piece of my father in the man I love." I wasn't sure what the fuck Kan was rambling about, but eventually, it would all make sense to me.

Slowly tiptoeing around the glass and pushing some of to the side to sit next to Kansas, she didn't waste anytime placing her head on my shoulder. Her tears had me feeling like shit, my sister shouldn't have been going through something like this.

"Everything is going to be okay, iight?" I said.

"I have to make it right first, everything. I can't go through this anymore, my body and heart can't take it anymore," she mumbled.

"I told you I would always protect you, sis, I'm sorry I failed you," I whispered, fighting back my tears. Kansas left eye was swollen shut, she couldn't make eye contact with me if she wanted to.

"It's not your fault, Clover, don't ever feel like that. When I'm hiding things from you and putting myself in dangerous situations like this, how the fuck can you honestly protect me?" She uttered, exhaling loudly.

"When I heard things in the streets, I should have run with it. You're a grown ass woman and I hate to be in your business like you're a child, but damn. This is this kind of shit that happens when I don't get in your business. I'm sorry, sis, don't hold this against me," I begged.

"Clover, even with a black eye and busted lip, I would never put this on you! I won't let you play the blame game because I tried to love and protect a man who didn't give a fuck about me."

"I didn't only make a promise to you, I made a promise to Daddy also. He told me to promise him that I would always watch and take care of you. Daddy is probably rolling in his grave because of me, I'm sorry, Kansas."

"No, no, no, NO, Clover, this is not your fault, and I can't let you feel like it is!!! The first time he hit me should have been the last time. I should have told you and Smoke when you asked me about it. It was my word against everyone else's. Being in love makes you protect people who don't always deserve protection. I knew if I told you two anything, that y'all wouldn't show any mercy on him. He's not a bad person and I couldn't have that on my heart, I just couldn't."

"Wait, you said he's not a bad person??? Are you dead ass serious right now, Kansas??"

"YEA, CLOVER, I'm dead ass serious right now. I've known Ryan for six years and he's really not a bad person, Ryan's a sweetheart. I've never heard of Ryan being abusive, or maybe I wasn't listening hard enough," she answered.

"Maybe you didn't hear anything because the other women kept quiet like you. Have you ever thought about that?" I asked.

"No, but at the end of the day, Ryan is NOT a bad jawn, I know that."

"Wow, just imagine if I went upside a broad's head like he does you. Do you think they would say I'm a good person? FUCK NO, and you know that, so, quit the bullshit, Kansas! Do you know this nigga is on drugs, Kansas??"

"Yes, I know he does coke, yes, I know he cheats on me, but I love him Clover. He loves me too, but from time to time he cheats and beats me," Kansas tried to laugh, but her emotions got the best of her. The tears ran down her face followed by snot racing out of her nose. Blood also came from her mouth, but that didn't matter to her. It sounded like Kansas would use her last breath to defend Ryan. For what reason, I probably never understand.

"It sounds like you're very fine with this, but tell me I'm tripping," I demanded.

"I just want to be …. LOVED, Clover, that's it. I see you and Smoke with someone and y'all are happy! Whhhhhhyyyyy can't I have that? I want someone to be home when I get there and to carter to me like the queen I know I am," she sobbed.

"A queen will attract a king, baby, you gotta realize that," I replied.

"Sometimes, queens fall short, Clover. I want a man to love me the way Dad loved Mom. Yea, he was in the streets a lot, but that didn't stop the love that pour from his heart. Besides, I've seen you and Smoke fuck over so many women, what's the difference when someone does it to me?"

"The difference is that I sold coke, not put it in my nose. Yea, I've played on a few smuts, but putting my hands on a woman is something none of them bitches could ever utter! You're my sister, not them, I care about YOU! Another thing, if their brothers allowed what we did to their sisters, they are some damn fools. You can't imagine how I felt when Star called me. She thought you were dead, Kan, fuckin' dead, yo!"

"Men cheat, that's what y'all do. Us women have learned to just accept it, even though we know it's wrong. I haven't come across a man yet that hasn't cheated on his woman," she spoke.

"Look, it doesn't matter if you're a man or woman, people only do what you allow them to do. If I did anything to a female, that's because she let me. Look at your fucking eye, Kan, you really have the nerve to defend him or any part of this. Wow, never in my life I thought I would see this day come," chuckling with my head down, I stood to my feet, walking through the room. Taking one look at my iron, I then put it on safety. Clearly it was no need for it, unless Ryan came back looking for some smoke. If he did, I didn't mind giving him what his heart desired.

"What do you mean?" She questioned, wiping her snotty jawn on her hand. Then she scooted closer to her bed using the hanging sheet to wipe her hand.

"I never thought I would see you so fuckin and weak, you're drawlin'."

"Weak, that's something I could never be, Clover. Now YOU'RE the one is drawlin," she said.

"Well, show me you're not, let's go."

"Go where, my body is killing me," she asked.

"Anywhere, but here," I replied.

"Okay," tucking Kansas hair behind her ears, I squatted to the floor, kissing my sister's forehead saying, "you know I'mma kill that noodle bull and if I don't, I'll come close to it."

"Okay," she silently cried. I had enough of seeing my sister like this and it was time we bounced. Scooping Kansas into my hands, I carefully rose to my feet, walking out of the room. Kansas held onto me firmly with her warm tears and blood soaking my black t-shirt. For some reason, I felt her pain, as if I was the one with the busted lip, bruised hip, and black eye.

"Are you hungry," I questioned, grabbing her purse from the countertop and closing the living room door. Trying to lock the door and still hold Kansas was hard, but I managed to do it. With every step I took, Kansas held my neck tighter. When I was finally able to open the car door and gently place her in, I pulled the shirt over my head tossing it into the car. After that, I ran around my car rushing to start it.

Adjusting her sit further back to recline, relax, and mostly hide from people, Kansas asked, "where is Manhattan?"

"She's home, sleeping, Hat has work in the morning," I replied, pulling out of the driveway.

"Oh, okay, I've been meaning to talk to you about something," she yawned carefully, trying not to cause any more pain to herself.

"About what, baby," I asked, while I adjusted the air conditioner to a cooler temperature.

"You and Manhattan, I love you two together, it's like she brings out the best in you."

"I feel like that too, I think I love her more than she loves me," I chuckled.

"What? Clover Porter using the L word, it's going to snow tomorrow," Kansas pushed out a few giggles, but stopped and held her chest.

"You good?"

"Yea, I'm good."

"Ard, but yea, the L word, we're in love, it would be hard to not fall in love with a woman like that," I spoke.

"Hey, nothing is wrong with that, there is no time frame on when you can fall in love. Trust me, I should know that. Just treat her right, Clover."

"You know I will, I have no reason to treat her any other way," I smiled.

"Okay," Kansas smiled, but rolled to her side, staring out of the window.

"Word to, everything is going a hundred with us, but it's that fuckin' Marcy, bruh!'"

"What'cha mean?"

"Shorty alllwwassyyyyysssss has my fuckin' name in her jawn. Hat can't even mention my name without her throwing salt on it, real talk. I don't want to disrespect her sister on the strength of her, but that smut is trying me. I don't take disrespect too lightly, everybody knows that."

"I feel you on that and I would hate for her to have to see that OTHER side of you. That UGLY side of you, it's not nice," Kansas chuckled a little.

"Trust me, I got into with the bitch a couple of months ago because of Gary. When she told Hat the story, you know she was the victim and I was the villain."

"Typical shit, G, but since she's doing all that talking, does she know what happened?"

"You know what, with all that talking that bitch does, she never told Hat what happened. Ain't that funny, right," I laughed.

"Very much funny, but someone needs to tell her. Just waiting this long will have Manhattan in her feelings."

"Trust me, I've thought about telling her a million times, but I don't know how to tell her," I replied.

"Uuuuhhhhhhh, just tell her how low down her knock-off jersey dress wearing sister is."

"Did you hear what you said, LOW DOWN, no telling how Marcy will flip this on me, Kan, Hat and I are good, yo, I don't want to fuck up what we have going on because of Marcy."

"Trust me, Clove, I feel that a hundred percent, BUT what if Marcy tells here before you do. Just imagine the extra lies she'll add to the story. I say tell her asap and thank me later for making you tell her," she smirked.

"You have all the answer to my problems, huh, sis?"

"That's what it looks like, but I can't answer my own," biting her top like to disguise the pain, I could tell Kan was in serious pain. She was a strong jawn, who hated hospitals and medication. She always had home remedies

"Kan, do you want to go to the hospital? After that, I'll get you a room for a few days."

"Yes, on the room, and no, to the hospital, you know I don't play that shit. Just give me a banana and some milk, I'll be straight," she laughed.

"Okay, superwoman, but I don't think it's a good idea for you to go home. Matter of fact, it's best you move from there. You can start looking for another place Monday morning. Let me know what you find, I'll have your money for the deposit and shit."

"What, Clover, it's Saturday, fuck, it's Sunday morning really," she said, sounding shocked, but I don't know why. It wouldn't be the first time I made her do something she didn't want to do. See, one thing about Kan, she respected my gangster and knew I didn't play when it was something like this. Eventually, she'll thank me and realize my decision was right. Until then, if she was upset with me, I didn't give a fuck.

"I'm glad you know your days of the week, but do you want to tell me what day comes after Thursday," I asked, laughing, but Kansas cut her eyes in my direction.

"Kansas, I know you're upset, but I'm only doing this because I love you. I know niggas who wouldn't give a fuck if something like this happened to their sister. You're my ONLY sister, I love you to the moon and back, girl."

"I know you do, Clover, but it's going to be hard starting over," she pouted.

"So, what, people start over every day, b, you're worrying about petty shit."

"What I'm really worried about is Mom finding out," she shook her head, uttering.

"As long as none of us tell her, she won't know a thing. I told Star to keep her jawn shut also and to get away from there for a while. I'm glad no one called the laws on y'all."

"You and me both, I don't need them in my mix making, reports and shit."

"That's the same shit I said to myself. When you get a chance, call Star, shorty is worried about you."

"Lord, I will, she always does this," Kansas thought by speaking under her breath that I wouldn't hear her, but I heard exactly what she said.

"Sounds like this ain't the first time she been in the middle of you and Ryan."

"No, it isn't," Kansas sighed, shaking her head and tears slowly filled her eyes. She tried speaking, but it was like her words couldn't come out.

"When he hit me with the slap, my head slammed against the wall and I screamed. That's when he ran out of the house, but Star also was walking across the street to figure out what was wrong. When she walked into the house, Star thought I was dead this time. She's seen me like this a few times, but I guess this time was different. I guess the neighbors decided to mind their business this rip too. After calling the cops and the bitch take the nigga back, fuck, I would mind my business too after a while."

"You know what? I would ask you how many times he knocked your ass out, but I won't. All it's gon' do is piss me off even more, yo."

"Clover, I want something nice, in your neighborhood, two bedrooms. Nice, but simple, ard," she said.

"You got that, anything for my queen," I smiled.

"Thank you, bro, I love you for life," she mumbled.

"I love you too, sis, I love you too."

"You're right, I sounded like a fool defending him, but that's only because I DO love him. My love for him didn't end tonight, but I wish it would have. It's going to take some time for me heal from this physically, mentally, and emotionally, but I can handle that. I'm more sorry than I'm portraying to be, yo."

"Everything is going to fall back into place, sis, and you know I got' cha back all the way."

"I know and that's why I love you so much."

Before I knew it, she was passed out sleeping. Five minutes later, she was snoring like she hadn't slept in five days.

For an hour, I drove through the streets of Philly, thinking about everything. Shit had to get better for my sister, losing her to domestic violence wasn't an option. If so, I be damn if my family would be the only ones crying in all black.

Chapter 6

Looking at the unknown Pittsburg number calling my phone, I was a Lil' hesitant about answering the call. Assuming it was a lick calling, I answered the called.

"Yyooooooooo!"

"Hello, is this Clover," the familiar voice questioned, it was Star.

"Yea, what up, Star? Is something wrong with my sister?"

"No, no, I was calling on my own behalf," she giggled.

"Oh, word, what's up?"

"Well, I just want to say thank you for what you did that night," Star uttered.

"You're welcome, love."

"If you weren't taken, I would ask to take you on a date," Star laughed.

"Too bad I'm taken, but let me get back to what I was doing. It was nice talking to you, beautiful."

"Same here, Clover, bye," ending the call smirking, I dropped the phone into my pocket. Lately, I got a lot of Lil' phone calls like this from bitches trying to see how far they could go with me. I didn't have time for the unimportant shit like this.

"Nigga, who was that," Smoke questioned me, with a curious look on his face. Smacking my lips and giving him the side eye, I replied, "that was Star, Kan's neighbor."

"*Kan's neighbor*, what does she want with you?"

"Damn, nosy ass boy, she just wanted to tell me thank you."

"Thank you for what, dicking her down? She probably ain't been fucked on in a Lil' hot minute," Smoke laughed, clapping his hands, I lightly chuckled. This nigga was a true clown, but I loved him to death.

"Nah, never that, I gave her a couple of dollars to move around that night that shit happened with Ryan."

"Oh, okay, but Hat better not find about that," he smirked.

"It's nothing to hide, I told her about it. Hat said it was nice that I paid for Star's hotel room."

"That shit sound nice, my brother," Smoke laughed, he didn't take anything seriously.

"You know what, seems like it's always one thing after one thing. I need a fuckin' break from reality and society, real talk."

After getting a fucked-up text message from Manhattan, it was only right I rushed home. News about Ryan getting his ass beat by some young cats, two days ago, spread like wildfire. Nearly killing him, all fingers pointed to Smoke and me. The news of him beating Kansas ass even made it back to my mom and she was pissed. I think she was more hurt than pissed, because Kansas hid the abuse for so fuckin' long. My mom couldn't look at Kansas without crying and neither could she. My mom started talking crazy when she said we needed to turn ourselves in. That shit was mad funny, yo. With solid alibis, they couldn't pin anything against us, even though they wanted to. The cops knew what was up and so did we.

I guess Ryan was solid, because he didn't go to the police station, I guess he took his lick like a man, shit, probably was the only time he's been a man in his life. On the other hand, it was his crazy ass family who took matters into their own hands. Four hours ago, the cops caught Smoke and me coming down Broad Street hacking us up. The laws knew us well and we knew everything about them from their schedules, hobbies, families, and what they ate for Sunday dinner. Since Smoke was a petty cat, he bagged a few of their wives and side bitches just to let them know who really was running the streets. The ones with wives, really didn't care, because they were too busy trying to keep their secret on the hush.

We were at the police station for two hours, being held for questioning, but they also tried to slip in some ole shit. Like always, I didn't know anything and wasn't saying too much without my lawyer being in the room. Cops hated when a street nigga mentioned anything about his lawyers. They assumed you only had money for clothes and to splurge on groupie hoes. They attempted to 'ruff' us up a Lil' bit, but that was Lil' bitty shit to us. Word to Mommy, Smoke and I have been through worse on a better day. We would never let something small like this fuck with our heads or paper. When Manhattan got the call, I was at the police station, her extra ass was all destroyed and left work. I told her it wasn't that deep, but she didn't want to hear that mess. In her eyes, it felt like death was knocking on her door. This was the shit I promised to keep her away from, but I was breaking promises already.

"This shit is crazy, word to Mommy," I said, laughing as Smoke and I walked up the driveway, approaching my front steps. Shaking his head, he replied, "God was with that Ryan that night, because I would have killed him with no problem."

"God and every other person we pray to."

"Fuckin' with that clown I could have been off in some pussy or something," Smoke laughed.

"Fuck, I could have been fuckin' my shorty. Man, I know Hat will have an ear full for me when I walk in the house."

"What the fuck she texted you, anyways," Smoke asked.

"Some shit about her people don't want us together. They heard what happened, now they hate me," I laughed at this, because it was funny to me. I wasn't crazy enough to laugh about this to Hat, she took this seriously.

"I can't wait until bitches learn how to mind their business. What does y'all business have to do with them? Hat is good with you."

"Same thing I'm saying, I would ever put Hat in any danger. From jump, I told her I would never bring any of my street life around her. Bruh, I don't even bring a blunt or lighter in the house when she's there," I chuckled.

"Fuck it, it can be y'all against the world and you know I got' cha back."

"Then that means it's you, me, and Manhattan against the world," I laughed dapping Smoke down. Right or wrong, Smoke always had my back.

"Fuck it, that's what it is then," he laughed a little louder opening the door. Finding Ryker sitting on the couch, flipping through an *Ebony* magazine, I nodded my head at her.

"Damn," Smoke whispered to me, but I ignored him.

"Hey, Ryker, where's Hat," I asked, closing the door scanning the house for her. Besides her keys and clutch on the countertop, there wasn't a trace of Manhattan in the house.

"What up, Spitta, she's in the bathroom taking a shower. That bullshit with her people really fucked her head up. On top of that, you getting questioned messed with her head a little. You know Hat ain't built for this street shit, that's why they made sidewalks, for pretty girls like her," Ryker laughed.

"You're sounding like me right about now. I didn't mean to get her all worried, this is small shit to a giant," I replied.
"Trust me, Clover, I already know that. I told my girl don't worry about you, but you Manhattan wasn't trying to hear that," slowly placing her hands on her hips, Ryker licked her lips, flipping her long brown hair. Even thought she was talking to me, Ryker couldn't keep her eyes off Smoke. I didn't have to look over my shoulder to know Smoke had his eyes glued to Ryker.

"Say, Clove, you ain't gon' introduce me to your home girl," Smoke said, slightly moving me to the side, he wanted a better view of Ryker's fine ass. Standing five feet flat, with hazel eyes, and facial frame that resembled a heart, Ryker was a gorgeous girl, but she couldn't hold a candle next to Manhattan. With his pockets in his hands, Smoke stared at Ryker like she was a work of art on display. By the way Ryker stared back, she was feeling the way Smoke eye-balled her. I guess she liked being on display for a real one.

"Damn, my bad, Ryker, this is my big bro, Smoke. Smoke, this is Manhattan's friend and co-worker," I said and they shook hands. Smoke was still eye balling Ryker and Ryker was still blushing like Smoke was the first man to ever lay eyes on her.

"It's nice to meet you, Smoke," she released his hand, tucking her hair behind her small ears.

"Likewise, beautiful, likewise."

"I hope Smoke isn't your real name, but if it is, I can learn to like it," she laughed.

"Nah, my real name is Clerk, Clerk Porter and no, I'm not kin to Rich Porter. I swear, we get that question every time we met someone new," he laughed.

"I'm glad you got that out the way," I laughed.

"If my real name was Smoke, you would learn to love it, not just like it," Smoke smirked.

"I can see you're funny already, Mr. Porter."

"Yea, but I can be a lot of things, depending on what you want," slightly rubbing his hands together with a smirk on his face, Smoke was talking that cash money shit females loved to hear. Just like Manhattan, Ryker wasn't the type to go for a street nigga, but I guess Smoke could change that. It wasn't much a nigga like him couldn't do, I witnessed that with my own eyes.

"Oh, yea, you're talking some big shit I hope you can back up," she laughed, flipping her hair again.

"Trust me, I do, and always will do that. You better ask about me, Smoke holds weight in the streets," flexing his big muscles, Smoke chuckled, seemed like that corny shit turned Ryker on.

"Instead of asking the streets, I'd rather ask you. You know the streets don't always tell the truth," using her long blue fingernails, Ryker rubbed Smoke's face. In that moment, I knew he was feeling shorty, because he NEVER let a soul touch his face.

"Well, how about I get your number and we can discuss how much my name holds weight?"

"I like the sound of that," she smirked.

"You have that brown skin thing going on like Nia Long. All you're missing is the short haircut," Smoke laughed, stroking Ryker's long hair that was all hers hanging to her hips. Ryker was in love with covering her face with make-up, but she didn't do that weave shit either.

"Alright, looks like y'all two got it from here, I need to check on my shorty. Walking away and jogging down the hall, I stood in front the room door, adjusting the collar on my Gucci shirt. Before coming home, Smoke and I blew a couple of blunts and I had to make sure I didn't smell like it. Knowing Manhattan, she probably smelled my Kush from the front door.

Knocking on the door, but slowly entering the bedroom, I found Manhattan sitting on the edge of the bed. When she rose her head, her face was covered with tears, something I never wanted to witness.

"Baby, what's wrong," I rushed to close the door to be by her side. Holding her hand softly I stared at her waiting for answers, but her eyes were glued to the floor instead.

"Whatever y'all did to Ryan, everyone knows, Clover. I don't know if my parents heard about it, or Marcy ran her mouth to them, but they know. Now they're saying they don't want to have any dealings with me if I'm with you. I love my family, Clover, but I love you too," she whispered, silently crying. Holding her tightly, I exhaled loudly, allowing Manhattan's tears to fall on me. I never wanted Manhattan, or any woman, to choose me over her family, but I couldn't let them come between us. Why, because they couldn't love shorty like I did. This was a different kind of love, the kind of love no family member, or man, could ever give Manhattan. It didn't matter how much her family CLAIMED to LOVE her, I didn't believe that shit. If they loved her like her family said they said, those jawns would never attempt to make her choose.

"What?"

"Clover, what did y'all do to him? I'm hearing all kind of stories, I'm not sure what to believe now, this is crazy!!"

"I don't know what you're talking about, yo, I didn't do that boy shit. When that happened, I was here, with you, watching re-runs of *The Nanny*. When the laws called you, you did tell them that, right?" I asked.

"You know I did, it's the truth, but you don't have to lie to me about anything."

"Baby, I'm not lying to you, but I have a good feeling that Marcy dropped that info into your parent's ears. Ole mess ass, but I have something to tell you about her."

"Oh, Lord, what happened now, Clover? It's like every second is something with her!"

"There's another reason Marcy doesn't like me, like before we got into it about Gary," I uttered.

"Ooookkkkaaaayyyyyy, tell me the reason, Clover," she demanded.

"Okay, I guess here goes nothing. Uummm, the night before that, I saw in Germantown with her crew. Marcy was high as usual, I guess she was tipsy too, because she was on that touchy shit."

"Touchy like what," Manhattan questioned, with an attitude.

"She was touchy like trying to see what that dick was like, but I wasn't feeling that. She hated the fact that I turned her down in front of her home girls and she started running off by the mouth. I tried laughing it off, but you know how your sister is. That's when I saw her again and the shit with Gary happened."

"So basically, my sister is jealous I have you and she doesn't?"

"I didn't want to say that, but yea, that's what it is. I guess Marcy isn't used of niggas turning her down. Since I'm much a 'hoe' like she says, Marcy was highly upset she couldn't get a taste of ole' Spitta's dick," grabbing my dick and laughing, Manhattan crossed her legs with her arms across her chest. The way her wet hair dripped on her body kind of turned me on, but Manhattan wasn't in the mood for any joking or loving.

"Clover, don't fucking play with me right now."

"Bae, be cool, I'm not playing with you, I'm just saying."

"Whatever, the thought of you and Marcy fucking is really pissing me off right now."

"What? I didn't even fuck that hoe. Were you even listening to anything I said?"

"Watch your mouth, Clover Porter, I heard everything you said. When were you going to tell me this, Clover?" She asked, rubbing the back of my neck. Kissing her hand to keep her calm, I replied, "I'm telling you know, but it been on my mind. I'm sorry I waited this long to tell you, but I didn't want Marcy to fuck up what we have. We have something good, I'm happy, and I'm in love with you."

"Marcy is already trying to fuck up what we have. That's no excuse for keeping something like this from me. Clover, I really thought we were better than that," she exhaled, shaking her head, I felt like shit.

"We are, bae, and once again, I'm sorry for not telling you sooner. I just don't want to come between you and your sister, shorty," I answered.

"Uhhh, I think you've already done that, but it shouldn't be like that. Who I'm involved with should have nothing to do with her. It's no secret Marcy has fucked half of the state, but I've never gotten in her business. As long as no nigga is beating her ass, she can fuck whoever she wants," Manhattan chuckled.

"Trust me, even when a nigga is beatin' their jawn, they still want you to stay out of their business," I shook my head.

"Like Kansas?"

"Shit, that was my prime example."

"Speaking on Kansas, how is she?"

"She's fine, I'm going to my mom's house later to check on her," I uttered.

"Oh, okay, that's good."

"Hat, check this out, guess who's making a love connection in the living room," I chuckled slightly, lying Hat across the bed. Rubbing her inner thigh just to make her feel comfortable and forget the conversation of Marcy ever happened, she sighed a little.

"Who?" Manhattan looked like she was dying to know. Before saying it, I had to laugh a little bit.

"Bruh, Ryker and Smoke."

"Ryker and Smoke, who??"

"How many Ryker's and Smoke's do you know," I laughed again.

"I only know your brother, Smoke, and my friend, Ryker, is that who you're talking about," kissing my forehead, Manhattan laughed with her eyes closed shaking her head. I guess the thought of Smoke and Ryker was funny to her.

"Bingo."

"Woowwwwwwwww, I'm kind of surprised, but then again, I'm not. Anybody is better than that boyfriend of hers," rolling her eyes, Manhattan kissed me again. Then suddenly were heard laughter floating from the living room. We locked eyes, laughing.

"I know damn well Smoke isn't that funny," Manhattan joked.

"He's not Chris Tucker, but clearly your homie thinks he's funny."

"Oh whatever, Clover," she smiled.

"Well, at least you're smiling and laughing now. I hate seeing you sad and crying, that shit fucks with my jawn, yo. Another thing, I think it's best you don't mention what I told you to Marcy."

"Why not?"

"Hat, I don't have time for the bullshit and drama every time I see your sister. It's only so many times I'mma let her throw juice on my white shell-toes," I laughed.

"Fuck her, you're all mines now," slowing rising and removing the damped towel from her body, Manhattan's perky, full, breasts, were slowly being exposed. I didn't know what the fuck she was doing, but seeing her naked body turned a nigga on asap. Her body was placed in front of me as if it was the Statue of Liberty. Examining every inch of her damped, but smooth skin, Hat easily turned me on by just standing there.

"Damn, girl, ummm, I'm going to holla at Smoke for a minute," I laughed, standing to my feet, but Hat playfully pushed me back onto the bed.

"Why would you want to leave and I'm standing in my birthday suit," she asked, with a grin on her face. Dropping my head with a smirk on my ace, I rubbed the back of my neck saying, "Baby, you have a nigga's dick rock hard. Whenever you're ready to give yourself to me, that's when we'll have sex. Until then, I'm still willing to wait, I want our first time to be right. No pressure, you dig?"

"That's the thing, I want to feel that pressure from you. I need to experience firsthand why all the women are crazy over Spitta," licking her lips in the sexist way possible, Hat stood over me with her breast dangling over my head. Having a clear shot of her pussy and breasts, my view was perfect. I was only getting hornier by the second, and ready to dick Hat down like I never dicked a bitch down. I'm surprise she didn't see my dick popping out my jawn.

"Are you sure you want to do this, baby," I asked squeezing her ass tightly, but also softly. My touch made chills form all over her body, plus the hairs on her arms stood up like toy soldiers. My dick was slowly getting hard, I sure hope Hat wasn't playing any pussy ass games with me for nothing. Even if she wasn't sure about finally having sex, I sure was going to persuade her let me slide nine inches of dick into her.

"Yes, I'm more than sure," with the black rubber band around my wrist, Manhattan pulled her hair into a high ponytail. Then, she pulled my Levi jeans and Polo boxers to my ankles. My big ole' dick stood tall, catching her by surprise. I could tell she ain't never seen a dick this big.

"Wow, all that's for me," Manhattan stared at my dick like it was made of gold. Once I finish dickin' her down, that's what Manhattan was going to think for life.

"Yea, all of it," grabbing Hat by the waistline, I placed her body on top of me. My view of Hat had to be of her riding my dick. It slid smoothly into her tight wet pussy, causing her to moan loudly. I smiled at the way she bit her bottom lip as she stared me in my eyes. Her long nails dug deep into my chest, but I didn't mind the pain. I was too occupied with the love faces Hat made.

"I love you, Clover Porter," she moaned, grinding her pussy softly on my dick. Hat's pussy felt so good, I couldn't even reply. I guess you say that pussy had a jawn speechless.

***

"Whatever I have to do to fix this mess, I will," leaning against his Range Rover, but also grabbing Ryker by the hips, Smoke pulled her closer to him. Ryker tried to fight him off, but his playa ways were too smooth for that. Besides, I don't think Ryker really wanted to fight him off. You know how women are though, they love playing hard to get with the men they love or even like.

"Stop," Ryker whispered, loudly, but it only made Smoke laugh. Ryker knew she was stunted so she had to laugh at herself.

"I'm serious, love, I'm gon' handle all this, ard?"

"I guess, Smoke, but I don't have time for all that messy shit. Keep that away from me and we'll be alright," she rolled her eyes, walking closer to him, nearly brushing her wide lips against his. Smoke stared Ryker in the eyes, blushing like he was crazy, but I didn't blame him. These days, a good woman was hard to come by. The only fucked up thing was that Ryker was in a relationship, which meant she and Smoke were creeping around. Ryker didn't go into too much details about her relationship, but the few details she did say, told me a lot. That relationship wasn't going to last long for a lot of reasons, mainly, Smoke. I also overheard her and Hat talking a few times, and Ryker never said anything good about this young bol. Even if he wasn't a youngin, he would be one in my eyes.

"I hope you have that same tone of voice, if your nigga come my way," he laughed.

"Boy, that's the last thing I'm worried about. No telling where his ass is anyways," Ryker prompted her hands on her slim hips rolling her eyes, but once again, she looked over her shoulders. Smoke laughed louder, and harder, making Ryker giggle with her head down.

"Fuck, I can't tell you ain't worried about him. Every time we're together, you're looking over your jawn and shit."

"That's because I don't want any problems, seem like we have enough of those with you," Ryker said, joking, making Smoke give her a stale face.

"See, it's not funny when the joke is on you, huh," she pointed at Smoke laughing. In a playful way, he nibbled on her finger giving her a kiss on the hand.

"Naw, it's not, but I was thinking we go inside. It's fuckin' hot out here and I don't want you sweatin' like a slave," grabbing Ryker's hand without giving her a chance to reply, Smoke and Ryker walked through the grass, entering the house since the door was wide open. Every time Smoked thought about what the fuck happened, he got heated. It didn't matter how much he apologized, he still did it every chance he got. Smoke had a good heart and never liked pulling anyone in his drama or mess.

"I'm really sorry about what happened earlier, I told that bitch we were done four weeks ago. Long before you came in the picture, I don't understand why this bitch is tripping now," Smoke paced back and forth through the living room, smoking on a cigarette to calm his nerves. It's like every time he thought about what happened, he got pissed off even more.

"It's okay, as long you pay for the damages that crazy bitch did to my car. I mean, I can't stay mad all fuckin' day about it," Ryker shook her head, wishing she smoked. If she did, Ryker would have smoked the entire pack of cigarettes in Smoke's pocket.

"I'm pretty sure this ain't how you wanted to spend your off day. I damn sure wouldn't want to spend my Saturday like this," Smoke released the smoke through his nose, feeling defeated. This wasn't the first time something like this happened, but it had to be the last fucking time something like this happened.

"You know how that goes, bro, bitches only want you when somebody else has you," I said.

Smoke's ex-girlfriend, Miranda, spotted him and Ryker together, and jumped deep in her feelings. That smut bust the headlights and three tires on Ryker's Jeep Wrangler. Miranda was an ole' crazy bitch I always said was overly obsessed with my brother. On top of that, the bitch was insecure, plus, mad annoying. When Smoke wasn't next to her, Miranda called his phone non-stop trying to figure out his whereabouts. If he didn't answer, she called whoever's phone Smoke was with, just to get in touch with him. If he still didn't answer, Miranda rode through the hood looking for him like a true stalker. This was one broad who didn't mind popping up to the trap like she had an invitation. Miranda and Smoke were only together for a year, but the bitch caused a lot of problems for no reason. My mom hated the ground that girl walked on, and her and Kansas stayed into it. Fucking around with Miranda's ass, a nigga took a lot of loses, but it was never anything we couldn't bounce back from.

"Exactly, and that's the shit I don't have time for, bruh. Too much shit is going on, I don't need any extra heat tagging to my name. I have enough jackets on me, real rap," Smoke spoke loudly, in a flat voice, that's how I knew Miranda had him beyond pissed.

"Shorty was out of pocket for that. You should have smoked that hoe, show her why they call you Smoke," I laughed.

Smoke and Ryker only been conversing for two weeks, but shit was real between them already. I thought I was a sucker for Manhattan, fuck, I had nothing on Smoke. He was so in love that he probably would have tossed roses at Ryker's feet every time she walked by. I don't know if it was lust or love, but Smoke's eyes lit up every time Ryker spoke, walked, or even breathed.

"Clover, watch your damn mouth. You wouldn't want anyone calling Kansas, or me, out of our names," Hat flared her nose, shouting.

"Exactly," Kansas said, as she dropped the box of towels onto the floor. She didn't waste any time ripping the tape from the box to open it and save the towels.

"My bad, baby."

"Uh huh, anyways," Manhattan sized me up, saying. I blew a few kisses at her laughing, and she laughed as well.

"Damn, girl, this is a bomb ass place you got here," Manhattan stood in the middle of the empty living room staring at every inch of the place. By the look in her eyes, I could tell she couldn't wait to decorate the place from top to bottom. I didn't mind paying for all that home décor shit, because it would keep Hat out of my face while

I did my trap shit. With four fuckin' killings in Harrison Project, the streets were hot, my only choice staying out of the mix. The last thing I needed was to be at the wrong place, at the wrong time, getting caught up.

"All thanks go to Clover, I'm in love with this place," removing the black sunglasses from her face to place then on the damped countertop, Kansas wrapped her arm around Manhattan's neck smiling. I was glad to see her black eye was gone and the swelling finally went down. No one's seen Ryan since that night, which was probably a good thing. Kansas said he attempted to contact her a few times, but she didn't reply. I just hope that was the truth and not another lie from my sister.

"You know it' all love, sis, anything to make you happy," I said.

"That's why I love you, brother," smiling while walking in my direction, Kansas gave me a hug and the kiss on the cheek. It made me feel good that she was happy and not a single tear was in sight.

"You know I love you too, sis," as I looked up, Smoke's eyes were glued to Ryker, who was fumbling through her phone. He smirked a little, but I could tell he was jealous. Knowing him, he probably thought she was texting her ole' man.

"Damn, must be a dope ass text message," Smoke said to Ryker, while sitting on the barstool. Ryker laughed, but she didn't raise her head. Once she was done, Ryker closed her phone, slipping it into her back pocket saying, "yea, it was, my little cousin from Florida will be in town next Thursday. Is there anything else you want to know, the airline she's taking or when her flight lands?"

"Don't play with me, Ryker," Smoked replied.

"Yea, that's what I thought," Ryker rolled her eyes, laughing.

"Smoke is in his feelings," I whispered, loudly.

"Naw, just keeping up with the opps," he laughed.

"So, Ryker, what's the deal you and this clown ass man of yours? Well, should I call him your boyfriend, because he's nothing, but a boy that's a friend," I said, laughing.

"There's no deal, I guess it is what it is at this point," shrugging her shoulders as she walked to Smoke, Ryker stood between Smoke's legs, with her arms around his neck. It looked like he wanted to say something, but her beauty had him stuck like a bad drug you couldn't shake.

"Don't worry, Lil' bro, I'll give her a Lil' jawn to shake that boy. Once she does, Ryker will be begging to become a Porter," Smoke licked his lips, laughing, but Ryker flared her nose, trying to fight back her smile. She knew what Smoke said was true, even if she didn't want to admit it right now.

"Ayyyeeee, do your shit, Smoke, I'm pretty sure Manhattan is ready to propose to me," I laughed.

"Boy, we all know that's a lie and it's the other way."

"Aye, lick's calling, Clove, let's go," staring at his phone screen with squinted eyes, Smoke then closed the phone to drop it into his pocket. He planted a kiss on Ryker's cheek, making her smile, but she also rolled her eyes. She liked the way Smoke made her feel, but Ryker also hated the way he had her feeling in a short period of time. Kicking it with Smoke was cool, but she knew it would only be a matter of time that her heart would be stretched between two men.

"Bet, baby, I'll be back, do you need anything while I'm out," I asked Manhattan, with my hands around her hips. She shook her head from side to side saying, "I just need you to be careful, that's it."

"You know you got that, I love you," I kissed her lips, and she replied, "I love you too."

　　　　Manhattan waited until Smoke and I were in the car, then she closed the door. She was a little quiet and Kansas noticed it from the jump.

"Hat, what's good," Kansas sat on the floor asking. Biting on her bottom lip and nodding her head, Manhattan said, "what's good with you, Kan?"

"I'm Gucci, but what's really good with you? You seem mad off today, what the fuck did Clover do?"

"She's right, Hat, what's up with that," Ryker asked.

"I don't even know where to start, but everything is a-1 between Clove and me."

"Okay, so, what's the problem," Kansas questioned.

"I'm drifting further, and further, from my family, and what Clover told me really has my head messed up."

"What happened, girl," Ryker asked.

"Clover decided to tell me how the argument between him and Marcy started that day in the projects."

"I thought it was because she tried to bust Gary's windows," Ryker questioned.

"Oh Lord," Kansas whispered, opening the box, but her comment caught Manhattan's attention. Slowly turning in Kansas' direction, with her hands on her hips, Manhattan spoke, "Oh, Lord, it sounds like you already knew about this."

"Hat, I did, I'm the one that pushed him to tell you sooner. Please don't be mad at me," she begged.

"Wait, I'm confused as fuck right now, can someone fill me in," Ryker asked.

"The day before that, Clover saw Marcy in the projects. Marcy was drunk, or high, trying to fuck him, but he didn't want to fuck her."

"What the fuck? Ole my God, not the Marcy who hates Clover so much because he's a hoe," Ryker covered her mouth, giggling.

"Yea, that same Clover, I nearly fainted and dropped my oowops," Kansas clapped her hands laughing.

"Get the gun and shoot it, like, are y'all serious right now? I know my second question is about to be stupid, but did she tell you about any of this?"

"Nope, and I'm still waiting."

"Are you going to ask her," Kansas asked.

"Nah, it's no need to, the bitch will flip it on Clover somehow. Shawty was salty because she couldn't get the dick. Marcy thought Clover was going to tell Gary, but he's too solid for that. That's the REAL reason she threw that juice on his shoes."

"Word to, I wanted to knock your sister's head off her shoulders," Kansas tossed her hands in the air, and threw her head back. Manhattan gasped, but she laughed as well. Maybe Marcy needed a good ass whipping to get her fucking mind right.

"Well, I'm glad you didn't, that would be awkward as hell now."

"Marcy gotta chill though, Clover doesn't bother her at all," Manhattan replied.

"Since we're speaking of men, how long are you going to be a playa, Ryker," Manhattan asked, laughing, but Ryker flicked her the middle finger. She didn't want to be a playa, but she couldn't help how she had feelings for two men. Smoke and her man were the total opposite, Ryker liked the way Smoke thugged her out.

"I am not a player, Smoke and I are just friends."

"Yea, that's how it always starts, but it's good to be friends first," Manhattan joked.

"Smoke's name is ringing like crazy right now, and this shit with Miranda, I'm not feeling. The last thing I need is my boyfriend knowing about this."

"What are you going to tell him about your car," Kansas questioned.

"I don't have to worry about that, he's out of town working. By the time he gets back, Smoke will have everything repaired."

"Let me tell y'all something, I love my brothers, but dating them aren't easy. Fuck, dating me isn't easy, I can tell you in the humblest way. I wish Ryan had a sister who could have told me the exact same thing. Real talk, I would have run the other way, all the way down Broad Street."

"What are you trying to say, Kan," Manhattan asked.

"I'm not saying anything bad, my brothers are good people. I know the world doesn't feel like that, but they really are. I've literally, seen Clover give a junkie the shoes and socks off his feet. Last year, Smoke gave out coats and his old clothes to the homeless. What I am saying is to be careful, and don't be a fool like me. When you see the signs, take it seriously, all of it."

"Can I ask you something, Kan," Hat asked.

"Yea, what up?"

"Why?"

"What, why what," Kansas questioned.

"Why …. Would…. You let him beat your ass like that? Kansas, that boy, because he isn't a man, he could have killed you. Then what? We would be at a funeral instead of moving into this nice ass house."

"I don't know, Hat, I really don't know. That's a question I've asked myself every night, but I do know one thing," she uttered.

"Yea, what's that?"

"Whatever it was, it couldn't be love. Love would never allow anyone to put a foot or fist to my head."

Chapter 7 (January 2009)

It all started back in 2009, on a Tuesday afternoon, when I stumbled into my favorite place to get Manhattan's lunch. On a snowy day like this, I wanted to be in my bed, but my baby had me running errands like a gofer. Money was blowing my phone up, them junkies didn't give a fuck what the weather looked like. They needed their fix, by any means.

Now running North Philly, South Philly, and Uptown, like a king, while Smoke had everything else on lock, I met Deaux Gates at Max's. Deaux was a bad motherfucker, looking like something straight out a UGK video. Even though Deaux was a bad chick, she didn't grab my attention when I walked in the door. On the other hand, dripping in swag, I had that bitch's full attention. Bagging her later that night, I already knew I could easily have mind control over shorty. Word around town was that Deaux was nothing but a smut, that got mad freaky for the right cats in Uptown. I didn't give a fuck about that, or any of them niggas in Uptown. The first day I met her, she hid my pills in her pussy with no problem. I needed a bitch like that in my life, Deaux was down to ride forever. I saw her a couple of times around town, but she had to have more than a fat ass to make me cheat on Hat.

See, Manhattan was still green to the street-life, just the way I wanted it to be. In her eyes, I was this thug in the streets, but a complete gentleman while in her arms and presence. Never in a million years, my baby thought I would cheat on her, I didn't give her a reason to think I would at first. No lie, I stayed faithful until I met Deaux, it was something about her that I couldn't resist. Maybe it was the street in her, and the way Deaux stroked my ego. Real rap, that dumb hoe would jump in front a bullet for me to prove her love and loyalty. I loved that shit, but that didn't mean I would do the same. A girl like Deaux could be replaced any day.

"Clove, when you get that, hit my line. My peoples in Pittsburg calling me non-stop for that straight drop. I gotta run to Fairmouth to drop my baby mama some money," Jimmy dapped me down, nodding his head. Jimmy Bush was my young bol from Strawberry Mansion, but he was about his paper like an old head.

"Which baby mama? You have so many," I laughed.

"Mannnnn, number four, but number five is getting on my damn nerves, bruh," he chuckled, rubbing his dry face. Jimmy was only twenty-three, but that Lil' nigga was laying pipe down since he was twelve. By his 14th birthday, he was on his third baby, but you would think he learned how to pull out.

"Stop dropping dick off every day and shorty won't be in her feelings."

"How I'm supposed to stop doing that? I love her, man, and I think she's pregnant again," Jimmy chuckled, dropping his head. Having multiple jawns was funny until that child support would kick in. Then he was going to need more than a couple of heroin packages throughout the month to make a living.

"Boy, you better slow your lil' ass down," I laughed.

"My nigga, you're like eighty-years old, when you gon' have some kids," Jimmy laughed.

"Eighty, bol, I'm still in my prime, ya dig, but in due time, I will. I'm trying to put one in Manhattan, fuck, maybe even two."

"Trust me, I'm a prime example of that shit is easy. I gotta get my tubes tied or something, these bitches trapping me," he joked.

"Keep your jawn in your pants and you wouldn't have that problem," I chuckled.

"Yea, yea, yea, I've been hearing that pussy ass shit all my life, and I still ended up like the *Brady Bunch*."

"Fuck around and look like them Amish families," I joked.

"Never that, I'll get my tubes snipped before that happens. Two of my kid's birthdays are this month and you know my baby mamas going out all just because it ain't their money. I gotta move that work asap."

"Real talk, that pack won't be dropped off until later, you can take your time," I said.

"Bet, bet, I'll be waiting, yo, fuck with me," dapping me down again, Jimmy grabbed his food walking out the building clutching his coat tightly. Jimmy was a wild cannon, so I always watched his back when I was around him. You never know when a nigga would rock out on him or catch him slipping without his stick.

Once he got into his car, I chuckled again once turning away. My youngin would forever be wildin' and living like he didn't have a care in the world.

"Say, Patrick, let me get the usual, and one for my girl. You already know how she likes her jawn," I stated, reaching into my pocket grabbing a fifty-dollar bill. A few bitches who were mad at me for curving them was in the building. Me being the show-off I was, I pulled out my stack of money to show off. I got the satisfaction of listening to them breath heavily and rolled their eyes. It wasn't me who they wanted, it was my dick and money; the two things I didn't give crusty hoes anymore.

"Youse want whole or half sandwiches, Spit," he asked, while wiping the sweat from his forehead. I thought about it for a second, then said, "Whole sandwiches and keep the change, yo."

"Ard, coming up," tapping the glass while walking off, Patrick walked to the register leaving me alone in my thoughts. A lot of shit was on my mind, but it wasn't anything that could stress me out. With the way that heroin, meth, and pills, were pumping through the state, I could feel a fuckin' drought coming soon. Everyone thought selling drugs was a piece of cake, but my nigga, it was far from a cake walk. Being popped by the laws wasn't the only thing you had to worry about. It was the opps coming in different shapes and forms to knock you off your game. Then you had bitches who would do anything to take what you have. Even if that meant setting you up for the next nigga to get a come up. Don't let me start on droughts and your plug getting popped. Shit can turn drier than the desert and fuck with your cash flow in a big way, word to.

"I guess you're too faithful to speak," someone said, as they walked out of the building with an attitude. Whoever she was, I didn't turn around paying her any attention.

"Your girl, huh," Someone said, but I didn't pay them any attention either. These bitches were mad annoying, yo and didn't want to take no for an answer.

"Helllllllooooo," she said again. When I did turn around, I felt a soft tap on my left shoulder. Now I was annoyed, with a mug on my face when I turned to the left saying, "What?"

"Youse getting that cheesesteak for your shorty, huh?" Smiling with her bottom grill showing, Deaux had my full attention right then and there, it's like a light bulb went off in my head. Slowly sizing her up and down, I smirked saying, "Yea, that's what I said, yo."

"Hhhmmmppphhh, I didn't think I would ever see the day Spitta would get cuffed," she smiled wider, shoving her hands into the front pockets of her denim jean jacket. It was cold as fuck outside, but Deaux still wore a Lakers' jersey, white booty shorts, with white shell toe Adidas, and a bright yellow bubble jacket.

"They didn't think there would be a man walking on the moon, but somehow they saw footprints."

"Wow, still slick by the mouth I see," she laughed.

"How would you know that, I don't recall telling you anything slick before?"

"I've seen you handle a couple of bitches and niggas before, that's why. I'm Deaux Gates, I just moved back to Philly a few days ago," extending her hand out to shake my hand and expose her long fingernails, I couldn't help, but to notice the gold Rolex on Deaux's skinny wrist. She had to be two things; a paper chaser or fuckin with one.

"Oh yea, where was you living like that?"

"I was in New York for two years, Spanish Harlem, but I was still coming to my neck of the woods. I can't forget about my hood, you know," she replied.

"Word to, I gotta couple of homies that way. Harlem and Carter Wright, do you know them?"

"That's your homies," Deaux asked, dropping her head.

"Listen when I talk, shorty, I just said that, but why?"

"Let's just say……. I taught Harlem a couple of things he won't ever forget. As for Carter's Lil' fast ass, I heard he's holding the streets down while his big brother is away. I can respect youngin for that, I might just give him a taste of pussy for his hard work," she smirked, patting her itchy head. The color of her hair made Deaux stick out like a sore thumb, as if she already wasn't sticking out. The cooper hair color and hazel brown eyes was something I called soul snatchers. It was kind of hard staring that bitch in the eyes without getting hypnotized. Now, if you were a sucker fool, the dead ass opposite of me, Deaux would have you hooked and in love just by her conversation.

"That's what he's supposed to do, but I don't think you should put that pussy on my lil' bro."

"Why not, are you going to be jealous," Deaux laughed.

"Fuck no, I don't need Carter being tender dick. Too much money to be made in the N.Y.C.," I laughed. Patrick handed me the sandwiches dapping me down and walked off. The look he gave me, I knew that meant leave Deaux the fuck alone. He's been giving me that look since I was a kid and he saw me chopping it up with a bunch of snake ass niggas.

"Speaking of money, I need to get back on my grind. I heard you got that connect on straight drop, no water whip. I need some of that in my life, money is good, yo," she spoke.

"Bet, bet, I got you, love, put my number in your phone and we can link up tonight to handle that."

"While you're handling that, you can handle something else too," slowly licking her big pink lips that were covered with a sweet strawberry lip gloss, Deaux raised her jacket slowly walking in a small circle. That tiny waistline, wide hips, flat stomach, and ass cheeks hanging out her shorts sure looked good. She dead ass wanted Spitta to drop of drugs, and I'm talking about that dope dick. With her hair styled in bantu knots and the baby hairs slicked down, she looked mad cute, yo.

"You're fine and all, but didn't I just say I gotta ole' lady," I asked, slapping Deaux on her ass. Watching it jiggle had my dick jumping and busting through my pants. Not for a split second I thought what if Manhattan would hear about any of this.

"I don't see a wedding ring on your finger, or am I going blind," with a smirk on her face, Deaux grabbed my hands looking for the imaginary ring.

"Nah, no wedding ring, yet, but that will change eventually."

"Yea, just what I thought, no wedding ring. Even if you would have had one, I wouldn't have been bothered," she laughed.

"Shorty, you must have a thing for married men, huh," I laughed, Deaux wasn't insulted by what I said. She laughed also, shrugging her shoulders.

"I just like what I like. If he's taken or married, what the fuck that has to do with me?"

"I guess, but hey, do your shit," I replied.

"I need to order my jawn, but here's my number," grabbing the pen and business card that was on the countertop, Deaux scribbled the ten-digit New York number on the back. Then she kissed the business card, leaving her lip print on it to press it against my lips. As she walked out of the building, I chuckled, sliding the card into my pocket, Deaux wasn't taking no for an answer. With a body and face like hers, she probably never had to hear the word no. I was starting to think she only came into Max's because of me, the bitch didn't order shit.

Since she knew Carter, mostly knowing Harlem on a personal level, I had to ask them about her. Harlem was on lock down, so, Carter had to give me the run down about Deaux. I had to make sure this jawn was legit before I sold her anything. For all I knew, this could be a setup, then I would be in the same situation as Harlem.

Walking out of Max's, I jumped into my car, turning it on. I didn't waste any time cracking the heater to warm that mutherfucker up. Looking over my shoulders to check my surroundings, I reached for my phone to call Carter, and on the second ring, he answered the call.

"Yyyoooooo, what up, four-leaf Clover," Carter said, through the speaker. The sound of noisy ass people in the background drowned his deep voice out. Once the noise faded a little, I said, "say, lil' bro, you busy?"

"Nah, at home, but what's up," Carter asked.

"Why the fuck you ain't at school," I asked, dropping the bag on the passenger seat slowly driving off. Jawns act like they didn't know how to drive in the fuckin' snow, that shit pissed me off.

"Man, look, it's like every day I'm dead ass fightin' somebody because of what Harlem did. Everybody knows I did it and people are mad at me! Clove, I didn't tell him to do shit, yo!"

"Carter, fuck that shit and what people say. You think if I did what you did, Smoke wouldn't have done the same thing?? You gotta stop letting that shit get to you, iight?"

"Yea, I hear you, but what up," Carter asked.

"I ran into this lil' joint a few minutes ago at Max's. She said she knows you and Harlem, especially Harlem," I replied.

"Oh, word, what's her name?"

"Deaux Gates, I thi—"

"Deaux Gates, mannnn, I know that hoe, real freaky," he laughed.

"By the conversation we had, I can tell shorty is a freaky. Her name is out there like a half of brick that's going for the low."

"Just imagine how it's buzzing down here. For the right block bleeder, girl get dumb nasty for them niggas out of Spanish Harlem and Tompkins Projects. One time, I walked in on her getting bodied by Harlem and the bitch wanted me to watch," he clapped his hands laughing.

"Deaux did say she lived in Spanish Harlem while staying down there. Deaux want that work and dope dick from me, she's legit on the hustle side?"

"Yea, I never really heard about her being a snake. She just like to suck a jawn's dick until the skin comes off," he laughed again, making me laugh. My young bol had no filter on what came out of his mouth at all.

***

Fucking Deaux in the front seat of my truck wasn't surprising to me. Carter and his homie told me enough about her, maybe a lil' too much. By the way she pulled on my zipper when she got in my jawn, I knew she wanted me more than I wanted her. What's crazy is that a part of me felt kind of bad for fucking her. Hat was at home sick with the flu, while I had Deaux's head in my lap, getting the best top I had in a while. Don't get me wrong, after I taught Manhattan how to give me head, she was a fool with it. Deaux, on the other hand, probably was a freak since birth, and a fool with the sloppy top. Shit like this could make a nigga sprung behind a bitch he doesn't even care about. I didn't know much about Deaux, besides her being a petty hustler out of west Philly. She had a couple of abortions and miscarriages for a few joes I knew out the hood. Carter's homie said Deaux was solid and knew how to keep a secret, that's the only thing I cared about. I had no intention to fuck with her beyond this point on a sexual level or to even get to know personal shit about her.

"Let me trap with you," she said, while slipping her panties on and wiping the nut from her lips.

"What," I laughed, brushing her comment off and pulling my boxers and sweatpants to my hips. Hearing my phone vibrate, I glanced at the screen staring at a text message from Hat. It was just to tell me she loved me and to be careful in the snow. Ignoring Deaux, I smiled and replied to the message. Once I was done, I carefully pulled off.

"I'm serious, Spitta, we can get this money together. I want to be down for you, I know the stuck-up bitch youse with can't hold you down in the streets like a bitch like me can," she worded.

"What?!"

"I SAID, I know that stuck-up bitch youse with can't hold you down in the streets like I can." If you said anything about Manhattan that I felt was disrespectful, youse got a reaction out of me fast. Deaux, got exactly what usually happened. Quickly putting my hand around her neck and pushing her head against the head rest, I then squeezed her neck tighter. Deaux was surprised, but it looked like the horny smut was turned on by the slight abusive.

Biting her bottom lip while grabbing my wrist, Deaux pressed my hand around her neck tighter. Then Deaux reached for my other hand, sliding it into her jawns. My hands had a mind of their own and they began to figure fuck her nasty ass at the stop sign. The way she moaned with her bottom grill shining made my dick rock hard.

"Never call my woman out her fuckin' name, ard?"

"I want that dick again, Spitta, give it to me," she begged. "Youse one nasty bitch, keep my dick hard and shit," I laughed, making her pull her jeans and panties to the floor. Finding the first alley near Reedland Avenue, I parked my jawn, leaving it running so the heater could keep the truck warm. Within minutes Deaux was on top of me naked, moaning, and finding any part of my body to dig her nails into.

"Damn, Spittaaaaaaaaa, I can feel that dick in my stomach," she grinned in a sexual way, grinding harder on my dick. I didn't reply, fuck, I couldn't if I wanted to. Instead, I tossed my head back gripping and slapping her ass like the big fine horse she was. Deaux's pussy was so damn wet, this shit was relaxing. I could stay in her pussy for hours in deep thought.

I can't lie though, fucking Deaux for an hour was mad good, but I couldn't stop thinking about Manhattan. If she found out about this, my baby would be dumb hurt by my actions. Everything Marcy warned her about would be true, but it was just this one time. I wouldn't dare cuff a smut like Deaux or let her come close to ruining what I built with Manhattan.

"Fuck, girl, no more pussy from you, I'm tired like a lazy bitch," I laughed, rubbing on her big thighs with my free hand. Manhattan called my phone twice, but I shot her a quick message saying I was in the trap. Manhattan understood that and didn't bother me anymore. It was 3:45 am, the usual time I did my shit in the trap, it was easy for me to lie to Manhattan,

"No more pussy for life, or just tonight," Deaux asked in a sexy way.

"Both, I told you I have a joint and I love her."

"I hear you, Clover, whatever you say. Sometimes love doesn't mean anything," she chuckled, slightly stretching her eyes.

"In this situation it does, I love the fuck out of that girl, I whispered.

"You know it's brick out here, I ain't seen a nigga on the block all night," I chuckled, looking both ways before crossing the icy street.

"One thing about them jawns in south Philly, they can't stand the snow or cold. Put that shit together and they are ready to get a blinky and body themselves," she giggled.

"You're right about that," I replied.

"So, will you let me trap with you?"

"Now why would I do that, I don't really know you like that?"

"Well, you fucked me twice without a rubber, it doesn't get any trustworthy than that, homie."

"It's nothing to take some antibiotics, my freedom isn't something I put in anyone's hands," I answered.

"Clover, do you see this ass and face? Niggas put their money, time, and freedom in my hands every day, b. I fuck with this nigga out of Southwest Philly who's getting' money, Marco. His bitch, name is Serious, she's the real bread winner though."

"Why, what's her hustle?"

"The bitch and her two sisters, Denim and Jaquelyn crack credit cards and set niggas up for their big brother, Rob. To me, Marco is like her pimp, it's a must she pops him off with half of what she makes."

"Fat nigga with the beard, drive that '07 red Range Rover," I asked.

"Yea, that's him, he's really who I'm trying to get at, but that nigga is like a ghost. Plus, he's the 'faithful' type, that nigga barely take a shit without his girl on his side," she laughed. Thinking about the shit Deaux said, had my mind running, but I wasn't into that jacking shit. I knew a couple of females who were into cracking credit cards, but none of them made a living from it. In my opinion, if they stayed out of the True Religion and Gucci store, they could pay a bill or two.

"Not everyone's dick gets hard when they see your fat ass and cute face," with a grin on my face, I softly pinched Manhattan, I mean, Deaux on the cheek. Little did she know, I was also reaching for my burner under the sit to see how she would act when the burner was to her temples.

"Trust me, it ain't too many niggas who don't get a hard on when they say this fat ass," she laughed.

"If you don't mind me asking, what happened between you and Harlem?"

"What' cha mean," Deaux questioned.

"Why did you two stop fuckin' around?"

"I don't know, to keep it a stack with you. It's no bad blood between us or anything, it's not like we had feelings for one another. Harlem and I are cool, I hate that the judge gave my boy ten flat. He's a stand-up guy so jocing will be light work to him."

"Yea, you're right about that, my dude is good people," I replied.

"His wife, on the other hand, that broad can't stand the ground I walk on," Deaux laughed.

"Hhhmmmm, I wonder why."

"It's no need to wonder, she found out about Harlem and me. Thanks to her messy ass sister, I forgot the bitch's name," Deaux answered.

"Yo, let me ask you something else, but it ain't about Harlem or Honesty."

"What up, Spitta," looking at the burner in my lap, I really didn't see fear in Deaux's eyes. That right that told me it wasn't much that she feared and it wasn't the first time Deaux seen a gun. I wasn't surprised by that at all.

"How do I know you ain't trying to rob, or set me up, like Rob and Marco," slowly raising the gun to Deaux's temples, she stared at the trigger. Then she looked at me saying, "If I wanted to do that, don't you think I would have done it by now?" For a minute, I stared at Deaux with my poker face on a thousand, but still pointing the gun at her. Deaux didn't show any signs of fear, but her heart damn neared pounded out of her chest. Thank God she had a bra on, if not, her heart probably would have fell to the floor.

"I guess so, but we'll see if you're about that gangsta shit you're talking," removing the gun from her head to tuck it under the sit, Deaux shook her head laughing. Then she turned away, staring out of the window with shaking hands.

In a few hours, I knew everything I needed to know about Deaux. Real rap, it was a major difference between her and Manhattan, the kind of difference that would never allow me to her make her my woman, or not even my side bitch. I was going to use the hoe for what she was worth, hood shit, that's it. This wasn't the type of bitch you wanted to be seen with in public because your niggas would clown the fuck out of you. Deaux couldn't come to family gatherings or Sunday dinner to meet my family. I was going to keep that smut exactly where she needed to be, in west Philly.

"You're shaking like a stripper, love," I laughed.

"Shut up, no I'm not," she laughed, but her hands were still shaking.

"I bet if I put a drink in your hand it'll turn into a milkshake."

"Ohh, Spitta, fuck you, I'm good, G," Deaux laughed.

Deaux never asked me about my dreams and goals, the type of shit Hat drilled me on. Not once did she call me Clover, Deaux always kept it street by calling me Spitta. Since she was so street and hood, that's exactly where I was going to keep her.

We rode through the city for a Lil' minute, joking and shit. I had to see where shorty's head was, which is wasn't in a good place. Deaux had the same mentality and tendencies like a street nigga. Just to see if Deaux was bout that gangsta shit she was talking, I had her set up some niggas from West Philly who owed me a couple of stacks. They were dodging me like a was a probation officer who wanted his dirty piss. I wasn't worried about the $3,500 dollars, that was chump change to me. It was the principle and respect I was worried about. If I let these niggas slide, that would let other niggas think they could short me out my dough. Now that shit, I wasn't having at all. With Deaux as my bait, my message was going to them niggas loud and clear.

Sitting at the corner of 59th Street, it was a little pass 5:00 am. Besides a few cars rolling through the hood, the streets were empty. In about an hour, the sun would be out, but it would still look dark because of the snow and rain that was coming in by 10:00 am. I sat low in my car with my black hoodie sitting right above my eyes. With her ass and hips swinging everywhere, I had a clear view of Deaux who strutted across the street. Somehow, which was probably easy, she conceived the clown to let her fuck at his place. If he only knew what she had in store for him, he'd probably kill her on sight.

"Yea, Deaux, do exactly what daddy said," mumbling to myself with my eyes glued on Deaux. Before walking into the house, Deaux winked her eye at me tapping on the dirty forty-five I gave her. It was show time ladies and gentlemen!

Chapter 8

After the night I had with Deaux, I needed plenty of rest, but that wasn't going to happen. Manhattan was an early bird, who woke up at 6:00 am, even on her off days. On top of that, my phone was ringing non-stop, but I didn't give a fuck who was calling. The smell of herbs, seasonings, and cleaning supplies, were heavy in the air. Manhattan was walking through the house, cleaning, and singing loudly offbeat, like always. To me, that was music to my ears. The way she horribly sang reminded me of the old saying, 'Only a face a mother can love.'

Deaux managed to get $5,000 from the opps, six ounces of coke, and a hundred Xanax pills. It was a lot to Deaux, but lil' bitty shit to me. Deaux only been back in Philly for a week and was living at different friend's houses until she got back on her feet. You would think she would have kept the money to bubble, but instead, she had to prove a point by giving it to me. To me, $5,000 was like a dime, I gave that to Manhattan to shop with.

"Sleepy Head, Sleepy Head, it's about time you woke up," walking into the bedroom, Manhattan clapped her hands to grab my attention. Pulling the earbuds out of her ears, Manhattan gave me a kiss on the forehead, smiling.

"Hey, baby, what time is it," pulling the cover by my body, the cool breeze gave me the chills. I quickly covered my body again, motioning Manhattan to get back in bed with me. Without saying anything, Manhattan kicked off her running shoes, climbing into bed with me. I didn't waste any covering her with love and kisses. Manhattan loved this type of shit and I never mind giving that to her.

"It's 5:00 pm, the snow is up to yonder, plus, it's still raining. Thank goodness I racked up on food and drinks two days ago. If not, we would be fresh out of luck," she laughed, kissing my neck.

"Damn, I guess I'll be in the house all day, but how are you feeling?"

"A little better, I didn't want to stay in bed all day."

"I feel that, but you need to listen to your body and relax yourself, iight?"

"Yea, I hear you, Clover Porter," she replied, yawning.

"What are you cooking," I asked.

"Your favorite, beef and vegetables soup."

"Nice shot, did you get crackers? You know I can't eat my soup without crackers," I laughed.

"Boy, that's like asking a smoker if he has a lighter," she giggled.

"I'm guessing that's a yea."

"It is, but I called you a few times last night, I'm pretty sure you saw me calling. I guess you were mad busy," she rolled her eyes.

"I'm home, aren't I? In one piece, just like you ask me to always come," holding Manhattan tighter, I kind of felt nervous and paranoid. Since I didn't shower yet, I wondered if she could smell Deaux's cheap perfume and pussy on me. I think if she would have, Manhattan would have spoken on it.

"Okay, Clover, next time, can you just pick up the phone and check in? I don't think that's too much to ask for."

"Okay, baby, I will," I said.

"Thanks, you're the best. I need to shower, I'll be back, baby," Hat implied, kissing my lips and rolling out of bed.

"Bet, but don't take too long, I'm going to start missing you," I smiled.

"Yea, yea, yea, it'll be a birdbath," as Manhattan walked out of the room, she blew several kisses in my direction. Once she walked into the bathroom, I reached under my fluffy pillow for my phone. I knew she heard my phone vibrating, but Hat wasn't the type to trip over that phone shit. She wasn't the type to dig in phones either, I guess Hat felt she never had a reason to do any of that.

Before I could return any of my phone calls, I got a call from Deaux. Clearly the bitch didn't listen, or forgot what I told her last night.

"Hello," I whispered into the receiver, praying Hat couldn't hear me from the bathroom.

"What up, Clove," Deaux asked.

"What the fuck, Deaux? I told you to never call me. I'll call you whenever I want to talk to you!"

"But, Clov—"

"Bye!"

"Who were you talking to," Hat walked into the room with her long hair wrapped into a towel. Tossing my phone onto the bed laughing, I laughed, saying, "Smoke's crazy ass, he ain't talking about nothing important though."

"Oh, okay," she replied, climbing back into bed naked. Since I was only wearing boxers and socks, I wanted to fuck Hat badly, but I couldn't do it. Hopefully, she didn't pull on my jawn or try to give me head.

"Your mom called looking for you earlier, but I told her you were sleeping," Hat said.

"Bet, I'll call her in a few. I need to shower, shit, and eat, I'm starving," I said.

"I bet you are you." Rubbing Manhattan's flat stomach, I stared at her saying, "I dream about you being pregnant with my lil' jawn."

"What," Manhattan laughed.

"I'm serious, baby, then I see you having this little chocolate baby girl, with long, curly, coal black hair. Her eyes are sparkly and the same color as yours. Her face is shaped just like a heart and she have the biggest, brightest smile in the world. It's crazy how I'm in love with someone who isn't even real. I guess because I want that so badly, it feels so damn real. When will you have my baby, Manhattan?"

"I don't know, Clover, I didn't know it was that important to you."

"It is, I think we should go for it. I know I ain't ever going anywhere and I'm not letting you leave me. I will rob and jack every nigga you get with after me," I laughed, making Manhattan gasp. She knew I was serious and about that gangster shit I spit.

"Are you serious right now, you really want a baby," Manhattan tried her best fighting back her smile, but she couldn't help it. Manhattan damn neared jumped into my arms over filled with joy. We talked about having kids often, but she was skeptical because of her family. Manhattan didn't want to deal with the lack of support they would give her, but I didn't give a fuck about that. She had me and my family in her corner, that's all Manhattan needed. In her eyes, that wasn't enough for her, but then again, I couldn't blame Hat for feeling that way. At the end of the day, having support from your family was priceless, yo. It seemed like the deeper Hat feel in love with me, the more her family pushed away from her. Sometimes, I heard her crying about it, but she always brushed it off. Manhattan wouldn't tell me the truth, but I knew that's why she would be depressed some days.

"I'm very serious, I love you, girl. I want to give you everything you want, dig?"

"Yea, I dig, but I think we should start now," laughing while kissing my forehead, Manhattan attempted to reach in my boxers, but I softly grabbed her hand, saying, "let me hope in the shower first. I'm mad I even got in bed after being in the trap all night."

"Okay, baby, but don't take too long."

Chapter 9

With the phone attached to my ear, I sat on the toilet in the bathroom talking to Harlem. I also had the shower running so Manhattan couldn't hear my conversation from the living room. No telling what Harlem and I would say while on the phone. With his sentencing hitting everyone by surprise, Harlem was in good spirits lately. Even though he didn't commit the crime, he still held his head up doing the time. I'll forever respect him for that, word to.

"What the fuck the money looking like," Harlem asked.

"Exactly what it's supposed to look like," I laughed.

"I like the sound of that, did you get into with dude from Brownsville?"

"Not yet, but I think I need to make a trip that way."

"Do what you gotta do, yo, it's always good to get off the scene for a Lil' while," Harlem said.

"Facts," I laughed.

"What's up with you, man, you still fucking with that bitch," Harlem inquired, making me laugh, I already knew who the fuck he was speaking of. Two weeks later, Deaux and I were still kicking it, I think she was falling in love with me. Fuck, I don't know why, because the feelings weren't equal. They were nowhere close to being equal, and I made that clear to Deaux. To me, Deaux was like one of the homies, my young bol, who I could kick it with. From time to time I could get some pussy and head from my homie. To me, that was a win, win, situation that I couldn't resist.

"Yea, Harlem, I'm still fucking with that joint like that."

"Why?"

"Because I benefit from it, ain't no love on this end," I murmured.

"You sound just like when I was fuckin' with that hoe. I'm telling you, Clove, leave that bitch alone before it's too late. Carter doesn't know that hoe like I know her. That bitch mouth runs more than a damn leaking faucet," Harlem spoke loudly, trying to get his point across, but it's like everything he said about Deaux didn't hold any weight to me. Like I said before, I wouldn't let Deaux, or any other hoe, fuck up what I had at home.

"Deaux said she don't know why you two stopped kickin' it, but y'all were still cool. She also said Honesty can't stand her because her sister told Honesty y'all were fuckin' around."

"Mmmaannnnnnnnn, that bitch is a fucking lie. Her and her sister were playing them phone games, that's how Hon found out about us. That's the real reason Honesty dragged that hoe when she caught her by Con's house getting some work for some nigga out of Spanish Harlem. Honesty dragged that bitch up and down the street like a rag doll," Harlem laughed.

"Hhhmmm, glad to know she's a liar too, but fuck it. I made it clear to her that I ain't messing with her like that. By the end of the month, I'll be done with her, and things will be back to normal. Trust me, bro, I have this under control." Everything Harlem told me about Deaux came from a good place and not on some hating shit. I appreciated him for that, Harlem was only trying to look out for a jawn.

"I swear, bro, you sound just like me. End that lil' thing asap, I promise you're going to thank me later. Deaux is the type that's always looking for a come-up in a nigga instead of hustling herself. Put it like this, Deaux would rob a nigga for her other nigga just to prove a point. That way, she done showed that man her loyalty and he's going to take care of her finically."

"All that sounds quite familiar, bruh, trust me. I gotta go though, those people coming in to count," Harlem replied.

"Alright, hit me up about noon, I'll be running the streets by then."

"Bet, Lil' bro, be careful out there," on that note, Harlem ended the call, leaving me with a lot to think about. Maybe some of what he said about Deaux wasn't true, but I had a strong feeling everything he said was a hundred. Shorty had no reason to lie to me, but Deaux did anyways. Brushing off what Harlem said, I jumped into the steaming hot shower, letting the water wet every inch of my body. Today, I didn't have time to take a long shower, so, I was out of there in five minutes. I had a lot of shit to do today and going to New

York was heavily on my mind. That thought didn't stay long, because once I walked out of the hot bathroom, Manhattan quickly reminded me why.

Humming to the R and B music that played through the house, Hat rolled the wet paint brush up and down the white walls. Before you knew, the living room walls would be covered with tan paint. At first, I refused to let Hat do that dirty work, but she begged me to. With the drama with her family because of me, painting was like therapy to her. If I would allow her to, Manhattan would paint the entire outside of the house. If painting is what my baby wanted, that's what the fuck she got. As much as we've been fuckin', I'm surprise shorty had an ounce of energy running through her body.

With a fresh towel wrapped around my waist, I stood in the middle of the hall, watching Hat do her shit. Man, that girl made everything look perfect and beautiful.

"You look good doing this, you should become a painter," I laughed.

"What," she laughed, turning around with the paintbrush in her hand. Pain dripped on the plastic under her feet and onto her dirty white Chuck Taylors.

"I said you look good doing this, you should become a painter."

"Boy, do not play with me on this early Sunday morning," Hat turned around laughing and continued painting.

"You know I'm joking," laughing and walking into the room, I dropped the towel at the door, standing there naked. Since Manhattan already had my clothes laid out on the bed for me, I quickly grabbed the green long sleeve shirt, boxers, socks, and jeans. Still naked, I walked out of the room, entering the living room grabbing Manhattan's full attention.

"Big, BIG, dick, Clover," Hat stared at my dick with lust in her eyes. Trust me, if she had the time Hat would fuck me with paint flying everywhere.

"That's not anything new, baby," I laughed, dropping the clothes on the couch to slip the black and white striped boxers on. Scanning the living room for some of Hat's lotions, I slightly jogged to the computer desk. Taking a look at the new color, I had to admit, I was impressed.

"This is nice, Hat, I guess I can put my pride to the side and say you were right," I laughed.

"Yea, because you know that pride is a bitch," Hat giggled.

"Yea, yea, yea. It's 9:45, Ryker didn't make it here yet? I thought her flight landed at 8: 30 am," opening the bottle on the cocoa butter lotion, I squeezed a large amount into my hand, lathering it on my body. After that, I slipped my clothes on, sitting back on the couch.

"I spoke to her thirty minutes ago, she landed. Ryker said she had something to tell me, Lord knows what will come out of her mouth. I sure hope she isn't pregnant for Kay'Jun, that's the last thing my friend needs in her life."

"Hat."

"What, Clover," Manhattan asked, still running the wet paint brush up and down the wall. My eyes followed every movement Manhattan made because I was memorized.

"When are you going to put a for sale sign on your house and move in for real? You spend more time here than there, moving here is plain ole' common sense."

"It is plain ole' common sense, but I'm not selling, or moving out, of my house. Especially not for a boyfriend I haven't been dating for that long," she murmured.

"Boyfriend, oh, that's all I am to you? Just a jawn you're dating, wooowww, that's crazy, yo." I know Hat didn't mean any harm by what she said, but her words did kind of rub me the wrong way. Sighing loudly and dropping her paint brush, Manhattan walked in my direction flopping on my lap. I pretended to ignore her my playing in my phone, but I was wishing Deaux wouldn't call. Today was one of those days I wasn't in the mood to lie to Manhattan about another woman.

"Get off me," I whispered, staring at the television. Hat laughed, she didn't take me seriously. As a matter of fact, I didn't take myself seriously either. If Hat would have really got off me, I would have chased behind her like the tender dick jawn I had become.

"I'm not getting off you, because we both know that's not what you want."

"I guess you're a mind reader, huh," I expressed, with a straight face, trying my best not to laugh.

"When it comes to you, you can call me Mrs. Cleo," laughing while wrapping her arms around my neck, I could no longer keep a straight face anymore.

"You're right about that."

"Baby, you know you're not just a boyfriend to me, you're like my best friend. It's not a secret I love you to the moon and back, but selling my house is something I can't do. It means a lot to me and I hope you will eventually understand that."

"Since I love you so much, I'll be understanding," I smiled, kissing her forehead and Manhattan's smile expanded mad wide. Then suddenly, my phone started to ring, I didn't think twice about sliding it into my pocket. Sometimes, Deaux called from different numbers or even private, that shit would dead ass piss a jawn off. It was clear this bitch didn't have any understanding, just like Harlem said.

"Thank you, Clover Porter, you are the B E S T," before I could respond, the doorbell began to ring. Jumping to her feet, Manhattan walked to the door without checking to see who was standing on her porch. Opening the door, Manhattan nearly fainted seeing Smoke and Ryker tongue kissing in the flesh.

"What up, bro? What up Hat?" Smoke said.

"Cooling, it's about time y'all got here, I was starting worry," I joked.

"Hey, Spitta, I smell paint in the air," Ryker laughed.

"Uummm, what the fuck is going on right now, on my jawn?" Manhattan asked, with a serious face. Kissing again, but quickly pulling away from each other, Ryker tucked her long hair behind her ears smiling. Then she gave Manhattan a tight hug, but Hat was too busy staring at Smoke, waiting for answers. He didn't say anything, Smoke just laughed dapping me down. Somehow, he wiggled his way into the house to sit on the couch.

"I'll explain everything to you later," Ryker whispered into Hat's ear as she closed the living room door.

"This must be how it feels when you enter the twilight zone," with a blank look on her face, Manhattan followed behind Ryker taking a sit next to her. Hat glanced at Smoke, then glanced at Ryker. Everyone laughed, except Manhattan. We all knew Manhattan wasn't upset, only confused and wanting answers pronto.

"Sssoooo, uummmm, how was your trip to Texas," Manhattan asked.

"It was good, real decent, but next time, I want you to come. The food is AMAZING, I think I gained at least twenty pounds the five days I was there," Ryker laughed, but she couldn't stop making eye contact with Smoke. Smoke was in a daze staring at Ryker, plus he was high. Manhattan really had to be caught off guard, because she didn't trip about Smoke coming in the house smelling like a pound of dro.

"Damn, Ryke, he's still going to look the same, I promise you that," Manhattan mumbled loudly.

"Don't be a hater, Manhattan, let her do her thing," stretching his arm out, Smoke grabbed Ryker's hand, gently stroking it. I could see the chill bumps forming on her left arm, shit was kind of funny to me.

"Bro, I need to holla at you about something. Let's go in the room," Smoke didn't say anything, he stood to his feet to give Ryker a forehead kiss, and followed behind me. Ryker blushed so damn much that she couldn't say much. Her red rosy cheeks told Hat a lot, but she still needed to know more. I knew Manhattan couldn't wait for me to close the room door so her and Ryker could gossip their asses off.

"Ryker?"

"Manhattan," Ryker giggled, flipping her hair, then she pulled it into a tight ponytail.

"Have I been half ass listening to you talk, or am I missing something here? You, Smoke, together in my house? Which means you two were in the same vehicle driving here. Which also means that you two had to talk in some way, shape, or form. Are y'all in a relationship?"

"We're always…. Kind of…. I don't know Hat, but I really like him. Like a lot and more than I liked Kay' Jun."

"Hold up a second and back it up!! I have soooo many questions, but let's start with you saying you LIKED Kay. Liked is in past tense form, which means Kay is in the past!"

"Yes, Kay'Jun is in the past and I buried him there. He's been in the past for three months now," Ryker said.

"What, are you serious, Ryker and why haven't you told me any of this? If you did tell me I don't remember and I'm sorry. With everything that has happened with Clover and moving, I barely remember to shower," she laughed.

"No, girl, you're good, I never mentioned any of it to you or anyone. I also told Spitta to keep quiet, because I didn't want to jinx anything between us. So far, things are going good between us and I think it's going to continue to go that way."

"Hhmmm, we all know he can keep a secret or two," Hat flared her nose, rolling her eyes.

"Don't start your shit, girl, but I'm sorry we kept you in the blind," Ryker laughed.

"Aww, you're good, girl. Before I become nosy and get into you and Smoke's business, what happened with Kay'Jun? Was it the whole situation with the daughter that came out of nowhere," Manhattan questioned.

"I wish that would have been the reason, but no it wasn't. I was right from jump and I feel stupid that I got played like a fool."

"What are you talking about?"

"Kay'Jun was cheating on me once again, in October, I know right, such a shocker," Ryker laughed.

"I hate to say it, but not at all."

"Same thing I told myself and Smoke. He used the situation with his daughter as a cover up. I spoke to the baby mama, and Kay'Jun has only seen his daughter like four times," chuckling with her head dropping, Manhattan was shocked, but she wasn't surprised much. Kay'Jun was a bullshit ass Muslim and shit like this was his m.o. Since we were yungins that nigga couldn't be trusted anything, he always had sticky fingers. We always told him to use them fingers to be trigger happy, but he was too pussy to bust a gun. I remember in the 8th grade, he stole this shorty's phone, then he turned around to help her look for it. That was the kind of things niggas out Strawberry Mansion did. That was the main reason I only dealt with a hand full of them on a personal level when it came to selling drugs.

"Noooooooooo!"

"Bitch, yes, and if I'm lying, I'm dying. Can you believe that, Hat? I got cheated on again by him, but not anymore. I gave him all of me, but I guess that wasn't good enough," Ryker started to cry, but she stopped and smiled. She had no more tears to cry for Kay' Jun, about fuckin' time, yo. Word to, I was tired of her calling Hat crying about that clown, then two hours later, she was taking him back. I know I wasn't the perfect man or boyfriend, but I could never be a scumbag like Kay.

"I have one question for you, does Smoke make you happy," Manhattan asked.

"Yea, he does, I feel like a different woman with him. I don't know, it's kind of hard to explain it. He's so real, it's crazy!" Just talking about Smoke made Ryker blush, and gave her butterflies as if he wasn't in the other room feeling the same way. Her face turned red and warm, her body told her she was in love with him already.

"Well, girl, fuck Kay with his tired ass. You know what I've been saying since day one, BE HAPPY! You are a great woman, you're solid, you're beautiful, and sexy as fuck. Any man would be happy to be with you, like Smoke for example," Manhattan smiled.

"I'm sorry you had to go through that again, but how did you find out he was cheating this time?"

"I was at work, but I noticed I forgot my charger. That day he was going back to work, but I thought he was on the road by that time. When I got home and walked into my room, a phone rang, but it wasn't his phone. It was this little flip phone that I had never seen before. Looked like some shit Smoke would use to trap on."

"Dead ass," Manhattan asked, laughing.

"Yes. Since it was an unknown phone in my bedroom, I felt I had every right to answer it, and I did. The only thing I could say was hello and the caller disconnected the call."

"Did the voice sound familiar?"

"Not really, and I didn't bother calling the girl back. I knew it had to be a girl, but I decided to go through the phone. I shouldn't have been surprised, but it was Kay's phone. I guess it was his little cheating phone. It was full of blurry ass pictures of different females showing every body part they shouldn't show a man in relationship. Some of the females I've seen before around town, but some I hadn't. One girl name was Tiffany and they talked a lot. He even talked about me to Tiffany, I wish Kay would have told me he wasn't happy instead of Tiffany," Ryker shook her head chuckling.

"What do you mean?"

"Kay' Jun constantly told Tiffany how he couldn't wait to leave me. Kay' Jun was going to do it one day while I was at work and never talk to me again. I swear, Hat, I never thought Kay would be that kind of person. I guess you really don't know the person you'll sleeping with every night. What hurt my feelings is how they laughed at the fact I thought he was spending time with his daughter. That poor little baby probably won't ever know her father. I don't know if any of those bitches even make him be in her life like I made him. Well, like I thought I made him be there for her."

"This shit is crazy, makes me want to rock out when I see his no-good ass," Manhattan shook her head, she was pissed off. Kay' Jun was never Manhattan's cup of tea and this shit only made her hate him more than Manhattan already did.

"Girl, I thought about breaking his nose and busting his windows, but his bitch ass isn't worth it at all," she smirked.

"When you confronted him about it, what did he say? I know it wasn't much explaining he could have done," she replied.

"You know that ole typical shit about how I'm tripping and that was his homie's phone."

"These niggas getting goofier, and goofier, by the second," folding her arms across her chest with lips tight, Manhattan had so much to say, but she changed her mind. She loved Ryker like a sister, but she didn't want to get too deep in her mix. In her mind, she couldn't relate to any of this, because deep down in her heart, Manhattan knew her man was faithful. Too bad that was ONLY a thought, and not the truth.

"Wait a minute, was Smoke the person with you on vacation?" Manhattan asked, with a curious face, but Ryker rolled her eyes laughing. That kind of behavior gave Hat the answer she needed.

"OMG, I can't believe this, you and God damn Smoke," Manhattan smiled. She loved this kind of shit, seeing her friends happy.

"Yea, he was there, well, he surprised me, actually. This vacation was like a detox and cleanse from all the drama with Kay'Jun, but I got more than a cleanse. That time with Clerk really showed me a different side of him, a side of him I feel in love with, instantly," she replied.

"Gggiirrrrlllllll, I feel so damn lost. So, when did you two start this relationship?" Manhattan asked.

"When Jarvis was killed, I had the urge to be by his side, but only as a friend. He was emotional and weak, I was able to see a different side of him. I basically got the pleasure to meet Clerk and not only Smoke. Smoke is a sweet, caring, and loving guy, something I never thought. It's crazy how I didn't cheat on him, but he had no problem cheating on me," she laughed. Back in mid-November, Smoke's homie from west Philly was gunned down walking out of his house one morning. He took the killing mad hard, but he tried his best to stay strong.

"Technically, you were cheating on him, but fuck it," Manhattan high-fived Ryker and they laughed.

"You're right, but at first, I pushed back from Smoke. I truly wanted to make things work between us. It didn't matter how much I tried, Kay and I weren't meant to be and I'll finally okay with that."

"That's good to hear, but I really hate that you had to go through this. On a better note, I'm glad you found the strength to leave him. Now you're all happy and glowing like you're pregnant. You're not pregnant, right," she asked.

"No, baby, Hat, but I'm glad I did find my strength. Kay' Jun wasn't good for me, just like poison. Clerk isn't perfect, but we have a good ass vibe and time together, Hat. Sometimes the L word wants to slip out and I'm not talking about like," Ryker began to blush again, but turned away feeling like a sucker in love.

"Are you serious, Ryke, you're falling in love with SMOKE?" Squealing like kids, Ryker grabbed Hat's hands, nodding her head. Ryker couldn't control the way she smiled, Ryker wasn't ashamed of it at all. It felt good to be truly happy and in love, two ways I should have always made Hat feel.

"Yes, I am, I love this feeling, girl. I was wrong about him the entire time and I wish I would have given him a chance from day one. It feels so good to be loved, the RIGHT WAY. I know it's real this time, I can feel it in my heart. I've never felt like this with Kay. I only felt heartaches, and heartbreaks, with him and that's not fair. Why do us good women go through the most shit," Ryker asked, that was a question she could never get a legit answer for.

Manhattan shook her head smirking. Then she rubbed Ryker's thigh and said, "That's because every time we get cheated on, we still try and find the good in that person. Do you remember my ex-boyfriend, Warren?"

"Ugh, how could I forget him? He hated my guts and he reminded me of that all the time," Ryker said.

"I know, and I'm sorry I let him disrespect you like that. Warren use to put me through HELL! Man, I swear, that boy was the devil dressed in Ralph Lauren. I always said he stayed with a fitted cap on so he could hide those horns on top of his head. After two years of being cheated on, I couldn't take it anymore. Before I met June, I jumped from relationship to relationship. First it was Kash, then Kacey, after Kacey was Jordan, then it was Warren. I was looking for love and I made myself emotionally drained. After I ended things with Warren, I promised myself I wasn't getting involved with anyone until I felt it was right. Don't get me wrong, for a year, I was lonely, but I didn't break my promise. I ask God to send me someone special, then I met Clover. I know how you feel about

Smoke, because that's how Clover makes me feel. Love is beautiful, and he makes me feel beautiful inside and out. Being with Clover makes me feel safe, and secured, that's one of the best feelings in the world."

"It is, and I hope I don't get this feeling ripped from my heart," Ryker replied.

"Besides those street ways, he's a good dude. Don't be afraid to be in love, or worry yourself about anything. Just enjoy the good company and being loved."

"I know, but it's kind of hard not to, yo," Ryker replied.

"If you feel like that, there's nothing wrong with taking things slow. Just make sure y'all are on the same page."

"What's crazy is that, I didn't even cheat on Kay with Smoke. Once I found out he was cheating, that's when Smoke and I took our relationship to another level. I'm glad I made that decision, girl."

"I'm really happy for you girl, now we're both in love and happy. Doesn't it feel good to be loved by a faithful man," giving Ryker a warm hug with a big smile on a face, Ryker felt bad that she couldn't agree with Manhattan. Rumors about Deaux and me were starting to spread, somehow, it made its way to her. I wasn't sure why, but Ryker hadn't told Manhattan about what she heard. Maybe because of Smoke, or maybe because Ryker wasn't the type to feed into rumors.

While Manhattan and Ryker talked, Smoke and I made our way out of the house to do what we made to do. Well, Smoke had business to handle, but I was going too. I got a high watching Deaux jugg different niggas, especially the ones who THOUGHT, I forgot they owed Smoke or me money. Shorty had to slow down with the jacking though, I didn't want her name buzzing in the streets already.

Smoke knew about me fooling with Deaux, he was pissed like he was the one getting cheated on. I tried to explain to him why

I fucked with Deaux, but big brother wasn't trying to hear that. He didn't want anything to do with that situation, or to even be in Deaux's presence. I couldn't understand why he had a lil' vendetta against her, but you know the truth eventually comes out. Deaux moved to New York because all fingers pointed to her robbing one of Smoke's young bols. Like any other snake ass nigga, or bitch, would do, Deaux denied it. Once I told him where I was going, I'm more than sure that's the real reason he had Ryker leave the house. Smoke never wanted Manhattan to think, or feel, like he condoned any of my cheating.

By 8:00 pm, Ryker was gone, and Manhattan was alone, waiting for me to come home. After what was sent to her phone via text message, Manhattan had a lot to tell me. Walking into the house at two in the morning, I found Manhattan sitting on the couch with a face full of tears. Her phone sat next to her, with a picture on the wide screen. I tried to ignore the picture, it was something I couldn't miss.

"What's wrong with you, baby," I rushed to her side asking, but she smacked her ashy lips, pushing me away. At this point, I was confused, well, I was playing like I was confused.

"I was worried about you, Clover, I called your phone a million times, but the calls were being forwarded."

"Baby, as you can see, I'm good, stop tripping. Is there anything to eat? I'm starving."

"No," she whispered, with her head down. I attempted to kiss her, but she pushed me away. Showing me the picture of me in bed passed out with Deaux smiling at the camera, caught me by surprise. While I was sleeping in the hotel bed, this bitch was plotting and playing phone games. At this point, I wished I would have listened to Smoke and Harlem, mostly Harlem.

"Babe, I can explain."

"Clover, are cheating on me," Manhattan burst into tears asking me. I didn't know what to say.

"Baby, it was only one time, I swear, and I was fucked up. I went to sell the bitch some coke, she asked if I wanted a drink, and I said yea. Next thing I know, I'm feeling dizzy so I asked her to lie down. I don't know why the fuck would she do something like that, it's not even deep between us. That's just some smut out the hood niggas use to do shit for them."

"Clover Porter, that is a bald face lie. She told me everything, when, where, and how y'all met. One minute you're saying it was a mistake, then you say it only happened one time!! Get your fucking story straight, Clover!"

"Hat, I'm sorry, I didn't mean for any of this to happen," speaking in a whisper, I dropped my head. I felt like a fuckin' fool getting caught up like this.

"Fuck your apology, Clover, that doesn't mean anything when someone breaks your heart. Tell me, do you love her," she asked, while holding herself with tears falling to the floor. Hat's sobbing broke a jawn's heart.

"Manhattan, I swear to God, I don't love that hoe, she's nothing to me. You think if I loved her, or had any feelings for her, I would still be here?? Come on now, that's mad stupid and crazy."

"I don't know what to think right now. You promised me, Clover, you promised me that you would never hurt me. You promised me that you would never cheat on me, and you did. I need some time to think, alone, thank God I didn't sell my house," standing to her feet, I attempted to grab Manhattan's hand, but she pushed me away, tossing her phone to me. Pacing through the living room, I didn't know what to do. Maybe I should have raced behind her, because shorty managed to pack her bag and walk pass me like I didn't exist. A part of me wanted to grab her hand and the bag, but I didn't want Manhattan to fight me off. Instead, I stood in front of the door, with tears rolling from my own eyes. Manhattan wasn't moved by my tears, I didn't blame her.

"Come on, Hat, don't leave, let's talk and work this out."

"Nah, I'm good, Clover, you did enough talking," pushing me to the side and opening the door, Manhattan didn't think twice about looking back.

"Manhattan, when are you coming back? Tell me something, don't leave wondering like this, please! I said I'm sorry, I'll do whatever I have to do. You know I don't want to lose you, fuck, man," chasing behind Manhattan while she walked to her car, I watched the tears still fall from her face. The way she tried to fight back most of her tears fucked with my head. On my mama, I never meant for any of this to happen, or go down like this, but Hat wasn't trying to hear any of that.

"I don't know, Clover, I might not ever come back. Enjoy the rest of your night," standing in the middle of the driveway, watching Manhattan drive off had me feeling empty and stupid. Besides that, I was ready to find Deaux and kill her stupid ass.

Chapter 11 (June 2016....... Eight years later)

"On God, Clover has more drama than on Love and Hip Hop," Cope laughed.

"I guess you can call him Hitman Stevie J," Smoke laughed, but I didn't find any of what they said funny.

"Mind your business, that's always the best thing to do," I replied, brushing them off.

"You better start praying to that white God y'all pray to," Cope crossed his heart saying, and Smoke laughed.

"White God, nigga, my God is awesome and black," Smoke said.

"Clover been going through the same mess and still hasn't realized what the problem is," Cope chuckled, shaking his head.

Riding through Strawberry Mansion with Smoke and Cope was something I always did, but seeing those red and blue lights weren't supposed to be a part of my night. I had a funny feeling about them pulling us over, and by the way Smoke looked at me, I could tell he thought the same thing.

"Fuck," he mumbled, with the burning cigarette hanging from the bottom of his lip. We weren't riding dirty, but we were still some nervous jawns. With all the innocent black men being killed by armed officers, you never knew when a traffic stop could turn deadly. The last thing I needed was to witness Cope or Smoke being killed or them seeing me gunned down.

"In the name of Allah, everything will go smooth. Clover, put your information on the dashboard," Cope quickly said, as he watched the stocky Caucasian officer approach the car. Of course, he clutched his gun tightly, waiting and probably tempted to bust that bitch.

"Fuck yea, Clove, we don't need him ASSUMING you were reaching for anything else. If that nigga shoots you for ANYTHING, it ain't no fucking peaceful protest! I'm going burn the whole state down so everyone can feel my pain," Smoke implied. Rushing to shuffle for my license, registration, and proof of insurance, I then placed it on the dashboard. After that, everyone placed their hands in the air.

"License, registration, and proof of insurance," the officer was cocky and I knew him well. Officer O'Nan Biggs found himself caught up in a lot of shit, but somehow made his way out of it. A list of corrupted cops was leaked last March, and best believe, he was number three on the list.

"Yes, sir, it's on my dashboard, I'm going to grab it right now," slightly looking over my shoulder, I reached for the papers, handing

it to the officer. Flashing his flashlight in the car, he was searching for something. Luckily, Smoke and I left our weed and iron at his crib.

"Officer, can I ask you why you pulled me over?" I asked, with my hands on the steering wheel.

"Hey, I didn't tell you to speak," he shouted, making us all paranoid. This clown was already on ten, for no reason.

"Why the fuck do you have that shit on your head, boy?" Right along with him, and number two on the list, was officer Timor Black. He approached Cope's side of the car ready to be on the bullshit. Rumor has it that Timor hated Muslims, because his daughter was killed during 9/11. For that, he always found his way harassing any Muslim in the city. I guess tonight, Cope was the one he could harass.

"It's called a Taqiyah, it's a part of my culture," Cope replied, he was pissed, but Cope wasn't a fool to react.

Clearing his throat while leaning against the doorframe, Timor stared at Cope, but Cope kept his head straight. He wasn't a pussy ass nigga, but in a time like this, he feared his life. What man wouldn't who has a lot to lose? Since the birth of his daughter in 2010, A'laysha, Cope turned his life around completely. He wasn't with that street life anymore, but he still managed to hang with his boys sometimes.

"I don't give a fuck what it is, it's a disgrace to MY country and culture," Timor shouted, with spit flying from his mouth. Cope then turned his head, eye-balling the white pig. For a white man to say this was his country, was a disgrace to us. The white man didn't build this country, but they could never admit that.

"Okay, officer, but nice evening we're having, don't you say?"

"Shut the fuck up!"

"Bet, bet," Cope replied, locking his fingers behind his head. I bet he was regretting getting in the car with us. Two Porter's and Muslim was a bad combination in Philly.

"What are you boys doing out at 4:45 am? Selling drugs or looking for trouble, which one is it," O'Nan shouted, tossing my information back. This niggas didn't even run my license plate, he was literally, just fucking with us because we were black.

"Selling drugs," Smoke asked.

"Looking for trouble," Cope questioned.

"Oh, no, sir, we're just vibing and killing time," I answered, but O'Nan and Timor wasn't trying to hear that. Before we knew they were opening our doors pulling us out.

"GET THE FUCK DOWN, BOY," as the white officer slammed my body to the ground, all I could think about was and how history repeated itself. Cops still hated anyone with the last name Porter, they even gave Kansas a hard time when they saw her out in the streets. That's why you hardly spotted her out at night, Kan wasn't trying to become a hashtag, or be on a shirt that said Black Lives Matter."

"Hands behind your fucking head," Timor yelled, as he dug in each of our pockets.

"What the fuck y'all pulled us over for, huh," Smoke shouted, but Timor dug his knee deep into Smoke's back. Then he used his flashlight to hit me in the back of the head. I prayed this night wouldn't end too badly, these jawns were drawlin'.

"For being BLACK and MUSLIM, Timor, I'm not the reason those plans crashed," before Cope could finish his sentence, Timor rammed his foot into Cope's hip. He screamed out in pain, this night was definitely going downhill from here.

Replaying what happened two hours ago in my head, had me lost. What turned into a simple and pointless traffic stop, turned into some whole other shit. After getting our asses beat like we were worthless pieces of shit, we were arrested for resisting arrest.

Just when I thought things couldn't get any worse, they did. Seeing Manhattan walk in the police station made me feel good, because we were already beefing. That showed me she would still come through, no matter what. When Deaux appeared from the bathroom, I knew I was fucked. I don't even know how this bitch knew I was here! After the drama she caused earlier, why the fuck would Deaux even show up at the police station?

"Wow," Manhattan stood at the door, laughing and shaking her head. I could tell she was embarrassed and felt like a fool.

"Damn, there goes the Mrs. and the mistress," Cope shook his head, turning to his wife, Oak. She was always team Manhattan, but hated Deaux with a passion. If killing was legal, I truly think she would have smoked Deaux years ago.

"That's my cue to bounce," Smoke shook his head, walking towards the door. Before walking out, he gave Manhattan a hug, she hardly hugged him back.

"Why didn't you tell me she was here, Cler,?" Manhattan whispered.

"Sis, I'm sorry, I didn't know anything about her coming here. He told me he called you to come here."

"Yea, he did, but I guess he called him backup plan also."

"Get me the fuck out of here, before I drag that hoe by the cheap ass weave," flaring her nose at Deaux, Oak and Cope walked out of the door. Oak purposely sized Deaux up and down, looking for trouble. Deaux wasn't crazy, she knew who, and who not, to fuck with. Oak was the bitch not many bitches wanted to fuck with. Back in the day, Oak had a reputation for causing hell. Now married and settled down, Oak was on her chill shit.

"Ugly ass Hijab," Deaux mumbled, standing closer to the bathroom door. Handing Cope her purse, Oak turned around saying, "bitch, speak up, what the fuck did you say?"

"Bae, chill, she didn't say anything," Cope said, grabbing Oak's hand pulling her out of police station. Even though Cope and Oak were outside, I could still hear her cursing and fussing at Deaux. Deaux's scary ass couldn't say anything to Oak, but probably had a mouth full for Manhattan.

"Hey, girl," Deaux waved from a distance, but Manhattan turned away, running out of the building.

"I swear, if we weren't here, I would beat your ugly ass like I did last week," pressing Deaux's body against the wall, I instantly put fear in the bitch's eyes. Lately, I found myself going upside her head all the time. This smut was asking for it though, like right now.

"Clo—"

"Shut the fuck up and get out of my face, yo," I said, racing out of the building.

"Manhattan, baby, wait," I shouted, as I jogged through the parking lot, but Hat didn't have a word to tell me. She just continued walking, like I wasn't chasing behind her.

"LEAVE ME ALONE!"

"Manhattan, I'm sor-."

"You're what, Clover, sorry, yea, you're a sorry ass nigga. God, Clover, when will it stop, WHEN WILL YOU STOP FUCKING EMBRASSING ME?"

"Hat, you gotta let me explain, you're drawlin, yo," I explained, grabbing her hand, but she aggressively pulled it away. Hat wasn't trying to hear shit I had to say, but I couldn't blame her.

"No, I don't have to do anything, leave me the fuck alone, yo," slapping me, before getting into her car, Hat drove off without trying *to hear me out. Seconds later, Deaux walked out of the police station. Snatching that hoe to the side of the building, no telling what I was going to do to her. I guess she wasn't tired of me putting my foot in her ass.*

"Bitch, what the fuck is your problem," wrapping my hands around Deaux long neck, I slammed her against my car, choking her out. She stared me square in the eyes, not saying anything, or attempted to fight me off. See, one thing about Deaux, I had my bitch trained and she knew better.

"Man, this is some bullshit, but all we can do is charge it to the game," Smoke mumbled, while placing the icepack on his eye. It was black, but it was swollen.

"I can't even think about that right now. I need to figure out what the fuck I'mma do, besides beat the fuck out of Deaux again. This bitch doesn't listen, just like a fuckin' child, yo," I shouted. getting more pissed than what I already was.

Years ago, I made a promise to Hat that I wouldn't cheat on her again, but I knew that was a lie. I wasn't purposely trying to hurt her, but somehow, I still did time after time. After a while, it felt like she accepted me creeping with Deaux, and Deaux accepted that she was the other woman. In Deaux's mind, I would eventually leave Manhattan for her. I'm pretty sure Manhattan thought I would eventually leave Deaux and it would just be us again.

"I don't have shit to say about that, you put yourself in that jawn. Anyways, yo, did you talk to Harlem yet? I tried calling him, but that Honesty said he was in the shower," Smoke asked, staring in the mirror at the bruise on his face.

"He shot me a text when he got home. You won't believe this nigga man, shit gone blow your mind."

"What happened, bro," Smoke asked.

"He's with Con's girl, Giselle," I laughed.

"What?"

"Same shit I said. All that preaching he did to me, he's cheating on his wife with his right-hand man's girl."

"You and Harlem need to get it together before all this bitches be y'all downfall. I'm talking about Deaux, Manhattan, Giselle, and Honesty. Bitter and mad bitches aren't anything to play with, y'all drawlin'!"

"There you go with this shit again."

"Yea, here I go," Smoke said.

"Look, we just got beat up by the cops for no reason Then this shit with Deaux and Manhattan fucking with my head!"

"You know something, Clover, eventually, you're going to have to choose one of them. I'm out, man, my shorty is waiting for me."

***

Sitting in the living room, wearing her pink fuzzy robe and the matching house slippers, Manhattan was an emotional wreck. You could see it in her eyes that she stayed up most of the night crying over me. Hat was so heartbroken, that she couldn't go to work. Because of me, my shorty was literally, sick to her stomach. I never wanted to make any person feel like that, but somehow, I still found myself doing that. Over the years, things changed between us, good and bad. The bad was mostly because of me and the dirty things I did to Hat. We often asked each other what the fuck we were doing and why we were still together? I don't know about Hat, but I stuck around because I was in love with her. It was kind of hard to believe that, because all the shit I did, but I was. Even if I tried to, it was hard to fall out of love with a woman you didn't want to stop loving. After all these years, Hat still couldn't do any wrong in my eyes. After all these years, she no longer looked at me as the same man she used to. Some nights, she went to bed acting as if I wasn't in the bed with her. That shit always did something to my jawn, no lie.

Shortly after I cheated with Deaux the first time, I proposed to Manhattan, trying to make everything better. She said yes thinking I would never cheat on her again. Fuck, I thought so too, but I couldn't. Deaux had too much information on me and always threaten to send me to jail. A lot of times I thought about what Harlem said when I first met Deaux. I wish I would have listened to him, man, fuck! It didn't matter how many times I said I was done with Deaux, she somehow found a way to pull me back in. Some days I wished they both would have left me alone, because seem like the only thing I did was hurt them. I didn't really care about Deaux's feelings, she was tough. It was Manhattan I worried about, if she ever hurt herself, that would be on me. That's the kind of shit I couldn't have on my heart.

"Hello," Manhattan cleared her throat, saying.

"Hey, girl, what are you doing," Kat asked.

"At home."

"At home, I thought you worked until five today," Kat questioned.

"I did, but I called in today, I wasn't feeling too good."

"That's perfect, I was passing through the neighborhood. I'm outside, girl," Kat said, while pulling in the driveway. Walking to the door unlocking it, Manhattan then sat down, staring at the clean carpet. My poor baby couldn't even think straight. Over, and over, she replayed in her head what happened in the police station. If she knew how I stomped Deaux to the ground because of that, she would answer the phone when I called.

"Okay, the door is unlocked," Manhattan said, with her phone on speaker, then she disconnected the call. Running her ashy fingers through her messy hair, Manhattan stared at the old picture of us on the wall with a sad look on her face. I often stared at the picture, wishing things could back to how they use to be.

Katera Washington, Manhattan's best friend, but everyone called her Kat for short. They've been friends for as long I could remember. They met years ago, when Manhattan spent her summers in Charlotte, North Carolina as a kid. Three years ago, she moved to Philly when her mom passed away in a car accident. Charlotte held too many memories because her mom was the mayor. Kat knew the best thing to do was move to Philly, because Manhattan would help her through her hard times.

They were different, but still the same in so many ways. Kat was more outgoing and loud spoken. Manhattan was quiet, and majority of the time kept her opinions to herself. Kat was a thirty-seven-year old, free spirit, who didn't give a fuck about what anyone said about her. Even though she was mad cool, the bitch was dramatic as fuck. Causing scenes in the poppi stores, starting fights at Max's, and even threating to kill somebody on the L-Train. That wasn't the only thing that made her dramatic. On a daily, Kat wore a leather coat in the middle of the summer just to show off the price tag. With her mom passing away, shorty was left a lot of bread. If it wasn't for Manhattan, Kat would have blown through that money a long time ago, no lie. Kat always said Hat was her peace, she sounded a lot like me when she said that. I fucked with Kat tough, because unlike everyone in Manhattan's life, she didn't get in our business or talk down on my name.

"What up, what up, what up, my jawn," Kat spoke loudly, walking through my house swinging her hips from left to right. Wearing a white cropped top, a short red leather skirt, black leather thigh high boots, and a blonde short wig, Hat stared at Kat like she was crazy.

"What's up with you and where are you going looking like a model who lost her way to Fashion Week in New York?"

"Zaammnnnnnnnn, shawty, I see someone woke up on the shady side of the bed," Kat laughed, sitting down next to Hat. Manhattan scoffed laughing, but she really wasn't in a laughing mood.

"My bad, Kat," Hat replied.

"No, what's bad is that hair and appearance of yours. It's 3:45 p.m. and it look like you JUST rolled out of bed."

"That's because I did just roll out of bed. I called into work last night, I was too depressed to get out of bed," she answered.

"Why jawn, what's wrong?" Pulling her wig and stocking cap off to place it on the couch next to her, Kat began to scratch her tampered fade haircut. With bright pink hair like hers, everyone looked at her twice, but in a dope way. Kat loved the attention anyways.

"Girl, you pulled that wig off like it was a snapback," Manhattan laughed.

"That's what it feels like, but what's up though?"

"Yesterday was our anniversary, and he was nowhere in sight. I called his phone all day, but he ignored my calls and text messages. About 8:00 p.m., Deaux is sending pictures of Clover to my phone, while he was in her bed, sleeping."

"What, this bitch is still with the childish games? I thought he was done with her and she was fucking with some dawn out of Yorktown?"

"I don't know about any of that, but that's not the end of it. A few hours after that, I get a phone call from Clover, saying he's at the police station and I needed to come through. When I walk in there, Deaux is walking out of the bathroom. She had the nerve to speak to me like we're friends or something. Oak was also up there because Cope and Smoke was with Clover. Oak was ready to snatch Deaux by that nappy weave of hers.

I swear, Kat, my feelings were so fucking hurt. Clover knew how important yesterday meant to me, but he didn't care. I guess spending time with Deaux was more important to him," with her knees pressed against her flat chest, Manhattan place her face on her knees crying.

"Girl, it's okay, but you know how this shit goes with Clover. Besides that, are they all okay?"

"Yea, they didn't beat them too bad, but what about me? I can't continue to go through this," she whimpered, trying her best to not make eye contact with Kat. Sitting closer to Manhattan, Kat rubbed her back saying, "come on, Hat, we go through this all the time. I can't let you cry about this, just like I can't let you cry about everything else he has done."

"I guess you're right, but what the fuck am I supposed to do?"

"You don't have many options and I can't tell you what to do," Kat uttered. I know she was tired of hearing this same ole shit and seeing those same ole' tears fall.

"I'm over talking about this, it's really pointless," Manhattan wiped her tears, mumbling.

"You're right, let's change the subject. Guess who I ran into today in Center City?"

"Who, Kat?" Manhattan questioned, yawning. Kat cleared her cluttered throat, saying, "your sister."

"Oh, okay."

"Yea, uumm, she asked about you and Katober. I told her y'all are doing good, she was happy to hear that," Kat answered.

"Oh, okay," Manhattan replied, in a dry tone. Dead ass, she didn't give a flying fuck about her sister or anything she had to say.

"Hat, you haven't seen or hardly spoken to your mom, sister, or anyone else in your family in years. That's not right, you all know that."

"Four years, four years to be exact, and I'm fine with that, Kat. I was fine when they stopped talking to me when I said I was pregnant with Katober, and I'm fine with it now. They're missing out on watching her grow up and being in her life, not me. I'm here watching her blossom every fucking day, that's facts!"

"I understand what you're saying, trust me, I do. I am going to say this though, one day, y'all need to talk before it's too late. People are dying every day, B, you don't want something to happen and you're not speaking to any of them."

"If they want to apologize and mend things with me, I'm not hard to find," Manhattan spoke, firmly. From the bottom of her heart, she really didn't care if she ever spoke to her family again. It wasn't because she didn't want to, it's because the way they treated her for loving me.

"Okay, Hat, I said what I had to say about the situation. Where is my niece, anyways? I've been thinking about her all day and ready to cover her face with kisses."

"She's with Smoke and Ryker."

"Awww, okay, I'll stick around until she gets back. You need me here," Kat smiled, giving Manhattan a hug.

"Thanks, Kat, I owe you for life."

"That's what friends are for," she smiled again.

After two miscarriages and an abortion, ya boy Clover FINALLY got what he wanted from Manhattan, a fuckin' kid, yo.

Katober Grace Augustine Porter, that little girl was truly the apple of my eye, my motivation, the fucking wind beneath my wings, and all that other mushy stuff I love to compare her to. I never thought I could love another woman more than I love Manhattan, but that changed when I laid eyes on Katober. I swear, she was a breath of fresh air, something I desperately needed in my life. Watching my beautiful baby girl grow up these past four years were dumb amazing.

When I told Deaux that Manhattan was carrying my seed, she literally, broke down in my lap crying. Too bad for her because I didn't have time for that. From jump, I made it clear that what we had was only a fuck thing. She desperately wanted a baby by me, but I made damn sure that would never happen. I care about Deaux, I had a couple of feelings for her, I even had love for shorty, but I wasn't in love with her. To me, Deaux was my street solider, like my young bol who did everything I demanded and commanded with no issue. Deaux was still the same bitch I met back in 2009. No goals, ambition, or motivation, such a sad case. The only goal she had was becoming the queen pin of Philly; why the fuck would I want to fuck that for life?

"If you were me, what would you do?" Manhattan questioned Kat.

"Hat, you know Clover is my boy and I fuck with him like he's my brother. Clover only does what you allow him to do, baby girl. I can't tell you want I would, or wouldn't do, because I don't know what I would do in this situation. When you love a man, yo, you do some crazzzzyyyy things."

"Never mind, forget I asked that. I'm loving that blonde bob on you, but I love the bald head look better. It goes well with your caramel skin tone, it reminds me of some fancy candy," Manhattan laughed.

"Thanks, girl, but I need to talk to you about something," Kat said, while unzipping her boots and kicking them off to the side.

"What's up?" She questioned.

"It's about Charlie, he's been acting real funny lately."

"Funny, whatcha mean funny?"

"Besides a few text messages, I haven't talked to him in three days."

"I mean, Kat, he is a married man, what did you think it would be like?"

"Naw, Hat, that doesn't mean shit. For a married man, Charlie is always available. I think he's fucking around, and if I find out I'm going to kill him. Come with me to his other crib across town."

"What, why?" Manhattan asked.

"I need to check a few things out, that's it!"

"I don't know Kat, you know that kind of stuff not my twist."

"Awww, come on, Hat, it's not like we're going to rob a Mac machine or Chinx," she implied, trying to convince Manhattan to, but she still didn't give in.

"Look, I'll think about it, ard?"

"Okay, thanks girl," she smiled, giving Manhattan a big hug, but she rolled her glossy eyes in return.

"Kiss my ass, Kat, you know I'm going to say yea," Manhattan flared her nose and rolled her watery eyes. She was ready to breakdown and cry, but her pride wouldn't let her do it.

"I have a question, Hat, and I want a serious answer."

"What's up, Kat?" Manhattan questioned her friend, exhaling.

"Do you ever think Clover will only be with you?"

"I don't know, Kat, I ask myself that all the time. Clover and I have been engaged for forever, I don't think I would ever marry that nigga now," she chuckled.

"If you feel like that, why do you still wear your ring?" Kat pointed at the huge rock on her finger. Staring at it for a few minutes, Hat then answered, "it reminds me of what we used to have, something I can never get back. I pray so hard at night for it, but the old days never come back. I guess it isn't meant to me."

Chapter 12

After crying for a few hours, balling out on my money, and having a dinner date at one of their favorite joints, Kat and Manhattan finally made it to Charlie's house. Forty-nine-year-old Charlie Peters was a neurosurgeon that everyone thought was in a happy married for ten years. I don't know how he found Kat, but she sure enjoyed every minute of knowing him. Fucking with a nigga like that would have you set for life if you played your cards right. Knowing Kat like I knew her, she was playing her cards right and moving light.

"I'm sleepy, full, and need to get to my child, Kat. I keep having this feeling that something will happen," Manhattan whispered, walking closely to Kat, who didn't have a care in the world. It was 10:00 pm and Hat was still ignoring my calls. At this point, I didn't know what to do, or how to fix this situation.

"Hat, you have to CHILL, yo, Charlie is out of town, Minnesota, I think," she replied.

"In Minnesota doing what?"

"Vacationing he said," using the spare key she had, Kat walked into Charlie's house as she owned the jawn. Hat, on the other hand, was dumb scared of what could happen if they were caught.

"Home sweet home." Tucking the key into her bra, Kat was tempted to pull her wig off like this was really were jawn. A lot of shit ran through her mind and she didn't know where to start looking for clues.

"I feel like a damn fool creeping and tiptoeing in this man's house. Charlie is going to kill us if he finds us in here, you know that nigga is crazy!! I'm talking Mad Max fucking crazy."

"Clearly, you don't know my hoe, Charlie wouldn't hurt a fly who sucked the blood out of his arm," as Kat fumbled through the stack of mail on the living room table, she laughed. As of now, she didn't see any signs that pointed to him cheating with another woman.

"I can't lie though, this jawn is nice, Kat," still tip toeing, but also holding onto the back of Kat's shirt, Manhattan stared at the house in an awe. White Persian rugs, high ceilings, pricey chandeliers, and bar full of over-priced champagne, whiskey, and wine, this nigga lived a good life. Well, at least, it looked like Charlie lived a good life.

"It is a nice place, but let's go upstairs and look around," exhaling loudly, Manhattan followed behind Kat running upstairs. Seconds later, they entered the spacious room, that resembled a luxury suite. Everything was white and gold, boss shit, that was fit for a king.

"Wow," Hat said, with stretched eyes looking at everything in the room. From the black dress shoes at the door, to the curtains hanging from the high ceilings, everything was designer.

"Fuck yea," Kat said, quickly closing the door and looking around. She then searched the room with her eyes, but nothing was out of the ordinary.

"Hhmm, let me check his closet," running to the closet door, Kat swung open the door not wasting anytime.
"Oh my, his closet looks like a mall, but where is his wife's things?" Manhattan asked.

"Girl, at her house," Kat laughed.

"What?"

"You know how that shit goes, they're together, but they're not together. Charlie and Diana have been together so long, that getting a divorce would be foolish. Diana does her shit and Charlie does his. When it's time for them to come together, they do. You know, for like holidays, soccer games, and birthdays."

"Bruh, relationships and marriages are getting pointless now."

"I always loved the fur coat, this jawn feels so good on my skin. Ayo, take me a picture so I can send it to my other nigga and make him jealous," Kat didn't wait for an answer, she handed Manhattan the white iPhone striking a sexy pose. Manhattan rolled her eyes tossing her head back, but she snapped the picture. Before Kat could strike another pose, their attention was grabbed by the opening door. Manhattan and Kat locked eyes and froze, they didn't know what to do.

"Shit, shit, shit, Kat, someone's here," whispering while tossing Kat her phone, Manhattan grabbed the root of her curly hair trying to figure out what to do. Kat rushed to pull the fur coat off, place it back on the hanger, and grabbed Manhattan's arm to hide. Dropping to the floor and rolling under the king-sized bed, Kat and Manhattan anxiously waited to see what would happen next.

Charlie, and an unknown man, busted through the door shirtless, kissing one another. Kat help Manhattan's hand tightly and her eyes grew huge. Manhattan slowly stared at Kat to make sure she saw what she was seeing, but ain't no way Kat missed this show.

"NOOOOOOOOO," Kat whispered, softly, with her mouth wide opened. Manhattan was surprised as well, but she didn't make a sound.

"I've been waiting for you all day, Teddy," Charlie smiled, still kissing on Teddy's neck.

"Me too, baby, you've been on my mind all damn day," unzipping his pants, Teddy dropped his boxers and pants to the floor. Then he fell to his knees, pulling Charlie's dick out of his pants. Stroking Charlie's dick and making him moan, had Kat and Manhattan sick to their stomachs. This wasn't something you saw, or wanted to see, every day. I could only imagine how Kat felt watching that shit. When Charlie rammed his dick in the back of Teddy's mouth, Kat nearly fainted making Hat silently laughed. Before she could scream, Manhattan covered her mouth, shaking her head side to side.

"You better not," Manhattan worded.

"Did, did you see that shit? Ted, Teddy, or whatever his name is, sucks dick better than me and I can suck a bullet straight out of the clip!"

"That nigga make you want to say Super Head who? I don't know if I should be grossed out or ask his for tips on giving head," Manhattan snickered, trying her best to stay quiet and hidden. She wasn't sure if Kat was hurt by this, but Manhattan couldn't take any of the situation seriously.

"Damn, suck that dick," Charlie tossed his head back, moaning louder. Charlie moaned louder than woman getting her pussy ate.

"He doesn't even gag, what the fuck?" Kat mumbled.

"I'm going to go downstairs to grab a bottle of wine, I'll be right back," Charlie said, making Teddy stand to his feet and kissing Teddy like his dick wasn't on his lips. Kat was ready to roll from under the bed and act a fool, but she knew that wouldn't be smart.

"Okay, baby, I'll be butt ass naked, waiting for you in the bath tub. Don't take too long, you know I don't like waiting," Teddy kissed Charlie again, then he walked out of the room, entering the bathroom. Once Charlie walked out of the bathroom and Teddy turned the water on, Kat grabbed Manhattan's arm, pulling her from under the bed. Dusting her clothes off with a racing heart, Manhattan mouthed, "What now?"

"Just follow me," Kat mouthed back, heading for the double doors. Then she slowly quietly opened the door and they walked out. Kat pointed to the staircase that was attached to the side of the house and Manhattan started to climb down. With raining pouring down hard, Manhattan felt like a fool, wishing she would have stayed her ass in the house. Once Kat closed the jawns, she did the same and they broke out running to her car. The Charger was only parked a few houses down, but it felt like they were running for miles.

"Girl, this why I don't fuck with you," Hat pulled on the door handle opening the door, but also looked over her shoulder to make sure no one saw them. Kat on the other hand didn't give a fuck, she hopped into her ride speeding off. She left dust, smoke, and rocks, everywhere.

"Oh my God, I can't believe this shit," pulling her wig off again, Kat tossed it to the backseat, laughing.

"This whole time you thought he was cheating with a woman and it was a MAN," Manhattan looked back, laughing.

"I'm going need a drink after this, but I wonder I his wife knows he's gay."

"She probably does and doesn't care," Manhattan answered.

"I need Patron, now, let's go to the bar or something."

"Not tonight, Kat, I just want to go home. I really had a long day and I want to climb in bed," Manhattan implied, making Kat annoyed. At this point, Manhattan didn't care how she made anyone feel.

"Suit yourself, I'll have fun by myself."

Finally making it home, Manhattan barely looked me in the eyes. To be honest, I didn't pay her much attention anyways, I guess we were on the same page.

"Where is my child," she asked, removing her kicks from her feet and the wet clothes from her body.

"My daughter is with my sister, Kan said she would keep her for the night. You were too busy running the street, no telling with who."

"Bet, I'll call her when I get out of the shower," she replied, walking through the living room and entering the bathroom. I hated how she ignored most of what I said. Lord knows I wanted to pick an argument, but I went into the room instead. A few minutes later, Manhattan entered the bedroom, sitting on the edge of the bed. The more she ignored me, I became pissed and ready to start something.

"Where the fuck were you, Manhattan?" I asked, with my eyes closed. I could hear her scoffing, but I didn't pay her ass any mind. Knowing her, Manhattan did that petty shit for my attention.

"None of your damn business," she replied, walking into the bathroom again, but this time, naked. Her smart ass comment made me open my eyes, now she had my fucking attention.

"What, you're fucking around now? If you were with Kat like you said you were, I know you were up to no-good. I'm telling you, Hat, don't-"

"Like I should fuck up Deaux, like that, CLOVER? YOU KNOW WHAT? LEAVE ME THE FUCK ALONE AND FIND YOU SO GOD DAMN BUSINESS, ARD," walking into the bathroom and slamming the door locking it. I thought about kicking that bitch open, but I was too tired to continue this argument with Manhattan. Closing my eyes again, I started to think, but also fall asleep, but out of nowhere, I felt something.

Manhattan sat on top of me, in the straddle position, with wild thoughts stomping through her mind. On a rainy night like this, we should have been making passionate sex and going half on another baby jawn name Clover Junior. Instead, I chilled peacefully, while she was headed for self-destruction. She couldn't stop thinking about Deaux lying next to her in our bed two nights ago, making sweet love to her man. The way she moaned and cried out I love you to me was oh too familiar to Manhattan. Why, because it's the same way she moaned and screamed I love you to me. She couldn't believe I would do something like that to her, but in my head it was all a game. I didn't think I was hurting anybody, because they knew about one another. If Manhattan couldn't get in contact with me, the first person she called was Deaux. I knew that shit would always fuck up her pride. I could only imagine how it felt to call the side bitch looking for your man.

"Wake... The fuck up, Spitta," the trembling sound in her voice woke me, I thought something was wrong. Well, I KNEW something was wrong. The only time she called me Spitta is when she was pissed, like zero to a hundred really pissed.

"Manhattan, what's wrong with you?" I mumbled, with my eyes barely opened. I didn't notice that tears were racing down her slim face because of me.

"You're what's wrong with me," before I could respond, Manhattan formed her hand into a handgun and placed the fake muzzle into my mouth. I was shocked, my eyes grew big. Manhattan was shaking, and I knew for sure that something wasn't right with her.

"I'm at my breaking point with you, Clover, I mean it this time. All those other times, I didn't mean it, but now I do. Imagine if this was a gun and I was about to kill you. Your heart would be racing faster than what it is.

Your life would flash right before your eyes, then you would think about all the things you haven't done in life. Like being faithful to me for once in your life muthafucka."

"What?"

"Imagine how your mom would feel if I killed your ass, right now, right this second! I think Deaux would cry harder than some of your family members."

"What the fuck, Hat, why would you even say some shit like that? Why would you even clown about killin' the nigga you love? You're tripping, for real, and I'm about to rock out on yo joe ass!"

"Shut the fuck up, Spitta, if anybody is gon' to rock out, please believe it's going to be me. You have the nerve to ask ME, how can I clown about killing the nigga I love, but how can you constantly hurt the woman you love? You fucked Deaux, in our bed, CLOVER, AND I WAS IN IT!!! I lied next to you and another woman. You didn't even change the fucking sheets, you nasty, bastard. I love you..... With eevveeerryytthhinngg in me, Clover Porter. You're my air and I can't breathe without you, but I have to change that. I can no longer love you the way I love you, because it hurts. Don't you see how you hurt me, baby? I'm dying inside, you don't even know it."

"Baby, I'm sorry, I swear, I'm sorry. I popped a perc with Deaux and I was tripping hard. I never meant to hurt you, but you can't leave me. Without you in my life, I won't function right!!! I'll kill myself if you leave me, and that's on Allah, please don't go." I started to cry, but I could see my tears didn't mean anything to Hat. With a chuckle sitting on her tongue, and a smirk on her face, she climbed off me, chunking the deuces. Once again, I was confused, but my baby couldn't be serious. She couldn't be leaving me without giving our relationship another shot. I know a nigga fucked up a lot, but damn, I really loved Manhattan, with everything in me.

"It's better you kill yourself than I do. I would hate to get blood on my hands. I'll be back for my things in the morning. Since you like Deaux in our bedroom so much, I'll call her to tell her she can move in. She's finally won, and now, she has you to herself. Goodbye, Spitta."

"Bye, see you later, Hat."

When the door closed, I rolled over closing my eyes. That fast, Hat gave me a major headache. I tried falling asleep, but Deaux was blowing my phone up like a junkie. After the fifth call, I finally answered saying, "What do you want, Deaux Gates?"

"I want you, Clover Porter, come though."

"Too bad because I don't want you right now," I laughed.

"What, are you dead ass serious right now," she asked."

"Dead ass, bye."

"What," I disconnected the jawn not letting Deaux finish what she had to say. Not even ten seconds later, Deaux ranged my phone again. Exhaling loudly, I answered the call saying, "What Deaux, what Deaux, WHAT?"

"Spitta, stop acting like a fool and selfish," she begged. For a minute I thought about Deaux wetting my dick with her big mouth. After all these years that bitch could still suck the skin off a dick like a high-paid porn star.

"Come here," I chuckled.

"Yea, that's what I thought, but come where, baby? I was thinking about you and I'm feening for you," she giggled making me shake my head.

"That's not anything new, but I'm at home. You would want to hurry up before I change my mind," ending the call again, I climbed out of bed walking out of the room. Still a lil' sleepy with my eyes half opened, I made my way to the kitchen, but first, I walked to the living room door unlocking it. My stomach was growling like a pitbull in desperate need to food. If Manhattan would have been home instead of thottin', I would have had a decent meal on the table. Fuck, or at least something that could get me through the night.

As I opened the fridge to grab my leftover sweet potato pie, the noise of a car grabbed my attention. Knowing it was Deaux's dumb thirsty ass, I sighed pulling the pie out of the jawn. Then I closed the fridge walking to the door that was opening. Sizing me up and down with a smirk on her face, Deaux kicked her Timberlands off at the door like she finally made it home from work. Hell, as much as Deaux crept in and out of here, you would thought it was her place of residence.

She looked good in her black tight jeans and even tighter white shirt, no telling why she was dressed up at this time of night. I always liked when Deaux wore her hair in the bantu knots witht the baby hairs laid. She did shit like that because she thought eventually one day it would make me be with her. Deaux was still a fool for me, a full blown full.

"Hello to you too, Spitta, my baby," she smiled kissing me on the lips. Replying, "what up, Deaux," pissed her off. You would think by now I would have gave the broad a pet name besides bitch, smut, thot, or hoe, but nah, I didn't. She expected me to be lovey dovey, calling her bae, but that wasn't me. At least that wasn't me with her, but eventually she would get that through her fuckin' head, yo.

"Where is your lil' girlfriend, somewhere reading a book," laughing while she kicked her shoes to the side more, I pushed Deaux making her laugh more. Closing the door behind her, I walked way to reenter my room smacking on my pie. Like a lost puppy, Deaux followed behind me with no problem. She wasn't bother by being in another's woman house because techinally, it was my house. Even if it wasn't my house, Deaux wouldn't have a problem. The first time I told Deaux to come over, she didn't question me about anything or felt insulted. She loved that kind of mess, Deaux called it bait.

"Shut up and mind your own damn business!"

"What, I'm just asking a simple, simple question. She might come home while I'm here, then what," laughing as she undressed to get into bed next to me, I pushed Deaux again. This time, it was a little rougher, but Deaux didn't mind the agression. I always said that shit turned her on and by the look she always had in her big eyes, it truly did.

"She's going to cry just like all the other times. Now, lie the fuck down before you piss me off," I demanded making Deaux do exactly that with a smile on her face.

"Lord, what did you do that girl, Philly, I hear it all in your jawn," she laughed.

"Since your nosey ass want to know, we got into a lil' jawn. I woke up with her sitting on top of me with the barrel in my face," I laughed. To me, this shit was funny because Manhanttan's lil' emotional stunt didn't put any fear in my heart. She probably wanted to turn around and come home, but her feelings wouldn't let her.
"What," Deaux eyes stretched gasping, but I laughed,
"Not a real gun clown, but she did her usual two-step. You know I'm never worried, she'll be back like always."
"She doesn't have to come back. You can move me in and we can live happily ever after," Manhattan whispered making me give her an ugly look.
"Bitch, she's the mother of my child, she ain't going nowhere. Manhattan Mullen is stuck with me for life, believe that," I laughed.
"Just because you two have a kid together doesn't mean yall have to BE together! I know plenty of people who co-parent with no damn problem, that's your excuse to stay with her!"
"Call it what you want, but any nigga after me I'ma get him ribbed or killed, I made that clear to her years ago," I laughed again, but Deaux rolled her eyes. I always talked about Manhattan to her like Deaux was the big homie. She hated these conversations, but I didn't care. That's the kind of shit that happens when you mention Manhattan's name without my permission.
"Clover, I want a baby, I'm not getting any younger here," Deaux whispered.
"That's funny," I uttered while taking a bite of the sweet potato pie.
"What's funny, Spitta, I'm dead serious?"
"That's what's funny, Katober doesn't need a lil' jawn unless it's coming from Manhattan's pussy. I made that clear to you a longgggg time ago, I don't know why we keep having this stupid ass conversation. You need to find you a man who will give you all that shit you want because it won't be me," I expressed with a smirk on her face.
"What does Manhattan have that I don't have? What makes her better to me and why won't you leave that bitch for me," standing to her feet shouting,
"Let me hurt your feeling real quick, Manhattan has me. She had my first and only kid, my heart, and Manhattan's probably going to have my last name. That's every fucking thing that you won't ever get from me! Now stop asking me about a baby that won't ever happen,

a relationhip that won't ever happen, and stop talking about Hat. If you don't I'ma kick your ass out this bitch naked again, try me if you want to. You already know how I get down, don't test me, Deaux." Sitting next to me with a stupid look on her face, Deaux couldn't say much. After the hurtful jawns I said, how could she? As usual, she always painted this picture of me being the bad guy, but the picture was also of her being a clown.

***

Making it to Kansas' house with a face full of tears and the crumbled pieces of her heart, Manhattan knocked on the door softly waiting for Kan to answer. Since it was 2: 00 am, she didn't want to knock too hard in fear of waking Katober. Manhattan drove around Philly for a minute trying to figure out what was the downfall of our relationship or why the fuck she even gave me her number the day we meant. It was too late for that part because we both were in too deep. Truth be told, I would never leave Hat, especially for another woman. I often felt like I couldn't live without her, but that was something I could never admit to her. To keep it a stack, the only person I admitted that to was Deaux. I purposely did it to give her a friendly reminded that she would never be number one in my life. Even if Hat EVER decided to leave me I always had to remind her she STILL wouldn't be number one. Some people said it was mean of me to admit that, but I call it the truth. That was some shit people couldn't swallow even when you spoon fed it to them.

After a few seconds of patiently waiting, Kansas finally opened the door yawning. Rubbing her skin against her smooth black skin, Kansas spoked, "Well hey sister in law."

"Hey, girl." Giving Kan a fake wave as she walked into the house, Kansas could sense something was wrong. Rushing to close the door, Kansas then followed behind Manhattan to take a sit on the couch.

"Girl, Tober had me watching Mickey Mouse all damn day, we fell asleep in her," she laughed.

"Oh, okay," Manhattan laughed turning away with tears in her eyes. Pushing a little closer to Manhattan, Kansas pushed Manhattan's hair out of her face saying,"Hat, are you crying?"

"No, I'm not crying, I swear, Kan," she said, sobbing dropping her head lower like a damn fool. I hated how she put my sister in our business which put a damper on our relationship. I'm talking a huge damper which made Kansas almost hate me most of the time. It kind of made me wish I would have never pushed for those two to become so fuckin' close!! Now, it was like I was the outsider and Hat was her sister. Her damn blood sister, ya feel me? Throughout the years, my cheating and dog days made Kansas slightly hate me more by the second. It also kind of made us distant, but I tried my best to keep our bond tight. If that meant throwing money at her to make Kansas mind her business, I didn't have a problem doing that. Besides, I was her brother and she should have been minding her business anyways.

"What did he do this time, Hat?" Kansas whispered giving Manhattan a hug. Sighing and wiping her tears away Hat would hardly speak. Kansas held Manhattan tighter as if being body to body to her would mend Manhattan's pain.

"It's okay, Manhattan, it's okay!" Still sobbing, Manhattan uttered, "I don't know where to start, like always. It's always some shit with Clover Porter. God knows I love him, but nothing in my heart tells me he feels the same way!"

"I know Spitta does some fucked up shit, but I would never say he doesn't love you, Hat. He's just a selfish ass jawn he will always put himself first. The streets corrupted his mind and train of thought years ago."
"Forget that, Kansas, I'm tired of hearing that. The streets can no longer be his excuse for the messed up things he put me through," jumping to her feet, Manhattan was mas pissed off. She was right though, the same ole' excuses I used were played out. The street had a little to do with why I began this fucked up person. On the contrary, I let my own mind and pride make me into a selfish man.

"You're absolutely right, but, Hat, you've dealt with it for so long. Now that you're starting to go against his word, he hates that shit."

"Fuck all that, I can't do this anymore, Kan!!! This shit is too much and someone is going to get hurt. Clover will be on *Forensic Files* or I'm going to be on *Snapped*. When you start feeling like that, you need to let that clown gooooooooooo!!!! This relationship is not healthy, Hat, we all know that. I think the only person who doesn't know that is Clover. He should be the mutherfucker shouting it from the top of the Trump Towers."

"I really need to end this before Katober can realize what is going on. How am I supposed to be a good role model for my daughter when I can't even leave the man alone who hurts me? Everyday it's the same ole shit with Clover and Deaux. She doesn't have any respect for me or my relationship, I hate that bitch so much!!! I swear, Kan, I wish that bitch would just drop dead."

"You should be wishing the same about my brother also if that's the case. It takes two to cheat, not just one. You can't expect a smut with no morals to respect your relationship when your man doesn't even respect." Sitting there with a blank look on her face, Mahattan couldn't say much because Kansas was right. Those words hit her hard in her chest, she felt every word Kansas spoke like a G. See, what fucked me up was how Manhattan never took responibilty for her part in all this. She allowed me to cheat, beg her to take me back, and believe all the lies I said about never cheating again. After the second time being caught, I knew I could continue doing it because Manhattan would take me back with no problem. Shorty would always take me back and I felt that in my heart. What I did know is that one day, she would get some tuff skin and put her foot down. Until that day came, I would continue to do my shit with no problem.

"At the end of the day, Kansas, Deaux won't leave Clover alone because she has a point to prove to me!"

"Okay, so what's your excuse for not leaving him? Please, don't say Katober because nothing is wrong with co-parenting. I know PLENTY of women who does it with no problem. I also know more women who are single parents and do that shit like it's easy, yo." Kansas answered leaving Manhattan stuck. Her pride prohibited her to admit the truth. Manhattan didn't want to leave me because SHE didn't want to leave me. I often thought that Manhattan was the one who didn't leave me alone because she had a point to prove.

"I don't want my daughter to grow up without both her parents in the household." Manhattan replied.

"Look, Manhattan, we've been down this road plenttyyyyyyy of times and I'm going to tell you this for the last time. Just…. Let….go……baby, just let know," she expressed loudly, but quickly lowered her voicetone when Katober began to move in her sleep.

"I love him though, Kan, I fucking love him," dropping her head into her lap, Manhattan sobbed loudly making tears form in Kansas eyes.

"Sometimes that love shit isn't worth our sanity. Sometimes we have to just say fuck it and let things go. You're going to drive yourself crazy trying to keep a man and compete with a smut. Deaux will go above and beyond to prove her love to Spitta, yo. Deaux and Clover are out of pocket, but you know what you have to do."

"Yea, pray." Manhattan replied. The look on Kansas face said it all and praying wasn't what Kansas was talking about.

"Girl, bye that's not what the fuck I was talking about!"

Chapter 13

"How was your trip back at home," Manhattan asked Kat as she reached into her pocket for her cellphone. Every second she glanced at her screen to see if she had a miss call from me. Little did she know, big daddy was doing the same thing.

"It was okay and quick. I didn't visit my mom's grave though. I don't have time for that depressing mess right now in life. I'm in a good place in life, I can't let my depression come back, that shit is no joke."

After the shit that went down with ole boy', Kat went back to North Carolina to visit and it also was the anniversary on her mother's death. Nowadays, was in a good place with her mom's death, but the pain will always be there. Today, was her first day back home and you know the first person she had to link up with was Hat. They act like Kat was gone for two months instead of two fuckin' days.

"I feel you on that, there's no need to backtrack." Hat said shrugging her shoulders.

"Not at all, but I swear, girl, this store gets all my money, well all of that dick suckers money."

Manhattan chuckled a little as she shuffled through the clothes on the racks. Joan Shepp Boutique was one of her favorite places to spend all of my damn money.

"Yea, I know right." Replying in flat tone, Kat could sense something wasn't right about her friend.

"You know that new Mexican restaurant they built across town?" Kat asked. Staring at herself in the long mirror, she held the black and white chevron pattern dress against her body.

"Girl, that looks like something my mama would wear. Put that shit back and try again." Manhattan laughed, but Kat laugh also placing the dress back onto the rack.

"Shit, maybe you should get it for your mama." Kat joked.

"Anyways, what about that Mexican restaurant?" Manhattan asked.

"Today they are doing their special, two for one Monday margaritas. I think we should go, it's not like we have anything to do. Besides, I could use a drink or four, these past few days have been crazy."

"My days have been beyond crazy. I should create a word, add some synonyms, antonym, and throw it in the dictionary. Do you have Noah Webster on speed-dial, we all know Kat Washington knows a lot of jawns."

"Is that a yes or a no, I don't read between the lines and fuck them antonyms." Kat laughed.

"I guess we can go, but I need to drop these bags off and change my shoes at my house. If you don't feel like going across town I understand, there should be some flats in my car." Manhattan implied.

"At your house, why not drop your things at your real house? You know your place is only collecting dust, I don't know why you don't put it on the market. Then some newlywed couple can enjoy it and make babies in it." She laughed.

"That house is my real house, that other place is for Clover."

"Okay, Hat, dang, girl, I'm just saying." She replied.

"Well, I'm just replying, but do you like this dress?" Holding a cherry red off the shoulder dress in mid-air, Kat examined the fitted dress with her hand on her chin. Suddenly, a smile appeared on her face and she said, "I can't wait to see that lil' fat ass in that dress. Katober gave you hips, thighs, and ass, thank you, sweet baby Jesus.

It's been two days since Manhattan left the jawn, and I really hadn't spoken to her also. I wasn't moved by that at all, real talk. By tomorrow she would be back home like always acting like everything is a hundred with us. Until then, I wasn't tripping on her ignoring my text messages and calls. The most she would stay away was four days, but that shit would drive her crazy. I didn't mind the peace and quiet, I needed to clear my mind anyways. Don't think I hit her line on some thirsty shit because I was never the thirsty type.

I only bothered her to see if I would get a response. World around town was that someone saw her leaving Max's with some joe, but I laughed at those allegations. Manhattan had to have a twin out there because the bitch wasn't stupid enough to play on my jawn like that. I be damn if I let a joint stress me the fuck out. As long as I knew Katober was straight, Manhattan could to whatever she wanted.

After shopping for two and a half hours, Manhattan and Kat were ready to get drinks and tacos at three in the afternoon. Kat didn't mind being tipsy or drunk at that time of the jawn.

"I need to pee so damn bad, is Clover home?" Kat and Manhattan walked out of the boutique with two completely vibes that they both could read. Besides answering questions that Kat asked her, Hat didn't say much. Kat knew her homie well and that something was bothering her. On the other hand, she didn't want to jump to any conclusion running off by the mouth.

"I'm not with Clover right now and I really don't give a fuck about where he is," fumbling for her keys in her purse, Kat stared at Manhattan with a confused look on her face.

"Why, sis," Kat questioned.

"I don't even want to talk about it, Kat. At this point in life, I'm disgusted with myself.

As Kat and Manhattan walked out of the boutique, Charlie was leaned against her Jeep Wrangler nervously waiting for her. Kat's first reaction was to go off, but she had to remind herself that she needed to work on her attitude and angry. On the flight going back to North Carolina, all she thought about was beating the dog shit out of Charlie. Kat always pretended like she didn't have much feelings for Charlie, but she did. Kat wouldn't admit it, but she prayed for the day he would leave his wife for her. Without his wife in his life, Kat and Charlie could live happily ever after. I knew she was heartbroken by what she witnessed at Charlie's house, but Kat was also disgusted. I could only imagine how she felt witnessing that shit. I can't relate though. if I would have walked down on Hat eating some bitch's pussy, I would have joined in, no questioned asked.

"OH loorrdddd, there goes the dick pleaser," Manhattan snickered with her bags covering her face.

"Call that nigga the dick eater, fuck the pleaser." Kat whispered back to Manhattan.

"Beautiful woman, hey." Charlie spoke with a charming smile scribbled on his face, but Kat wasn't following for that sweet shit today. She had shit to get off her chest so, Kat had to forget about that smile. His smile always suckered her back into his arms and he knew that.

The closer Kat and Manhattan approached the Jeep, Manhattan said, "uumm, I'll let you to talk, take your time."

"How are you doing, Manhattan?" Charlie asked smiling waiting to shake Manhattan's hand. She could hardly make eye contact with him, so, Manhattan shook his hand while looking pass Charlie. As she walked off, she answered, "i'm doing, Charlie, that's about it." Manhattan's world and vibe didn't sit well with Kat, but she let her enter the Jeep without saying anything. Once Manhattan closed the door, Kat rubbed her fresh tampered fade sizing Charlie up and down. He was astonished by her alluring beauty that Charlie didn't realize the evil look on her face.

"What the fuck do you want and how did you know I was here," aggressively pushing Charlie out of her way to place her bags in the jeep. Then she slammed her door as if it wasn't her vehicle. Kat was fucked up like that, a true clown.

"Since you used my card, I got the alert, I figured you were shopping in the area." He laughed brushing his hand against her let hip. Usually, this would have turned her own, but Charlie couldn't do that anymore. She could no long look at him as the same man. At least not as the same straight man Kat used to.

"Oh yea, I forgot it was yours, but here, I should have maxed the bitch out," Kat reached into her pushup bra pulling the card out and handing it to Charlie. He was confused, but no worries, Kat would unconfused him in a heartbeat.

"Katera, what the fuck is your problem? Is there a reason I haven't heard from you in two days, Katera? I've been calling, texting, and even emailing you like I'm some damn stalker, what's up?" He asked staring Kat in the eyes, but she didn't reply. All she could do is shake her head and think about what she saw.

"Is there something you want to tell me," she asked sliding her hands in her back pockets. Just the thought of the nasty shit Teddy and Charlie did when Kat and Manhattan left made her want to vomit on his Stacy Adam shoes.

"What?" He asked still confused.

"You know what, Charlie, I don't even know where to start with you."

"Start from the beginning so we can fix this!! I don't want to lose you, baby, is it about my wife? I told you we're getting a divorce soon, this shit takes time!!!"

"IT'S NOT ABOUT YOUR FUCKING WIFE, CHARLIE, IT'S ABOUT YOU AND WHAT THE FUCK I SAW!!!!!" Kat shouted at the top of her lungs causing a few jawns to look at her who was walking by. Once Kat stretched her eyes at them with an attitude, they rushed to walk off.

"What are you talking about, tell me now," Charlie attempted to pull Kat by the arm, but she quickly pulled away forcefully. Her actions shocked Charlie, but it was going to be her words who cut him deeper.

"For the past for weeks, you've been acting mad strange. I tried to brush it off, but it felt like by the day you were getting stranger. The shit starting driving me crazy and I had to figure out what was going on. I knew if I asked you, you wouldn't tell me the truth, Charlie. So,

I decided to go snooping in one of your houses while you were away. Two days ago you lied and said you were out of town, but I know for a FACT you weren't out of town! Now, just come clean, Charlie, I don't want to expose the truth because every time I think about it my stomach becomes weak." She begged.

"Kat, I was out of town, you know that!" He replied loudly.

"CHARLIE, I WAS IN YOUR HOUSE WATCHING YOU SUCK SOME MAN NAME TEDDY'S DICK!!! Before you try to lie again, I had Manhattan with you. Yea, she saw exactly what I saw," pushing Charlie out of her way again, Kat reached to open her door startling Manhattan. Then Kat pulled Charlie by his tie saying, "Manhattan, please let this nigga know what we both saw. He's 'claiming' he was out of town, but WE all know that isn't true." Kat had a tight grip on Charlie's tie, but he wasn't a fool to complain. Kat was so heated, Charlie could hear her cold heart pounding. See, it was niggas like Charlie who scarred bitches for life. I know I wasn't a saint, but what Hat never had to worry about was watching me on my knees sucking dick.

Charlie stared at Manhattan with wide eyes hoping she could read his mind and lie for him. Too bad Manhattan wasn't going to lie for him and could get the sex images out of head.

"We saw what we saw, Charlie, you can't lie." Hat replied.

"Shit!" He whispered and dropped his head. That made Kat even more pissed, she was ready to kill that nigga with her bare heads. Instead, she slammed the door releasing his tie. It's crazy how she went from rage to crying in a matter of second.

"Kat, I'm, I'm sorry, I'm so sorry." Charlie could barely speak as he rubbed his aching neck.

"You don't even understand how I felt seeing that shit, Charlie!!!!! The fucking man I love is…..the fucking man I love is nothing, but a gay nigga!" She whispered loudly covering her mouth. The way she cried and sobbed made Manhattan want to come to Kat's rescue, but she changed her mind. She already was in there business and she didn't want to be an inch deeper in it. I am not gay, Katera, don't ever call me that shit!!"

"What, what the fuck do you call a man who sucks another man's dick? Please let me know because in 2016, we call that gay! GAY, GAY, GAY, GAY, BOY YOU ARE GAY AND ACCEPT IT!" She replied, still sobbing.

"I am not gay, stop saying the shit, Kat, for real. You're about to piss me off, real talk! A gay man is someone who has been with multiple men and soft! They wear purses and talk like lil' bitches, that's not me, and you know that, Kat!!!! I'm a masculine man, I've ALWAYS BEEN that."

"Wow, how can you be so ignorant and say any of that? The man that's standing in front of me right now, is that the same man I loved?" Kat asked, but to keep it a stack, she really wasn't sure what the answer to that question was. It's sad to say it, but the man that stood in front of her was always 'that' man.

"Look, I've known Teddy for years, since my Sophomore year at Temple. At the time, my parents had to file bankrupt and I was on the verge of being pulled out of college because they couldn't afford anyone. Teddy was there for me……in ways that kept me finically straight. I had to learn how to survive and he taught me how to do that."

"Woowww, so Ted has been your gay lover?" Squatting to the ground, Kat began to gag and whimper. While it felt like bricks were sitting on her chest, it felt like a rope was tied around her flat stomach. Purposely hurting her by the second without any remorse.

"He's is not my fucking gay lover, Kat!!!"

"Does your wife know about you being an undercover homo? Does she know you're an undercover homophobic homo? That shit doesn't even make sense, but that's exact what you are." Kat uttered.

"Baby, please get up, people are starting to look at us. Besides, you're ruining your pretty make-up and I know how you feel about your face beat." He begged attempting to pull Kat to her feet, but she tightly tucked her arms between her thick thighs.

"NO, leave me the fuck alone, I mean it. I don't care, Charlie, let them fucking stare!!!! On God, I wish they could have seen what the fuck Hat and I saw. Then they would look at you in an entirely different lighting."

"Baby, I am still the same man you met a year ago and fell in love with.

"Does your wife know about you being downlow and don't lie to me. You can at least tell me some kind of truth, please." Begging in a soft tone, Kat used her wet to wipe her wet face. Mascara smeared all over her hand and cheeks, but she didn't care. The only thing Kat cared about was getting the truth, but it felt like she wouldn't get that from Charlie.

After a few seconds of standing in silence while Kat cried, Charlie knew it was time to come clean and give Kat the answers she needed. Inhaling loudly, Charlie then exhaled taking a sit next to Kat on the curb with his hands deep in his pockets. He didn't know exactly what to say, but whatever he did say, he prayed it kept her in his life.

"Katera, I honestly do love you and I'm in love with. Besides being sexy as hell, you're intelligent, funny, easy to talk to, and a go-getter. Any man would be lucky to have you in their life and it's crazy how I am that man. I know we hooked up in a fucked up situation, but everything I promised you I would do, I will do. You wouldn't even understand how much I love you and probably never will. Every day I counted the days I would be divorced and all yours."

"You would have been living a lie because you fully wouldn't have been mines. You said all that shit, but you still haven't answered the one question I asked you." She stated. Exhaling again, Charlie uttered, "yea, she knows, she found out about two years ago."

"So, that's the real reason you're getting a divorce, not because of me. This whole time I was afraid of losing you to your wife, but now I see it's to another man." Kat began to cry louder, but Charlie gently grabbed her by the face replying, "no, I filed for a divorce because the moment I met you, I knew I had to have you in my life forever." Charlie was literally pouring his jawn out to Kat, but her thoughts were so far gone. She didn't give a fuck if he shouted to the world how much he loved, her, Kat's thoughts could never change.

"How did your wife find out about you being gay?" Kat questioned Charlie as she turned to face him. She had to make sure Charlie had a clear view of her red eyes and tears. He could hardly look Kat in the eyes without feeling like a piece of shit.

"Imagine being out of town, in a city where you think you can be open with your sexuality, but your wife is also there cheating with your co-worker. He doesn't see you kissing a man, but your wife sees it. Kandi and I looked each other dead in the eyes without saying a word. I guess the looks on our faces said it all. My flight landed home that Monday and Kandi's landed that Wednesday. When we were finally face to face again, she didn't say anything. I'll never forget that day, Kandi took a hot shower, read her bible, said her prayers, and got into bed. The next morning, she gave me my usual morning kiss, and left for work. A couple of weeks after that, I met you and decided to file for divorce. Still today she hasn't questioned me about it and I'll never understand why."

"Hhmmm, I can tell you exactly, it's called love. It makes us accept things we never thought we would accept. Kandi would do anything to keep you in her life, but I can't blame her. You were always a good man to me, a great man actually. I wanted to be your wife so damn bad, but some lucky man will be that. I can't believe I'm losing you to a man." Dropping her head on his shoulder, Kat began to cry again. Makeup damaged her white t-shirt, but that was the least of her worries.

"Kat, you have to believe me, you're not losing me to another man!!!

"Charlie, I saw the way you looked at him, you're in love, but you can't admit it to yourself. I feel bad for you, you need to be honest with yourself. You are a gay man, Charlie, and I hope you accept that one day." Kat whispered.

"Katera, I'm not gay, I wish you would stop saying that! Teddy is the only man I've been with, I don't get turned on when I see a man."

"Charlie, just give it a rest, YOUR'RE GAY! I don't know if I should be upset that you suck dick better than me or that you didn't teach me how to not gag." She expressed shaking her head. It's crazy how Charlie really thought he wasn't a gay man, but eventually he had to admit that to himself and everyone.

"I, I don't know what to say at this point, baby. I love you, I really do love you and I always will. It's fucked up how no matter what I say, it won't change the damage that is already done." A few tears dropped rom Charlie's eyes, but he wiped them away laughing. Then he gave her a kiss on the cheek, that would be the last kiss forever. Kat's eyes were blurry, but she still managed to hold his hands giving him a wet kiss on his lips. Even though he used those same lips to suck dick, this last kissed she would remember for a life time. Kat felt every ounce of love she had for Charlie lingering on lips, but it slowly left her heart. Kat prayed that eventually the love and pain would leave soon, she couldn't tolerate the pain of a heartache. Letting go Charlie would be dumb hard, now I understood how Manhattan felt. To let go of someone you truly love feels impossible, maybe that's the reason why I couldn't let go of Manhattan. Trust me, I hated seeing her cry, Allah knows that I wanted to stop the pain I caused frequently, but I just couldn't let her go. I wanted to let her move on and find a better man, a man that would love her exactly how Manhattan wanted to be loved, but I couldn't let her go. The idea of another man caressing her sweet body or making her laugh in that unique giggle drove me insane. I've should've gave

Manhattan her heart back years ago, but I didn't want another jawn making her happy. Yea, I'm fucking selfish, so what?

"It's really not much to say at this point, just our goodbyes. I loved you so much, Charlie, so much that I was willing to wait for you. After seeing what I saw, there is no more waiting and it's damn sure no more us. I-I-I can't even look at you anymore, it's killing me inside, bye forever," wiping her eyes while jumping to her feet, Kat rushed to get inside of her Jeep to speed off. Hat didn't know what to do or say. She cried hysterically, Kat couldn't even drive much which made her pull to the side of the road. Manhattan began to cry, but silently. Kat's tears and pain was oh so familiar, it made her heart ache and open the love wounds that Manhattan thought were closing.

"It's going to be okay girl, I promise it will." Hat stated attempting to grab Kat's hand, but she shook her head pulling away.

"It hurts so fucking bad, Hat, I don't see how you do this shit! I really had plans for Charlie and I. The big house, two kids, a poodle, and the white fence to surround our house. I love that man, this shit cuts so deep!" She shouted sobbing ugly. Right now, Kat was crying ugly with drool hanging from her plump lips. She was wearing every emotion on her sleeves without a care in a world.

"I don't know, but don't be a fool like me.

"How, how do you leave a man alone who you honesty have no intentions on wanting to leave?" Kat questioned.

"I can't answer that question just yet, but it's coming soon, Kat. It's hard, God knows it so damn hard to leave a man alone that holds your heart in his True Religion pockets. Then you have the bitch or bitches who are also fighting for his love waiting for you to give up. They are waiting for you to break, but your heart is holding your emotions together for some odd and dumb ass reason. At the same time, you have your mind telling you to let go, it's no love lost, but how? How can your mind tell you that when indeed, it was once love there. It was pure like Colombian cocaine, it was the ONE thing that made you feel secure. Now that same love have you feeling like Willie Lump Lump, you feel isolated, and you feel just like a damn fool." With tears filling her eyes, Manhattan began to whimper in a low cry. She was dumb upset with herself for crying and making everything about her, but she couldn't help it. She knew Kat wouldn't judge her, but it was still hard to express her feelings. Manhattan knew even her own best friend was tired of hearing the same old sad stories. Especially when Kat knew Manhattan wasn't going to leave my trifling ass. Still being the good friend she was, Kat stayed a listening ear and gave Manhattan the best advice she could possibility give. Unlike my sister and everyone else in Manhattan's ear, Kat still didn't bash me after all the fucked up shit I did. Kat knew how it felt to be stuck between leaving a man, but also loving that same man.

"Okay, Hat, this is no longer about me, I've been catching this vibe from you all day. What the hell is going on?" Kat questioned.

"Girl, it's just been so, so much shit with Clover and I. I know it's been the same shit between us, but I'm finally reaching my breaking point." She sobbed softly with drool dripping from her bottom lip. Breathing heavily, Kat replied, "Hat, what happened this time and don't lie to me."

"It's so much shit that I don't even know where to start," reaching for a napkin, Hat wiped her nose shaking her head. She felt like a fool for what she was about to say, but she didn't give a fuck anymore. She needed to vent and if she would be judge for her poor decisions, Manhattan didn't give a fuck.

"When he got arrested, Deaux was there. I felt like a fucking fool running to his rescue. A few days before that, I was lying in bed and he came stumbling in the house with Deaux at 3:00 am. Clover was out his mind and really had sex with this girl in our be…" Manhattan tossed her hands in the air with a cracking voice. The tears rolled from her eyes, but she turned away staring out of the window. Kat and Manhattan both felt like a fool and couldn't give one another straight advice.

Gasping loudly, Kat placed her hands over her mouth. This was the first time she wanted to go off about me, but how could she do that when Kat was crying over a joe ass nigga who was gay?

"Manhattan, tell me you're not serious, Clover wouldn't do any fuck up shit like that, yo!" She yelled shaking her head, but lets be real, Kat knew the answer to her question. It's crazy how through all the shit I did, Kat always tried to find good in me. She always made excuses for my immature behavior, but the older we became, she stopped doing that. I guess it was time for me to grow up and responsibility for my actions.

"I wish I wasn't being serious, but lets be real, when Clover is full of lord knows what, he doesn't give a fuck. When he's sober he doesn't give a fuck! Kat, he really fucked her, NEXT to ME, the woman he swears up and down that he loves with all his heart."

"Did he fuck her better than he fuck you?" Kat mumbled, but immediately felt dumb for asking that question.

"Nah, Clover could never fuck anyone the way he makes love to me, but forget all that. I feel like a damn fool, Kat, I really can't do this relationship anymore. I love that nigga, but I be damn if I let him make bitter and scorn. I want to know what love really is because, this isn't it! Love is supposed to make you feel like you're on cloud nine and not having withdrawals." She spoked.

"I feel everything you're saying, but you have to do what's best for you. I know you're thinking about what's best for O'Retta, but what's best for you is what's best for her. She's the most innocent person in this crazy situation and she deserves to not be in any toxic places."

"Every day I think about that." Manhattan whispered.

"Besides, step dads are taking over for the 99's and 2000's." laughing with streaks of dry tears and make up on her face, Kat reached into her purse. Grabbing a blue packet of makeup wipes, she began to clean her face to remove the ruined makeup. Once she was done, Kat pulled the long bleach blonde wig off her head. Manhattan laughed shaking her head.

"Here, Hat, throw that wig in the back." Driving off in silence, Kat still managed to clean her face, but when she came to the first red light in her path, she asked, "where is he now?"

"I don't know, I guess he's in New York by now. His homie Harlem just got of the pen, so, he went visit him."

"Uumm, Deaux is also in New York." Kat mumbled.

"Wait, what, I didn't know he took her with him?"

"Damn, there my big mouth goes again, I'm sorry, Hat." Feeling foolish, Manhattan wiped her last tear away chuckling. When her phone began to vibrate with a call from me, she didn't waste anytime ignoring the call. Yea, reality of leaving me was kicking in.

Grabbing her phone, Kat rushed to open her Instagram app to find Deaux's Instagram. Slowly scrolling through her photos, she found the picture of Deaux standing next to me with a heart emoji over my face. It wouldn't take a rocket scientist to figure out it was me in the picture. Especially with that big ass tattoo of Manhattan's name on my arm. See, that's how fucked up Deaux was, there I was in the picture, not paying attention with my girlfriend's name on my arm, but Deaux was still in love. What the fuck was she so in love with, I had no damn clue, yo.

"Wow, really, Clover?"

***

Standing outside of the Sylvia's restaurant in Harlem, I looked over my shoulders to make sure Deaux's nosey ass wasn't ear-hustling. I had to make a trip to New York to handle some business and holla at my nigga Harlem since he was finally free. The way the money was pouring in, I knew I wouldn't get much time to escape the city without missing a dollar.

Like the joe I was acting like, I was still blowing up Manhattan's phone and she ignored every call. I was ready to kill that bitch for ignore my calls, ME, CLOVER FUCKIN' PORTER, YO! Real spill, who the fuck did Manhattan think she was or playing on my jawn like that. She had me putting my pride to the side and shit for no reason.

After calling for the hundredth time, I decided to do some more fuck boy shit and leave a voicemail. Manhattan was going to hear what I had to say even if she didn't want to hear it.

"Baby, I know you see me calling your phone, PICK UP. I don't know why you're tripping, that's not even me in that picture with Deaux. I love you, iight, please call me back," That lie rolled off my tongue smoother than slick, everyone knew that was me in the picture. Even the groupie ass bitches who dropped hearts and the emoji eyes under the picture knew that was me. They just wanted Deaux to drop a name for clarification, but that hoe wasn't a fool. The first and LAST time she pulled that mess, let's just say it didn't end pretty for her.

"Baby, are you done talking to Smoke," kissing me on the back on my neck, Deaux stood on her tiptoes smiling at me. Glancing over my shoulder, I slightly rolled my eyes. It's crazy how after all these years Deaux's touch still didn't have an affect on the kid. If Manhattan would have done that, chills would have traveled to my ankles. That's the kind of affect she had on me, dig? I couldn't stop thinking about her making some random nigga from southwest or north Philly feeling the same way. Her hands were meant to be on my body, my body only.

"Nah, give me a minute, I'll be in there."

"Okay, but don't take too long, I'm going to miss." Kissing me on the cheek with a smile on her face, I only nodded my head in return. As Deaux walked off, I began to dial Manhattan's number again, but this time, my pride stopped me. Damn, my pride should have stopped me when I called non-stop five times. Yea, I know I said I wasn't tripping about the lil' rumor I heard, but we all know that was a full-blown lie. Between this and her ignoring me, Manhattan Mullen was driving a nigga crazy!! I stalked Manhattan's Facebook, Instagram, Twitter, and Snapchat just to see if she would drop hints about a new nigga. Either she was too smart to put her business on social media or their wasn't a nigga in sight. I even had Smoke stalk her house and job a few times to see if anyone besides her girlfriend would be there. Once again, not a nigga in sight and all this extra shit I was doing had me feeling like a fool. Maybe my conscious was starting to eat me alive or the fact that Manhattan would truly leave me had my head gone. Either way, I had to shake this feeling off asap, yo. If Manhattan wouldn't give me any answers, I know who would. It would be hard, but it was worth calling her. Sighing loudly, I quickly dialed Kansas phone number and the third ring, Kan answered smacking her lips.

"Come on now, Kan, don't come on the phone with that negative energy!" I demanded, but Kan wasn't trying to hear that jawn. When she cleared her throat, I already knew shit was about to go dumb.

"What the fuck do you want, Clover?" Kansas shouted through the speaker on the phone making my ear ring. With an attitude like this, I already knew why she was upset with me. Which would make my next question harder to ask. Kan would probably laugh herself into a coma, but I needed some kind of answers.

"Kan, don't hang up, please, I need to ask you something." I replied. "Ask me what, Clover?"

"Is Manhattan fucking with some nigga?"

"What?" She questioned me loudly. I could tell that bitch was upset with me already and ready to end the call on me.

"I asked you if Hat is fucking with some nigga? I heard some shit through the streets and I want to know if it's true. You don't have to lie to me and worry about hurting my feelings." I uttered.

"My nigga, did you REALLY wake me out my sleep for THIS stupid ass question. Clover, get off my line and ask her that yourself. Aren't you in New York with Deaux anyways, why the fuck are you worried about Hat? I wish she was fucking with another nigga, I would love to be the first to hurt your feelings with that tea." She laughed loudly.

"Look, it ain't even like that, chill out! I told that smut I was going to holla at Harlem and she begged to come along. Fuck that though, does that mean she is?" I asked feeling the pace of my heartrate increasing, this conversation had me nervous. If Hat was fuckin' with another jawn, how could she do that to me? She knows how much I love her pale ass!

"I DON'T KNOW, ask her your damn self." She argued.

"If I wanted to ask HER, I would have, Besides, you're my sister, you should be on my side anyways, yo, real talk." I said making Kansas laugh, but it wasn't purposely. She laughed because I was being a fool.

"I'm you're sister, I'm well aware of that, we have the same blood pumping through our veins. Picking sides because of blood has never been my steelo, you know. Right is right and wrong is wrong, you've been on the wrong side for a very long time!!!"

"Kan, can you chill the fuck out with all that, damn! I'm trying to make shit right with Hat, but it's always some shit going on." I expressed, hoping Kansas understood where I came from. Knowing her, she wouldn't, go-figure.

"How are you trying to make things right when you fucked DEAUX while Manhattan lied in bed. Then the bitch is at the police station while she was there, and now you're in Harlem with her. I just don't understand how she hasn't pushed your shit back yet."

"What?" I shouted.

"You heard what the fuck I said, I don't understand how she hasn't pushed your shit back yet! A bitch like me would have killed you a hot minute ago, yo." She implied. Kansas had my blood boiling, but I wasn't going to say anything crazy. I needed to get back on her good side pronto.

"Kansas, I really didn't call you to hear all this jawn."

"Look, Clover, it's time for you get your shit together and choose a side. You can't continue to play these rock head games with these women, it's wrong!! Even though I hate Deaux with every bone in my body, she doesn't deserve to be strung along for this emotional ride. A situation like this will get someone hurt, I can see it now."

"What the fuck are you talking about, Kansas, you're drawlin'?? I am getting my shit together and no one is going to get hurt. I'm always telling Deaux I don't want to be with her and she can find her a man. That bitch wants to stick around praying I'll leave Hat, but that won't EVER happen."

"Maybe if you mean what you say and stop fucking the broad, then she'll fully understand. I have to go, hubby is calling, bye." Ending the call without giving me a chance to explain myself, I could have slapped Kansas through the phone. Who would have thought Kansas would be married with two kids. She talked all that shit about being against motherhood and marriage, but love changed that. Besides my mom and Manhattan, Kansas was the best mom in the world.

Right about now, I didn't know how to feel, my emotions were on a thousand. Before walking into Sylvia's, I sighed tucking my phone into my pocket. I was hardly four steps into the building, but Deaux had a huge smile on her face. I don't know why the smut was smiling, there was no reason to be so damn happy.

"Baby, I hope you and Smoke were jawning about a million dollars. You took long enough out there." She chuckled.

"Yea, something like that." I replied sitting down and reaching into my pocket. I had to make sure I didn't miss any calls from Manhattan, but there wasn't a missed call on my screen.

"Something like that, but what are you going to order? Hand me a menu also." Pointing at the menu, Deaux quickly reached across the table to grab the menu. Her tiny wife beater rose showing majority of her lower back. A nigga two tables down with his homies had his eyes glued on her ass and small waistline. Knowing Deaux, she knew the jawn was watching her and she wanted to give him a show. If he wanted a piece of Deaux's ass, he had to pay some serious bread and I wasn't talking about a couple hundred of dollars. You had to come off some stacks to fuck shorty and that's how Deaux got down. The spacious restaurant was crowded with people, I'm surprised Harlem wanted to meet at a place like this.

"Here you go, baby," handing me the menu, Deaux was still smiling and it annoyed me.

"Thanks, but what are you ordering?" I asked.

"I'm going to get fried chicken and mustard greens." She replied twirling her clear straw in the glass of cold water.

"Take a bitch to Harlem and she still orders fried chicken and collard greens." I laughed flipping through the menu.

"Oh, whatever, but what are you getting? I hope it's something I like and that way I can have like a two for one special." She chuckled dropping her head on my shoulder.

"I don't know, I'm not really hungry, but I'm going to get the fried pork chop with mac and cheese. I might get a lil' appetizer too, probably the coconut shrimp."

"Take a nigga out of Philly and he orders a porkchop. For someone who isn't hungry, you're sure ordering a lot of food." She laughed softly making me laugh for the first time today.

"Fuck you, Deaux, this is my jawn every time I come to Harlem. It's a must I get the coconut shrimp, dig?"

"Spitta, I can make you some coconut shrimp if you want that." she giggled.

"Nah, I'm good, I'll get Manhattan to make me some when I get back home."

"Manhattan, yea." In a low tone and a sad look on her face, Deaux slightly pushed away reaching for her phone that was on the table. I could tell her feeling were hurt, but fuck, she'll be alright. She's been through wayyyyy worse in life.

Sitting at the table waiting for Harlem and Honesty to walk in, all I could think about was Manhattan. For a jawn who claimed he didn't give a fuck about anything, I sure let Manhattan drive me crazy. The thought of another man running his hands against her smooth skin had my blood boiling. Fuck, I was too busy daydreaming that I didn't realize the dirty looks Honesty had on her face when she spotted Deaux at the table.

Sitting there as if she was confused, Deaux glanced at everyone without saying anything. Harlem nodded his head at Deaux, but he rushed to turn away when Harlem sized him up and down.

"Harlem fuckin' Wright!!" Honesty spoke loudly through her tight mouth. She didn't want to cause a sense, but Honesty was pissed. The way she huffed and puffed, I was ready for her to blow the building down.

"Harlem, did you really bring me to lunch and THAT bitch is here? You told me he was bringing his WOMAN, not some smut he's fucking! I should smack fire from your fuckin' mouth!" Honesty was pissed, but Harlem laughed not taking her serious.

"Why would you want to smack fire from your husband mouth? Chill out with all that, Hon, real talk." He implied, but only pissing Honesty off more.

"Real talk my ass, Harlem, why would the fuck you lie and bring me around this bitch? I didn't like the bitch then and I DAMN sure don't like her now. I hate you bottom of the barrel hoes, always looking for the next come-up. If Clover wasn't stack paper like he is, we all know this bitch would be in Germantown, Queens, Spanish Harlem, or even in Frankford ready to suck dick for a dollar." Honesty stood there with her Chanel bag attached to her arm and her long electric blonde hair hanging to her back. Her skin glowed brighter than a hot day in Harlem, but the mug on her face was far from bright. It looks could kill, we probably slumped over at the table.

"*Bitch*, Honesty, I know we've had our differences in the past, but calling me out of my name ain't called for. I have never disrespected you so I think I deserve the same in return." Deaux replied with an attitude, but she kept calm. She knew Honesty was just as crazy as Harlem, so, Deaux really wasn't trying to go that route with her.

"Girl, shut up, you disrespected me when you fucked MY HUSBAND and bragged to the world about it. Haven't you mom talk you to leave married men."

"Wwwoooow, you're still tripping on me fooling around with Harlem? Honesty, that was years ago and let's be real, I wasn't the only jawn screwing your husband." Deaux answered.

"Deaux, just be quiet and chill out, I didn't come here for all that." I replied making Honesty flared her nose at me. She hated my guts for the same reason my sister did.

"No, I'm not going to chill out! Are you really going to sit there and let her talk to me like this?" Crossing her legs and arms tightly, Deaux turned to me waiting for an answer, but I started to laugh. Deaux's tight face became soft with sadness written on it. She had no reason to look at me for rescue, no one told Deaux to run her mouth. We all know Honesty is a crazy jawn who doesn't bite her tongue.

"Once again, BITCH, I have other reasons to not like your dog ass." Honesty began to talk a little louder causing attention to our table. Now she was the one was drawlin', Harlem and I didn't need any attention on us.

"Harlem, get your woman, she's VERY disrespectful! Your problem should be with Harlem and this nigga, not me. I can't help it that playas get chose!"

"Keep my name out of your mouth, Deaux, I don't have shit to do with yall arguing." I said.

"I guess you just loovveeeee being the side bitch, huh?"

"Come on now, Hon, don't do all that." I expressed. Honesty stared me up and down ready to throw a fist at my face.

"Clover, play with Deaux, my nigga, don't play with me. I never really liked your sorry ass anyways, Manhattan deserves better than you and I really hope she finds that! Harlem, let's fucking go now!!!" Clutching her handbag tighter to her hip with her nose flared, Honesty began to walk away, but Deaux said, "if you and Manhattan would learn how to please yall men, they wouldn't step out." Abruptly stopped, Honesty turned around and Harlem already knew what was about to go down. Before he could say anything or grab Honesty, she rushed for the glass of water throwing it on Deaux. Splash everywhere and laughter spilled for Honesty's mouth.

"OH MY GOD!" Deaux shouted jumping to her feet and now all eyes were on us.

"Play with me next time and it's going to be more than water. Let's go Harlem!" Honesty walked off with her hips swinging from left to right.

"Damn, my bad for that, I didn't thin she would trip like this." Before walking off, Harlem handed Deaux a stack of napkins, but out of anger, she tossed them to the floor.

"What the hell am I going to do with that?" She shouted at me, but gave her a stale. I don't care how mad she was, Deaux knew not to play with me.

"You should have shut up like I told you to."

Deaux looked at me searching for answers, but I couldn't say anything. She looked like a damn fool covered in that ice cold lemon water. Her makeup was sliding down her chubby cheeks and her long false eyelashes were hardly on. I told her about wearing all that dumb shit on her face, but the broad didn't listen. I bet right now she wished she listened to me.

"OMG, are you okay, mam?" The friendly waitress asked with a panic looked on her face. Deaux didn't reply, but nodded her head up and down.

"Yes, I'm fine, thanks for asking because it seems like no one else down." Cutting her eyes in my direction, Deaux rolled her eyes at me. I guess Deaux wanted me to do the waitress's job and make sure she was straight, but it wasn't that deep. It was just a little water, it's not like it Hon tossed gasoline on her. I guess next time Deaux will watch what the fuck goes from her dick suckers.

"Mam, let me clean this water for you." the waitress dropped to the floor with towels rushing to wipe the water. Everyone was still staring at us thanks to Honesty and Deaux.

"Thank you so much, but can I get some more napkins?" Deaux asked the waitress as I stood to my feet. The waitress pulled out a stack of napkins handing them to Deaux.

"I'll be right back man." Jogging out of the restaurant, I scanning the parking lot searching for Honesty and Harlem. When I spotted the white sundress and red bottom swinging on the jawn in the Red Polo shirt, I continued jogging to Harlem's white Range Rover.

"With'cha dumb ass, Harlem, just plain ole dumb," Harlem didn't take Honesty, her lil' punches were light weight to him.

"Get in the truck, son, you're drawlin'." Laughing while opening the door, Harlem gently pushed Honesty in closing the door. He was still laughing, which had Honesty pissed. She was ready to pull the door off to fight Harlem again.

"What the fuck was that, we didn't even order yet." I laughed. Meeting me halfway, Harlem replied, "I sure had a taste for those short ribs, but I guess Manhattan was thirsty instead.

"Man, I was ready to smash those short ribs, but I guess Honesty was thirsty instead. Son, why didn't you tell me you were bringing Deaux? If we were bringing side bitches, I would have brought Giselle instead." Dapping me down laughing, Harlem look over his shoulder to make Honesty was still in his truck. Since he was fuckin' his best friend's Consequence girl, Giselle, he had to keep that under wrap until he figured out who he wanted to be with. Knowing Harlem, he would be with the both of them until the end of time or unless until Honesty found out and explode on the both of them.

"I didn't think it was a big deal, I thought Honesty was over that shit." I chuckled.

"Honesty will never be over any bitch I fucked, but how long are ya'll staying?" Harlem questioned.

"It was supposed to be more two days, but I need to get back home by tomorrow afternoon. Shit is bad back at home, yo." I said.

"Word, do we need to clear the business with some niggas?"

"Nah, not like that, I'm talking about with Manhattan. I think shorty is really ready to dip out on the kid. Every time I turn around this bitch Deaux is pulling some lil' jawn. This bitch posted an off-guard picture of me and her, but she blocked out my face. With this big ass Manhattan tattoo on my arm, everybody knows that's me!! Now Manhattan is ignoring all my calls and I'm hearing she's fucking with some nigga. If I find out that's true, on my mama I'ma kill that boy."

"Word, she's really stepping out on you like that, son?" Folding his arms across his chest, Harlem stood there shocked. If you didn't know any better, you would think Manhattan was his bitch instead.

"Exactly, can you believe that shit? As much as I love her, why the fuck would she hurt me like that? Manhattan knows how much I love her pale ass! Just because I cheat on you doesn't mean she has to cheat on me. I don't love Deaux, I never did and everyone knows that. Fuck, even Deaux knows that, but in her mind, one day I'll fall in love with her." I laughed.

"Yea, and live happily ever after with you, but that shit won't happen. We don't cuff hoes, you know that shit. What you need to do is keep that hoe in check, every time I look on Instagram the bitch is doing some wild shit. See, I don't have that problem, Gigi knows how to stay in her place. If not, I'll stop that heffas teeth out of her mouth." Harlem laughed, but he still spoke in a whisper making sure that Honesty didn't hear a word he spoke.

"It's no happy ending with Deaux and I won't ever cuff no hoe! Don't even come at me like that bro." Gently punching Harlem on the arm, we both chuckled.

"Yea, yea, yea, I heard that plenty of times. Then niggas are calling me asking if I can get their baby mama wacked for the low." He laughed again slapping his hands.

"Well, I love my baby mama and I'm not one of them niggas. Real talk, I feel like shit is changing between us. Hat really may be at her breaking point with me, I can't handle that shit."

"You know that girl will never leave you, just like Honesty will never leave me. We can fuck as many hoes as we want. If they find out, we have to kiss their asses until they forgive us. It's the circle on life, my nigga." Harlem laughed, every word he said was true, but for how long though? Harlem would never say it, but how long would Honesty and Manhattan put up with our bullshit?

"Maybe she won't but if she doesn't, things won't be how they were when we first met." I implied.

"Check this out, if you can get rid of Deaux, come fuck with me by Con's crib. You can kick back and clear your mind. That nigga still ain't came back yet." Harlem laughed.

"I'm guessing you're still fucking his joint behind his back." Shaking my head laughing, this nigga Harlem was brick!! He didn't give a fuck who feelings he damaged, just plain ole reckless. "Does a dog have four legs?" Harlem questioned.

"Duh, my nigga, well that's your answer."

Chapter 14

By day three, I knew Manhattan would be home, but too bad I had other plans. I tried making peace with her, but Hat rather play these lil' fuck ass mind games. Really drawlin' and shit for no reason. I said I was sorry a million times, but she didn't believe me. So, me being me, I didn't give a fuck and continued doing what I was doing. I can't lie, I hadn't been home for a week, I missed Manhattan like crazy. The whole jawn I spent in New York, I couldn't get shorty off my mind. Even lying in bed with another bitch couldn't get Manhattan off my brain. I can't lie, I wanted to shower her with love, but I know that wasn't going to happen. Love and affection was probably the LAST thing she wanted from me.

It was 10:45 am, Thursday morning when I rolled out of Deaux's bed to go home. I wanted to rush home once I landed, but once Deaux wrapped her fat lips around my dick, I couldn't leave. I decided to teach Hat a lesson and spend a few days with Manhattan when I got back to Philly. Of course, she had to mention Manhattan's name and we got into an argument fucking up my mood. I almost punched the bitch to the ground for calling Manhattan out of her name, but I left instead.

At this time, I figured Manhattan was at the park doing her morning jawns; lunges, squats, crunches. You know, all that shit I like she does to keep her body tight and right. I'm more than sure I was jogging through her mind since she left the house that night. To be thurl, the last thing on my brain was if she was worried about a nigga. When I attempted to make things right, she didn't want to. Manhattan knew if something was wrong or shit got hectic in the trenches, my lawyer Flores would hit her line. Besides chasing bread, I was in my bag with Deaux, chillin, you know? Her nagging ass cried all week about spending real time with me, I had to give her what she wanted. The lil' bitch worked hard for that time. All it took was me dicking Deaux down for days straight to get her ass to stop nagging me for a while. I knew by the end of next week she would be back to the same shit.

I ignored Manhattan the whole time I was there, she called my phone at least fifty times, left ten voicemails, and eighteen text messages. I wasn't moved by any of that shit, I would come home when I felt like it. Knowing Manhattan like I did, she was tempted to call Deaux looking for me since Smoke and Kansas didn't know where I was. They were solid with her and would rat me out in a second. The way her pride was set up, she would never do that again.

Walking into the house, still tired, I headed straight into the kitchen to brew a cup of coffee. Since the smell of fresh coffee danced in the air, Manhattan had to already be back home. Leaning against the countertop in a black and pink two-piece spandex workout outfit, Hat nibbled on a fresh red apple. Music by Tink blasted through her Beats headphone, so, I already knew what kind of mood Hat was in.

A steamy cup of brown coffee sat next to her near the sink with her Keisha Ka'oir waist eraser. Just by looking at my baby I could tell she hadn't gotten much rest. With her hair pulled back into a tight ponytail, her red baggy eyes were visible for me and the world to see from a distance.

I approached her attempted to kiss her lips, but she gave me her cheek to kiss. I could tell Hat barely wanted to do that, but she probably was tired of playing hard to get.

"Yizzo, Hat, good morning," I said as walked to the cabinet for a clean coffee cup, but Hat grabbed my wrist saying, "What's up, really Clover?? Your ass wasp in here casually after being M.I.A for days and all you can say yizzo? Naw, you have to say a little more than that if you're trying to get back on my fucking good side!!!"

Manhattan held my wrist so tightly that I could feel my pulse throbbing and a vein popped out. Has was drawlin' already, I was ready to haul ass.

"What'cha want me to say, my baby? You look nice, by the way, but you know that already." I chuckled slowly trying to pull my wrist from her hand, but that made her hold it tighter. Her nails dug in my arm, but that didn't bother me. She usually did this kind of stuff when he made passionately love or had rough sex.

"Clover, do not fucking tamper with my feelings talking that sweet mess," she shouted through her closed mouth, but quickly lowered her voice tone. She then placed the half-eaten apple on the countertop to get a better grip of my arm. Before I could tell her anything, she sized me up and down with a mug on her face.

"Manhattan!"

"Clover, I said don't fucking play with me, but you still do it anyways!!! Where the fuck was your joe ass at? Let me guess, you were still with Deaux? I guess that mini vacation in New York wasn't enough for you."

"You have one more time to call me something that isn't my name!"

"Or what, you're going to choke me out how I heard you do Deaux? I hear from time to time you go upside her head to get your point across. The bitch is so in love with you that she thinks you're beating her ass out of love. She probably gets wet when feeling she feels your shoe against her face."

"Feling my size ten shell toes against her jaw doesn't get her pussy wet. Nah, it's this big black dick that does that. Can't you tell by the way that bitch act, she's dick whipped. Kind of how I'm pussy whipped behind you." I laughed pulling on my dick. My actions and words pissed Hat off, but to stay calm, she laughed.

"Oh yea, bitch?"

"Yea, but I wouldn't dare lie a finger on you. Even though sometimes you need a beaten or two," I laughed.

"Keep it up, Clover, you're going to regret every word you said, believe that," she answered, but I ignored her walking out of the kitchen heading to the living room. Like I knew she would, Manhattan followed behind me. I wasn't in the mood to argue, but clearly, she was. The only thing I was in the mood for is sleeping. Deaux's freaky ass wore me out, I had to stay away from her for a few days. Her pussy was becoming like coke, ADDICTIVE. I sold that shit, I didn't need a hit of it.

"I don't regret shit, that's why I do what the fuck I do!"

"Excuse me, did you really just say that," she asked grabbing the back of my t-shirt, but I pulled it away making her feel stupider than what she already felt. Seriously, I would NEVER hit Hat, but boy, was she pushing my buttons to put my hands around her throat.

"Yea, that's what I said, but keep pushing me. I'll stumble back to where I came from."

"Hhhmmphhh, and where was that Mr. Honest," she asked knowing the answer already. Knowing Deaux, I mean Manhattan, she wanted to hear it from my mouth so I could be the one hurting her feelings. In reality, she knew the truth and was hurting herself.

"Go head, yo, you know where the fuck I was. Why hurt your damn self trying to play tough and you no you're not," rubbing the back of itchy head I searched for the remote throughout the living room. Manhattan spotted it under the fluffy pillow and rushed to grab it. I smacked my lips exhaling loudly, Manhattan was becoming more annoying than Deaux.

"Give me the remote," I demanded, but she tossed it against the wall causing the remote to fall apart. Tears began to fall from her eyes as she dropped to her knees crying. Seem like this same routine happened when Deaux's name was mentioned. It was like ...... Deaux had mind control over Manhattan and neither one of them knew it. You would by now Manhattan wouldn't still get emotional, Deaux didn't have shit on her

"Come on now, Hat, get the fuck off the floor and stop being dramatic. I hate when you start acting like this, especially behind Deaux This must be some North Carolina shit Kat taught you. I'm not in the mood for this, bruh, I just want to go back to bed!!" Ignoring everything I said, Manhattan continued to sit on the floor, but her whimpering became louder with her face covered.

"Four days, Clover, four fucking days I thought about how to murk your black ass. I thought about going to Deaux's house to burn the place down. Waiting for you to come home just to poison you crossed my jawn six times. That was too easy, I want you to feel some pain. Then I thought about running you off the road the first chance I get, smothering you in your sleep, or simply putting a bullet in your head. Either way, it would finally put a stop to all this because lord knows none of us will. I want you to suffer, Clover, I want you to feel how I feel when you hurt me. I'm far from a killer, but killing you I would do it with pride. Just as much pride floating around at a gay parade. FINALLY, the toxic waste in my life would be gone and I could move on with my life. It's really sad to say it, but if we don't let go, we'll all be tied into each other forever. That's not something I can deal with or handle for another moment. I'm too good of a woman to deal with the shit you drag me through. Yes, I love you, Clover, but I can't be stupid anymore."

"I'm not holding a gun to your head to make you stay. You can leave whenever you feel like it, Hat."

"You're right about that, the gun isn't pointing to my head. The gun is pointing to my heart, my heart, Clover, and it's not fair," Manhattan began to cry again, but I still wasn't moved by her tears. They were familiar, just like the words she always cried out to me.

"Are you done, I need a shower and a nap," I asked.

"No, bastard, I'm not done with you. Once I am, you can sleep off whatever drugs you're on and wash Deaux's dirty pussy off you.

You have her so fucked up in the brain that she actually thinks you love her. I'm no better than her though, I thought the same thing. As the years went by I loss hope that you would change. I figured because you love me and didn't want to lose me that you would change. Boy, was I wrong, I was sssooooooooo wrong. Clover doesn't love anyone, but his damn self, it has always been like that."

"Anything else, Hat, I'm a lil' pressed for time?"

"It's time I admit all this to myself and stop pretending I'm special to you. You don't have to care because I know you don't. JUST LIKE YOU DON'T GIVE A FUCK I DON'T GIVE A FUCK ANYMORE!!!!! Fuck you, Clover, she can have you, all of you!!"

"You're done," I asked knowing she wasn't serious. Manhattan did this at least three times a month and I never believed her. Sometimes she even packed her stuff just to get to the door and turn around.

"Yea, I am and this time you'll see it for yourself. I should have killed you that night, damn!! I blame my stupid ass heart for not allowing me to pull that trigger. BANG! Just like that you would have been gone," still crying, Manhattan used her arms to climb to her feet and walk away to the bedroom. I didn't have to follow behind her to know what she was doing, which was packing her shit. A bunch of loud noises came from the bedroom, but I still didn't enter the room. Instead, I walked to the corner of the living room gathering the pieces of the remote controller. Then I flopped on the couch putting the remote back together. Manhattan was still in the room, acting crazy and dying for my attention. A few times I laughed because she was a true clown. I didn't want to hear that shit so once I powered the t.v. on, I turn the volume loud as possible.

A few minutes later, Manhattan walked into the living room pulling her red suitcase and a few bags on her arms. Wiping her tears away, she continued walking, but stopped to toss me the house key, OUR house key. That was the first time she did that, kind of mind blowing. Still, I wasn't going to beg her to stay or chase behind her.

We both knew in two days she would be back home like nothing ever happened.

"You know what's funny, Clover?"

"What, Hat," I questioned sighing loudly while flipping through the channels.

"Last night I was on the phone with Honesty. She said if I ever needed someone to talk to that I could call her. I was crying so much I could hardly get my words out."

"Honesty who, Harlem's girl?"

"Yea, dickhead, how many Honesty's do you know? Wait, I'm pretty sure you know a lot of Honesty, all the pipe you lay down through Philly. I told her what happened and she told me to leave you before I end up like here. She refuses to watch me be in my forties, divorced, and trying to find love again. After all the shit Harlem did since he been home, even divorcing her, SHE still took his ass back. After leaving her for some bitch name Giselle and getting her pregnant while he was still married, SHE STILL TOOK HIM BACK. Now Harlem is looking crazy because Giselle left him for some joe ass nigga from Long Island. I guess karma really is a bitch, but that didn't mean anything to him. Two weeks ago, she caught him in a hotel with some chick name Rebecca. Clearly Harlem didn't learn his lesson, just like you. You two are friends for a special purpose and there are two seats in hell with yall names on it."

"How the fuck can she give YOU advice when she's been getting cheated on since the 90's," I laughed, but Hat didn't find my statement amusing. She only nodded her head and continued talking.

"Maybe that's why she told me to leave you. She has already been down that road. I deserve wwayyyy better than what you dish out to me. I rather no man instead of a pathetic piece man."

"Are you done talking this time, for real," I chuckled folding my arms across my chest. As I kicked my Nike slides off, Manhattan mugged me like I was her enemy.

"Tomorrow I'll remove my car from your insurance and everything else. When you want to see your daughter, contact Ryker or Kansas. I don't have anything to tell you."

"Now you're going too far to prove a stupid ass point. All you're doing is wasting your time, we both know you ain't leaving me. Just deal with who the fuck I am and stop bitching all the time, damn!"

"I love you, Clover, you know that, but I can't do this anymore. A nigga like you will make a bitch turn into left eye real quick. I swear, if my daughter didn't live at the house, I would burn this bitch down, TO THE GROUND. You don't understand how much hate I have for you right noow, good bye."

"Bye, Hat, see you in a few days and tell Kat I said yizzo. Oh yea, kiss my daughter also, I would love to spend time with my baby tonight. Check this out, get Ryker to drop her off and tonight you can go meet that nigga I'm hearing you're fucking with."

"Fuck you, Clover, right about now, you can drop dead. The only reason I didn't kill your ass is because of our daughter." Manhattan uttered making me laugh. Since the jawn wanted to say hurtful shit, two can play at that game.

"Ard, but if I really drop dead, don't be at my funeral fighting with Deaux to sit next to my mom." My loud laughter and hurtful words made Manhattan slam the living room door aggressively, but she pissed herself off. She knew better than to tell me some crazy shit like that. I already had niggas in the street hoping I drop dead, the last thing I needed was my shorty hoping the same thing!

"I wouldn't go to your funeral anyways and I can promise you, whoever THAT nigga is, he'll love me better." She shouted from outside and continued walking. Every bone in my body told me Hat wasn't coming back easily this time. I guess only time would tell how she really felt.

For ten minutes, I sat on the couch daydreaming at the flat screen television that was mounded on the wall. I can't lie, some of Hat's words cut a nigga deep. I don't know why she said some of the jawns she said and Hat knew she didn't mean a word she said.

As I began to fall asleep, a knock on the door woke me. Before I could ask who was it, Smoke said, "open up, lil' bro."

"Ard." Stretching while I stood to my feet, I dragged to my front door opening it. Smoke exhaled the smoke from the cigarette and tossed it into the wet grass. Then he walked into the house closing the door.

"What's up with you, fool?" Dapping me down, Smoke flopped on the couch next to me. Then he reached for the remote flipping through the channels for Sports Center.

"Nothing, bro, chillin'.."

"It's quiet in this bitch, where's Hat?" He asked checking his surroundings. Laughing softly, I replied, "she left about thirty minutes ago, we got into an argument. Typical shit, but I ain't sweatin' Hat, you already know how this shit goes with her."

"Didn't you just get back home from being laid up with Deaux and on vacation? What the fuck you excepted when you got home, a home cooked meal with roses on the floor?" Smoke chuckled shaking his head. His tone told me he was about to go in on me, but I wasn't in the mood or that shit. First Deaux, then Hat, now Smoke, naw, that wasn't going to happen.

"So what, what does that mean? I don't want to hear that same shit from Hat. Like Harlem said, Hat won't ever leave me, I can do what I want." I laughed.

"Eventually, my nigga you'll stop taking advice from a nigga who lost his bitch to the same nigga twice. Harlem is the LAST person I would take advice from, yo. It's time for you to stop playing these lil' rock head games and choose one. You're always saying you don't like Deaux like that, but yet, you still fuck with her."

"I fuck with her because she's beneficial, that's it." I said.

"Naw, you're in love with her and you don't want to admit it. You can't do this shit forever, someone is going to get hurt. Then what, Katober loses a parent or maybe even both?"

"Yea, whatever, Smoke."

"Yea, whatever, Spitta, you need to get your mind right and stop playing all these lil' mind jawns. Manhattan, that's my nigga, man, and that girl loves you. Probably more than she loves herself because of how much shit she puts up with you." Smoke replied.

"Well, since you feel like that, you date her." Placing my feet on the wide coffee table, I laughed pissing smoke off. He took one look at me, pushed out a chuckle, and stood to his feet. Then he tapped my shoulder saying, "I'm out, my nigga, it's too much ignorance in the room."

***

Standing at the door of her home, Manhattan dropped her bags crying. Her heart ached, it was heavier than a mutherfucker. I truly hated being the reason for her pain, but it's like I couldn't stop being the no-good nigga everyone said I was. For years, Hat let me do whatever I wanted and I got used of that. To be real, Deaux was the only woman I cheated with. Maybe that's why it hurt Manhattan tremulously. In arguments, she often said it wouldn't hurt so much if it was multiple women. That way, she would know I was out here doing shit for fun and not looking for love. Fuck what Smoke said, not a bone in my body held love for Deaux. I proved that to her plenty of times and she knew that. To me, Deaux was like the homie I could fuck from time to time. She would never admit to herself that I didn't love her and I don't know why.

Manhattan stared at the empty living room feeling out of place and like she didn't know where she was. Yea, this was her house, but this wasn't home. Home was with me, the place she made memories with my daughter and I. Yea, that was home because that's where her heart was. To be honest, mines was there also. She stood there crying for a few seconds, but wiped her tears closing the door. Manhattan wanted to cry more, but her phone began to ring. Rushing to collect herself, Manhattan then answered the phone saying, "hello?"

"Girl, I'm in front of Clover's house, do you want me to bust his front two tires?" Kansas questioned. It's crazy how she called me Clover like I wasn't even related to her.

"Kan, no, go home, it's damn near midnight, fuck your brother." Manhattan replied dropping her bags. Then she wiped her eyes again walking to the fridge opening it. The only thing she spotted was an expired gallon of milk, two old bananas, and old fries from Chi-Fil-A. Slamming the door, Manhattan turned away walking out of the kitchen feeling frustrated.

"Are you sure, he never has to know it was me?" She laughed.

"Yea, I'm very sure, but thank you. Is anyone there, like a familiar car or something?" Wiping her runny nose, Manhattan heart rate slowly started to increase because she was nervous. Even though she 'moved on', Manhattan was still worried about another woman being at home. When I said another woman, I meant Deaux.

"No, Hat, no one is there, Clover isn't here. Him and Smoke or together, doing what, I don't know. Ryker gets off soon, so, you know his ass will be in the house." Laughing as she jumped back into her car, Kansas drove off regretting that she didn't bust my window. With the way Kansas was acting you would have thought I cheated on her instead of Manhattan.

"Oh, okay, thanks, girl. I just got home and I'm tired, I'll call you later or tomorrow."

"Bet, I love you, girl, get you some good rest." Kansas begged.

"I love you too and I'll try, bye." Ending the call, Manhattan began to walk to her room, but a knock on the door made her turn around. It was no need to ask who it was because Manhattan knew it was Ryker. If it was me at the door, the bitch probably would have pulled it off the hinges. I know, I know, I know, I should have chased behind her, but there was my pride again taking over.

Opening the door, Manhattan found Ryker in a pair of red spandex shorts and a blue sports bra. Her hands were filled with bags, but Manhattan didn't have the energy to help Ryker. Instead, she nodded her head and turned around.

"Hey." Manhattan spoked softly.

"Hey, girl, I got here as fast as I could, what's up? I also brought you some iHop, I wasn't sure if you were hungry or not." Dropping her handbag and bags on the countertop, Ryker gave Manhattan a tight hug. That was the kind of hug my baby needed from me and not one of her homegirls.

"It's just too much with Clover, I don't even know where to start. I'm tired of having this same conversation with everyone, I know ya'll are tired of it also. This is not how I predicted my life would be, it's not, Ryker! I'm supposed to have a house full of kids, married, in love, and living the best life I can. Instead, I'm getting my heart broken every other day by the man who swears he loves me more than life!!"

"Just because someone loves you doesn't mean you have to tolerate the pain they cause you. I salute you, girl, a bitch like me would have BEEN killed Clover for playing with me. I can't stand his black ass, that's on my life!! Don't get me wrong, Smoke isn't perfect, but I made sure he knew I wasn't playing any of that cheating bullshit when we made it official. No one was going to humiliate me in these Philly streets.

Ryker and Smoke played this lil' game for years before making it official three years ago. Smoke didn't call it a game, he just had to get his shit together before making Ryker his girl. Ryker and Manhattan were total opposite when I came to relationships. Ryker didn't play that cheating shit, which explains why she has only been in three relationships, including Smoke.

"Clover is all I know, I love him, Ryker."

"Fuck love and fuck Clover, Manhattan. You're acting like you're just some regular bitch who can't get a man. You're a bomb ass woman, you're beautiful, sexy, and all that other shit men love to brag about with their woman.

"I know I'm not just some 'regular bitch', Ryker, but I love me some Clover. Lately, I haven't been liking him, but that's because of the extra bullshit we've been going through. Maybe one day all this will stop and Deaux will disappear. Then things will go back to normal between Clover and I."

"Manhattan, you sound dumb and crazy as fuck saying that. If not Deaux, it's going to be some other chick causing you hell. We all bitches like Deaux are replaceable, but a woman like you aren't. " Ryker expressed herself freely and every word cut Manhattan deeply. You know they say the truth always hurts, which is why Manhattan didn't like telling Ryker shit. Most of the time, she only told her because Manhattan knew the tea would get back to Ryker. Then she would be pissed that she had to hear it from someone else. Even though I didn't like Ryker most of the time, I didn't blame her for hating me most of the time. I Manhattan bad, yo and all Ryker did was lace Manhattan with truth. Wouldn't you want your homies to do the same thing, yo?

"That's true but at the end of the day, I just want things to be like they used to. I fell so hard for Clover and he did the same as well." Exhaling loudly, Manhattan ran her fingers through her loose hair. Her tears had a mind of their own and started to fall freely again.

Manhattan was so sick of crying, but she couldn't help herself at this point.

"Look, Hat, I'm sorry to say this, but things won't ever be the same between you and Clover. It doesn't matter how much you beg God at night or even ask Clover to change his dog ways. Even if Clover decides to wake up as a changed man, the damage is already done."

"What the fuck am I supposed to do then, start over at my age?" Burying her hands into her lap, Manhattan sobbed shaking her hand. Her heart ached in so many places, I could only imagine how she felt. I can't like, if Manhattan would have put me through half the things I've put her through, I would have killed her years ago.

"Manhattan, you are not a sixty year old woman, you can start over. Plenty of women you're age start over and meet the man of their dreams. Look at Beyonce's mama, you think she let Matthew stop her from loving?" Ryker rolled her eyes as she crossed her long legs tightly. The crying and sad stories from Manhattan was getting old.

"I'm not Beyonce's mama, Ryker! I really don't know what to do."

"You damn sure can't continue to let Clover hurt you, it's not right. You don't see how it's taking over your life, mind, and body. Those headaches you're having is because of his no-good ass, but you can't admit it to yourself. Let's not talk about the weight you're losing in all the wrong places." Tilting her head towards Manhattan, Ryker pointed at Manhattan's breast, then slowly pointed at her hips. Katober gave Manhattan the kind of body you way for, but in the past month, Manhattan started to lose weight. Everyone knew it was because of stress, but Manhattan was too shame to admit that. See, the difference between Ryker and Kat is that Kat always minded her own business. Ryker on the other hand, she didn't'. She always told Hat the truth, even when she knew it would hurt her. Ryker wasn't trying to hurt Hat's feelings, but it was no reason to hide the truth Manhattan. It's not like Deaux wasn't running her dick suckers about everything we did.

"I know, I know, Ryker, I know. I never thought love would become my enemy, especially with Clover! When we first met, things were totally different, the love was REAL!! Clover was my best friends and my everything, that's all I knew. I've went against friends, co-workers, and family defending him and our love, now I understand what everyone was talking about. All the whispers and mumbles, bitches pointing when they're looing at me. Fuck, they probably were fucking him also, but at this point I don't even care. Love have me looking like a damn fool." Hat said.

"Love makes us do crazy things, Hat, but love also shows us our strengths AND weaknesses. Clover, he's your weakness, but it's time to show him that you are your own strength. It's time to let him go before you lose your mind. Clover nor Deaux is worth your damn sanity."

"It's not that easy, Ryker, I love him so much and you know it's not easy to leave someone you love." Manhattan expressed, but Ryker laughed shaking her head. Yea, Ryker was officially over hearing these tired ass jawns about love and me. Ryker probably wanted to smack the shit out of Hat and make her come to her senses.

"In the words of a famous woman, 'what the fuck does love have to do with it?'"

"Girl, I don't ever recall that being Tina Turner's exact words." Manhattan laughed.

"Hell, close enough, but I'm serious, Hat. Love isn't always important, you need to use your brain. Stop using your pussy and heart in this situation, there is life after Clover Porter." She worded with a straight face.

"Yea, that's the hard part I have to admit to myself. I never thought I would want to move on from Clover, never thought he would push me to do this. I just wanted to have a family and marry the man I love, Ryker. He can't tell me that was too much. You want to know what's crazy, yo?" Manhattan asked.

"This doesn't even feel like my home, that's crazy, yo. I only come here when things are bad between Clover and I."

"I guess you better start making this place home again. Some new curtains, furniture, and maybe new flooring will do this place some justice. Yea, you'll feel like you're living in a new home." Ryker smiled.

"Maybe you're right, how about we go to the furniture store tomorrow? The one on Germantown Avenue, Isabella Sparrow. Sounds like a broad's name, but I heard they have nice shit." I laughed.

"Fine with me, I get off at 2:30 pm, but what about you?" Ryker asked.

"I get off at 4:00 pm, thanks for everything, Ryker."

"You know I'ma be real, it doesn't matter how much I have to see you cry." Giving Manhattan a hug, Ryker knew this wouldn't be Manhattan's last time crying about Clover Porter.

⸜

Chapter 15

With Katober clinging to her right leg, Manhattan strolled through the fancy furniture store search for some legit jawn to put in her 'home'. She was tired as hell and dealing with a bad ass child wasn't making her mood any better.

"Ko-Ko, we are not one, let go of my leg." Manhattan worded to Katober, but she held her leg tighter laughing at Manhattan's words.

"Mommy!" Laughing while fully exposing her two missing front teeth, Katober's smile made Manhattan warm inside. She hadn't felt like that in a while.

"What, little girl, what do you want now?" Manhattan questioned laughing.

"Daddy, I want daddy."

"I want a million dollars, but it hasn't fallen from the sky yet." Manhattan joked.

"If that falls from the sky it better rain men also. Some fine ass men, not those little joe ass niggas from around the way." Rubbing her flat stomach, Ryker stared at a few of the price tags and felt insulted. It didn't matter how much money Smoke and Ryker made, she was still a cheap hoe. Smoke on the other hand loved to blow through money because he knew he could always make it right back. Now that he was out of the dope game and making legal money, he really felt like he could blow through it with no problem. Even though I didn't want him to get out of the dope game, Smoke was a changed man. I was proud of my big brother even though he changed his entire life for a piece of pussy.

"Bitch, $150 for a lamp, this mutherfucker better light up my entire house."

"I kind of like this lamp, it was made in Greece."

"What the fuck that's supposed to mean? Like I said, it better light up my whole house. Shid, better light up the whole Greece." Ryker laughed, then she flipped her long Peruvian bundles like it was her own hair.

"You ain't just like this nigga, I swear." Manhattan laughed.

"Hey, I'm just speaking the truth."

"Girl, I need a stiff drink when I get home. Today was not a good day for me, the animals were going crazy today. I was fine when the poodle peed on me, but when that parrot took a crap on my shoes, I was ready to ggoooooooooo. " Yawning as she laughed, Manhattan carefully stared at the row of sectionals, but none caught much of her action.

"That girl would have been dead, just like on *Martin*." Ryker and Manhattan laughed loudly drawing a little attention to themselves, but they didn't care. If it would have been Kat, she would have spoked and laughed louder to get more attention.

"You are so damn ignorant." Manhattan laughed softly.

"I think you should get that white couch we saw when we first got here. We've been here for two hours and you still haven't decided on anything."

"Girl, we've only been here for TEN minutes and besides, white with Katober? Nah, you must be smoking dope, girl." Staring at the blue couch, Manhattan continued to examine it, but continued walking. The two piece set wasn't her style at all.

"What about this leather sectional, I like this? Black, leather, easy to clean, and Katober proof!"

"I like it, but you need something BRIGHT, ya know? Something that will blind your eyes when you walk in the house." Ryker laughed.

"Maybe they have this in another color." Manhattan continued to examine the sectional, but she couldn't help, but to notice the joe staring at her from a distant. His 'charming' smile made her nervous, but I don't know why. To me, she looked her best when she was tired, straight beautiful.

As the guy leaned against the countertop, he stared at Manhattan trying to give her a hundred percent of his attention, but she continued to turn away. If it wasn't me, Manhattan didn't like attention from men. I guess she was so wrapped up in loving me for so long that attention from other men wasn't important to her.

"Where the heck is the salesman in here? If we were stealing I bet they would be walking behind us like soldiers. You know how them white folks are in this area." Ryker flared her nose saying and Hat nodded her head agreeing.

"I'm tryna tell you."

"Anyways, have you spoken to you know who?" Ryker asked as she adjusted her belt through the belt loops. Exhaling softly, Manhattan said, "only about KoKo, but other than that, we don't have much to talk about."

"Just watch, God is going to send some fine ass man your way. Then you're going be like Clover who?" Ryker whispered laughing.

"Yea, one day, but I don't see that happening any time soon." Manhattan laughed shrugging her shoulders. Yea, she laughed, but the truth she felt cut deeply.

"Hi, I'm Christopher Dunn, do you need help with anything?" Turning around, Manhattan and Ryker found a goofy looking nigga standing about six feet tall with a beard screaming, "trim me!" He wore a crème colored dress shirt, a brown tie, and a pair of creased brown slacks that matched his tie to perfection. Since he was so light skinned with curly hair, he reminded me off a knock off version of Drake. He was one of those big muscle bound joes that probably did steroids as a hobby. This clown wasn't Manhattan's type at all, I was her only type.

"Damn, I just felt the heartbeat in my pussy." Ryker mumbled while biting her bottom lip. Her eyes were glued to the salesman, but his eyes were glued on Manhattan. This nigga looked like one of the mama's boys from *I Love New York* and he wasn't playa made like me.

"Hi, yes, you can help me. I'm Manhattan and this is Ryker."

"Nice to meet you two ladies. Who is the one shopping?" Christopher pointed at Ryker, than Manhattan with a smirk on his face. Before Hat could say anything, Ryker pointed at her saying, "she is, my SINGLE fine ass friend, Manhattan is. Right, Manhattan." Gently tapping Manhattan on the hip, Ryker slightly pushed her towards Chris. Brushing against him, Chris started to blame, but Manhattan was a little embarrassed.

"Uumm, I'm so sorry about that, but I'm the phone who is looking for new furniture."

"That's cool, ma, but did you just move in a new home?" He questioned.

"No, it's time for new furniture in my home. Do you have this sectional in a different color?" Manhattan pointed to the sectional asking.

"Yea, we do, it comes in royal blue, brown, and maroon."

"Okay, I'm thinking royal blue and the price is $1,500?" Manhattan questioned.

"Yea, but I can give it do you for $1,200 because you have a nice smile, shorty." Smiling again, Chris softly grabbed Manhattan's wrist, then slowly released it. Suddenly, Manhattan's pale cheeks turned red and she cracked a small smile.

"Damn, what can she get more some good puss—"

"Ryker!"

"What, girl, I'm just asking?" She laughed.

"NO mama, not daddy."

"Girl, be quiet and let your mama talk." Ryker said grabbing Katober, she knew some fuck shit was going down.

"You know a nice smile can go a long way." Christopher implied with a big smiler making Manhattan blush.
"Since I don't see any wedding ring on your finger, I'm assuming you're single." Ryker smiled as if she was the one trying to bag the nigga.

"No, I'm not married, and I'm also single. What about you, pretty lady?" Chris asked Manhattan.

"You know what's crazy, my beautiful friend, Manhattan Mullen, just got out of a really bad relationship. Maybe you two can become a little more than friends. Slowly pushing Manhattan towards Chris, Ryker took a step back smirking. Manhattan flipped her hair slightly looking over her shoulder to cut her eyes at Ryker. She had Hat looking dumb thirsty, Manhattan was far from a thirsty chick.

"Oh, word, I always find it crazy when I see a beautiful woman like yourself single." He cracked a smile.

"Well, maybe you two can take a cup of coffee or even lunch to discuss why she's single."

"Uumm, excuse me for a second, Christopher, we'll be right back." Manhattan replied.

"No problem, shorty, take your time." Giving Chris a fake smile while she pulled Ryker and Katober to the side. Ryker started to laugh, she already knew why Manhattan pulled her to the side.

"Girl, what the fuck are you doing, I JUST broke up with Clover not even two days ago?"

"Aawww, calm down, Manhattan, it's just a little fun we're having. Besides, that nigga is fine as hell and that's clear as day, yo." Ryker wanted to look over her shoulder to take a glance of Chris, but Manhattan already had her eyes on him. Of course, he had his eyes glued to Hat like she was the prettiest girl in the world. Well, she was, so, that nigga had every right to look at her that way.

"Yea, he is, huh?" Manhattan mumbled trying not to make eye contact with Chris, but it was hard not to. He literally didn't take his slanted eyes off her and every time they locked eyes, he began to smile.

"Duh, we're looking DEAD at him. Seems like he's interesting in Manhattan and I'm not talking about the New York City Borough. I'm talking about your fine ass, girl, a little conversation with him won't hurt." Cocking her head to the side with her hand on her left hip, Ryker tucked Manhattan's loose strands behind her ears. Then Ryker dust the lint from Manhattan's work scrubs to make sure she looked nice when she turned around.

"Why do you have to be so extra, Ryker, but maybe you're right. A little conversation wouldn't hurt, beats sitting in the house crying about you know who." She mumbled.

"Exactly, you can thank me later or for your wedding." Ryker laughed, but Manhattan shook her head. She tried not to laugh, but Ryker always said some crazy shit.

"Anyways, I need to get my furniture before I be planning anything." Turning around while holding Katober's arm, Ryker followed behind Manhattan.

"Back so soon." Christopher stated rubbing his hands together.

"Yea, I would like to pay for my furniture now and I guess I can give you my number."

"That's fine, I was going to look at your contact information to get your number." Chris laughed, but he covered his mouth because his bitch as blushed like a girl.

"Isn't that like a crime?" Manhattan chuckled.

"Yea, but it wouldn't be my first time committing a crime. A lil' joint like you would be worth a lil' bid."

"Wow, I'm liking you already." Ryker smiled.

"Yea, anything for my future lady." He said.

"Yea, I like you for real." Ryker dapped Chris down smirking.

"Yoooo, shorty is wild, but let me get your paperwork started. You can meet me at the cashier when you're ready."

"Okay, thanks." Manhattan gave Chris a little wave as he walked off. Then she rubbed her neck with a smile on her face trying to play it cool, but she couldn't help it.

"See, things always work out in your favor. I told you that you had to kiss a few frogs to get to your prince."

"Ryker, we don't know that man from a can of paint. He can be some ole' crazy ass nigga from southwest Philly." Manhattan implied.

"Girl, stop clown, I have never seen him in the hood or on the news. You do know you have to date people to get to know them." Ryker replied rolling her eyes.

"I guess, Ryker, but I'm not trying to make him my man tonight."

"That's not what I'm saying, but get to know the guy. I'm just trying to make you feel better, girl, he could be a great friend, you never know."

"You know what, you're right about that. What if he's gay though?" Manhattan snickered asking.

"Well, if he's gay we can go to the nail shop with him." Ryker laughed loudly leaning on Manhattan's shoulder, but when she noticed me in the parking lot, her laughing faded away.

"There goes your baby daddy?" Ryker flared her nose as she cut her eyes in my directions. I wasn't in the mood for Ryker's slick and petty comments. Like I said, besides talking about Katober, we didn't talk much, but she did let me see her when I pleased. I knew if I spend more time with KoKo, I would see Hat just as much. Even if it was for only a few minutes, seeing her ravishing facial features was worth it.

"Hey, Ryke." I said in a flat tone, but instead of replying, Ryker nodded her head. Then she mumbled, "uh-huh, I let you too talk." Ryker said as she walked off. Man, if she wasn't Smoke's ole' lady, I think I would have strangled the bitch to death.

"Daddy! Daddy! Daddy!" Jumping up and down with her ponytails swinging, I scooped Katober in my arms giving her a big hug.

"Hey, my baby, I missed you, do you want to visit grandma before we go home?" Clover asked.

"Yes."

"Her bag is in my car if you need it. Clover, please do not give her any sweets, she's going to be bouncing off the wall. We both know you don't what them problem." Manhattan spoked.

"It really doesn't matter if she bounce from wall to wall. When we leave from here I'm going to my mom's jawn. Ya know, spend some time with her and eat, she cooked a beef stew. I can bring you some when you leave from here. I can also pick you up a water ice, it's really not a problem at all, yo."

"I know your mom cooked, she texted me earlier. I'll stop by myself and grab a bowl." Manhattan uttered.

"Are you sure, Hat, it's really no need for you to go cross town?" I questioned making Manhattan exhale loudly.

"Alright, I'm just making sure, baby."

"Like I was saying before, if you need her bag, it's in the car." Manhattan implied with a straight face giving Katober a kiss on the cheek.

"What about me, can I have a kiss?" I chuckled asking, but Manhattan rolled her eyes.

"I don't need that bag, Manhattan, I'm not a fly by daddy, yo." I could feel the tension in the air and I laughed by trying to lighten the mood, but that didn't work. Manhattan stared at me with a straight face and zero passion in her eyes.

"That's one thing I do know, Clover Porter, but anyways. Her medication is still at your house, give it to her before bed." Manhattan replied.

"Okay, but our house."

"No, that's your house, not ours." Manhattan said.

"Don't do that with her right here, it's not that deep."

"Hey, I'm just speaking the truth, you know you don't hearing the truth." With a smirk on her face, Manhattan flipped her curly bob. She truly knew she had the upper hand on me and enjoyed every minute of it. I can't lie though, it kind of turned me on how Manhattan didn't want to be bothered with me.

"I hear you, baby, I hear you."

"Manhattan, you can call me Manhattan, but Clover, I'm telling you now, Clover Porter, don't have my child around anyone and yes, I'm talking about Deaux." Manhattan said in a serious voice getting her point across.

"Come on now, Manhattan, when have you ever heard of me letting her be around Katober?"

"Clover, at this point with you, I don't know what you're doing behind my back. Any who, baby girl, be good for daddy, okay? Mama will see you after work tomorrow."

"We love you too, mommy." I smiled, but Manhattan scoffed saying, "like I said, don't have her around anyone I don't approve of, bye." As Manhattan walked off, a lil' pain hit my chest. My main joint was really acting funny with me, yo. Yea, I've done some fucked up shit, but bringing my daughter around another woman wasn't my steelo. Katober had one mother and she didn't need another one. Since I respected her in that way, I hope she did the same behind my back. If I ever find out Manhattan has Katober around any man, let's just say they all will die. Even when Deaux begged me to meet Katober, I nearly slapped the taste out of her mouth for that shit. Since I felt Manhattan would be the only woman I could be with, there was never a reason for Katober to meet anyone.

***

Sitting in the half empty iHop restaurant at 7:00 pm on a Sunday, Ryker scrolled down her Instagram Timeline until the waitress came back with their food. The way she snickered had Manhattan curious so she asked, "girl, what's so funny?"

"Biittcchhhhh, Honesty is in Jamaica with Juelz and her kids! Harlem ass is all in the comments being petty and shady. Talking about, "did that, done that, try a new location nigga!" Girl, if you don't call Clover and tell him come get his homeboy, delete his social media and throw his phone in the Delaware River."

"What?" Sitting up in the booth, Manhattan snatched Ryker's phone from her to see what the fuck she was talking about. The shit Harlem said under the comments had her gasping and laughing loudly.

"First of all, Honesty's body is snatched, hunni. Second of all, it's crazy how niggas can tell the next nigga fuck bitches, then he's all under his ex-wife's comments in his feeling." Manhattan shook her head laughing as she handed Ryker her phone.

"Exactly and I overheard Smoke on the phone with him. Giselle is back with Consequence living in Queens, baby the tea was over pouring while I pretended to slumber and sleep." Ryker laughed so much that she started to snort and tears fell from her eyes. When you think about it, this shit was funny as hell. Just when I thought I had drama going on, Harlem topped me every time. This nigga literally was commenting under every picture Honesty posted. Since Honesty got back with Juelz, Harlem claimed Honesty as his wife more than ever. He talked all that shit, but was losing his mind because of Hon. I guess Smoke was right, Harlem was the last person I should have ever taken advice from.

"Wwwhhhattttt, are you serious?" Manhattan eyes grew big as she took a sip of her coffee. Nodding her head up and down slowly, Ryker answered, "if I'm lying, I'm lying on what I overheard HARLEM AND SMOKE SAY."

"Biittccccchhhhhhhhh, Honesty did exactly what Harlem thought she wouldn't. Now he's looking like a clown probably ready to slit his wrist in four pieces. That's who Clover looks up to, child, why, I don't know."

"I'm guessing since he looks up to Harlem, does that make you Honesty?" Ryker's nosey ass asked. For some reason, her question made Manhattan feel uneasy. The thought of Honesty moving on and living happily ever after kind of scared her. Harlem was really the only man Honesty loved, but when she had enough, she had to move on from him. It made Manhattan wondered, why she couldn't move on like that and get the love she truly deserves?

"I ain't with that nigga now, huh?"

"Barely, but carry on with your story." Ryker replied laughing.

"Well, that's your answer. If Honesty can leave her HUSBAND and the father of her children, I can leave my boyfriend I have one child with." Manhattan laughed raising her eyebrows.

"Preach sister, preeacchhhhhh." Raising her glass in the air, Ryker chuckled as she raised her eyebrows. Even though Manhattan slowly found herself getting over me, she didn't need her friends making her feel worse than she already did.

"I hate you, girl." Manhattan laughed.

"What's the move the 4th of July? I'm trying to be on someone's beach this year and not in Philly. It feels like we've been in June for thirty-two days, it's only June 18th."

"Hell yea, I had to look at the calendar twice at work today. I could have sworn it was June 27th."

"Shit, that's how I was feeling yesterday." Said Ryker.

"About the 4th, I'm going to take off tomorrow for four days. I don't care where we go, as long as we aren't here looking at these clowns."

"Miami?" Ryker smiled raising her eyebrows with a smile on her face. Smiling back, Manhattan raised her shoulders replying, "let me get on this lemonade diet like Queen B did. Hey Maybe we should invite Honesty also, make it into a little girls trip."

"Hell yea, what about Kansas, do you think she'll be able to come?"

"I'll ask her tonight and I'll text Honesty. I sure hope she leaves that drama home. I don't have time for that drama, I have enough of my own." Manhattan replied rolling her eyes. Then she took a lil' sip of her coffee. The last thing Manhattan wanted was to be in sunny Miami dealing with her drama and Honesty's drama.

"Harlem can get these hands just like Harlem can. I would say ask Kat but, lord." Snickering while locking eyes with Manhattan.

"Chilleee, I'll ask her, I guess."

"I don't even know who's the stupidest person at this point; Kat, Harlem, Consequences, or Clover." Ryker stated.

"Girl, I can't believe Kat, I don't know if I should still be laughing or mad at her." Adding a little more cream to her coffee, Manhattan reached for the black stir to mix her steaming cup of coffee.

"Yea, it has to be Kat. It's one thing to catch your man cheating and take him back. It's a wwhhoolllee different jawn when you catch your married boyfriend cheating with a man. People are really drawlin' in 2018." Ryker laughed. While Ryker and Manhattan were downtown, they spotted Kat with her boo, but the look on her face was priceless. After all that clowning she Kat did, I couldn't even believe she took that nigga back.

"How can she kiss that man after she saw him deep throat a dick?? Bitch, there was no way I could do that, but hey, we can't help who we love."

"Man, this baby isn't doing my skin any justice!! Last night, Smoke popped the pimples on my back, it was so romantic." Laughing as she stared in the big spoon to get a view of her face, Ryker was low-key annoyed with looking at herself. She attempted to pop a few of the pimples while at the table, but Manhattan grabbed her by the wrist cutting her eye. This baby had her with the nastiest acne that I've ever seen.

"Eeww, can you stop picking at those bumps and pimples, you're going to ruin my appetite.

"I'm sorry girl, I just hate this acne. I didn't have this shit as a teen and now I have to experience it. That's what I get for waiting to have a baby at this age." She laughed.

"At least you're not one of those big pregnant women. You barely look four months pregnant, probably because you're carrying in your ass." Manhattan laughed.

"Right about now, I rather be big instead of looking like I have cookie crumbles on my face."

"You should have asked your doctor for something when you say him today. Baby boy is giving you the blues, that's messed up." Manhattan said, but she barely paid attention to what Ryker said. Even though she attempted to, Manhattan couldn't shake off this lil' jawn she felt in her body. Ryker knew Manhattan well and could sense something was wrong.

"Okay, ladies, blue berry pancakes topped with whipped cream and extra butter bacon extra crispy, and scrambled eggs." The happy waitress placed the hot plate in front of Ryker's face making her smile. Then she rubbed her belly reached for her knife and fork digging into her pancakes.

"Strawberry pancakes with bacon, and your eggs sunny side up." Placing the plate in front of Manhattan's, the waitress then reached for her cup to refill it with coffee. Manhattan didn't reply, but gave the waitress a friendly smile instead.

"Anything else for you, ladies?" She questioned them.

"No, we're fine, thank you." Manhattan said as she took a bit of the eggs.

"Okay, I'll be back to check on you ladies later." The waitress walked off leaving Manhattan and Ryker to enjoy their food. Manhattan pretended to be hungry, but she didn't have much of an appetite. She only agreed to get out of the house because she knew Ryker would talk shit if she didn't. Then somehow, Clover would be the blame for it, like always.

Every time Ryker stared at Manhattan, she saw this defeated look on her face. A defeated look Manhattan couldn't explain if someone asked her to.

"Girl, are you okay?" She questioned Hat who was nibbling on the sandwich. She didn't make eye contact with Ryker, but she replied, "yepppp."

"Hat, it's me you're talking to, be honest."

"You want me to be honest, okay, I'll be VERY honest. Somedays, I want to kill myself just so I can ruin Clover's life. That nigga couldn't last ONE day without me on this earth. Other days I want to kill him and Deaux because I want to live on earth peacefully. I'm the one that deserves him, NOT HERE!!!! That hoodrat doesn't deserve to even be in the presence of my man, you understand what I'm saying. I'm the one who loves that nigga for who he is and not what he has or for any of that street shit!!! That bitch is fucking every nigga who flashes a dollar, but doesn't want to let Clover go because she has a point to prove." Manhattan expressed with a tone full of emotions. You didn't know if she was happy, sad, angry, or bitter. Knowing Manhattan, she was a little of both.

"The smut has a point to prove to you and I don't know why. Clover would literally leave that hoe out in the rain on a Friday and the Sunday she'll be acting like everything is cool when he calls. I swear, that bitch will DIE trying to proof a point to Clover and the world. She wants to be a ride or die so bad, baby, it ain't that serious."
"Preach, sista, preach, Deaux better listen to some Tink and boss the fuck up." Manhattan laughed.

"Bitches be in love until a nigga go back to his baby mama. Now she's in the shower with a razor blade at her wrist listening to *Treat Me Like Somebody*."

"Oh my God, bitch, you're so fuckin' stupid, yo, not the razor blade at her wrist." Manhattan replied laughing.

"Yes, blood dripping down her leg like a horror movie." As Ryker and Manhattan laughed, Ryker attempted to take a sip of her Dr. Pepper, but the soda started to come out of her nose. It burned a little, but they continued to laugh. Ryker was glad Manhattan had happy tears in her eyes and not tears of pain, courtesy of me.

"Clover has been trying mad hard to get me back in the house. I guess that's what has me in my feelings, I haven't seen him like this since we first met."

"That sounds cute and all, but I wouldn't fall for it. Clover is Clover, let's not forget ANY of the things he has done, iight?" Ryker implied.

"I hear you, girl. How I'm feeling, I want to move completely out of this state. This shit with Clover and Deaux is taking over my life!! Every time I go somewhere a bitch or joe is whispering some shit about Deaux. I have people literally coming up to me asking if I'm the side chick!!! The fucking side chick, Ryker, that shit is so humiliating."

"Look, Hat, you have to stop letting that shit get to you!! talking about DEATH because of Clover made me sick to my stomach and you don't even know it."

"I know, let's just drop the subject."

Entering iHop immediately searching for Manhattan, Ryker waved at Chris to grab his attention. With all that white on trying to look godly, you couldn't mis that nigga. Once Ryker grabbed his attention did, she pointed at Manhattan whispering, "there goes your boo!"

If I didn't know any better, I would think Ryker wanted to fuck Chris instead. She was so ready for Hat to move on that Ryker would hook her up with any jawn who had a heartbeat.

"Girl, shut up, that is my friend that I don't know much about." Manhattan whispered.

"If you don't know much about him, what the hell are ya'll talking about on the phone? You better not be on the phone with him crying about Spitta!"

"Girl, fuck you and Spitta, what the hell do I look like mentioning his name to Chris. His conversation is totally different from Clover's. We talk about politics, books, astrology, and things like that. I mean, Clover and I would talk about things like that, but somehow an argument would occur. It kind of feels good to be single, never thought I would say that."

"Like I told you before, plenty of women start over at your age. It may feel like it's the end of the world, but I promise it's not. This little storm will pass and when it does, you'll be, Clover who?" Ryker giggled.

"That's the thing, Ryke, we share a child together, I still have to deal with this nigga."

"I hear you, Hat, but Chris seems like a good guy. It won't hurt you to give him a chance, you never know what good things can come from him." Twirling her fork in several circles, Ryker bounced her shoulders with a smile on her face. Stuffing a small piece of the bacon into her mouth, Manhattan uttered, "Clover was a nice guy when we first met and you see how things turned out."

"Enough with Clover, are you really going to let him ruin you like this? Clover has been having a reputation since BEFORE you met him. Stop comparing Chris ad Clover because they are two different people. You know I did a lil' jawn on Chris, he's good people." Ryker said.

"What, when and why are you just telling me this?" Manhattan questioned.

"I was going to tell you tonight, but I had to make sure my source was one hundred." She laughed.

"Ard, so what did you find out about Chris? Any crazy ex's or baby mothers I should be concerned about?"

"I don't think so, but Christopher Bradley Dunn graduated Temple three years ago studying marketing. He's the manager at the furniture store and is in the process of opening his own clothing store in Fishtown. He lives in East Falls, moved there when he graduated from Temple. Oh yea, he drives a Jeep Wrangler, a black one, all black. You know how much you love those Jeep Wranglers. Just imagine that silky brown hair blowing with the top down." Ryker chuckled again.

"Wwooww, I wonder why he didn't tell me any of that. Well, he did tell me he lives in East Fall, I forgot about that." Manhattan thought.

"So, you don't know anything personal about that man?" Ryker questioned.

"To think about it, not really, but maybe because I'm too busy dwelling on Clover's ass!"

"Ding ding, I'm glad you said it, but I did throw it in Clover's face about meeting Chris tonight." She chuckled.

"Oh , really, what did Mr. Porter have to say?"

"Girl, he was like, "the nigga from the store?" I told him yea and he said, "ohhh, that's why he kept staring at you in the furniture store. The look on Clover's face was priceless." Hat smirked while running her tongue across her pearly perfect white teeth. That bitch really enjoyed making me sick to my stomach.

Manhattan didn't waste any time telling me about Chris even though they've only known one another for three days. For some reason, this nigga kept a smile on her face. The same smile I used to have scribbled on her face.

Entering iHop immediately searching for Manhattan, Ryker waved at Chris to grab his attention and when Ryker did, she pointed at Manhattan whispering, "there goes your boo!"

"Girl, be quiet, that's my friend."

"Yea, a very fine ass friend." Ryker batted her eyes saying.

If I didn't know any better, I would think Ryker wanted to fuck Chris instead. She was so ready for Hat to move on that Ryker would hook her up with any jawn who had a heartbeat.

"He is looking pretty fine in all that white, damn." Staring at Chris with lust in her eyes, Manhattan gave him a flirty wave as she bit softly on her bottom lip.

"Fine is not the word, baby, but do you, Hat, I'm behind you all the way." Ryker laughed. Approaching the table, Chris stared at Manhattan with love in his goofy eyes. Manhattan couldn't control the goofy look on her face also and Ryker enjoyed all of this cornball shit.

"Well, well, well, hello, Miss. Mullen, you're looking nice." Chris was right, Manhattan looked good in her fitted sundress that was coral. Her hair was pulled into a slick and tight ponytail rocking big and gold hoop earrings. Manhattan loved wearing her beautiful feet out so, she rocked a pair of gold sandals with white toenail polish.

"Hello to you also." Still with a smile on her face, Manhattan slightly pushed her plate to the side standing to her feet. Wrapping her arms around Chris' neck to give him a hug, Manhattan couldn't help, but to inhale the Gucci Guilty he wore. I didn't like the nigga, but like myself, he had a good taste in cologne. Hat loved a nigga who wore good cologne, that shit was her weakness.

"What's up Ryker," Chris said to Ryker, but he couldn't take his eyes off Hat. I don't know what it was about him, shit, maybe the way he licked his lips at Manhattan, but homie sure had her undivided attention.

"You have a unique name, the only time you hear the word Ryker is when niggas going to jail." Chris laughed as he took a bite of Manhattan's pancake. Then he gave her a sweet look that made butterflies form in stomach, I hated it!

"I know right, you could never get me confused with anyone." Ryker laughed rubbing her foot against Manhattan's leg under the table. Manhattan locked eyes with Ryker with her weird smile on her face trying to place it cool, but she wasn't good at that. Manhattan could never hide her true emotions, she always wore them on her sleeves.

"What, is something wrong, yo?" He looked at Manhattan then look at Ryker.

"No, not at all, now that Chris is here, I'll be leaving."

"Shorty, you don't have to leave, I think your friend rather you here." Christ laughed a little as he sat next to Manhattan. She softly rolled her eyes, but chuckled a little taking a bite of her bacon.

"Yea, Ryker, stay." Manhattan implied, but Ryker shook her head maneuvering her way to her feet.

"No, no, I need to go home before I fall asleep at this table. Then Smoke is going to kill my behind and I don't think we want that right before my birthday." She laughed.

"Ugghh, okay, girl, but let me know when you make it home." Manhattan demanded.

"Yes sirrrr, ya'll have a good night." Reaching into her clutch, Ryker pulled a crispy twenty-dollar bill and dropped it onto the table. Then she smiled at Chris and Hat saying, "ya'll are so cute together, it's like a match made in heaven." She laughed walking away. Now alone with Chris, Manhattan was a lil' nervous, but that nigga was far from feeling that way. He loved the vibe he got from Manhattan, even though it was there first time meeting in public. He loved talking to her over the phone like he was some lil' young bol in love.

"You know your friend could have stayed, it wasn't a problem." He spoked softly wrapping his arm tighter around Manhattan's neck. She blushed a little, I bet real coming from a 'real man' felt good to her.

"She knows that, but she wanted to leave. That girl falls asleep in the middle of a conversation." Manhattan laughed taking another bite of her food.

"Damn." He laughed.

"That's what kids do to you, but this is the easy part. The more they grow, the more you become tired. I swear, Katober drinks coffee all day, shorty be non-stop."

"I'm guessing your daughter is with her father since she isn't here."

"Yes you are correct." Manhattan chuckle a little, she was hella nervous.

"Bet, bet, but how was your day? I couldn't ask you that earlier since we hardly spoke."

"I'm sorry about that, but my day was great actually." Manhattan turned to Chris smiling.

"That's what's up, you have the prettiest eyes." Slightly moving the loose strains of hair from Manhattan's face, Chris smile grew bigger. This nigga had a serious thing for Hat already.

"There you go with the game running, trust me, you don't have to do that." Manhattan pushed a chuckle out, but Chris gently grabbed her by the chin saying, "I'm serious, but you look at yourself in the mirror every day, yo, you should know that."

"I do and thanks." Still holding Manhattan's chin, Chris stared further in her eyes, Manhattan could feel her heart race increasing. Chris had her feeling nervous, but also calm and Hat looovveeddddd that feeling.

"No problem, but what if I wanted to kiss you?"

"What if I wanted to kiss you back?" Hat asked and without giving Chris a chance to reply, Manhattan leaned forward giving Chris a wet kiss on his fat lips. Then she grabbed the back of his head pulling him in for a deeper kiss. I can't lie, Chris was a gentlemen and kept his hands in the appropriate places. Things like that turned her on even more.

After kissing for a few seconds, Manhattan pulled away saying, "hhhmm, that was nice." She smiled.

"You think so?" He smirked.

"Yea, something I haven't had in a while."

"If that's the case, it can be more of that." He replied.

"I think I like the sound of that, but I don't want to rush into anything. I've been through a lot in my last relationship, I can't go through any of that again."

"My mama didn't raise me to disrespect women in any kind of manner. I'm not going to sit here and say I haven't hurt any women before, but I've always been a man about my shit. Before I continue to hurt you, I rather end things with you, ya dig?"

"I hear you, but I need to SEE that also, friends before anything?" Manhattan questioned.

"Hell yea, but you haven't told me much about your situation. Is there something you don't want me to know? Are you single or taken a lil' bit?" He asked.

"Not really, I'm just so over him and all that, it's really no need to talk about Clover. Too much damage has been done and I don't bring that baggage into anything new." She replied.

"Clover, as in Clover Porter?" He asked.

"Yea, that Clover."

"Wow, small world, I didn't think ya'll were still together. So, you're the Manhattan I'm always hearing about." He stretched his eyes a little taking a sip of Manhattan's coffee.

"That's about right, but what do you mean the Manhattan you're always hearing about?" Turning to face Chris, Manhattan wanted answers, truthful answers.

"I hear shit about how Clover treats his girlfriend. I must be losing my mind because I damn sure didn't put two and two together. That damn sure explains why he was mugging me in the store, but Clover don't want this Smoke."

"Clover is……. I don't even know half the time, but I don't want to make everything about him."

"I feel that, but how long have you two been separated?" He asked.

"About a week."

"What, about a week?" He laughed asking, Chris seemed dumb confused.

"Yea, but things have been rocky between Clover and I for a very long time. At this point, I'm scared to move on, but moving on is my only option. I'm ready for news things, but I can't lie, I'm scared."

"Scared of what, new things are always good?" He asked.

"I'm scared of being a fool again, I guess I'm scared of loving again. You can give someone the world, but they don't always do the same. That was the situation between Clover and I."

"Damn, well, don't be afraid to move on, even if it's not with a fly nigga like myself." Sucking his teeth in a sexual way, Chris hit Manhattan with a smile that made her cheeks turn cherry red. She tried speaking, but her words fumbled over one another. Thy both laughed making one another blush more.

"Uumm, what if it was with you?"

"If it was with me, I promise to love you in a way that would make you forget all the pain Clover caused. We don't have to rush into anything, like you said, friends first, and whatever comes after that I'm fine with it." Kissing Manhattan again, but on the cheek, she could feel a million butterflies in her stomach. For a second, she had to pressed against her flat stomach to calm herself down.

"You make it sound good, we shall see hoe this go."

"Can I ask you something?" Chris asked taking another sip of the coffee that was now cold. Instead of replying with words, Manhattan nodded her head waiting for him to speak.

"Why are you so ready to move on already? You don't feel like it's any hope between you two?"

"Hell no, for years I wanted Clover to change, for the sake of himself, me, and our daughter. It's been eight years with no change, it's just time for me to move on." She answered.

"Are you honestly ready to move on, it's fine to be real with me?"

"Am I ready to move on, no, of course not, but am I ready to move on from Clover, hell yea? You said it yourself how you've heard about the way he treats me. It's embarrassing and I'm tired of it, I want to be loved like in the movies."

"Do you want a love Jones?" Chris asked.

"I want my own love story, but I can't rush into anything. I have a daughter and I refuse to let her see me with different men. You did say you didn't have kids, right?"

"Yea, no kids."

"At your age if you don't have kids, I'm assuming you don't want any."

"It's not that I don't want kids, the problem is that I don't want kids with any ole smut. Trust me, I've seen that shit go sour too many times and I'm not trying to be a statistic." Chris uttered while sipping on his ice tea. The shit he said had Manhattan impressed, this was the kind of things she didn't hear from a man too often.

"Trust me, I feel you on that, not many men are think like that. The don't mind climbing in bed with any big booty hoe they see. Then when the bitch gets pregnant, they are mad at the world. I promise you I never understood that mess." Manhattan laughed.

"Tell me more about yourself, the part that doesn't include Clover Porter." He smiled.

Chapter 16

It's been two weeks since I really spoken to Hat or seen her. When I say, 'seen' her I mean touching, fucking, and smelling that Paris Hilton body fragrance on her silky skin. Sleeping alone wasn't fun, but sleeping without her wasn't my steelo at all, yo. Even though Deaux literally begged to spend every minute with me, I wasn't feeling shorty on that level anymore. Maybe because she didn't turn me on anymore or probably because she was the main reason I lost my main joint. Either way, I had to figure this shit out, I couldn't lose Hat for good.

Besides a few text messages discussing Katober, like always, we still didn't talk much. I tried making small conversation with her to slowly make my way back in her good graces, but youngin' wasn't having that at all. Manhattan shut me down every single time the conversation shifted into another direction. I wasn't sure if it was because of Chris, the people in her ear telling her shit about me, or maybe Manhattan really was getting over me. Either way, I couldn't deal with this shit and I slowly found myself changing my dog ways that Manhattan once begged me to do. I was entertaining Deaux as much and Deaux noticed it from jump. I couldn't accept the fact that I was losing the love of my life for some hood rat like Deaux, what the fuck was I thinking. Those two weeks without her was weird, I can't lie. The closes thing I could get to her was Katober, which made things better between my daughter and me.

In those short fourteen days, word rapidly spread about Hat being seen with another man. Some people attempted to make me the victim of being cheated on, but that was crazy as fuck, yo. As much cheating as I did on Hat, I was the LAST person who could have cried wolf.

"Clover, can you grab the cake and bring it outside?" Manhattan pointed at that pink and white, big three tower cake that sat on the kitchen table. Rushing out of the house through the back door, Manhattan didn't give me a chance to reply. I didn't say anything back, but I carefully grab the cake with both hands walking to the backdoor. Hat made me spend $200 dollars on a fuckin' cake, but it was worth it and anything for Katober on her special day.

Carefully placing the cake on the table, I searched through the crowd searching for Manhattan. When I spotted her, she was staring at her iPhone with a big smile on her face. With a smile that wide and cheesy,

Today, daddy's little girl made five years old and Hat had to talk to me, plus be in my presence. Since she didn't want many people to know what we were going through, she had to pretend like everything was fine with us. By the cold shoulder she gave me and short conversations, everyone knew what the fuck was up. On top of that, Manhattan refused to give Katober's party at my house. If that wasn't enough on my plate, Deaux's annoying ass called me non-stop. The bitch didn't understand that I didn't want to fuck with her anymore. It didn't matter how clear I made it to her, but I could no longer do this anymore. I had to get my family back some kind of way and fast, if not, Chris would be laid up with my woman. As bitter as Manhattan was, she probably would allow Katober to call Chris daddy, but I fa'sho wasn't letting that mess happen.

"As-salamu alaykum, my brother." Approaching me with a smile on his face and a four foot barbie doll tucked under his arm, Cope dapped me down. Of course on his arm was his daughter and Oak. I didn't waste my time speaking to Oak because I knew she wouldn't reply and if she did, it was be a nasty comment. Today, I wasn't in the mood for her or Ryker's shit. Nowadays, even Kate was on the negative shit when she spotted a nigga.

"Mualaikumsalam. What up, Cope, what the hell you have under your arm?" I laughed glancing at the box. Pulling it from under his arm, he showed off the barbie doll. It was something Katober wanted for months, good looking out, Cope.

"Some expensive ass life size doll I like Laysha choose for Katober. She's going to be playing with that thing until she's thirty." Cope said making me laughing, but I shook my head also.

"Daddy, where is KoKo?" A'laysha asked rubbed her eyes. By the puffiness and redness surrounding her eyes, I can tell she just woke up from a nap. Cope handed the gift to A'Laysha, then he spoked, "put this on the table with the rest of the gifts."

"Yes sir." She replied, attempting to run off, but Oak stopped A'Laysha to adjust the collar on her dress. Then she spoke in a whisper saying, "hey, don't act a fool here, I wouldn't want to make you shame." Oak said, then she motioned her daughter to continue walking.

"What up, O?" I asked Oak. Slowing turning to me flaring her nose, Oak replied, "shit, that's what's up, yo." She kissed Cope on the cheek saying, "baby, I'm going in the house to find Hat."

"Ard." As Oak walked off, she sized me up and down sucking her teeth. If you thought Marcy and Ryker hated my guts, Oak's hate for me was on a whole different jawn. Which is why Hat didn't tell her many things I did. That bitch attempted to knock my head off my shoulder every time I made a tear fall from Manhattan's eyes.

"Damn, bruh, if looks could kill." Cope laughed dropping his head.

"Yea, I would be dead right now because of Oak."

"Is shit still bad between you and Hat?"

"Is water wet?" I chuckled asking.

"Yea and it can be wet and cold." Cope clapped his hands laughing.

"Hat is strictly cold with me, ice cold, my nigga. I don't know what to do at this point."

"First, you need to leave that hoe Deaux alone, I told you that the first time I saw you with that bitch. Every time I see shorty I get a bad vibe, like a dark cloud follows her around." Cope expressed, I felt every word he said.

"Brody, I ain't been with that hoe in about three weeks, no lie." Pulling my phone from my back pocket, I rushed to unlock the screen to show Cope how many Deaux blew me up. I couldn't help, but to smile at my lock screen. It was a picture of Hat and Katober six months ago lying in bed. The smiles on their faces were priceless, that really wasn't something money couldn't buy. Six months ago, things weren't the best between Hat and I, but fuck, they were better than what they are now. Six months ago, I could put a smile on her face, but I could hardly get her to look at me for six seconds without wanting to cry or punch me.

"Damn, the bitch even left ten voicemails." Cope laughed scrolling through my call long. Then he pointed to the numerous times I called Manhattan and the call was ignored.

"Seem like Deaux isn't the only stalker around here." He laughed.

"Cope, if it isn't about Katober, Hat won't give me the time of day."

"Well, you better try harder because seem like that Chris nigga is sweeping her off of her feet."

"Fuck that joe, I won't let some random ass nigga who sells rugs and love sofas take my woman from me. Nah, I ain't letting that shit happen, but I'll figure it all out."

"You do that, but I gotta take a piss." Cope dapped me down walking off and leaving me in my thoughts. He was right, I had to try harder, but I wasn't used of that shit.

While everyone was enjoying themselves surrounded by a bunch of kids, I stood back watching everything. Everyone was happy , but deep down inside I wasn't. Sitting back watching Hat and Katober laugh and smile without me kind of fucked me up. It truly was a slap in the face and showed me how Hat didn't need me for happiness anymore.

"Daddy, daddy, daddy!" Holding a white and pink cupcake in her hand, Katober hopped my way exactly like a bunny. Kansas followed behind her yawning with a tiresome glare of her face. I laughed a little saying, "what's wrong with you?"

"Katober has some bad ass lil' friends, yo."

"Trust me, I know, how do you think I felt for her slumber party last year?" I laughed.

"This is ten times worse." Kansas spoked using the back side of her hand to wipe the sweat from her big forehead.

"Daddy, today is my birthday!" Katober shouted.

"I know baby. Happy birthday, beautiful girl, daddy loves you." Jumping into my arms with a big smile and a few missing teeth, Katober didn't know she had a nigga feeling a lot better. If I was a weak jawn, I probably would have cried like a lil' joe about Manhattan ignoring me.

"Thank you daddy, I love you." Katober gave me a big kiss on the cheek making me feel warm inside. I knew if no woman loved me on this Earth, my daughter damn sure did. In her eyes, none of my mistakes mattered.

"Aawwww, I love you too, baby girl." I replied giving her a wet kiss on the cheek. Standing behind me clearing her throat, Manhattan tapped me on my shoulder saying, "I hope you don't have any plans to leave. We were about to serve the food."

"Come on now, Hat, why would I leave my daughter's birthday party? Everyone who's important to me is at this party, right Koko?" I asked my daughter slightly tickling her stomach and she laughed loudly. Katober laughed exactly like Manhattan that she even tossed her head back.

"Hhmmm, it's not like I haven't heard that before, but anyways. In about five minutes we'll start serving, iight?" Manhattan said.

"We're doing what?" Cope and Oak asked as the approached us. I noticed how her dress was a lil' twisted and Cope's True Religions were unzipped. Knowing these two freaky mutherfuckers, they were fucking in the closet. After all these years of being together, Oak and Cope still acted as if they just got together. You know, that stage in your relationship when everything is perfect

"Not today, Hat, please." I begged staring Manhattan up and down, but not in a bad way. In a simple cropped white t-shirt and plain dark denim Levi's, Manhattan looked great. I loved when she wore her toes out painting them in a bright white polish and her hair pulled into a tight ponytail. Even though she put on a little weight, the little belly fat turned me on. By the look I gave her, Manhattan knew exactly what I was thinking, which is probably why she had that mug on her face. I couldn't help myself though, her jeans looked like someone sprayed painted them on her body showing off every curve.

Her appearance reminded me of the old Manhattan, the plain jane Manhattan I fell in love with. Not this Hat who wore makeup and weave all the fuckin' time, I guess the natural Manhattan was back temporarily.

"Hat, you look nice today, I remember buying you those jeans two years ago." I smiled, slowly examining her body again, but Hat was already flaring her nose at me to say, "yea, right around the time Deaux was posting videos of herself from your page. Good times, Clover Porter, real good times." Giving me a face smile and turning away, I really couldn't say two words without Hat reminding me of the foolish choices I have made.

"No, no, mommy, be nice to daddy, it's my birthday." Waving her little finger at Manhattan, Katober always had my back, even when I was wrong. Manhattan cracked a smiled at Katober exhaling, then she laughed giving her a soft kiss on the lips.

"Okay, baby, but tomorrow isn't his birthday, which means mama can be mean to him."

"That also means you're going to be talking to me tomorrow." I smiled.

"Yea, I'm going to need to pick up Koko from your mom's house tomorrow. Chris is taking me to this cycling class, I need to drop a few pounds. I guess all that crying and eating ice cream caught up with me." She smirked, slightly flipping her ponytail at me. I smacked my lips, but I didn't want to say too much in the presence of my daughter. When I wasn't around Hat and her bitter friends were probably filling her head with crazy things about me.

"Man, it's hot as hell out here, remind me to never throw a party in July." Cope wipe his sweaty bald head laughing. Today, the temperature was at ninety- nine degrees, but it felt like a thousand degrees. My clothes were damn near stuck to my body and I could see Manhattan's big nipples piercing through her top. If she wouldn't have worn a bra, everyone would have had front row seats to the titty show. Manhattan had huge breast now and when we were on better terms, I couldn't keep those bitches out of my mouth.

"Hat and Kan, where is Ryker?" Oak questioned while taking a sip of the refreshing punch. Wiping the sweat from her forehead again, Kansas replied, "

"Her and Smoke should be on their way, you know Ryker's aunt's leg had to amputated yesterday."

"Ryker has eight brothers and sisters, plus sixteen damn cousins, but it seems like her and Smoke are the ones taking care of her." Manhattan said looking at her watch.

"I don't know about ya'll jawns, but this mommy needs to step out tonight. My man and I are going to paint the city red." Kansas smirked.

"Must be nice." Manhattan replied.

"Yea, it is, and you know that. You've been hanging on the arms of that fine ass man, Chris." Oak replied. Slightly nudging Manhattan in the hip, Oak then stared at Kansas who rolled her eyes at Manhattan.

"I guess." Manhattan mumbled. She enjoyed spending time with Chris, he was a breath of fresh air, but that nigga didn't have her heart like I did.

"Chris is so head over heels, he's probably at the jewelry store choosing an engagement ring now." Kansas laughed making Hat's cheeks turn red.

"Girl, one minute Hat likes Chris, then the next minute she's trying to brush him off. The jawn is crazy, Clover had officially rubbed off on her." Kansas answered.

"He's so in love he can't even feel the cold shoulder she gives him. That man be all over Hat like white on rice, I love that shit. Now you finally get to feel REAL love from a man." Oak laughed.

"Yea, real love." Replying with an awkward laugh and smile, Manhattan hated when her homies talked down on me, but praised Chris. Besides the things Hat told him and meeting Chris a few times, they hardly knew him. Just how I was the perfect guy when Hat and I first met, Chris could be doing the same thing.

Manhattan was a little uncomfortable with the love and affection Chris gave her. Her girlfriends on the other hand, they thought it was the 'sweetest' thing and Hat actually got love for the first time. I know I've done some fucked up shit, but saying Hat was never loved by a man cut a nigga deep. It didn't matter how much Chris showered Manhattan with love, until she was ready to receive love from Chris, simple things like a kiss on the cheek from him would put her in an uncomfortable mind state.

After so many years of loving and tolerating the same jawn, Hat really didn't know how to love another man. Hat's guilt sometimes ate her alive because she felt as if she owed a hundred percent of her loyalty to me. I could be a selfish mutherfucker and say Hat did, but not an ounce of her loyalty belonged to me. Truth be told, I should have lost it years ago. Matter of fact, the day I met Deaux is when I should have lost it and never gained it back

"I think you should have invited Chris to the party." Oak mumbled folding her arms across her chest. She knew what the fuck she said was foolish and would make Manhattan explain herself like a nigga who got caught cheating. Kind of like me when I get got caught cheating for the first time.

"Everyone assumes that I'm mad at Manhattan, but for fucking what, yo? Oh, let me guess, because she dropped a zero and snatched her a hero? The fuck I'm going to be upset for, I'm not fucking Clover." Kansas laughed leaning against Oak's shoulder who was also laughing loudly. If we weren't at my daughter's party, Oak would have made sure I heard every word she spoke about me.

"She's not fucking him either, well, anymore." Oak laughed again cutting her eyes in my direction. I wasn't in the mood for any bullshit with Oak, so, I turned away.

"Manhattan!" Squealing with a few gifts in her hands, Honesty's thick ass was excited to see Manhattan. She was so excited that she nearly dropped the gifts attempting to hug Hat. Juelz walked behind Honesty as if he was her fuckin' bodyguard with a straight face. I could tell he wasn't too excited about being here, but he loved giving Honesty exactly what she wanted.

Walking over to Manhattan pissed off, I tapped her shoulder, but in a smooth way she brushed me off hugging Honesty.

"About damn time, girl, I thought you were somewhere lost." Manhattan laughed.

"I'm sorry, Hat, I took a wrong turn even though Ju told me six times don't turn on Broadway." She laughed.

"It's all good, you're here and that's all that matters. What's up, Juelz, thanks for coming."

"Glad to be away from home for a lil' while." He laughed.

"That's the same mentality I was going to have on our girl's trip." Manhattan giggled. Both opening their arms, Manhattan and Juelz embraced one another with a warm hug.

"Oak and Kansas, looking like the two baddest bitches I know." Arming her arms widely, Honesty hugged Oak and Kansas making them laugh. Oak was a freaky lil' somebody, so, she grabbed a handful of Honesty's ass making her giggle even more. Harlem always said if Honesty could fuck a woman, she would give Oak the best time of her life.

"There you go, keep it up and we might take you back to New York. Right, baby?" Honesty laughed.

"Hhhmmm, don't threaten me with a good time, baby." Oak wicked her eyes joking. Then she glanced at Juelz, but he laughed shaking his head.

"Oak, don't get fucked up." Cope said calm and softly, but Oak laughed it off blushing.

"Aawww, baby, be cool, you know I'm joking." Oak raised her eyebrows laughing again.

"Girl, that lil' weight is looking good on you. What great things love does the body." Kansas smirked, she knew that feeling oh so well.

"In my neck of the woods we call it happy weight." Honesty twirled in a small circle showing off her curvy body in the red spandex dress. The red lipstick made her lips appear fuller or maybe it was the sleek ponytail that made her lips stand out. Honesty's body was tone, but sexy as hell. With the upper part of her back being revealed, the tattoo of Juelz's name on her back was exposed to everyone. She hadn't looked this good since she's been with Harlem, now I understood why Harlem was so damn salty. Him and I were in the same boat.

"Well, whatever you want to call it, you look freaking amazing." Oak replied.

"Thanks, girl, thanks." Still twirling a little, Honesty turned around smiling at Juelz. He blushed more than her, but Juelz also pulled Honesty closer to him. Then he kissed the back of her neck giving Honesty chills.

"I love you, sexy ass." He smiled.

"I love you too, baby."

"You two are so damn cute. I'll be right back though, I need to get some things out of the house." Manhattan said.

"I'll help you, hello to you too, Honesty" I said knowing damn well she didn't want to speak to me. Sizing me up and down, Honesty said, "uh-huh."

"Wow." I shook my head laughing following behind Manhattan. I couldn't wait until we stepped foot into the house, I had a few choice words for her pale ass.

As she opened the back door stepping into the house, Manhattan turned around saying, "Clover, I don't need any help, but thanks anyways."

"I don't need any help, Clover, but thanks anyways. Damn, Manhattan, I wish you shut up sometimes and stop bitching!"

"Clover, who the fuck are you talking to?" Manhattan turned around cutting her eyes in my direction with a mug on her face. That fast, she quickly reminded me of who the fuck I was speaking to. Why the fuck would I piss her off and I wasn't even back on her good side.

"Clearly, I'm talking to you, but I'll just say no one since you're acting like we aren't the only ones standing here!"

"Yea, that's what you BETTER SAY and don't ever question me about anything again." Rolling her eyes and turning away, I exhaled loudly taking a few steps back, but I still had shit to get off my chest.

"Why is that nigga here, Manhattan, I don't recall sending that clown an invite?" Biting on Katober's cupcake, I stood next to Manhattan pissed off. She was handling me like I was a joe ass nigga.

"You would want to leave me alone, Clover Porter! You barely got an invite, don't clown yourself!" Grabbing the case of juice that was on the countertop, Manhattan used her shoulder to push me out of her way. I stumbled back a little, but I had to laugh it off. How the fuck could she tell me I was barely invited and I'm the one who literally paid for everything in this jawn.

"What?" I asked.

"You heard what I said." She shouted as she walked away. I can't lie, the way Manhattan acted turned me on! It didn't how much she played tuff, that shit was cute as hell to me.

By the look on her face, Honesty knew something was up. After taking a few sips on her punch, she asked, "girl, what's wrong with you? Walking out of the house like incredible Hulk."

"Who else would annoy me this much?" Dropping the juice onto the table, Manhattan then wiped the sweat from her forehead rolling her eyes. Honesty took one more sip of her drink, then turned around glaring me. Shaking my head, I turned away as if I didn't see her.

"Are you two back—"

"No, I told you I'm good on Clover, things are a lot better without him." She snapped.

"Damn, girl, it was just a question, but where is your boo, Chris?" Honesty questioned with her hands on her hips and a smirk on her face. Manhattan attempted to keep a straight face, but she couldn't.

"I haven't seen you smile like this in a while, girl. Smiling is good for the soul, I always said that." Honesty implied.

"Chris is at home, we all know it wasn't safe to invite him. Besides, he hasn't met Koko yet and I'm going to keep it like that for a while."

"You know what, Hat, I don't blame you. It's best to keep it that way for a while."

"How long though, when do you honestly move on completely from the one you love? I hate that my daughter will eventually be in the presence of another man. That was never in the plan, Hon." Manhattan whispered.

"Trust me, Hat, I know, things like that are never in how plan. I damn sure didn't have getting divorce in my plan. Despite Harlem 'leaving' me for Giselle, I still loved his ass and took him back after that."

"I don't want to move on, Honesty, I really don't, but I can't do this anymore, I just can't!" Trying to fight back her tears, Manhattan dropped her head hiding her trembling lips. Honesty quickly picked her head up telling Manhattan, "hey, it's hard, I KNOW it's hard. Some days I still pick up the phone to call Harlem to work things out, but I would be a damn fool. Over and over, Harlem has shown me that he wasn't good enough for my love. Some days, I still cry about us being divorce, Harlem is the only man I wanted to love. Don't get me wrong, Juelz is a great man, I swear he is, but Harlem was my first love. Something Juelz can never be."

Five hours of dealing with crazy kids who were high on cake, candy, and ice cream, everyone was finally gone and I had Hat to myself. To her, that wasn't a good thing, but to me, fuck, that was everything. We needed to have a serious conversation about us and our future, if that was anything to even talk about. The living room was covered with ruin decorations, leftover food and drinks, and gifts that would last Katober a lifetime. I could see how sleepy Hat was, but knowing her, she wanted to keep busy to avoid me.

At 8:30 pm, I wanted to be in bed with Hat, rubbing my dick against her big booty and making her cum until her body shook. Wishful thinking, huh, I already know, but wishful thinking isn't bad for a player who's in love.

"Today was a good day, I can't lie, I had fun." I chuckled.

"Yeeeppppp, but I know Katober's stomach will be killing her in the morning. I caught that girl eating cake with her hands like it was potato chips." Manhattan laughed drying the dishes off, still looking good even though her clothes were covered with stains. Standing two feet next to her, I cleaned against the countertop, I couldn't take my eyes off her. I always said in her natural beauty, shorty was the best.

"I caught her too, but I couldn't tell her stop. She's just too damn cute. It's kind of hard to tell her no for anything!" I laughed again.

"Those chubby little cheeks and big brown eyes will be the death of you. I can imagine how many things she will get away with when she becomes a teenager."

"A lot of things, if you ask me, that's forever daddy's girl." I smiled.

"You know what's crazy, we were dying to have a baby. Now we have to raise her in this crazy world and it scares me, Clover, it really does." After drying the last dish off, Hat used her already damaged shirt to wipe her wet hands. I didn't want her to see me staring at her with love in my eyes, but she did. Seem like Hat was stuck between being uncomfortable and confused.

"What, why are you looking at me like that?" She questioned.

"Uumm, no reason, but we can't think like that, babe, uuhhh, I mean Hat. We just need to enjoy raising her the best to how ability." I spoked.

"I know, but every time you watch abc6, someone was killed. I can't be that parent crying on the news begging my daughter's murder to come forward."

"Hey, that won't ever happen, stop thinking like that." I demanded.

"You're right, I'm going to literally drive myself insane."

"Hat, can you please talk to me?" I leaned against the countertop eating ice cream trying to make eye contact with Hat, but she didn't. Manhattan continued cleaning like I wasn't in in the room. Since she moved back home, it was my first time being here, I wouldn't mind standing the night. I knew that wasn't going to happen and I wasn't going to waste my time asking.

"Talk about what, Clover, and can you grab the rest of those dishes off the dining room table?" She questioned.

"Sure." Rushing to grab the plates, I turned around to hand Manhattan the plates. Still refusing to make eye contact, she whispered, "thanks."

"No problem, but you know that." Smiling hoping Manhattan would smile back, but she didn't.

"If I knew what you were talking about, I wouldn't have asked you, duh!" She worded.

"Manhattan, have you had Chris around my kid?" I questioned.

"No, Clover, Chris has not been around Katober." Manhattan replied in a flat tone and for some reason, I didn't believe shorty.

"To keep it a stack, I don't believe you."

"That's on you, I don't care if you believe me or not." She responded laughing, which made me not believe her even more.

"Maybe you're doing this on some get back shit, but you got it all wrong. Manhattan, I've done some fucked up shit, but bringing Katober around Deaux isn't something I've ever done. Yea, she has begged me plenty of times to meet her 'step daughter', but I shut that shit down a long time ago."

"Her fucking what?? My child and Deaux does not share the same blood or family tree. There is NO hoe in her damn blood, YOU GOT THAT, CLOVER??"

"Hey, calm the fuck down, Manhattan, like I told you, I put a stop to that shit a long time ago." I uttered.

"You should have put a stop to a lot of things a long time ago, but homeboy, you fuckin' didn't!!!! You just kept doing, and doing, and doing until I couldn't take it anymore, CLOVER!!!! NOW LOOK AT US, I CAN'T EVEN TOLERATE BEING IN THE SAME ROOM WITH YOU, CLOVER!!!! I LITERALLY CAN NOT STAND BREATHING THE SAME AIR AS YOU AND THAT'S SAD. EIGHT YEARS AGO, YOU COULDN'T CATCH ME SAYING ANY OF THIS, NOW LOOK AT US." Tossing the glass plate into the soapy hot water, Manhattan wiped her wet hands on her ripped jean crying. A few tears fell down my jawn, I swear man, I hated seeing Hat cry. As much crying as she did, it still fucked with my head. With every tear that stumbled down her face, I felt the pain that pumped from Manhattan's soul.

"Hat, i-I'm sorry, I swear, I never meant to hurt you. You think I like seeing you hurt and shit, fuck no!! That shit fucks with every time I can't hold or even touch you at night. Believe it or not, since you left me, I've been sleeping alone and I hate it. We both know I can have any woman in my bed, but I rather it be you."

"How can you utter those words, Clover, when you've been hurting me for years? You know it's times I look at you and I don't recognize the man I once loved. Now, you're just some random jawn to me, thanks to you. You can let yourself out, I can't even look at you anymore." Still crying, Manhattan wiped her runny nose charging down the hallway. Once her bedroom door slammed shut, I sighed covering my face. I could no longer have a decent conversation with Manhattan and that was my fault, damn. I couldn't leave with us on these kind of terms, so, I slowly walked down the hall quickly trying to gather a few words to say. Once I made it to her door, I softly knocked saying, "Baby, please open the door. I know you don't want to talk to me, but I really need to fix this."

"Fix what, Clover, the damage is done? Some things will never be the same and that's all YOUR fault. Do you really think I want to move on from you, this shit kills me every day." She sobbed.

"Fix us, the mistakes I made, and everything else I need to fix." Turning the doorknob, Manhattan still had the door locked.

"We're here, alone, just Katober and me, and I hate it!!! When you're not with Katober, you're all she's talk about, Clover. That little girl loves her some Clover Porter, just like I used to love you.

"You can still love me, Hat, we can start over." I spoke, but Manhattan didn't say anything. For a minute, it was dead silence, until the door finally opened. My heart raced, I wasn't sure what was about to go down.

"It's not supposed to be like this, BUT you made it this way. You can't fix mistakes, they shouldn't have been made in the first place." Manhattan replied. Staring Hat deep in her eyes, for the first time, I both couldn't say anything. For everything I did wrong, she had me feeling it all in this moment.

Chapter 17 (August 2016)

Manhattan: Clover Porter.

The message flashed across my screen saying. I was eager to text Hat back, even if it was something simple.

Clover: What's up, Hat?"

Manhattan: What is my child doing?

Clover: We're watching Mickey Mouse Club House, of course.

Manhattan: Oh, okay, I'll let you two continue what ya'll were doing. Tell my baby I love her, thanks.

Clover: Of course and you're welcome.

Tossing the phone next to me, I smiled like a lil' kid.

"You're mama said she loves you." Looking down at Katober who had her head planted on my chest. Spending time like this with Katober made me realize it wasn't nothing in those streets, but rats, hoes, and problems. Lately, I've put all the hustling on my yong bols, I slowly had to make my way out of the game. Harlem on the other hand, wasn't feeling that at all, but my decision was final. The times I was out creeping with Deaux should have been spent with my family. Too bad I couldn't get any of that time back, but now I gave every second I could to Katober.

"I love her too, daddy, but when is mommy coming home?"

"After work, baby, she'll be here to pick you up." I spoked.

"No, daddy, when is mommy coming back home?" She asked and this time, I knew what she meant. The questioned caught me by surprise and I wasn't sure if I should lie to my daughter or tell her the hurtful truth.

"Uummm, eventually baby, okay?"

"Okay."

Ring! Ring! Ring!

Stretching and yawning, I grabbed my iPhone from the table to see who was calling me. The number wasn't saved, but I knew exactly who it was. Clearing my throat to say, 'yyooooooooo,', but shorty was already running her mouth.

"Damn, Clover, a simple text message would have been nice. I haven't spoken to you in three days." Sitting on my couch rubbing my face, Olivia, my new lil' friend, annoyed me through the phone like always.

"What?" I questioned her, laughing, which probably pissed her off more than what she was.

"You heard what the fuck I said, Clove, why haven't I heard from you in days? I thought we were going to the movies or something tomorrow?" Olivia questioned.

"I thought so too, but I changed my mind, shorty."

"Well, you could have told me you changed your mind. Can I see you today though, please?" She begged in a joking way. I was lying like it was going out of style. A nigga had no intentions on going anywhere, especially with Olivia or any other woman. Well, unless it was Manhattan and by the way things officially were between us, that wasn't happening. The night of Katober's party, I thought things Manhattan I were getting back together. Maybe it was because we made sweet love, but I was wrong. It's like every time Hat stared at me, she couldn't get pass the mistakes I've made. I couldn't blame her, I probably would be the same way if the shoe was on the other foot.

Manhattan portrayed that she was happy with Chris and had everyone fooled. Deep down inside, I knew she wasn't because Chris wasn't me. It didn't matter how good he was to her, some people couldn't make you feel how others did. If she didn't have her homegirls in her ear, maybe she would have taken me back.

"What?"

"Ugh, I asked if I can see you today?"

"Naw, I'm good, I have shit to do today."

"Damn, Spitta, not even for a few minutes?" She questioned.

"Not even for a few minutes, but I hit you up later." I ended the call without giving Olivia time to say anything.

Olivia Jenkins, a twenty-seven year old jawn I met on Popular Street two weeks ago and O was head over heels already. Shorty was from Southwest Philly, born and raised, O's name ranged through Philly like the Liberty Bell. O was a stripper, worked at Onyx, and she was proud of that. The strip club was all she spoked about, seem like that was her biggest accomplishment. Olivia reminded a lot of Deaux, which is why I couldn't fuck with her the long way. O was cool though, I treated her like she was the big homie, but Olivia hated that. I wasn't looking for love, a new woman, or anyone to replace Manhattan. Life without Manhattan was……..different, but I slowly became adjusted to it. Even though I was ready to make a serious change, little did I know, Hat love wasn't the same for me. She made that clear every time I saw and spoke to her

While I was home depressed, Manhattan lived the best life she could live. Every time I stalked her social media, Manhattan was out thotin' with Kat. Now, she was fo'sho going on dates with niggas here and there. Manhattan was a different woman now, the kind of woman I never thought I would turn her into to. The bitch wore shorter dresses and she even cut her hair. That was her way of cutting of the bad in her life, which was me. Manhattan gained a lil' weight, but it was in the right places. Man, I missed her so much, but Manhattan didn't want to hear that.

As I flipped through the channels, a knock on the door stopped me. From the couch, I had a clear view of the living room window and I would see who it was. Doing a light jog to the door, I then unlocked it letting Smoke in. It was hot as fuck outside, so, I rushed to close the door. The sweat was already forming under my armpits and forehead. Smoke had sweat covering his body, but he didn't waste any time using his rag to wipe himself off in the cold air.

"Uncle Clerk!" Katober whispered from the couch.

"What's up, bro?" Smoke quickly dapping me down to place his full attention on Katober. Smoke loved his niece and since Ryker recently found out she was pregnant, Smoke wanted all the practice he needed.

"Shit, chillin' with the seed."

"Katober, hey uncle baby. You look so pretty today, I know your daddy didn't dress you like that." Kissing Katober on her forehead, Smoke made her laugh just like he always does.

"Actually, I did, Youtube can teach you a lot when you actually pay attention." I laughed stroking Katober's long ponytails. I wasn't the best hairstylist, but I could hook up my baby girl with three pigtails a tie it down with some pretty pink bows.

"Uncle Clerk, do you like my hair?" She asked.

"You know I do, pretty girl." Smoke smiled giving Katober a kiss on her cheek and she blushed.

"Baby, go in your room so Uncle Smoke and I can talk." I said sitting on the couch.

"Okay, daddy." Katober said running off. Once she closed her door, I flopped on the couch continuing to flip through the channels.

"Daddy duties, I see." Smoke smirked staring down the hall while he sat across from me. Nodding my head, I replied, "you know it."

"Where is Hat on this Sunday afternoon?" Smoke questioned, I had a feeling her already knew where she was.

"She's at work, but she's 'supposed' to be going on a date after that." I laughed shaking my head, but Smoke's eyes widen.

"On a date with who, YOU?" He laughed joking around, but I didn't find that shit funny.

"Nah, with some nigga that ain't Chris, but I think she's lying. She'll tell me anything just to piss me off." I spoked.

"The question is, ARE you pissed?" Smoke asked laughing.

"Hell yea, I'm pissed, wouldn't you be pissed if Ryker stunted on you like that? Have you been watching Hat on Snapchat, looking like she belongs in a UGK or Lil' Boosie video."

"Yea, I see her, but what did you think would eventually happen, bro? Hat really loved you, she took a lot of shit from you and that she moved on you're mad?"

"Man, I don't want to hear that, you would be the same way!"

"Correction, lil' bro, you know I take my lick like the big dog I am. If you wanted to fuck around, you should have let shorty go to do your shit." Said Smoke.

"I didn't want to let her go."

"You sound real selfish. That woman is single, you know she has the right to date anyone her heart desires. Just like you were doing when yall were together."

"Don't act like I was out there fucking every smut. I just fucked Deaux from time to time." I uttered.

"What, from time to time, mmaaannnnnnnn, are you serious right now? Is that what you're calling it nowadays?" Smoke laughed.

"Forget that, man, what if she's serious?" I asked Smoke as if he was a mind reader.

"Lil' Brody, you made your bed, continue to sleep in it."

"Yea, whatever, I don't mind sleeping in the bed I made, just not alone." I replied.

"See, that's the gag, you gotta sleep in it alone. I've been there twice before and I'll never go back to that." He answered.

"Really though, what am I supposed to do? I haven't had sex since Hat and I had sex for Koko's birthday. I really thought we were getting back together, but something or someone always reminds her of what I've done to her."

"See, that's the thing with making mistakes, you can never really depart from them. You think I wanted to kill that nigga in Germantown in 2000, no, I didn't. Every time I see his girl and kids, I can feel his blood splattering on my face and shelltoes. I swear, Clover, I really didn't want to kill. Seeing his three kids growing up without a father because of ME, will always remind me of my mistake." Smoke answered.

"Damn, I think about it like that. That explains why she can't even look at me half the time."

"That could be why, but I need to holla at you about something else. Something I know fucking well you ain't doing." He laughed.

"What's up?" I questioned.

"What am I hearing about you fuckin' with the lil' stripper hoe out of southwest?"

"Stripper hoe, who are you talking about?"

"Uumm, I think she goes by Champagne, but she more like a malt liquor."

"Who, O?" I asked knowing damn well he was talking about her.

"Nigga, yea, Olivia, but what the fuck is that?"

"It ain't about nothing, but clearly she can't keep her fuckin' mouth shut."

"Regardless if she can't keep her mouth shut, why are you dealing with that?" Smoke questioned.

"Be cool, it's not what you think. The lil' bitch loves to smoke, sometimes I need a lil' joint to blow and kick shit with. That's it, trust me, ain't nothing else going on with O and me. Besides, I have her pumping coke all through Onyx for me, without giving her the dick." I laughed loudly making Smoke smack his lips. Since he was faithful and junk, he didn't want to hear the foolish I often uttered.

"You better be careful with that lil' hoe, I heard she belongs on the police department. That bitch does more rattin' than John Gotti, that's facts."

"I haven't exposed her to ANYTHING. The few times we blew was in my car riding through the hood. You know I had to get me a Philly cheese and I didn't even buy her one. I literally heard her stomach growling." I laughed.

"Typical, Spitta, always and only thinking about himself."

"Yea, whatever the fuck that's supposed to mean." I spoked.

"Aye, I also heard Deaux can't stand Olivia already, I'm guessing you're still fucking lil' homie." Smoke shook his head saying.

"This time you're wrong, I haven't touched Deaux in a minute. Most of the time when she answers, I don't call. I told her dumb it's over and I don't want to fool with her anymore."

"Bro, you can't look me in my eyes and tell me you ain't dicking Deaux down."

"Boy, I put that on mama I haven't fucked that hoe since then. Deaux ain't shit to me and was never shit to me, it's about time she realized that."

"You say all that, but you made that smut feel like she did. Maybe you're not fucking her, I don't know because I'm not holding the camera."

"Like I told you, it's no fucking between Deaux and me. Can we talk about something because Deaux shouldn't be the topic of discussion."

"Cool with me my nigga, you know I never liked Deaux and I'm damn sure not trying to get to know Olivia on any level." Smoke said.

"Me either, I should get out the house tonight instead of sittin' in here depressed. I should be surrounded by some fuckin' bad ass strippers tonight. You rolling with me or not?" I questioned Smoke.

"Hhhmm, to go the strip club and leave my pregnant girlfriend at home? I think the fuck not, nigga, but I'm out. Hit me up later."

"Bet, I love you, boy." I said as Smoke dapped me down standing to him feet.

"I love you too."

***

Besides going to jail a few times on some petty charges, I never really laid down in the can for longer than a few days. This jawn, it might be different because Hat wasn't in the picture to handle my business. By the look of things, these few hours might turn into days, then weeks. It felt weird without her, to keep it a stack. Before I could tell the officer my jumpsuit size, Manhattan was there with the bond money to get me out. How the fuck did I get stopped in traffic with a dirty pistol while on parole? Right before I was supposed to drop of a package, but my gut feeling fold me something else. That was truly some flunky shit that never happened before. I began to think someone had voodoo on me or it was a case of bad luck. Either way, I couldn't change what happened, I could only deal with it. It's crazy how before the cops pulled me over I received six phone calls from Olivia, then it stopped. Something told me that bitch had a lot to do with it and Smoke was right about her.

Deaux on the other hand, well, that was a fuckin' different jawn. This joce made me realize how stupid the bitch was. I haven't fucked with her in months, but she still came to my rescue. Slow like she moved, I could have kept Deaux where the fuck she was. Nothing, but a pretty face and fat ass in tight jeans. If she kept snow out of her nose, Deaux would be able to handle my fuckin' business like Manhattan did. I guess my mom was right, Manhattan was the best thing to happen to me.

It took Deaux a week to leave her homegirl's house in Germantown, all those bitches did was snort powder and pop pills. Deaux didn't know what to do, she never had to handle any of my important business. Deaux hated to do this, but she had to be the one putting her pride to the side to holla at the one person she envied.

As Manhattan hopped out of her ride with a few grocery bags in her hand, Deaux approached her brushing her fingertips against red nose. Manhattan took one long at Deaux by lower the brown sun shades on her face. Deaux looked a messed, which made Manhattan laughed, but she continued walking to the house. Like a puppy with an attitude, she followed behind Manhattan wearing the same jeans and cropped top she had on two days ago.

"Manhattan." Said Deaux, but Manhattan ignored her.

"Manhattan!"

"Deaux, why are you here," Manhattan exhaled turning around with an attitude. Deaux flared her pointy nose sizing Manhattan up and down like she was the problem.

"Look, I ain't here on some friendly shit, I'm only here because I need your help!"

"Girl, bye, you don't need my help or shit from me. Now, gon, head about your business!!"

"I need your help getting Clove out of jail. I never had to do annnnyyyy of this shit and I don't know what I'm doing," sliding her hands into the back pockets of her black skinny jeans, Deaux waited for Manhattan to reply. Instead, she dropped her bags on the chair laughing, then said, "that's not my problem, hunn, Clover and his bid don't have shit to do with me. You wanted to take him from me, but I gave him to you instead. Now you have to deal with him and getting him out of jail, congrats, it's all a package."

"You didn't give me anything, we all know where Clover heart is. The same person he's with now, which is me," Deaux flipped her short bob laughing, but Manhattan laughed as well. Deaux's false words didn't mean a shit to her, she knew none of it was true.

Removing the Chanel sun glasses completely from her face, Manhattan took a few steps closer to Deaux with a big grin on her face. Still playing with her nose, Deaux cocked her head to the side waiting for Manhattan to hit her with facts like always.

"It's like every time I see you, you ALWAYS have this cold, baby girl. You need to get that checked and you're looking a lil' thin in these streets, but that's another conversation for a different time. Back to what I was saying though. I don't WANT Clover Porter anymore, so, I gave him to you, I knew you would be grateful for my problems, headache, and sloppy seconds. I'm happy without him, but he just doesn't get the picture. Maybe once I'm married he'll see it, but knowing him, he still won't."

"You can't call it sloppy seconds when I was eating off the plate too," Deaux said with a smirk on her face, which made Hat laugh louder nodding her head.

"Touche, touche, mama always said feed the poor and homeless. Let's get this clear for the last time, you didn't take anything from me. Side chicks are winning this year and in your head, Clover was the best prize you could ever get! Since no one else wants your ass or would make you into their woman. What I can say positive is that ….. I wish you two the BEST IN life and have fun doing whatever yall do. Oh, yea, tell him stop calling me after hours and don't drop the damn soap. We all know pretty boys like Clov have to fight for their bootyhole in jail," Manhattan giggled while walking away leaving Deaux with a dick look on her face. Once Deaux gathered her thoughts, she said, "you're always calling me the side chick—"

"That's because you are the side chick, dummy," Manhattan reached for her bags unlocking the door. Before she could take a step, Deaux uttered, "you swear you're so much better than me, Manhattan, but you ain't."

"Bitch, yes, I am," she laughed.

"That right there tell me you are no different or better than me. We're both in love with the same man and both refuse to let go because of the what ifs. You're always saying he was YOUR man, well let me tell you something about YOUR man. I fucked YOUR man in YOUR bed while YOU laid there crying like a fuckin' fool. You just laid under the covers instead of getting your dumb ass out of the room. What kind of woman are you really," she chuckled louder. Deaux thought her words would cut Manhattan deep, but they didn't. I had already cut her so deep that nothing could hurt her anymore. She just stood tall with a smirk on her face. Deaux continued to laugh waiting for Manhattan to swing a punch. She would be waiting forever, Manhattan wasn't a fighter and wouldn't hurt a fly.

"The difference between you and I is that I finally know better and I'm doing better. Where was nothing good coming from being with Clover Porter, we both know that. What kind of woman gets in another woman's bed while she's in it? That's the better question, smut! You're more disgusting than him if you ask me."

"I didn't ask you!"

"I'm telling you though because it seems like no one else is telling you the truth. I would never get involved with a man who is taken, that's what also makes us different. You don't care who you get in bed with, you'll get in bed with the devil if you have to. Where the fuck are your standards and common sense, Deaux? When are you going to realize Clover is only using you and stringing you along? When are you going to realize he'll never get over me? I've moved on with my life, but he still haven't let go. How many charges will you take for him, this nigga make you bond yourself out!! It doesn't matter how much coke, crack, pills, or heroine you stash in your bra, he will NEVER BE WITH YOU!"

"You're saying all that, but he's with me now," she smiled.

"No, he's in jail, sweetheart, he's with no one. Once again, if he was with you why is he still holding on to me? I've moved out of the house and he hasn't moved you in yet. I tried giving him his keys back, but he has every issue when it's to get them. Please, teach your man how to move on. That's the only thing I'll ask YOU to do. I'm not interested in any of his sob stories, how sorry he is, or apologies he sends through Smoke or Kansas. I know he was sorry when he got in bed with you. Now get the fuck from around here before you see a side of me you didn't know existed," slamming the door in Deaux's face, Manhattan felt good.

She was slightly pissed, but it felt good to tell the one person off who ruined her life. Not once did I tell Deaux we were together or going to be together. I knew she would come through since Manhattan avoided most of my calls. Even when I called to speak to Katober, I tried to make small contact with Manhattan, but she wasn't having it. Since she assumed I lied about still dealing with Deaux and hearing the rumors about Olivia, Manhattan made it clear that we would never EVER get back together. It's crazy how she 'moved' on, but was upset at me for only kickin' it with a lil' smut. It didn't matter how much I attempted to explain myself, Manhattan didn't want to hear shit I had to say. If her stupid ass would listen and not talk to fuckin' much, she would understand all this wasn't what she thought. Until then, I was digging my grave deeper finding myself further from her good side.

"Stupid ass bitch!" Manhattan said to herself as she pulled the milk and cereal from the plastic grocery store bag. At first, the petty argument with Deaux was funny, but the more she thought about it, it wasn't funny. Now Manhattan was ready to pull Deaux's fuckin' head off her neck.

Ring! Ring! Ring!

Stopping in her tracks, Manhattan placed the second bag of grocery on her kitchen table searching for her purse. Once she found it, Manhattan shuffled through her purse searching for her phone. Staring at the screen, she smiled because it was Honesty calling. Manhattan had to tell Honesty about this shit and make her laugh. Run ins like this was all so familiar to Honesty, but now she could laugh it off. Just like I was a thing of Manhattan's past, so was Harlem. He took it to a whole different level pulling some stunts I would never pull. The same man who left his wife for his big homie's woman was now stalking his wife. Plenty of times I called Harlem just to holla at him, but he was too busy creeping around her and Juelz home in the middle of the night.

"Hello?" Manhattan said with the phone on speaker. Then she shuffled through her purse again, searching for her headphones. Finding them quickly, Manhattan didn't waste any time stuffing the white earbuds into her ears.

"Hey, chick, what'cha doing?" Honesty questioned.

"Girl, I just got home from the grocery store, but what are you doing?" Manhattan questioned.

"I'm getting ready for my big day tomorrow. I have to carter this sweet sixteen tomorrow for some rapper's daughter out of Queens. I don't know the lil' cat, but the kids do and they are excited about tomorrow. Since they are so excited, I'm making there lil' asses work." Honesty laughed.

"Ohhh yea, I forgot you told me about that. What's his name again?" Manhattan questioned.

"His name is Boy Young, why is it Boy Young, I don't know, but he's making that dough. This nigga gave me a $4,000 tip."

"$4,000 for a tip, damn, girl, what kind of catering are you doing?" Manhattan laughed.

"I don't know myself, but I sure hope this help builds my resume a little more. He said he would recommend me to some of his friends, they need catering for a few upcoming events."

"That's good, but I sure hope they aren't crazy and wild." Manhattan described.

"Girl, they can be Mike Tyson crazy if they're giving tips like this. I'll just pack a blicky when I go to the events." Honesty chuckled.

"Do your shit, but let me tell you about this bitch!"

"Who, bitch, spill the tea, you know my cup is always empty." Honesty laughed.

"Deaux's ugly ass, this bitch shows up to my house trying to ask ME FOR HELP!"

"What, help for what?" Honesty questioned.

"She needs my help with getting Clover out of jail. That shit didn't go too well, she was about two seconds from getting hit in the head with a gallon of milk."

"Oh my God, bitch I was I was down there! What the fuck was said, spill the tea!!"
"We past a lot of words, some shit we both needed to hear. Clover swore up and down that he was done with Deaux, but clearly, that was a lie. Now I'm hearing about him fucking with some lil' stripper hoe name Olivia." Leaning against the countertop, Manhattan ran her fingers threw her hair exhaling. A few tears started to fall from her eyes, but Hat rushed to wipe them away. She wasn't in the mood to let her emotions get the best of her today or any other day for that matter.

"Ookkayyyy, why does that matter to you? You've moved on, right?" Honesty asked, but Manhattan didn't say anything.

"Heellooo, Hat, are you there?"

"Yea, Hon, I'm here, I guess it matters because a small part of me still thought he would have changed. No one knew that, but I feel like a damn fool for thinking Clover would change. I heard this new bitch isn't that much different from Clover, I guess he has a type. Clearly I'm not his type at all, I don't know what I was thinking when I got in bed with him. Stupid ass, stupid ass Manhattan!!!" Slapping her forehead, Manhattan released more tears from her eyes attempting to cry silently. Honesty would be the last person to judge Manhattan, but she still felt crazy for crying.

"You did what??" Honesty asked, even she was shocked.

"Don't jump down my throat, but Clover and I had sex the night of Katober's party. It wasn't supposed to happen, but we both were in our feelings. I didn't want it to happen, trust me. I love him, Honesty and I don't know what to do!!"

"I know that feeling all too well, Hat, I did the exact same thing you did. Harlem hit me with this lil' thing about we needed to spend some time together for the sake of the kids. Lord knows that I didn't want to go because of my feelings but I wanted co-parenting to go smoothly, so I agreed. I really went because I wanted to spend time with Harlem and save my marriage. Of course Clover had me in my feelings reminiscing about the past. I wanted to be with Harlem so bad, Manhattan, I thought the whole divorce thing went out of the window that night, but it wasn't."

"Moving on isn't something I want to do, Hon, but everyone is pressuring me to do. Why can't I just be alone until I figure everything out? I don't understand why it has to be so damn HARD!! Then I have to look in Deaux's face and she thinks she can tell me about Clover!! The nerve of her to tell me we are alike, that hoe and I are not alike in ANY way!"

"I know you don't like fighting Hat, but I'll do it for you. Let me beat Deaux's ass one time, that's all she needs. I know I'm a bad bitch, but you're too pretty to fight garbage like that. I'll drag that bitch up and down Broad Street." Honesty uttered.

"That's becoming very tempting, but if I go to jail, I would be too shame."

"Look, I'm not shame to go to jail. I'm so sick of that girl and I'm not the one who's fucking Spitta. I can't tell you be with Spitta and I can't tell you to not be with him. When you love someone, YOU LOVE them. Especially when you not only invested time, you've invested a child and love in this person. Some people and things are like bad habits that you can't shake off. The only advice I can give you is to do what your heart tells you and fuck what anyone has to say. I love you girl and I'm going to always be here for you. I don't care how many times you cry over him, I'll listen every single time.

"Thanks, girl, I love you too." Chuckling while wiping her tears away, Manhattan's attention was caught by the sound of a car pulling into her driveway. Rushing to peek through the blinds, she didn't recognize the car.

"Uuummm, Hon, let me call you right back."

"Okay, girl, bye." Manhattan ended the call as carefully unlock the door to open it.

"Chris, what's up?" Manhattan was a little surprised to Chris standing at her door with a single white rose and a big cheesy smile on his face. Her cheeks became red and warm, I don't understand why she was so nervous. It's not it was her first time seeing this clown in the flesh.

"Hello, beautiful, this is for you." Handing Manhattan the rose, Chris had Manhattan blushing even more. Even the kiss on the cheek had her feeling like a kid again.

"Hey, what's up, I thought you were out of town until the weekend?" Manhattan questioned Chris while taking a sniff of the rose.

"I was, but I had a change of plans. I wanted you to be the first person I see." Leaning against the door with a little smirk on his face, Chris held Manhattan hand. She couldn't control the way she blushed, but being happy made her feel good.

"Aawwww, that's sweet, but how was your trip to New Jersey?" Manhattan questioned.

"New Jersey was good, but I missed you a little. I think it would have been better if you were there." He laughed.

"I bet it would have been, but come in, come in," gently grabbing Chris by the wrist, Manhattan lead Chris into the house which surprised him. Manhattan never invited him in her house before, I guess things were changing.

"Me, come inside, wow, that's a first time."

"Oh, whatever." Manhattan laughed closing the door.

"Where is your daughter?" Chris questioned making Manhattan sighed as she flopped on the couch next to him. Then she ran her fingers through her hair saying, "with Clover's mother, but I'm going to get her in thirty minutes."

"Oh, okay, are you good, ma?"

"I'm perfectly fine, but why did you ask me that? Do I look like I'm not fine?" Manhattan laughed.

"Oh, trust me, you look more than fine, but your daughter's father did go to jail. Maybe you are feeling some type of way or at least on the strength of her."

"To be honest, I don't feel anyway. When she asks about her father, I tell her he's at work. Besides, it's not he's going to be in there for a while."

"Okay, I understand that, but how is your day going so far?"

"My day, it's going, I really can't complain, but I want to talk to you about something."

"Okay, talk about what?" Chris asked.

"You and I, and where are we coming with this." Manhattan stated.

"Where are we going with this?"

"I don't know, but think I'm playing with you. It's just......complicated and we shouldn't rush into anything. I can't take getting hurt again and I wouldn't want to hurt anyone how I was hurt."

"Shorty, I feel that, but where is this coming from? Does it has anything to do Spitta going to jail, be real with me?" Chris asked.

"No, it doesn't at all and I don't want you to think that. It has to do with me and how I'm feeling."

"Okay and like I told you at iHop we don't have to rush into anything. This is your show and I'm following you." Kissing Manhattan on the lips, Chris had Hat eating out of the palm of his hands. I had to admit it, he was a smooth talking somebody. That's the kind of jawn I wanted my daughter to stay far away from because he could talk her into doing ANY!

"I know, but I just wanted us to be on the same page, with everything." Manhattan spoke.

"We are on the same page, we don't have a reason not to be on the same page. I like you a lot, Manhattan, regardless if you don't feel the way I do. I enjoy your company and being in your presence."

"I feel the same way, Chris." Pushing herself a little closer to Chris, Manhattan stared at him with a throbbing pussy. She wanted to remain the lady she was, but Chris was looking too good in Manhattan's eyes. She began to kiss Chris again, but this time, she sat on his lap in the straddle position. Chris sat there like a fool not knowing what to do. He had all that ass in his hands, but didn't touch it. Maybe he thought Manhattan was tripping and didn't want to overstep his boundaries.

"What are you doing, shorty, you don't think this is moving too fast?" He whispered nibbling on her ear. Even though he wasn't sure if Hat wanted to have sex, his ashy hands still traveled under her low cut shirt. Caressing her full breast for a few seconds, Chris then grabbed Manhattan's ass. Pulling her shirt over her head, Manhattan tossed the black shirt to the floor and stood to her feet. Manhattan bit her bottom lip as she stood to her feet making Chris do the same.

"I don't think we're moving too fast, I call it perfect timing." Manhattan softly grabbed Chris by his dick, which was standing tall. Then she lead him into room where she didn't waste any time coming out of her clothes. Before you knew it, Chris and Manhattan were naked, touching one another in places I never thought she would touch another man. Manhattan lied butt ass naked across her bed, ready to give her body to a joe she hardly knew. It's crazy how from day one she made it clear to me she wasn't ready` for any sex, but gave Chris her body after a short period of time.

With his two fingers massaging Manhattan's clitoris, her legs were wide open as she moaned loudly for Chris to slide his dick in her pussy. He continued to tease her until Manhattan couldn't take it anymore. Manhattan begged for his dick, she literally begged for it. I guess the morals she had finally went out of the window.

Chapter 18

Tonight was Ryker's birthday and everyone she loved gathered at her favorite joint, Vernick food and Drinks. Tonight was also my first day home, but I wasn't sure if I wanted to be in the presence of too many people. Besides, seeing Manhattan would have made me feel like a sucker fool. I was missing shorty badly, but that didn't mean anything to her. Those three weeks away from her and Katober felt like hell, but I was glad to be home. Deaux was no help on getting me out, thank Allah for Smoke and Kansas.

Entering the building feeling like all eyes were on her, which they were, Manhattan's heart raced like crazy. She tried to ignore the whispers and stares, but they always fucked with her jawn. It's like my sweet baby couldn't win or lose when it came to love and her soul. Manhattan was talked about if she was with me and Manhattan was talked about when she wasn't with me. People had their own speculations on why we weren't together but that wasn't anyone's business, but ours. Shid, if any one asked me, I told them we were still together and everything was Gucci between us. That lie didn't hold much weight when people saw Manhattan booed up with that Chris nigga. She told Kansas they weren't official, but they damn sure looked like it. On top of that, Manhattan made sure she told everyone we were no longer together. This time, I had to get my lady back, cutting off Olivia and Deaux was a must. Dropping them hoes wasn't a problem for me anyways.

"Hat just walked in." Someone whispered from a far, but Manhattan ignored the comment.

The one person who mainly had their eyes on Manhattan was Marcy. Since she heard Manhattan and I were no longer together, Marcy attempted to reach out. Too bad Manhattan wasn't trying to hear anything Marcy had to say or wasn't trying to mend anything with Marcy or anyone else in the Mullen family Knowing Marcy, she only wanted to tell Manhattan I told you so a dozen of times. To keep it a stack, Manhattan was probably tired of everyone telling her.

"Hey, Hat, what's up, sis?" Smoke approached Manhattan giving her a hug and a smile. His droopy eyes told her he was either drunk, high, or a lil' bit of both.

"Hey, bro, what up?" Manhattan said as she pulled her short dress down.

"You look nice, sis."

"Thanks and you don't look bad yourself." Slightly tugging on Smoke creased white Polo dressed shirt.

"I do a lil' something, but where is your plus one? I thought you were bringing Chris?" He asked.

"He was coming, but he's at his house, we decided it was best he didn't come." Said Manhattan shrugging her shoulders.

"Word to, why, you know I don't have a problem with dude?"

"I know that, Smoke, but I didn't want things to be awkward tonight. Tonight is about Ryker having a good time for her birthday, not me and my men." Manhattan laughed. They acted like Manhattan was a celebrity, all she needed was to be on The Shaderoom.

"Girrrrllllllllll, it's about time you made it here. It's already 7:00 pm."

"I know and I'm sorry, Ryker."

"Where is Chris?" She asked.

"Like I told Smoke, Chris is at home, I didn't need the extra attention tonight. He did say to tell you happy birthday."

"Awww, tell him thanks, I wish he would have come." She stated.

"Damn, baby, you're really rocking this lil' dress. Where did you get this from again, Fashion what?" Smoke asked making Manhattan and Ryker laugh.

"It's called Fashion Nova, baby."

"Well I'm trying to push them panties to the side in that Fashion Nova dress." Smoke grinned while he pulled Ryker closer to him by grabbing her hips. Ryker began to blush, Smoke still had that kind of jawn on her. They began to tongue kiss exchanging heavy saliva making Manhattan uncomfortable. Their public display of affection was always a lot to handle, but Manhattan laughed it off like always.

"Uuumm, ard, you two, we are in a public place. Save the love faces for the bedroom." Manhattan stated still feeling uncomfortable.

"The way this liquor have me feeling, I don't think I can wait for the bedroom. Baby I'm trying get some of that pregnant pussy in the bathroom stall." Chuckling a little while grabbing a handful of Ryker's ass, she squealed a little laughing. She loved when my brother did freaky things like this, especially in public. Even though Ryker got on my last nerve, she looked good tonight in her all black dress. It was simple, but the royal blue sling back heels and mahogany colored bundles made her stand out. Yea, she stood out, that was until Manhattan walked in the room.

Wearing a short haltered top hot pink dress with lime green six inch opened toe shoes, and her gold clutched tucked under her arm, Manhattan stood tall. Her tone legs and muscular things probably had plenty of dicks on hard tonight. With her blond hair cut into a blunt bob, Manhattan was not only looking like a new woman, she felt like one. To top it off, she wore that nude lipstick that I adored.

"See, jawns like you are the reason why I hate using public bathrooms." Manhattan replied.

"Hey, Manhattan, can I talk to you for a minute or two?" Manhattan entire mood switched when she felt those fingers touch her elbow. By knowing voice and afraid look on Smoke and Ryker's face, Manhattan knew it was Marcy. She couldn't control how her eyes rolled on their own or how her heart raced.

"Why is she talking to me?" Manhattan stared at Ryker feeling like she was a part of this. When Manhattan said she didn't want to talk to Marcy or anyone in her family, she meant that shit.

"Hat, talk to your sister, it's my birthday and that would be the best gift ever!" Ryker begged.

"Damn bitch, I brought you that new pot set you wanted, that wasn't enough for you?" Manhattan asked, but Ryker smacked her lips not replying.

"Come on, Hat, talk to your sister." Smoke implied, exhaling loudly.

"Manhataan, please, I just want to talk to you for a few minutes." Marcy begged. After debating with herself her a few seconds, Manhattan finally turned around sizing Marcy up and down. Marcy had a huge smile on her face, but Hat damn sure didn't. Shit, Marcy, even reached out to hug Manhattan, but Hat wasn't with all that. It made Marcy feel bad, but now she got a taste of what Manhattan felt over the pass years.

"Well, we'll let yall talk alone, come on, baby," Smoke carefully grabbed Ryker by the hand leading her back to the table. Even though Ryker wanted Marcy and Manhattan to speak alone, Ryker kept her eyes glued to them.

Marcy was nervous, but Manhattan was already irritated and ready to end the conversation that hadn't started.

"Hat, you look, AMAZING, like always, I love your hair. I never thought you would cut your hair or wear weave. You can rock any look, I always said that." Marcy reached her hand out to touch Manhattan's blunt cut, but Hat stepped to the side. With her arms folded across her chest with an attitude, Manhattan replied, "uh-huh."

"I thought you would have had Katober with you. She's getting so damn big, I can't believe it."

"Yep, that's what happen when you age." Hat spoke in a firm tone, she had no reason to speak nicely to Marcy.

"I would love to meet her, Smoke and Ryker showed me some pictures of her yesterday. I saw them at the mall, spending bands like always." Ryker awkwardly rubbing her hands together and smiling. Hat knew exactly how to make Marcy feel uncomfortable in the smallest ways.

"Girl, you could have met her years ago, like the day she was born. I remember blowing your phone up and you denied every single call. All because I pushed out a baby by Clover Porter."

"I know, Hat and I'm sorry, it's been too long and I apologize again." Marcy insisted.

"Fuck an apology, Marcy, I NEEDED YOU THERE, but you weren't. You weren't there because you were too busy worrying about who I was laid up with. You talked all that mess about Clover when we first, but you failed to tell me why you REALLY didn't like him." Manhattan said.

"He, he told you that?"

"Yea, he told me everything, but it SHOULD have been YOU telling me. What fucked my head up is that I had to hear that shit from him. You down talked Clover so much because you were jealous and not because you wanted the best for me." Hat shouted through a tight mouth.

"You're right I was jealous, but it's not like I was the only person who felt that way."

"Girl, fuck how everyone else felt!!" Hat slightly shouted drawing attention to her and Marcy, but Manhattan didn't care.

"No one ever saw Clover so crazy in love until he met you. Then he started cheating on you and I was confused." She expressed.

"It was nothing for you to be confused about! Him cheating with Deaux had nothing to do with you disowning me!!"

"Yes, it does, Manhattan and one day you're going to have to be a woman and admit that. Clover had you in these jawns looking like a fool, yo. Do you think anyone wants to see their little sister getting treated in a random smut from the projects? Fuck no, you're a queen and that's how I want to witness a man treat you."

"It's crazy how you wanted the same man. You did a lot of shit talking about him because you wanted him, but you couldn't have him. I HAVE HIM AND EVEN WHEN I'M TRYING TO GET RIDE OF HIM, I CAN'T!" Now, Manhattan was doing a lil' more shouting. Including Ryker and Smoke, everyone stared at Manhattan and Marcy. They were startled by her loud outburst and Ryker wanted to interrupt the conversation, but Smoke stopped her saying, "No, bae, let them handle their shit, it's been long overdue." Manhattan wasn't much of a fighter, but Ryker knew things could escalate at this point.

"What if they start fighting, Smoke?" Ryker rubbed her belly asking and with a smirk on Smoke's face, he said, "just hold Marcy down so Hat can beat that ass."

"Ard, big homie, I love the way you think." She laughed a little.

"Manhattan, it wasn't only that, I really felt like you deserved way better than Clover. He did exactly what I knew he would do, I only tried to protect you. Why can't you see and understand that?" Marcy questioned.

"Because, Marcy, I didn't need you to protect me. I can protect myself, what I needed was my sister to be there with me!! Okay, you got that? When Clover was doing lord knows what with Deaux and I was home alone with a crying baby, THAT'S when I needed you. Not for you to tell I told you so every time he cheated on me, which we all know was often. What I needed you to do is to not play follow the leader with ma and dad. What I won't do is hold a grudge against you, but I won't forever forget how you let me alone. I done caught a fucking headache and I'm done with this conversation." Before Marcy could say anything, Manhattan walked off with tight jaws. She rushed into the restroom and Ryker followed behind her waddling in her heels. Marcy did the same, but Ryker stopped her at the door saying, "no, Marcy, just give her some time, Hat had a lot going on."

"Ard, but can you tell her I love her and I really want to see Katober this week?"

"Ard, and I'll try to make that happen, but I can't make any promises. You know how Hat can be." Ryker spoked low.

"Trust me, I know and thanks, girl. Enjoy the rest of your birthday."

"Thanks for coming, talk to you later." Smiling as she closed the door, Ryker rushed to Manhattan's side. Manhattan leaned against the bathroom sink staring at herself in the mirror frustrated. Then she pulled her clutch from under her arm dropping it on the wet countertop.

"The nerve of Marcy, I don't understand how she let even a portion of those words slip from her mouth." Running her tongue across her teeth, Manhattan was pissed the fuck off. Marcy really had

Manhattan upset. Fuck, she had me upset and I wasn't the one she had the conversation with.

"Are you good?" Ryker rubbed Hat's slim back asking. Still staring at herself in the mirror, Hat answered, "now that Marcy's out of my face, yea, I'm good. I can't believe this bitch, after all these years she still wants to play the victim wrong. Like she was concerned about me, but the whole time Marcy was jealous!! If I could go back into time, I would give Clover to Marcy and he could ruin her life."

"Nah, Clover didn't ruin your life, if that's how you're feeling. He actually did you plenty of favors, we should be thanking his ass." Ryker stated.

"Oh, yea, like what?" Turning around to stare Marcy in the eyes, Manhattan was like Curious George trying to figure out what the hell Ryker rambled about.

"If it wasn't for Clover, you wouldn't have this beautiful little daughter that we all love so damn much. You also wouldn't be the strong woman you are now and thanks to Clover, you know how you want to be loved. Tonight, fuck Clover and Marcy, enjoy yourself and get drunk enough for the both of us. I love you, girl," laughing while giving Manhattan a hug, Ryker held Manhattan closer to her chest. Manhattan was emotional, but she didn't want to make tonight about her and her usual drama.

"I love you too, Ryker." Turning to look at herself in the mirror, Manhattan ran the palm of her hands against her hair. Then she adjusted her dress a little to cover the bottom of her ass and they walked out of the restroom. Eyes were on Manhattan, that shit made her uncomfortable, but she brushed it off taking a shit next to Smoke.

"Are you good, sis?" He questioned her with a glass of red wine in his hand.

"Yea, couldn't be better, oh, there goes Kansas." Waving to get Kansas attention, she smiled at Manhattan walking their way. Once she approach the table, Kansas gave Smoke, a hug saying, "what's poppin', big brother?" Then she kissed his cheek.

"Cooling, baby, cooling." Replied Smoke.

"Happy birthdaaaayyyyyyyyy, sis!" Rubbing Ryker's stomach, Kansas pulled a big envelope from behind her back handing it to Ryker. Shaking it a little, Ryker said, "Hhhmmmm, smells like money, my kind of gift." Ryker ripped the card opening it to read it out loud, but the two hundred dollar bills caught her by surprise.

"See, I always knew I liked you for a reason, thanks girl. Here, baby, hold this." Handing Smoke the money and envelope to Smoke, Ryker gave Kansas a big hug.

"Attention everyone, I would like all you jawns attention." Smoke raised his glass higher grabbing everyone's attention.

"Okay, Smoke, come through with the speech." Kansas whispered to Manhattan and Ryker making them laugh.

"Ryker, the day we met, that's a day I won't ever forget. I was eager to get to know you, but on a personal level. The kind of level that would transform to a bond that no one could break. It took some time, but that happened. In a short period of time, you've become my best friend, and I don't know what I would do without you. The love I have for you is colossal and I've eager to know, will you marry me," dropping to his knee while pulling a small box from his back pocket, Smoke made everyone gasp. Fuck, even people who didn't know Ryker were gasping and in tears.

"OH my Lord." Manhattan whispered covering her mouth, a big smile appeared on her face. She wanted to say more, but her throat was cluttered. Kansas cried as if it was her man down on one knee.

"Oh my God, Clerk, ar-are you serious right now," with tears ruining her make-up Ryker stared at Smoke who had the most humble smile on his face.

"Fuck yea I'm serious, baby, will you do me the honor of being my baby, forever," he laughed. Wiping her runny nose, Ryker shook her head up and down saying, "yes, Clerk, yes I will marry you." Awes filled the background as Clerk slipped the eighteen karat ring onto now fiancé's finger. Ryker stared at the ring shaking her head, it looked good on her finger.

"Alright, nah, ya'll congratulations!" Kansas said giving Ryker and Smoke a hug.

"Is this real, you two are getting married?" Jumping for joy, Manhattan gave Smoke and Ryker a hug. Members of our family and hers crowded around Smoke and Ryker showering them with love.

"My baby is finally getting married, I'm so proud of you, son." My mom grabbed Smoke by the face planting a kiss on his cheek with tears in her eyes.

"Thanks, ma."

"Where is your brother?" She questioned.

"He's at home, but he no one knew about the engagement. I wish he would have come though."

"Well, we'll give him a past since it's his first day out."

"Yea, we'll do that, he'll be iight." Smoke laughed.

"Excuse me everyone, I would like to say something else," tapping his fork against his glass that was full of ice gold water, Smoke stood to his feet. Like the boss he was, Smoke instantly held everyone's attention.

"What now, bro?" Manhattan laughed.

"Drinks on me, I'm getting fucking married!" He laughed giving Ryker a big kiss on the lips. Everyone laughed clapping and cheering Smoke on. The rest of the folks wanted a glimpse of Ryker's ring. The white stone centered diamond engagement ring was hand crafted in New York, costing Smoke a pretty penny. When it came to Ryker, money literally didn't mean a thing to Smoke and it showed tonight.

"I think he a lil' past drunk and I like it." Kansas whispered to Manhattan laughing. Manhattan laughed back, but she didn't say anything.

"Congrats, yall!!" Oak tipsy's ass tried to give smoke and Ryker a hug, but she stumbled laughing.

"This is why I don't let her drink in public, a whole clown." Cope laughed.

"Another Ryker." Smoke chuckled.

"Hell yea, but congrats, bro, you're finally joining the club," chuckling a little, Cope dapped Smoke down taking a look at Ryker's ring. He pretended to be blinded by the icy rock on her finger making her laugh.

"Thanks, bro, it was only right I put a ring on it." Smoke said grabbing a handful of Ryker's ass making her jump a little.

"I love you sssooooo much, baby, I couldn't ask for a better man. I'm going to be Mrs. Porter, I can't believe it, God knows how long I've waited for this day." Squealing while holding her hand out to examine her ring, Ryker then she kissed Smoke again making his heart flutter.

Seeing Smoke and Ryker together had Hat deep in her feelings. It reminded her of what she wanted with me, but it also reminded her of what we would never have. Well, in her eyes, but I still hadn't let go and one day she would be Mrs. Porter also.

"It's crazy how we all thought you and Smoke were only a fling, now look at you two! Freaking engaged, in love, and with a baby on the way!! I'm so proud of you, bro, you turned out to be a good man, I worried for a while." Kansas laughed.

"Awww, sis, you were supposed to always have faith in me." Smoke laughed.

"I'm too damn old to be pregnant, but it's what Smoke wanted," Ryker said rubbing her little belly.

"You don't look a day over twenty, baby, but I'll be right back. Let me holla at Cope about something."

"Okay." Ryker carefully watched Cope and Smoke walk off conversing, then she turned to Manhattan sizing her up and down. Manhattan was a little confused, but laughed it off saying, "what, Ryker?"

"How are you doing with the whole Clover thing? Have you seen him since he's been out," Ryker asked.

"When you have a middle man, you don't have to deal with his kind. To answer your question, no, I haven't seen him and I plan on keeping it that way for a while." Manhattan laughed.

"You know I'm not for that shit with Clover, but you don't think you two should talk," Ryker questioned flipping her hair. She waved at a few people who were looking at them, probably trying to ear hustle. Knowing Ryker, she wanted to flip her middle finger at them.

"Not really, I can truly say I've evolved as a woman. The new Manhattan Mullen knows her worth, she's over Clover Porter and his drama. So, Olivia, Deaux, and whoever else can deal with that, I wish them well."

"Hat, I know you still love Clover and that's okay." She uttered.

"I know you all do, I don't portray that I don't." Manhattan replied.

"Look, we both know I hate Clover, I hate him because of how he treated you. I also hate seeing you like this, you can't fool me, I know you're still hurting."

"I'm not hurting."

"Yea, you are, you can fool Oak and Kansas with that mess, maybe even Honesty, but you can't fool me at all. Between you and I, he's really hurting about you and him not being together. The lil' Olivia chick was just a lil' joce, honestly, he was using her to pump coke in the strip club. As for Deaux, he hasn't dealt with her since the last time he went to jail, which was in June." Ryker rubbed her stomach saying.

"Okay, what's your reason for telling me all this?" Manhattan questioned Ryker with her hand on her hip. Right about now, Manhattan was desperate for those answers. As much as Ryker bashed me and pushed Manhattan on Chris, all of this had to make sense.

"Because, maybe you should consider working things out with him."

"WHAT?"

"Why are you so loud, hun, I'm standing right here?" Ryker laughed.

"Ryker, you literally pushed me to get with Chris and every time you spoke about Clover, it was something bad. Now you're standing here, the night of your engagement telling me I should take Clover Porter back? Wwoowww, I have officially entered the twilight zone."

"I'm just saying, you should—"

"No, no, no, we're not making tonight about me and fuckin' Clover's ugly ass," she whispered.

"Come on, Hat, you're my girl and it's my job to make sure you're straight." Exhaling loudly and scanning the room to make sure no one was watching her, Manhattan then worded, "I don't know, I don't know how I'm supposed to deal with this."

"What do you mean," Ryker asked pulling a chair closer to Hat. Then Ryker sat down kicking her heels off to massage her swollen, red feet. Dropping her head and chuckling a little, Hat then said, "a part of me really want to say fuck it and act like I never met him. Then there's a small part of me that misses him, I hate feeling like this. Ryker, I feel like a damn fool for loving this man, but I can't help it. I just wish these feelings would DIE!"

"Girl, you're not a fool or a damn fool. You just fell in love with a man like most women do. Yea, shit got bad between you two, but when it was good between you two, it was good. You have to always remember if you want to take him back, that's your business. I just want you to be happy, even if it's with or without him."

"Congrats, girl, I think I'm jealous, I should have snatched Smoke back in the day when I had a chance," Kat joked with opening arms giving Ryker a big hug. Rolling her eyes, but also laughing, Ryker said, "I swear, I can't stand your bald ass head, but thanks, girl." Charlie hung onto her arm trying his best not to make eye contact with Manhattan. If it was awkward or him, I know it had to be awkward for Ryker and Manhattan.

"Baby, can you give us a minute to chit-chat?" Kat asked Charlie.

"Sure, I'll be at the table waiting for you." Giving Kat a peck on the cheek, Charlie then walked off with Ryker and Manhattan's eyes glued to him. All Manhattan could think about was what she witness at Charlie's house that day. The way Manhattan and Ryker stared at Charlie made Kat feel uncomfortable, it was time for her to finally talk. Since she was caught with Charlie, Kat hadn't mentioned anything about Charlie and also tried to avoid some contact with her friends. Fuck, I didn't blame her I would be ashamed also if I was her.

"Look, I know what ya'll jawns are thinking." Kat whispered.

"What are we thinking, mind reader?" Laughed Ryker.
"Shut up, Ryker, Charlie isn't gay anymore and his divorce is finalized. Finally, I have Charlie to myself, how it's supposed to be. I want ya'll to respect my decision on being with Charlie. Just how I would do if ya'll was in my shoes."

"Hey, that's your life, Kat, I have problems of my own." Manhattan rolled her eyes flipping her hair.

"I don't have men problems, but your business is your business, sis. Whatever makes you happy, I wouldn't be a fool to stand in the way of love." Ryker replied.

"Tonight, we're going out and enjoy ourselves, ard? No Smoke, no Clover, just you, me, and Kat."

"I don't know, Ryke, I'm not in a clubbing mood. I just want to chill and *watch Orange is the New Black* on NextFlix," Manhattan replied, but Ryker rolled her eyes replying, "girl, fuck them horny inmates, we haven't been clubbing in forever. You've been so wrapped up in this Clover shit that you're forgetting to take care of yourself. One night out won't hurt you, I promise to have you in the house by breakfast," she laughed.

"Breakfast, now you're drawlin, but okay, I'm down. We're not to a club, Smoke would kill you, me, and KAT!" Manhattan laughed.

"Instead of pretending like you're happy on social media just to make Clover jealous, it's time for you to actual BE happy."

"It's crazy how he's falling for everything I put on Instagram. Clover is so dumb, but I miss his ass, I can't lie." She laughed patting her face to make the tears go away. Manhattan spent hours on her make-up and refused to ruining it crying behind my dumb ass.

***

Standing outside in the cool air smoking a blunt, my head was fucked up. Seeing Manhattan looking better than a supermodel, but I couldn't touch her, had my deep in my feelings. I missed my baby, but I doubted that she missed me. Manhattan didn't look at me one time in the restaurant, not even when I kept my eyes glued to her. Everyone noticed the distance between us, but I wish they didn't.

The attention had me feeling out of place and I couldn't stand being surrounded by all those people. I desperately wanted to talk to Hat, so, standing outside for an hour wasn't a problem for me. As soon as Manhattan spotted me leaning against the building, she exhaled loudly rolling her eyes. While shuffling through her clutch for her keys, Manhattan kept her head down walking. Taking one more hit of the blunt, I then tossed it releasing the smoke from my mouth.

"Manhattan." I said, but she ignored me.

"MANHATTAN!"

"CLOVER, WHAT?" She shouted back.

"Damn, can I talk you?"

"Talk about what, Katober?"

"Us, I want to talk about us." He spoked.

"There isn't really much to talk about."

"It's a lot that needs to be talked about. How are you," I asked awkwardly laughing, but Hat stood there with a straight face folding her arms across her chest.

"I'm wonderful, Spitta, couldn't be any better."

"Spitta, wow, did you just call me that, I laughed.

"Yeeepppp, that's what they call you, but what do you want?"

"I wanted to uummm, see how you were doing. I want to make sure the mother of my child is doing fine."

"Like I said, I'm good, but if something ever happens to me, I'm pretty sure Kansas or Smoke will let you know." Said Manhattan.

"I'm sure they will."

"Look, Ryker is begging me to go out with her and Kat tonight. Can you keep Katober until the morning? Or do you and Deaux have something planned, trapping and shit, you know yall are Bonnie and Clyde," she laughed rolled her eyes.

"Of course I can keep my daughter, I was going to ask you that anyways. Where is she?"

"At a friend's house, but I'll send you the address. She'll be waiting for you to pick her up." Trying to grab Manhattan's arm with a smile on my face, she pulled away shaking her head.

"Thanks, but don't touch me."

"Damn, it's really like that between us," I asked.

"Yea, always and forever."

"Manhattan, why can't we focus on starting over? I'm literally begging you, I'll get on my knees, right now."

"Look, the only thing we need to focus on is Katober. I want to raise my daughter to the best of our ability. God forbids she meets a man like you, I pray every night she doesn't."

"Fuck man, why can't you just believe me and give me another chance!!!! I LOVE YOU, MANHATTAN AND I DON'T WANT ANYONE ELSE, BUT YOU!!! I- I -I-I I'M SORRY, I'm sorry for every piece of pain I have caused you. All the times I didn't come home, having you worrying about me, the cheating, ALL OF IT! I'm so, baby, but you have to take me back. I'm going crazy without you, Hat."

"No."

"Damn, Manhattan, you're going to be cold like that to me?" I questioned.

"Yea, now you see how it feels."

"Can I at least take you out to dinner soon?"

"I'll think about it, but I'm not ready to be in your space again." She said.

"I want to be in your again."

"The aching pain you witness in my droopy eyes are from you!! The horrible choices you've made, the belittling, cheating, lies, and everything else you've have done to destroy my heart. I swear, JUST STOP!!! Stop hurting me, how much do you think I can take?! For years..... you've mind fucked me making believe that no other human being would love me the way you do. That no other human being would never touch nor caress me the way you do. Maybe that's a good thing because your love is toxic, so damn toxic. I surrender, I surrender to no longer loving you. No longer giving you my heart, tears, body, mind, plus soul. I surrender baby and it's time you know that. It's time I make myself believe I can live without you because lord knows I told myself I couldn't over the years. I promise you one thing though. You're going to miss me when I'm gone for good, KNOW THAT!!"

"Manhattan, Manhattan, wait!" It didn't matter how many times I called her name or begged her to take me back, Manhattan stood on everything she told me. For the first time ever, I honestly felt like she was done with me. Maybe I broke her heart for the last time.

Chapter 19

Maybe it was the prayers or all the begging I did, but Manhattan finally gave in and decided to have dinner with me. Every time I glanced at her, I had a smile on my face, I couldn't believe she was sitting across from me. I know she wasn't excited like I was, but that didn't matter to me. We were taking a step together in the right direction, a nigga was pleased with that.

Sitting at the dinner table in the dim restaurant, I had a clear view of Manhattan. With her long, soft hair pulled into a high bun, it exposed how perfectly shaped her face was. Embracing her beauty like this always made me fall for her a little harder, a little more than before.

"You are so......breathtaking." I mumbled making Manhattan say, "did you say something, Spitta?"

"Uuuhh, no, just thinking out loud, you know me. My mind is always on a thousand, trying to figure out how to turn a dime into a dollar." I laughed.

"Yep, sell those drugs, Spitta." She raised her eyebrows saying, but Manhattan also shook her head side to side.

"Speaking of selling drugs, I've fell back a lot from the streets." I said.

"What?"

"A long time ago, you told me to leave them streets alone, that's what I'm doing. I wanted to talk to you about something, we both can benefit from it."

"What is that, Clover?"

"I want to open a business, it really doesn't matter what kind. I'll put the money behind it, you can handle all that."

"What, are you serious right now?" Manhattan attempted to hide her smile and expression, but she couldn't. I adored the way she cracked a corner smile with her lips trembling from excitement. It made me feel good knowing I still had the ability to make her smile again.

"I'm dead ass serious, yo, when we first got together you said you wanted to owned a children's boutique. I think this is the perfect opportunity now, but stop me if I'm wrong."

"No, you're not wrong, I'm just shocked, I guess you were paying attention to the things I said." She smirked still looking at the menu.

"Fuck yea I was, from those big pointless brown hangers you wanted and even the door sign. I pay attention to everything, Hat, trust me. It's about time I start washing this dirty money, you're entitled to most of it anyways." I said.

"Yea, I kind of am." She giggled.

"I have $20,000 you can start off with, but I'll give you the other $30,000 next week."

"Okay, I'm fine with that, business partner." She cracked a small smile, but quickly made it fade away.

"Bet, business partner." I smiled, but I had no reason to hide it like Manhattan did.

"What made you change?" She asked.

"Huh?"

"I asked what made you change, I begged you for so long to leave those streets alone. Now you decide to, what's the change?"

"You, Manhattan, it was you, thank you for the change." I spoke.

"Me, well, you're welcome Clover Porter."

For a few minutes, Manhattan and I sat quietly, but I had more to say. The conversation we had was going well, I just hope I wouldn't say something that would make her leave the table.

"What are you getting, baby," I questioned Manhattan staring at the thick menu. With her head cock to the side Manhattan flipped through the menu ignoring me.

"Call me Manhattan, please," she expressed still looking at the menu, but I knew Manhattan. She was ordering Spaghetti with clams and kale, like always.

"Okay, Manhattan, what are you getting," I asked again. Biting on her fat bottom lip, she pointed to the corner of the menu saying, "I'm going to get the spaghetti with clams and kale." I smiled to myself, I knew my baby better than I knew myself.

"Bet."

"What are you getting, Clover," she asked.

"Eeehhh, I'm going to try something different and get marinated mushrooms with the crispy kale," I said.

"That sounds good, can I have a bite," she closed the menu smiling.

"Like always, you know you can." I laughed.

"Good answer."

"Look, Hat, I know I haven't always been the best boyfriend or man to you. That doesn't mean I don't love you because I do, I really do love you with all my heart. Before you say it, I know my actions have said otherwise, but I can't change the past. If I could go back in time and change everything, I would without a problem. Deaux has never meant anything to me and what's crazy is that the bitch knows that."

"What about Olivia?"

"I used her for what it was worth, she wasn't anything to me." I spoked.

"Why do you give these low lives a piece of you, Clover? The piece of you that only I deserve."

"That's a question I can't answer, I won't sit here and lie to you, but it won't happen again. I just want to take things slow and start over with you. I want to fall in love again with that girl I met at the bank in 2008. Let's be friends again, you know, kickin' shit like we used to." I worded.

"That sounds nice, but 2008 was a long time ago." Said Manhattan.

"No one will ever understand how beautiful you were to me the day we met. Too bad we can't freeze time on that day."

"Time after time you broke my jawn like I meant NOTHING TO YOU!!!"

"I'm ready to be the man you want, Manhattan. I'm going to stop talking about it and show you with my actions."

"That's the thing, Clover, when I wanted you to be the man I wanted, you didn't want to be," Manhattan replied.

"That's not true, Hat, from day I wanted to be the man for you. At one point, I was that man, that's all I wanted to be," staring at the table because I couldn't look Hat in the eye, I chuckled a little. I didn't because what I said was funny, I chuckled because everything started to make sense.

"Somehow, you became the total opposite of that, Clover Porter. When I told you I loved you for my soul, I truly meant that. Clover, you had the audacity to fuck another woman in my bed while I was in it!!! You were nowhere to be found for our anniversary, and you cheated on me time after time. From the moment I met you, I embraced you with love, but I guess that wasn't enough. You want to know the hardest part I dealt with," she asked.

"What?"

"The hardest part was that I had to admit to myself is that I was missing something Deaux had. Clearly she had something that kept you there for all those years." Said Manhattan.

"Manhattan, it was never that and I wish you would believe me. I can look you in those winsome eyes and honesty tell you Deaux doesn't mean shit to me. Shorty never meant anything to me. The bitch did so much dirty shit for me in the streets that I felt like I was obligated to fuck with her. I also felt like if I stopped fucking with her that she cross me, I didn't need that extra drama in my life."

"You never considered how I would feel when you cheated on me. Walking around feel like a damn fool because no telling how many people know about you and Deaux." In a sad tone, Manhattan dropped her head turning away. Her eyes were now glued on the young couple sitting three tables away from us. A miniature smile appeared on her face with a single tear rolling down her cheek. I wasn't sure why Manhattan was crying, but being the emotional creature she was, I could take a good guest.

"I bet they are in their early twenties thinking they have everything figured out. About love, life, and everything else that makes their role go round. Little does she know, he can break her heart at any given minute. Little does he knows, every single time he breaks her heart, she'll always forgive and take him back. They could be you and I in the next couple of years, crazy, right?"

"Manhattan, how many times go I have to say I'm sorry? Just tell me how many times and I'll do! With no problem, just tell me and I'll do it. It's literally killing me not being with you!! on several different occasions, I didn't want to get out of bed, I never felt love sick until YOU left me. Man, if I knew life would have turned out this way because of my cheating, I would have walked pass Deaux and never looked back. You really mean the world to me, I just hope you'll see that again one day."

"Clover, I know you love me, that's one thing I won't ever take away from you. I love you, Clover, I really do and I will never understand why you've hurt me to my breaking point. I don't want to give up on you and I damn sure don't want to give up on us. You're my best friend, my child's father, and the love of my life, it's hard to throw all that way." Said Manhattan.

"I know, baby, we're going to figure this out together. I'm going to Detroit for the next few days, I'm leaving tomorrow night, but I would love for you to be home when I get back. I'm not expecting you to move back in, but I would love for to see you and Katober there. Just something for old times sakes, please. You making breakfast in your lil' workout jawns." I begged with a smirk on my face.

"You know what, that doesn't sound too bad, I was going to ask you that anyways." Said Manhattan.

"Word?" I asked laughing. Taking a sip of her drink, Manhattan stared at me through the glass replying, "yea, this might sound crazy, but I think I have a stalker, Clover." Manhattan stated.

"What?"

"I don't know, I could be tripping, but I've seen this car passing around my house a few times." She said.

"What kind of car, tell me right now so I can clear the business!"

"Clover, calm down, but I've seen the car even parked a few blocks down. I could be overreacting or maybe they're looking for someone else." Manhattan explained, but I wasn't buying that shit. I could tell this lil' stalker of hers had her scared.

"What kind of car?"

"Uummmm, it was a blue or Honda Accord, 2012."

"Blue 2012 Honda Accord, bet, bet. Next time I see that car, you already know what it's gone be." I chuckled raising my eyebrows. It's been a minute since I upped a tool on a nigga and I was tweaking to draw down on a nigga.

"Thanks, baby, you know I kind of like when you talk that gangster mess.." Manhattan smirked, but she tried not to blush. She knew exactly how to get a nigga all in his feelings.

"Baby, oh yea?" I asked smiling.

"Maybe, but time will tell, again."

"Manhattan." I said.

"What, Clover Porter?"

"You know I love you and I won't ever stop loving you. Rather if you take me back or not, I want to remain friends with you. I also want us to raise Koko in the best environment possible." I stated.

"I know, and I love you too. No matter what, we'll always put her first, she deserves that."

"What about this Chris nigga?"

"What about him?" She questioned me.

"Do you love him, be honest with me?" I asked Manhattan.

"No, Clover, I don't love him and most of the time I'm not really sure if I like him. He's a good person, but I feel like I'm wasting his time already. I don't want to waste anyone's time or drag them into my mess." She replied taking another sip of her wine.

"I feel that, even though we're sitting at this lovely dinner table talking about you and another nigga." Flaring my nose feeling a little uncomfortable, I didn't want Hat to see me sweat.

"It's 6:00 pm, by the time we are done here, it'll be about 8:00 pm. I need to run by the store and my house, but after that, I'll be there waiting for you."

"That's a bet, I can't wait."

"I'm pretty sure you have a few things to do, so, 11:00 pm you'll be HOME?" She smiled grabbing my hand. Smiling back, I shook my head saying, "11:00 pm and not a minute later, baby."

Manhattan and I talked and joked for two hours at the restaurant, then we departed from one another with smiles on our face. Before we said our good byes, we decided to spend a few minutes at the park just to enjoy some more of one another's company. It felt good talking to Manhattan and holding a real conversation with an actual adult. When I say an adult I mean in the mind and not just the age.

Walking into the trap house with a big smile on my face, Smoke and Cope couldn't help, but to notice it. Nudging Smoke on the arm while shuffling the deck of cards, Cope said, "something good must have happened in his life, like Manhattan finally talking to me." Cope's words made me laugh, but before saying anything, I grabbed the stool taking a sit next to Smoke dapping him down. Then I stretched across the table dapping Cope down, still with a smile on my face.

"Something better than her just talking to me. Manhattan Mullen-Porter and I just came from a date." I smiled bigger.

"Whhhhhattttttttt?" Smoke and Cope pushed back, shocked as fuck. I shook my head fast, I couldn't wait to share my jawn with them.

"Yea, I mean, I had to beg her for four days, but she finally said yea. We talked about a lot of things, got some shit off our chest, and we're finally moving in the same direction."

"I hope that's the right direction because I'm tired of hearing you cry about Hat." Cope laughed.

"Nigga, it is, we're going to make things work and I'm definitely keeping my dick tucked into my pants."

"We'll see how long this last, Deaux will be popping up out of nowhere before we know it." Smoke laughed shaking his head. He was tempted to bite his finger nails, but that was a bad habit Ryker was dying for him to break.

"Naw, it's nothing with me and Deaux, that's dead. Two days before I got out of the jawn, I made it clear to Deaux that it was nothing between us. I said it loud and clear that I was going to chase after Manhattan and to get her back at any cost." I replied making Smoke clap his hand.

"No funny shit, I'm proud of you, lil' bro, go after your woman."

" I'm going after my woman so much that I hit up my jewelry, tomorrow we're meeting."

"Meeting for what?" Smoke said taking a sip of his Gin and Juice.

"It's time I make Manhattan a Porter, well, she is a Porter, time to put that on paper."

"Are you talking about marriage?" Cope questioned me making me shake my hand. Cope and Smoke's gasping told me that they were shocked as hell, but I laughed it off.

"Ding, ding, ding, you have the right answer. I have to show Manhattan that I'm serious about making things right."

"Wwooowwwwwwwww, you're dead ass serious about this." Cope uttered.

"Fuck yea, this is my last shot with her, it's a MUST I fix my wrongs. I know I can't take back the things I did in the past, but I can love her so much better that she'll forget about the past." I explained.

"I'm here for you doing right, bro, it's about damn time, but congratulations. When are you doing the big proposal?" Cope questioned.

"Thanks, but I was thinking in the next month or so. I want everything to be right with us before I drop down on one knee."

"Bet." Cope replied.

"Hit me up when you go, Clove, I'll come with you. Ya know, be your support system and shit." Smoke replied.

"Thanks, bro, I appreciate it."

Just as Smoke opened his mouth to reply, Deaux and her ratchet friend walked through the door like someone invited them here. Everyone's mood changed, here goes the drama.

"Spitta, let me holla at you for a minute." Making her hips swing aggressively from left to right as she walked, Deaux approached me with her hands in her back pockets. Her booty shorts slowly rose revealing her pussy lips, but know Deaux, she didn't give a fuck. I didn't make eye contact with her, I glanced at Cope saying, "deal the cards, bro, what are playing, booray?"

"Yea, but back to what Clover and I were talking about."

"What was that?" I asked.

"Clover, are you really going to act like I'm not in your presence?" Deaux slightly grabbed me by the shoulder, but I pushed her stupid ass away. She felt insulted, but that wasn't the first time it made her feel stupid like that. She had no reason feeling insulted or even coming here for that matter.

"Yea, you can get the fuck now, BYE!"

"My nigga, don't talk to my friend like that! I don't know why you deal with this clown ass nigga, girl!" Her friend said making Cope, Smoke, and me laugh.

"She doesn't deal with me, but you know it's legal to beat yo hoe, huh?" I laughed a lil' harder dapping Smoke down. Then he lit his fat blunt ready to put one in the air.

"Spitta, I ain't Manhattan or Deaux, don't play with me." Anna said, but that shit didn't move me.

"Yo, get you people and get the fuck out of here. I'm not in the mood to argue with any bitch tonight."

"Come on now Anna and Spitta, it's no need for this extra shit ya'll are doing. I passed by your house and you weren't there, where were you?" Deaux asked making me smack my lips.

"I was on a date with my woman. Your services are no longer needed."

"No, I'm your woman, YOU got the game fucked up!!" She shouted.

"Deaux, you got the game all fucked, I made it clear I didn't want to be with you. At least not in a serious relationship or giving up Manhattan for you, that would be crazy, yo. Hat, in exchanged for YOU, bitch, you must be crazy," I laughed clapping my hands. Cope and Smoke shook their heads laughing, but they didn't say a word. Manhattan glanced at Anna, who sized me up and down, with tears forming in her eyes. I tried to get her off my lap, but she became dead weight like a damn dummy. Deaux attempted to fight back the tears, but they still traveled down her face. With her mouth tight and closed, she shouted, "why are you treating me like this, Clover? I held you down when you were in jail, I've been having your back for years and you still won't be with me! You come home and run straight to that bitch, Manhattan, IT'S NOT FAIR!!! I deserve you, NOT HER!"

"Deaux, I don't want to argue with you, but get the fuck off my lap. The last thing I need is someone saying you and I were together. Matter of fact, you need to leave or at least get from around me," trying to push Deaux from my lap, she wrapped her arms around my neck tightly. I sighed loudly, this bitch needed to haul ass before I snap on her.

"Why, because of Little Miss Perfect Manhattan," she asked trying to kiss me, but I turned away. Deaux felt like a fool in front of her friend, but she brought this on herself.

"Yea, that's exactly why, now get the fuck before I drag your damn ass out of here! You know I'm good for that type of shit, yo, go head!"

With tears on her face crying hysterically Kansas rushed into the trap house searching for me. No one said anything, but Smoke and Cope reached under the table for their iron. Trying to jump to my feet, Deaux applied her body harder on my lap saying, "NO!" Then she wiped her tears away sniffing.

"Kan, what's wrong," Smoke asked while jumping to his feet. He stretched his arm across the table grabbing his other burner, but Kansas began to cry harder. Her body was shaking, Kansas could hardly breath and the few words she attempted to speak, no one could understand.

"Deaux, get the fuck off my brother's lap, I need to talk to him," she sobbed loudly. From jump, Kansas hated Deaux and what she should for. Deaux still tried to be

"What, I'm not going anywhere," Deaux rolled her eyes flipping her weave. I aggressively pushed her off my lap standing to my feet. The closer I walked to my sister, she cried harder shouting, "Clover, it's Manhattan." What, what about, my shorty?"

"She was, she was found …….. dead, Clover! She was found dead at her doorstep. Someone killed her Clover, someone killed Manhattan," I know I was wrong, but I started to laugh. This was funny and had to be a joke, there was no way my baby was dead.

"Wait what?"

Chapter 20
"When it rains, it pours……. Blood."

"Man, can ya'll please stop calling my fuckin' phone, yo!" I shouted staring at the phone screen. Unsaved numbers ring my line, but I was too skeptical to answer it. I knew it wasn't licks calling my phone and anyone I knew, I wasn't in the mood to talk.

For five minutes, I sat in my driveway sobbing like a bitch with my head against the headrest. My eyes were closed tightly, but I could feel the vibration of my jack ringing like crazy. The text messages, voicemails, and phone calls, didn't stop, even though I desperately begged myself for them to. Arriving to Manhattan's house replayed in my head a dozen of times already. It didn't matter how hard I tried to erase it, it just continued to play like a bad record. A fuckin' horrible, horrible, HORRIBLE record!!

My phone continued ringing, but this time, it was Kansas. I didn't want to answer it, but I knew she was worried and wanted to know my whereabouts.

"Hello?" I could hardly say. Kansas whimpered through the phone making more tears charged down my face. I could feel the stress taking over my body, yea, I could feel it.

"Hello?" She tried to say.

"Kan, what up?"

"Cl, Clover, where are you?" She asked, but before replying, I used the back of my hand to wipe my runny nose.

"I just got home, my phone is ringing non-stop, man, FUCK!!"

"Mines too, but I'm coming over." She replied sniffing.

"Ard." I disconnected the call throwing my phone on the floor. I wasn't in the mood to speak to anyone.

I walked into my house feeling lost, empty, confused, and hurt. I've seen plenty of crime scenes before, but this one was mighty different. Especially when it's someone you know and truly love from the bottom of your heart. Familiar and unknown faces surrounded Manhattan's home be concerned, but to also be nosey. When I saw cellphone being taken out for pictures and videos, best believe I flashed on every jawn! How disrespectful could these mutherfuckers get? Manhattan was only found dead an hour and a half ago, but the news about her dead circulated fast. I had people from New York, Detroit, Baltimore, and Florida calling me asking if it was true. Social media was already flooded with *Rest in Peace Manhattan* statuses.

"Uuhh, ma, where you at?" I sobbed closing the door with tears dropping from my chin. Rushing out of my bedroom, my asked, "Clover, what did they say, please tell me it wasn't her?" I dropped to my knees burying my face into my lap crying harder. I couldn't answer her question, at least not right now.

"Mom, where is my daughter, I really, REALLY, just want to see my daughter,"

"Okay, baby, but tell me something, was it her?" She questioned me with her entire body shaking. Attempting to speak again, my words stumbled over one another, but somehow, my mom understood what I said.

"Nnoooo, nooo, no, no," she cried out stumbling to the couch with her hands covering her mouth. I wanted to comfort my mom, but fuck, I needed comfort also. I needed someone to hug and tell me it would be okay, even though I wouldn't believe a word they would say.

"Mom, when I got there, cops where everywhere. I can still see the red and blue lights flashing in my eyes. She was shot dead in the face like some kind of animal. Ma, she wasn't a fuckin' animal and they did her so wrong!! I actually saw Manhattan, my fuckin' girl be zipped in a body bag like she was a fuckin' piece of clothing. MA, that's not right, it's not right at all."

"Baby, let's just pray about it, please." She begged.

"NO, I don't want to pray, I won't her back!!! I went there praying to God that it wasn't her, ma, but it WAS!! Clearly praying doesn't work, so fuck praying and fuck the God that we're supposed to pray to!"

"Clover, what happened, please tell me what happened and don't talk like that?" My mom cried out, but I shrugged my shoulders in return. It's crazy how I often portrayed to have the answers to everything, but not this one question.

"Ma, I don't know, the police aren't saying much besides it was a homicide." I replied.

"That's is, who found her dead?" She questioned.

"A neighbor heard four gun shots coming from Manhattan's house. When she ran outside she saw two people running, but by then, they were fleeing to their car. Carmen didn't see faces, but she thinks it was a black or dark colored car they were in. It could have been a Honda or a Camry, fuck, I don't know. I one thing, every car I see that fits the description I'm sending bullets in it, ma!!"

"No, Clover, don't get yourself in trouble, you have to let the police handle this." She begged.

"Let the police do what??? If I don't take matters into my OWN hands, Manhattan with be another cold case, I can't have that. Letting the police 'handle' this will never sit well."

"Clover, I will not let you LEAVE this house to do something crazy." She said.

"I have to go." I answered wiping my wet face and climbing to my feet. I felt weak, but somehow, I had to pull myself together. I couldn't do it collapsing to the floor again. My mom cried out harder looking around the living room for answers. I don't know why she did that, it wasn't any answers here.

"Why, what are you going to do, Clover?" She questioned me.

"The police want me to go downtown for some questioning, I should be back in about an hour." Wiping my tears away again, I slowly rose to my feet heading for the door, but my mom held my hand asking, "why do they want to question you?"

"Ma, I'm supposed to be the last person who saw her. I had to be the last person she was with. After we left from the park, she went to the grocery store to pick up a few things. Her purse and grocery bags were swimming in her blood, so, she couldn't have went anywhere else. I know Manhattan, if she would have went anywhere else, Hat would have told me. We were just together TWO hours ago and it felt like everything was back to normal. Ma, she agreed to work things out with me and get back together. I told her I was going to Detroit tomorrow and I wanted her to stay at the house tonight. I was shocked that she agreed to, but she also told me that she had a lil' stalker."

"Wait, a stalker, like a serious stalker? Clover, you have to tell the police that!"

"I don't know if it was a real stalker, she wasn't even sure if it really was someone stalking her, but that's the reason she wanted to stay at my house. I guess it kind of freaked her out." I sobbed covering my mouth. My tears and wild emotions made my mom break down, but she rushed to collect herself. One of us had to be strong, but dam sure wasn't going to be me.

"You need to tell them that, all of that when you get there, okay?"

"I will, ma, I just need to catch my head first, I feel like I'm in a bad dream. I'm in a bad, bad dream and I can't wake up! My head is spinning, I can't deal with this, NONE OF THIS!!"

"Baby, it's going to be okay, we're going to get through this together." She implied.

"Ma, before I would have left for Detroit, I was linking up with my mans to get an engagement ring. I was going to propose to Hat next month. On the ride to the trap house, I thought about how I was going to do it and all. I can't do that now, ma, because she's dead. What the fuck am I supposed to do now, ma? Ma, I had it down to the venue, what I would say, and what I was going to where. How the fuck could this mighty God we serve take all of that from ME, I'm not a bad person, ma? I just wanted to marry her, ma, and make her happy. Was I wrong for that?"

***

It only took a few hours for the world to blame me for Manhattan's death, which was mad wild, yo. Word through Philly was that Clover Porter had a debt he couldn't pay, but paid it with Manhattan's blood. Another rumor was that they rushed into Manhattan's house searching for money, but that wasn't true either. Me, the man that she loved and who loved her back, was the reason!! Can you believe that false shit?? These rumors had my head all fucked up, but it's what it did to my heart I couldn't handle it. The only rumor I kind of believe was that Manhattan got caught up in a robbery gone bad, but with her purse still full of money, that didn't make sense either.

Slowly walking into my living room, Kat cleared her throat saying, "Hey, Clover, can we talk?" She asked with heavy, read eyes that were ready to let out big tears. Kat was wigless and wore jogging clothes, you could tell shorty was going through it.

"What's up," I asked without turning around keeping my eyes at the window. I didn't have the strength or energy to pull myself from that chair and my bedroom window. Being in that weak state of mind I was buried in from guilt, I couldn't let anyone see me this way.

"When are you going to come out this jawn? You've been in here for three days, you need some fresh air, yo."

"If I want some fresh air I'll open this window, Kat. I know how to open a window, yo." I mumbled.

"Come on, Spitt, you need to get up, take a shower, get out this house, and get some fresh air. You can't be in this house all day, it's going to drive you crazy," she replied.

"I don't want to be here, but I feel like I need to be here. I keep telling myself she's going to come home one day and I if stay by this window, I won't miss her pull up. She made a promise that she would come back home, Hat wouldn't break her promise."

"I'm sorry, Clover, but she's not coming back. I -I wish she would, but my best friend isn't ever coming back. It hurts, trust me, I knooowwwwww, my heart is aching like a mutherfucker. I don't want to get out of bed sometimes, but it's only going to make me feel worse than I already do. It's only been three days, THREE DAYS, CLOVER and I feel so damn post without her. Hat keep me focused and in line, who the fuck is going to do that now?" Crying silently, Kat used the back of her hand to pat her puffy eyes, but the tears continued to fill her round eyes.

"I don't know what to do, people are really blaming me for this, but I know this isn't my fault. I would never put Hat in any danger, at least not purposely." I spoked softly, still staring out of the window. My backyard was perfect, these were the kind of sunny days Hat, Katober, and me spent all day in the backyard enjoying the peaceful atmosphere. Just us, no drama ruining our vibe, just like I liked it.

"I know this isn't your fault, don't think like that, bro."

"How can I do that when people are literally texting and calling my phone saying this shit?" I shouted.

"Fuck them, Clove, we all know that shit isn't true!! You really need to get out of this house, you're driving yourself crazy with your thoughts!"

"It's hard, Kat, it's fucking hard, yo!!! Manhattan was the only woman I ever loved, I ain't loved none of them bitches at all. How the fuck, man, Kat, how the fuck am I supposed to tell my daughter this? H-How, how am I supposed to fix my mouth to tell her I'm the reason her mother is dead," I whimpered trying to cover my mouth, but at this point, I didn't give a fuck about hiding my emotions. Before grabbing me by the face, Kat wiping her tears saying exhaling loudly. Then she said, "Clover, there is not a bone in my body that believes you're the reason Manhattan is dead. Shit isn't adding up, but it will, sooner than we think."

"I ready to kill any and every one. I tried reaching out to her mom and Marcy, but those dumb bitches cursed me out like a dog. They're probably the ones who start those fuckin' rumors!!"

"Speaking of them, I'm going to Marcy's house in a few minutes. She wants me to help with the funeral arrangements. Don't worry, Spitt, I won't let them fuck over you in that part, you have my word." Kat said.

"Thanks, Kat, I owe you big time, but I have to go. I'm coming back, but I don't want you sitting here, ard?"

"Ard." I cracked a fake smile while fighting back my tears.

"Before I go, do you want to know something?"

"What's that??" I questioned.

"She called me while in the grocery store. Manhattan told me how much you two had a good ole' time and she couldn't wait until she got home. She meant your home, that was always home for her. Manhattan also said how she knew people who talk about her, but she wanted to work things out with you. For some reason, she felt like you were sincere about changing."

"Kat, I was going to get down on one knee next month. I only told Smoke and Cope about it when I got to the trap after our date. I told Manhattan how I was ready to get out of the street and let her invest my money in something. When we first met, Manhattan had dreams of owning her own children's boutique. Katera, I was ready to make everything right with her." I cried.

"Clover, I'm so sorry. Have you spoke to the detectives again?" She asked.

"Nah, it's really not much to talk about. Every lead they get is a dead end, I told my mama them clowns won't get her any justice."

"Damn, okay, let me know if you hear anything new, see you later." Wiping her face again, Kat then gave me a hug and walked out of the house. I still didn't make a move until I heard footsteps at my door.

Knock! Knock! Knock!

"Who is it?" I shouted.

"It's Deaux, Clover." Walking to the door swinging it open, I stared Deaux up and down trying to figure out what her stupid ass wanted. I hadn't heard from her since the day Manhattan was killed, I was actually glad.

"What the fuck do you want?"

"Look, I know the last time we saw one another wasn't good." She spoked softly with her head down.

"It sure fuckin' wasn't, what the fuck do you want?" I asked Deaux.

"Clover, I just want be here for you. I know Manhattan and I didn't get along, but I didn't hate her enough to wish she was dead. Look at you, you need someone to be here for you. I know you need someone to help you with Katober, let me help." She begged holding my hands, but I pulled away mugging her even more.

"I don't care if Manhattan is dead or alive, you will NEVER be around my child."

"Okay, Spitta, that's fine, I'll come when Katober isn't here. I can't leave from here knowing that you are like this. Look at you, you're a mess, baby! I'll cook whatever your heart desires and I'll clean for you. I'll suck your dick all night if that will make you feel better." Chuckling at Deaux's ignorance, I grabbed my Air Force Ones that were at the door slipping them on. Then I grabbed my keys and pack of cigarettes that sat on the end table. Two months ago, I quit Smoke, but since last night, I ran through two packs of cigarettes like a breeze.

"At this point, I don't give a fuck about anything or what you do. Move out of my way." Literally pushing Deaux out of the way, I walked out of the house heading for my car. Deaux stood there looking lost, but slowly walked into the house closing the door behind her. I didn't waste any time pushing my car to start and speeding out of my driveway. My hands were shaking right along with my lips. I couldn't gather myself, it didn't matter how hard I try. I wasn't sure where I was going, but I needed to go somewhere. Something had to make me feel better. I was hardly two streets from my house when I spotted Marcy at the gas station. I wanted to speak to her, but I wasn't sure how Marcy would react when I approached her.

Marcy was being hugged by an unknown person while she cried tears on the woman's shoulder. Slowly pulling into the gas station, I parked my car a few feet away from Marcy's car hoping out. Marcy's glare at me for two seconds with the ugliest look on her face. It seemed like her tears faded away as she slowly broke free from the woman. I could tell the lady was confused at what was about to happen, but so was I.

"Marcy, I know I'm the last person you want to speak to, but I really need to talk to you." I approached Marcy saying. Charging my way, Marcy sized me up and down again shaking her head.

"IF YOU DON'T GET THE FUCK OUT OF MY FACE!!! NIGGA, YOU'RE THE REASON MY SISTER WAS KILLED, BUT IT SHOULD HAVE BEEN YOUR ASS. I PRAY TO GOD THAT THEY KILL YOU NEXT." Clearing her throat, Marcy released a large amount of spit from her mouth making sure it landed on me. Then she unscrewed the top on her drink tossing on me.

"What the fuck, man?" I shouted ready to go off, but instead, I hopped into my ride speeding off to my house. Within five minutes, I was back home regretting that I took Kat's advice.

Walking into the room covered with Marcy's spit and Strawberry Fanta soda, I wasn't in the mood for anything or anyone. If Marcy wasn't Manhattan's grieving sister, I would have beat that bitch like a clucker who owed me money. It was one thing to throw soda on me, but to spit in my face was disrespectful, yo. Maybe they should have named her Spitta instead of me. That smut clearly lost her jawn when she lost her sister. I wasn't the blame for any of this, but Marcy didn't want to believe that. My lifestyle wasn't the cause of Manhattan's death, but everyone had a good way of making me feel that way. Now, if Manhattan would have committed suicide, I would have taken that charge like the man my mama raised me to be.

"Hey, baby I didn't think you would be back so soon." Deaux said, but I ignored her sitting on the edge of the bed. That quick, this bitch got comfortable like this was her house. Like always, I had a rude awakening for her. Before kicking her ass out, I kicked my shoes off and peeled the smelly clothes off.

Burying my face into my hands, I exhaled loudly tempted to scream. To keep it a stack, I was an inch from losing my fuckin' jawn because of all this shit. Hat hadn't been dead a week and I was ready to literally lose my mind.

"I know I'm not talking to myself, I said, hey, baby." She spoked softly lying across my bed in her bra and thong. A few months ago, I would have been all over Deaux getting' some head, but now she couldn't turn me on

"Do me a favor, Deaux?"

"Anything, baby, what's up," pushing the blanket from her body while kneeing in the bed to come to me. Deaux sat behind me rubbing my shoulders. Gently pushing her off of me, I pointed to the living room door saying, "go home, I didn't even tell you to come here, you need to understand I'm done with youse dog ass. I don't need you here or ever, I don't need you to be my crying shoulder. All I need from you is to stay the fuck outta my way, yo!"

"Wait, what, I was ju—"

"You were just leaving, that's what the fuck you were doing, be out!" Without saying another word, Deaux climb out of bed slipping her cropped top sweater, Timberland boots, and skinny jeans back onto her body. Ignoring her, I walked to my closet searching for a fresh pair of sweat pants, boxers, and a t-shirt. Deaux slowly walked out of my bedroom, hoping I would turn around, but I didn't. Bypassing her, I walked down the hall, then entering my bathroom. A few seconds later, I heard my door slamming, but I brushed her ignorance off by turning on my shower. Within seconds, I was in the shower lathered in water and body wash brainstorming. A nigga like me was ready to kill, I craved to have blood on my hands. I didn't care who blood stained my hands, it would be well worth it.

Standing in the shower with the warm water hitting my back, of course I was thinking about Manhattan also. Maybe it was the hot water making my body tingle, but I could something taking over my body. Naw, it couldn't be that, the chills that traveled down my body could only be one thing. Well, should I say only ONE person...... Manhattan.

"Say something to me, Hat, let me know what to do!"

I stood there for five minutes waiting for a sign or anything, but I didn't get it. I started to cry, but a knock on the door stopped me. Turning the water off, I jumped out of the shower wrapping a towel around my waist. Then I rushed out the foggy bathroom grabbing my gun that was secretly stashed down the hall. Peeking out of the window, I exhaled a lil realizing it was Smoke at my door. Opening the door, I said, "boy, you almost got your head blown off."

"I doubt it, youse ain't living like that." he laughed closing the door.

"Yea, yea, yea, youse know how a nigga is coming." I faked laughed closing the door behind him. Disappearing down the hall, I hurried to put my clothes on and reentered the living room to run it with Smoke. We had a lot to talk about.

"What up, lil' bro?" Smoke questioned with the loosie hanging at the corner of his fat lips. Waiting for me to reply, he exhaled the smoke from his mouth searching for an ashtray.

"Shit, cooling, that's it." I sat down saying.

"Bet, but did I just see Deaux leaving from here? Come on now, bro, Hat ju—"

"Look, it ain't what you think so, don 't even say that shit!! I've been sitting in the house in that chair since Hat died. Kat came over about an hour ago to talk and get me out of the house. Then Deaux popped up when I was leaving, I saw Marcy at the corner store, and that shit didn't go well. The stupid bitch threw a soda on me and spit in my face. I swear I saw red, but I had to remind myself that bitch was grieving." I said.

"Lord, don't let that get back to Kan." Smoke shoot his head.

"Unless Marcy tell someone, Kan won't hear it from me, yo."

"Fuck Deaux and Marcy, besides hearing these lil' bullshit ass rumors, you haven't heard anything else?" Smoke questioned me.

"No, I was about to ask you the same thing."

"You know I don't believe any of those rumors, bro. Especially the one about Hat being robbed, it don't add up."

"What if it does?" I asked.

"It doesn't, but best believe we'll figure it out. You know I'm standing behind you all the way."

"I was going to do the right thing, bro, I swear I was. Manhattan was the only woman for me, now I don't have her anymore."

Chapter 21

For hours, I sat on Kansas couch watching all of Manhattan's favorite television shows, listening to her favorite music, and watching her favorite movies. Being at home wasn't an option anymore, at least for right now. Too many emotions and feelings ran through my mind when I was alone and I couldn't handle that pressure. Yes, for the first time in life, Mr. Clover Porter was folding under pressure. It was things like her loud laughter and snorting that I missed and desperately needed back in our home. That high pitched laughter would bounce from wall to wall when she was on the phone early in the morning. At first, I hated it, now I missed it so much fuckin' much.

Katober didn't fully understand what was going on, but I knew my daughter was missing her mother. With a personality and smile like Manhattan, I wouldn't blame Katober at all. Manhattan was truly one of a kind and that was the God honest truth. She still didn't know her mother was dead, but what she did know was that her mom was away. It was time for me to tell her the truth, but I was still trying to figure out how to utter those words.

Walking out of her bedroom, Kansas rubbed her eyes to clear her vision. Then she wrapped her pink silk robe tighter around her body to cover her private areas.

"Boy, I thought youse were sleeping, yo." Even half sleeping, Kansas heavy Philly accent was thick as hell.

"No, sis, I'm just up watching movies and shit. If I woke you, I'm sorry." I spoked softly.

"Of course you didn't, I got up to pee and I saw the television was on. I figured you were up like me, I can't sleep. I tossed and turn so much I know Byron is annoyed." Kansas laughed sitting next to me. She gave me a warm hug, then she reach for the bag of pretzels I had taking a handful.

"Oh, ard." I answered, also taking a handful of the pretzels to stuff them in my mouth.

"What were you watching?" Kansas questioned.

"*The Nanny*, I never realized how much Manhattan laughed like Fran." I chuckled.

"I thought you knew that. You could hear that laugh from the Hudson River." Kansas laughed and slightly clapped her hands. The living room was dark, but I could see the tears filling.

"Please, don't start crying, sis." I begged Kansas placing her head on my shoulder. I felt a few of her tears fall on my bare shoulder because I was shirtless and I could also hear her sniffing. Kansas gently cleared her throat replying, "I'm sorry, bro, I just miss her so much. Manhattan was literally a sister to me and she's gone." Wiping her wet eyes and face, Kansas whimpered loudly, but covered her mouth.

"Ssshhhhhh, I know, I know, but we have to be strong. We all have to be strong, Kan." I replied.

"It's kind of hard to be strong when you DON'T want to be strong. It's like Hat was the backbone of everything and all of us. Clover, whoever killed Hat, make them joes pay for it!! they have to fell every little thing we feel, ard?"

"Trust me, they will feel every emotion I feel. I'm so fucking lost right now, I wouldn't know if I was coming or going." I scoffed shaking my head, but slightly laughing.

"Some of that has to do with you not sleeping. Clover, you haven't slept since Hat was killed."

"I know, it's kind of hard to, every time I close my jawns, I see her. I want her to talk to me so bad and tell me what happen, but she always disappear." I replied.

"Clover?"

"What's up?"

"When are we going to tell Koko what happened? Eventually she has to know the truth, what are we going to say when she really starts to notice her mother isn't here?" Kansas questioned.

"I've been thinking about that every second of the day and I don't know, Kan."

"Hey, you know you don't have to do it alone, I want to be with you when you tell Katober." She demanded.

"This shit is hard, Kan, I can't sleep, eat, or even drink with feeling sick to my stomach. How could someone so pure and sweet be caught up in a vicious act like this?" I sobbed a little, but quickly stopped, I didn't want Kansas to get emotional because of me. If we both began to cry, neither one of us would have the strength to pull the other one together.

"Bro, I love you to death and I hate seeing you like this. Get you some rest, for me, iight?" Kansas requested.

"I'll try, sis, but I can't make any promises."

"As long as you try, that's good enough or me. I'm going back to bed, I love you." Kansas still had tears traveling down her face, but she managed to smile while giving me a kiss on the cheek. As Kansas stood to her feet, I said, "I love you too, sis."

"I don't know when, but all of this fuckery will make sense soon." Kansas walked out of the living room and from behind, I could see her wiping her tears away. Once she made it into her bedroom closing the door, I silently cried covering my mouth.

For twenty minutes, I sat in the dark crying, crying like the lil' bitch I turned into.

"Come back, Hat, just for one night, so you can fix all of this." I whimpered. Maybe I was high, drunk, or drawlin, but the silhouette that sat next to me looked exactly like Manhattan. I rubbed my eyes a few times to make sure they weren't playing tricks on me, but them bitch's were.

"WHAT THE FUCK!"

"Clover, calm down," she smiled reaching for my hand. My mouth opened, but not a jawn came out of it. With shaking hands, I reached for Manhattan's other hand, but I couldn't feel a thing. She simple placed her hand on top of mines as if we could actually hold hands. Hat smiled at me in a way I never seen before, it almost mad me sad in a way.

"Ma-Ma-Man-Manhattan, what the fuck is going on?" I asked feeling nervous and scared, but Hat giggled a little.

"What's going on is that I'm here, in spirit sitting next to you. That's what you wanted, right, you were just begging me to come back and fix all this?"

"Y-Yea, but I thought that was only wishful thinking, I didn't think you would actually come here!! Manhattan what happened, I need to know because the streets are playing me like a fool?"

"What happened is that.......someone killed me, but it wasn't a robbery, it wasn't because you owed anyone money, or any of that foolishness people are saying." She answered, still smiling and now, I kept crept out.

"Who killed you Manhattan, tell me right now so I can kill them?" I demanded making Manhattan sigh loudly.

"You need to look in your front view mirror and not your back mirror."

"Huh?" I asked.

"You'll catch on, but when the timing is right. Grieve a little, it's okay to grieve, baby, I was the love of your life. If you died, I would until the death I died." She expressed.

"That's what I plan on doing for the rest of my life. I miss you, Hat, this shit is eating me up inside. Knowing that your killer or killers are walking around here like they didn't do anything drives me crazy."

"Killer."

"What?" I asked.

"You said my killer or killers. One person killed me, but they were accompanied by someone."

"Manhattan, are you really going to sit there and not tell me who killed you?"

"Do you remember the first time we met, Clover?" sitting on the bed comfortable as if she was still alive, Hat wore the humble smile on her elegant face.

"That's a crazy question, you know I do. You had a jawn going crazy on the first day and you didn't even know it. I talked about you all…..damn…….week, I know I was driving Smoke and Kansas crazy." I laughed.

"What the fuck are you doing? Are you serious right now, joe ass nigga?"

"I'm dead ass serious right now. Beautiful woman, can I have your name," I asked her while leaning against the window trying to grab her hand. Hat wasn't having that shit and didn't waste any time sizing me up. Pulling away quickly with a mug on her face, Hat replied, "Nigga, no, I don't know you!"

"Girl, stop playing, I know you know me. Shit, you at least heard of me in these Philly streets," I licked my black lips smirking.

Removing the big brown sunglasses from her face, Manhattan said, "I've heard OF you, but I don't know you, Clover, is it?"

"Yea, Clover Porter, but my jawns call me Spitta. Can I have your name so I can stop holding up traffic?"

"I'm Manhattan, Manhattan Mullen, but my jawns call me Hat," she replied flipping her long, brown bouncy hair trying not to smirk. By the way her lips trembled, she struggled not like a mutherfucker.

"It's nice to meet you, Hat." After waiting for me to move, cars started to drive pass us sticking me the middle finger. I could only laugh, talking to her was worth every middle finger flipped at me and curse word. It's not like I haven't been called a black mutherfucker before. Hearing that was like music to my ears, yo.

"Damn, you're going to have the whole city pissed off, you drawlin at nine in the morning," she laughed flipping her hair again exposing the entire beauty of her face. If you ask me to describe Manhattan .... I turned into a square quick, bro. She was breathtaking with plump pink lips that she never embraced. I always told her to be secure about the things she saw as flaws. Though I saw them as something to praise on the daily. Her innocent behavior was precious to me, Manhattan could never do any wrong in my eyes. Now, some people didn't think she was all that and as beautiful as I always described. Some defined Manhattan as plain because her backside wasn't pumped with ass shots, she wore her real hair, and rarely covered her face with a touch of make-up. I loved her that way, Hat's clear skin was flawless, it was perfect to me.

"Fuck them joes, your conversation is worth it," I smiled.

"Oh, really." She spoke sarcastically making me raise my eyebrows with a big grin on my face.

"Very much so, but do you have a boyfriend? I don't want to have to beat up anybody for talking to their girlfriend."

"No, I don't, I've been single for a while now," she stated looking in her side mirror at the traffic. With every curse that was thrown at us, Manhattan snickered a little bit more. I guess after hearing black ass bitch a dozen times it became funny to her.

"Damn, a girl like you shouldn't be single when a man like me is walking this earth," I smiled.

"Boy, you have a way with words," she rolled her eyes placing the sunglasses onto her face. Slowly grabbing her hand, neither did she pull away this time, I replied, "I'm just being honest, maybe I can change that one day."

"Why would you want to change that, Mr. Porter, I like being single."

"I bet after spending a few hours with me, that will change," I licked my lips again stating. By the way Manhattan hesitated, but smiled at me, I already knew she was feeling a nigga big time, yo. It didn't matter how much she thought she could hid it, I could see the love in Manhattan's eyes already.

"I don't do good with bets, homeboy," she laughed.

"Shit, I'm glad to know that, but do you want to know something else?"

"What, Clover?"

"I think …… you should put my number in that phone, we should talk on a daily, I take you on a date every week, we fall in love, then we can live happily ever after."

"Bol, is that all the game you got," she laughed.

"It's not game, Miss Manhattan. I would love to take you out to dinner and talk more, we can go wherever you want to."

"I don't know about all of that fall in love mess, but I'll give you my number," grabbing her phone from the passenger's side and handing it to me, I didn't waste a second programming my number *into her phone. Once I was done, I handed it to her saying, "Now you're stuck with me for life," I laughed, but smacking her lips, Manhattan said, "Once again, you're drawlin, but I like your style. You gotta lil' flavor to you," she laughed.*

"Just a lil' bit, stank," I laughed as well.

"Yea, just a lil' bit, but before we get ran over, I need to go. It was nice meeting you Mr. Porter, have a nice day," blowing me a kiss and laughing, Manhattan drove off in her red Mustang with the top back. Her hair blew in the wind like she was in a music video or something. I was left standing in the middle of Walnut Street blushing, but hoping she would call me soon.

See, what Manhattan didn't know is that I've watching her for a lil' minute now. What else she didn't know is that I knew she was watching me too. She wasn't the type of shorty to approach a nigga like me, but I couldn't blame her. With the reputation I had ……. I probably wouldn't approach me either.

Finally hoping into my car speeding off, I grabbed my phone to see if Hat called yet. She didn't, I felt mad thirsty, but brushed it off turning my music up. On a day like this, the temperature was right, and it had me feeling good. All I needed was a bad bitch on my side, but none of these hoes could keep my attention after I caught a nut. It was still early in the day, you never know what will happen when the sun sets, and the street lights come on, on a Saturday night.

Chapter 22

A week later.

I knew I was wrong for smoking a loosie in a church's bathroom stall, but I needed that loosie badly. Majority of the people in the church hated my guts, whispered when they saw me, rolled their eyes in my direction, and gave me the direst looks I've ever seen. My mom and Kansas were ready to pop off because these bitches were drawlin' too much. Truth be told, I wasn't surprised by anyone's actions. Hearing people whisper things like, "murder, why is here, or even why is he here," kind of made me feel some type of way. I had every right to be in their presences, I love Manhattan just as much as everyone did and probably more. Maybe they were right though, I should have stayed home because everyone made it clear that they didn't want me here. It was only so many times I would allow people to handle me like I was a joe. A nigga was tempted to rock out at St. Augustine Church.

"Bro, throw that loosie away and the fuck out that stall. Ma and Kan are looking for you." Smoke said tapping on the door. Sitting on the small toilet, I shook my head exhaling the smoke in the air. I was smoking that cigarette like it was an oowops.

"Give me a minute, bruh, just onneeee minute." Tapping the loosie on the bottom of my Stacey Adam shoes, I then reached into my inner pocket to grab a small bottle of Axe body spray. I usually didn't buy this cheap shit, but right about now, I didn't care and it got the job done.

"You know you're out of pocket for this shit, huh?" Smoke laughed tapping on the small again. I knew I was wrong, so, I laughed with him.

"Yea, I know I'm drawlin', but people are drawlin' too. Now I see how Jesus felt when they crucified him, yo." Spraying a lil' more body spray on my suit, I walked out of the stall finding Smoke standing ten toes down. His arms were folded across his chest waiting for me to walk out.

"Nigga, did you compare yourself to Jesus, thee Jesus Christ, my Lord and Savior?" Smoke laughed.

"Yea."

"I can't believe this joe ass nigga." Hitting my shoulder a little, Smoke laughed, then he adjusted the cufflinks on his suit. Even though he was laughing, I couldn't help, but to notice the redness that filled his droopy eyes. Smoke wasn't the type to expose his emotions, but Hat's death hit him hard also. Smoke considered Hat to be like a real sister to him and their relation extended beyond her and I. Besides being a sister to him, Smoke considered Hat to be a good friend. To him, it didn't matter if her and I were together or not, Smoke would always remain type with Manhattan.

"Yes the fuck I just did compare myself to my lord and Savior. I'm not telling this shit anymore, bro, Motherfuckers are looking at me like I'm the one who blew her face off. This shit is not my fault, bruh, it's just not!" thinking about the hurtful jawns people said sent me in a rage of emotions.

Bam!

Breathing heavily, I punched the concrete wall releasing my frustration. With the skin instantly tearing over my knuckles, blood started to pour out. even though my hand was over in blood, I pulled back to punch the wall again, but Smoke stopped me by bear hugging me. I didn't have much energy to fight him off, but I still tried to. I was numb to the pain and could punch that wall for hours. "Smoke get off me man, this ain't right!!!" I shouted out, but he ignored me holding me tighter.

"I know, lil' bro, but you can't keep flashing out every second. This not the time or place to be showing your emotions like this Besides, I need to talk to you about something and it can't wait."

"Talk to me about what, man? The way everyone is treating me is ass wrong and you know it. I loved Manhattan with every bone in my body, everyone knows that. I would never put my baby in any harm, Smoke, you know me."

Finally breaking free from Smoke, I leaned against the wall crying like a lil' bitch. As I slowly slid down the wall, I covered my face to disguise the sobbing I was doing. They say men didn't cry, but I beg to differ. This pain I experienced was past undesirable and something I wish money could make vanish. What made me feel worse is that Manhattan had to have a close casket since most of her face was blown off. When her mom had to identify her body, Mrs. Mullen could hardly recognize her own daughter. If it wasn't for the clovers she had tattooed on her wrist, Mrs. Mullen wasn't believing that was her precious Manhattan lying on a cold table lifeless.

"Lil' Bro, I know you're hurt. Fuck, I'm hurting too and with you, but you have to shake this off temporarily. We have business to handle, SOME MANHATTAN KIND OF BUSINESS." Slowly removing my hands from my face, Smoke opened the left side of his jacket revealing his tool to me. It didn't matter what and where was the occasion, Smoked stayed strapped at all times.

"Nigga, why do you have a blinky at a funeral?" I asked.

"The same reason you were smoking a loosie in the bathroom. I know mama didn't raise us like this." Said Smoke and we laughed.

"Hell no, but what'cha mean some Manhattan business, bro?" I asked.

"My homie out of Harrison Project said he heard some shit through the wind. Some young bol from Fairmouth is bragging about killing some bitch last week. Supposedly it was a robbery turned homicide, but when he shot her, lil' nigga didn't even stay to see if the body would drop." Said Smoke. Imaging the love of my life body hit the floor and swimming in a pool of blood made every strand of body hair stand up. I've done some fucked up shit in my life and probably made some more fucked up shit to do, but killing women and children wasn't my steelo. Some things I could never carry in my heart, yo.

"Smoke, don't play with me right now, are you for real?" I questioned using my sleeve to wipe my wet face.

"I'm dead ass serious, bro and my homie told me where the lil' nigga be. Right there on Popular Street and Master Street. Tonight, we're dropping iron on that nigga and I care if he's out there playing booray with his mama, sister, or favorite cousin. Rock the fuck out on everybody, I ain't showing no mercy!" Smoke whispered loudly.

"Shid, I'm trying to rock out ASAP Rocky, it's not like anyone wants me here." Sighing loudly, I stared at the ceiling and I could feel my eyes filling with tears. My lips, they trembled uncontrollably and my heart paced in an unsteady beat. The feeling of being weak and defended wasn't something I adored on any level. To pull myself together would be hard, but I had to do it. Besides my dad, and a few homies out the hood, I never lost anyone this dear to the heart. The thought of her never coming back made my heart ache. Just hearing her name made my heart heavy and ready to explode with emotion.

"You know you turn me on when you talk that gangsta shit." Smoke laughed nodding his head. Wiping my face again, I chuckled a few times saying, "man, whatever, but I think I'm ready to leave, for real this time. I need a perc and a blunt."

"Like always, your wish is my command, I got a blunt in the car." Putting his hands together like prayer hands, Smoke laughed. Then he gave me a hug, but once again, I was crying like a lil' broad with a broken heart.

"Smoke, I really did love her, I miss her so much. This can't be real, I have to wake up from this dream because I'm losing my mind." I silently sobbed still trying to keep my emotions in check, but I couldn't.

"Trust me, Clove, I already know you loved Hat. Never let anyone tell you anything else, she couldn't tell you any different." Said Smoke.

"Well the fuck everyone else can't see that?"

"They do but they don't want to admit it. Everyone wants Clover to be the bad guy so they can get some kind of peace in all this. It's all good though, you don't have to prove a point to any one of these fuckers, yo. Especially those Mullens, I swear, they're pushing a nigga's buttons."

BOOM! BOOM! BOOM! BOOM!

The banging on the bathroom door ended our conversation fast making Smoke and I paranoid.

"Get that nigga out of this church, NOW, or will have the police escort his no-good ass out of here!" Marcy shouted still banging on the door. Every time I saw this smut or even heard her name I formed a headache.

"Marcy, don't do this here, please. Let my child go in peace!"

"Ma, leave me alone, you don't want him here just like I don't!" Marcy shouted.

"MARCY, I AM NOT THE ONE YOU WANT PROBLEM. JUST BECAUSE YOU'RE GRIEVING I BE DAMN YOU CONTINUE TO TALK TO MY BROTHER CRAZY!!!"

"Didn't I tell you I didn't want you here, but you still dragged your ugly ass here!!!! GET THE FUCK OUT!!!!!!" Marcy shouted making everyone stare at me waiting for my next move. Standing in front of me anxiously waiting for Marcy to make a move, Kansas held my wrist tightly. At this point, I had no more fight in me and ready to give up on everything.

"Have a good day, come on, Smoke."

***

"Let me gather the information, I'll text you." Deaux said softly through the receiver.

"Hurry up, bye." I ended the call frustrated. Pulling the tie from my neck, I paced through my living room trying to get my head straight. I drove around for a few minutes trying to figure out everything, but as usual, nothing bad sense!! I couldn't sit in the house any longer, especially once I thought about the conversation I had with

Manhattan. I wanted to tell someone, but I knew everyone would have thought I was losing my mind.

"Marcy has one more time to play on my jawn like that!! I'm telling you, I'ma smack fire from that bitch's mouth. I don't know who the fuck she thinks she is." I tossed the tie on my couch, still pacing like a maniac.

"I swear, Marcy is going to make me smash her face in!! That bitch is really pushing it, yo. She wants to play the role of the grieving sister, but she can miss me with that! I was more of a sister to her than Marcy was. Where was Marcy when Hat needed someone to drop Katober to the babysitter, doctor appointments, and everything else Hat needed help with? It was Oak, Ryker, and ME, not her!! That was OUR sister and that bitch better stay in her place." Kansas' full chest expanded up and down as she took big gulps of her Hennessy. She was so pissed that she drunk it straight, without a chaser. Kansas sat on the counter top tapping her legs on the bottom cabinets, she was going to need more than Hennessy to calm her nerves.

"On my mama, Marcy was two seconds from getting her fuckin' head pulled back at the funeral. The only thing that saved her was that we were at Manhattan's funeral. OH, but please believe if it was someone's else funeral, I would have cut the fuck up!" Oak rolled her eyes saying. She never really liked Marcy anyways. "Don't worry, we'll see that bitch in the streets and she better have that same energy." Kansas interrupted.
"Thank God you didn't rent that suit, I can smell your sweat from here." Oak said laughing. I could feel the sweat forming under my arms.
"Really, Oak, really!" I said.

"Baby, do you want anything to drink or eat? Clover still has some of the gumbo I made him yesterday." Ryker asked rubbing Smoke's back, but he ignored her pushing the Smoke out of his mouth.
"The only thing I'm thinking about it a one eighty seven. I can't even eat or drink anything right now." Smoke shook his head.
"I understand all that, but, baby, you haven't eaten anything since last night." Ryker whispered.
"Ayo, Deaux just text me back, with the information." I said to everyone.

"What did she say?" Oak asked.

"Ronan Reece, nineteen year old youngin' from Fairmouth, and he has a thing for jacking. Especially women who he thinks live alone. Supposedly, he thought Manhattan and I weren't together anymore. He's been watching her for the past two days waiting for the right time to rob her. Manhattan put up a fight, which is why he shot her."

"Bet, that's who we go and kill." Smoke took another hit of his blunt saying.

"Deaux said the lil' nigga have a thing for her, she can set the whole thing up." I replied.

"I guess hoe ass Deaux came in handy finally." Folding her arms across her chest, then crossing her legs, Kansas smirked a little. I could only imagine what she would do when she spotted Marcy out in public. I sure do hope she has that same energy she had.

"Look, Clover, we all know I can't stand your guts, but what Marcy did at the funeral was wrong. Youse loved Manhattan just as much as her family did, but by the looks of things, you loved her more. WE all know you loved Hat, you just couldn't keep your dick in your pants." Oak spoked grabbing my shoulder to comfort me. Coming from her, it was the sweetest thing she ever said to me.

"Thanks, Oak, that means a lot coming from you. Your words were kind of, eehhhhh, but you got your point across." I laughed and so did she.

"Hat always told me I had a way with words. I don't want to cry, Lord knows that's the only thing I've been doing, but what the fuck am I supposed to do without my best friend, Spitta? If it wouldn't been for Hat I would be in someone's jail by now. Here I go, crying again, I'll be back." Oak stood to her feet crying to the bathroom with Cope following behind her.

"See, this is what I can't deal with. None of us are strong, none of us can go a minute without crying. All because this lil" Ronan cat, Smoke and Clover, make that nigga answer for what he did to my sister." Jumping from the countertop and wiping her tears away, Kansas took the last sip of her drink walking outside. Everyone was fucked up.

Chapter 23

Staring at myself in the bathroom mirror I could see the outcome of a long night scribbled on my face. My eyes were heavier than ever filled with redness. Besides a few hours of sleep, I hadn't slept much, but now, rest screamed my name. For a black ass nigga, I looked pale as fuck. I didn't mind the bodies I caught a couple of hours ago, but lying next to my daughter after it made me feel low down and dirty. News was slowly beginning to spread about the killings, but I was bothered or moved by it. Clearly Smoke wasn't either because Ryker said he was sleeping like a baby. Smoke and I would never get caught or tied to the murders. We wouldn't tell on one another, but Deaux on the other hand, I couldn't say the same. Eventually, I would have to keep her mouth shut for good.

Still staring in the mirror, Manhattan slowly appeared with an unpleasant look on her face.

"Youse dead and still mugging me. I swear, yo, this shit is crazy, no funny shit."

"Yea, yea, yea, youse still giving me a reason to mug you. Even in the afterlife you're getting on my nerves. My LAST damn nerve, Clover Porter." Leaning against the wall, Manhattan placed her hand on my shoulder laughing.

"In the words of Manhattan Porter, yea, yea, yea. I wish I could actually feel your hand on my shoulder. It's simple things like your touch I'm dying for." Leaning forward on the bathroom sink, I dropped my head laughing. I stared at my bare chest hoping Manhattan didn't see some of blood droplets on my chest. Knowing her, she probably spotted it, but waited for me to speak on.

"Manhattan Porter sounds waaayyy better than Manhattan Mullen." She laughed, standing directly behind me.

"It does, I had this whole plan, baby, I was ready to do the right thing. Next month, I was going to ask you to marry you. You know I was going all out for it, I had to top Smoke. I wanted us to live happily ever after, but now that's ruin." I sighed staring back at Manhattan in the mirror.

"I know I didn't do any wrong, but I'm sorry. Since I met you, all I dreamed about was spending the rest of my life with you. I remember after our first date, I gave Ryker a play by play of our wedding. I probably sounded like a fool in love, but I couldn't help it. I love you so much, Clover, that won't ever change."

"You didn't do anything wrong. I want to understand this situation and not question God, but it's hard not to. You are a good person, why did he have to take you? He should have taken Deaux if he wanted to take something."

"Eventually he will." She mumbled.

"What?" I turned around asking.

"Nothing, but Clover Porter, do me a favor." Manhattan demanded.

"What, baby, anything, youse know that?"

"Take care of our daughter and keep her away from niggas like you. Katober deserves the world, all of it, okay? It's going to be hard raising her without me, but don't get discourage. You have plenty of help; Kansas, Ryker, Oak, and even Kat. Shit, Smoke and Cope will be there to help along the way." She laughed.

"You are truly, the most beautiful woman I have ever laid eyes on, Manhattan, just look at you."

"Thanks, but, Clover, that young bol on Master Street didn't deserve to die in front of his mama. The other boy from TNT damn sure didn't deserve to be pistol whipped." Manhattan spoked softly.

"Oh yea, I didn't deserve a lot of things. Like the way Marcy has been handling me. I'm telling you, Hat, she's pushing every button I have." I uttered hoping I didn't upset Manhattan with any of my words. By the simple look on her face, I guess I didn't.
"Trust me, if I could rise from the dead and kick Marcy's ass for

doing that, I would. We all know she's doing the absolute most. Matter of a fact, keep that bitch from around my child."

"Copy that, ten four. I also didn't deserved for them to take you from me!! How the fuck do you think I feel? You being KILLED, is literally tearing me up inside. Let's not talk about how I feel lying to Koko about your whereabouts."

"It's time you tell her the truth, waiting will only hurt her. I watch and pray over my baby every night, Clover. Make sure she knows how much I love her and I'm sorry I left her." Manhattan dropping her head with a cracking voice. I turned away, I couldn't watch her cry at all.

"Manhattan, please don't do that, I can't hold you while youse crying." I begged with tears chasing one another down my cheeks.

"I'm sorry." She whispered.

"You could have did this same two steps before the funeral. I couldn't even tell you goodbye, Hat."

"I'm here now, in spirit and that's all that matters, you're the only person I can come back to. The others won't be able to handle that. Youse like the strongest person I know, baby." She smiled reaching for my hand, but her smile disappeared when she got a lil' taste of reality.

"Me, the strongest, shit, I don't know about that. I'm all over the place, baby, I can't even lie to you. I swear I'm trying to be strong, but every time I think about you, I get emotional as fuck. Any one who gets tied to your name is catching a bullet."

"NO, you have to stop that. Deaux is still playing you like a guitar, but I want YOU to figure it out on your own. Bye, Clover Porter." In a blink of an eye, Manhattan was gone leaving me clueless to what the fuck she just said. Still staring at the mirror, I exhaled loudly walking out of the bathroom quietly. It was still early in the morning and I didn't want to wake Katober.

At 6:45 am, I found myself in deep thoughts that would drive the average person straight to the mental house. A lot of shit with Manhattan's death wasn't adding up, I began to feel like none of it would make sense. Too many rumors still floated in the air making me feel like the whole city hated my guts. With all this blood on my hands, it was only a matter of time someone linked me or my young bols to one of the murders. At this point, I don't know if I was chasing revenge or clearing my name to prove I had nothing to do with Hat's death.

Carefully climbing into bed, I pulled the covers over my body finally closing my eyes to get some sleep, I let motion coming from Katober's side of the bed. Dang, so much for getting some rest.

"Daddy, daddy, daddy!" Katober shouted my name while jumping on my stomach with a big smile on her face. With the sun rising and slowly dancing on her face, I could literally see Manhattan living through her. It almost brought tears to my eyes, but I didn't want my daughter to see me in tears. Clearing my throat and using my long fingernails to remove crust from Katober's eyes, I said, "good morning, sunshine, how did you sleep?"

"Good, daddy, but I want mommy to make me some oatmeal."

"Baby, daddy can make youse some oatmeal." I exhaled softly.

"Okay, but will you put the little apples in it like mommy does?"

"Yep, whatever you want." I replied.

"Good, but I want mommy." She stated, breaking my heart.

"Sweetness, mommy isn't here right now."

"When is she coming back?" she asked.

"One day, baby girl, but when you sleep at night, you might see her." I smiled, making Katober smile expand.

"Really?"

"Yep, you sure will and I want you to remember something." It didn't matter how many times Katober asked for Manhattan, it still brought tears to my eyes. On beat, like always, she wiped the tears not questioning why I was crying.

"What, daddy?"

"I want you to remember that your mama loves you to death. Never let anyone tell you different, you were her world, she did anything to make you happy."

"Okay, but daddy, can I have some orange juice with my oatmeal? Hold the pulp, please." She giggled.

"Girl, what do youse know about no pulp in your orange juice?" I laughed.

"I don't know, uncle Smoke taught me that. He told auntie Ryker that he doesn't like pulp. Daddy, who is pulp and why doesn't uncle like him?" I laughed again.

"Baby, I don't know."

Knock! Knock! Knock!

The knocking from the front door caught me by surprise, but I played it cool. Katober wasn't bothered by it, but asked, "daddy, is that auntie Kansas?"

"Uummm, maybe so, but let daddy find out. Don't come out of the room unless I tell you to, ard?"

"Ard, daddy."

Putting a fake smile on my face, I rolled out of bed heading straight to my Teflon that was tucked secretly in the hallway closet. Then I slowly tucked it behind my back walking to the window taking a peek. The new red Bentley truck didn't look familiar and made me nervous. Slowly opening the door a little, I peeked my hand out saying, "what's good, my nigga?" Chris stood on my porch dressed in a long sleeve shirt with khaki pants. I sure hope this fool was going to work and this wasn't his everyday attire. It was too hot for that shit. We locked eyes for a few seconds, then he said, "uuumm, can I holla at you for a minute?"

"About what?" Opening the door wider to expose my blicky to Chris, his hands shook a little as he took a few steps back.

"Manhattan, I wanted to offer my condolences."

"Oh yea?"

"Yea, I know I'm the last person you want to see, but I would feel less of a man if I didn't come here."

"You really didn't have to do that, lil' homie, it ain't that deep." I replied.

"To you, but you were a part of shorty's life."

"The autopsy showed that Manhattan was four weeks pregnant, did you know?"

"Naw, she hadn't told me that yet, I'm not even sure if she knew. Damn, in one night, I lost my baby and my woman, this can't be real." Sighing loudly with his hands on his head, Chris words didn't sit too well with a nigga.

"Nah, my nigga, youse just lost your baby. I'm sorry for that, I truly am, but you didn't lose your woman. Hat was my woman, you only borrowed her for a few weeks. Now, get the fuck off my porch." Waving my gun a little, I closed the door shaking my head. Rushing down the hall to saved my Teflon, I opened the room door to find Katober sitting at the edge of the bed watching *Dora the Explorer*. Damn, she literally was Manhttan's twin.

"Are you ready to eat, baby?" I asked climbing back into the bed next to my daughter.

"Daddy, can we go see mommy at the place she's at?" Katober smiled, but it was her high pitched voice.

"Uuuummm, baby, daddy has to tell you something."

"What is it, daddy?" She asked staring me dead in the eyes. Yea, this was going to be way harder than I thought.

"Do you know what death is? I know it isn't something your mom and I taught you. I guess we didn't because we never really had a reason to." I said clearing my throat.

"No, daddy."

"Okkayyyy, do you know what heaven is?" I asked.

"Mommy told me that grandpa is in heaven because he's an angel. Is that right, daddy?"

"Youse correct, but to become an angel, God has to call you home. Home is heaven, okay?"

"Okay." She nodded her head looking confused.

"So, with that being said, the real reason mommy isn't here is because God called her home. Daddy doesn't have the answer for it, but mommy left you loving you so much."

"Daddy, did you know she was leaving?" Katober questioned.

"No, baby girl, I didn't know she was leaving. I had to find out on my own."

"Did mommy want to leave?"

"Of course she didn't, she never wanted to leave us." I answered.

"Well, why did she leave?" Man, Katober hit me with the questions back to back, she needed to know everything.

"Because, baby, God needed her more, just like he needed grandpa." I replied.

"Are you mad that mommy didn't tell you she was leaving?"

"No, mommy really didn't know she was leaving."

"Daddy, I'm sad, I didn't want mommy to go home." She started to cry with her head slowly falling into my lap. Pulling lose hair back into a ponytail, I wiped her tears saying, "I know, baby, me either. Just know one thing, daddy is here, and I'm not going anywhere."

Chapter 24 (October 2016)
The aftermath, minus Doctor Dre and Slim Shady.

Twelve people, in approximately two months, I killed a total of twelve people trying to figure out who killed Manhattan. Not all twelve people I pulled the trigger, but their cold blood was still on my smooth hands. I wasn't sure who to trust with this jawn, but I had to tell someone eventually about what I did. Keeping this shit to myself would drive me crazy, I was ready to explode, I was still pissed and heart at who killed Manhattan. Jealously was a fuckin' crazy and thing and I never thought it would be the reason someone would kill my baby.

Rushing into my house, I ran into my room peeling the wet bloody clothes off my body. Seem like after I pulled the trigger letting those bullets go, the rain came down harder. It was only Manhattan crying because of my vicious act. If she was here on earth, I could only imagine how she would feel about my actions. The cold looks she would give me would probably leave me frozen for days.

Right about now, I couldn't even look at myself in the mirror without wanting to break down. Not because of what I've done, but because nothing changed. After killing Syn and Deaux for killing

Manhattan, it still didn't make me feel better and it damn sure wasn't bringing my baby back.

Now naked with a pile of wet clothes on my clean carpet, I paced through my room plotting my next move. It was time my daughter and I got out of Philly to start a new life, the life I should have lived a long time ago.

"Clover Maurice Porter."

"Manhattan," I jumped, but gathered myself quickly. Manhattan stood behind me with the saddest glare on her oval face. I dropped my head sighing, she didn't have to say how she was feeling. I knew her too well.

"I was there the whole time, Clover. I saw and heard everything you did, that's a side of you I never wanted to see. You had no reason to make them beg for their lives the way you did," she uttered, but I turned around attempting to ignore her.

"I would hate to lie and say I'm sorry because I'm not. Syn and Deaux got what they deserved, it should have been more! That bitch killed you because she wanted to be YOU. You had what she could never had, so she took one of the things that would leave me hurt for life."

"What now, you feel better because I know you don't!!! I know your heart, Clover, it's still aching, this will only make you feel worse. Did it bring me back, Clover," she asked.

"No, it didn't," I mumbled.

"So, what was your purpose of doing it," she asked sitting on the bed, calmly crossing her legs.

"Because now everyone she loves can feel the pain I felt, Manhattan!!!!! You don't know what it feels like to lose the one woman you love, your best friend, your fuckin' everything, man. I walk around like a zombie all day just hoping this isn't real and you'll come back. Not as a ghost, I'm talking about the real you, I just want to hug you so damn bad Manhattan!!!!! That's all I want from you and I would never ask for anything every again, I promise."

"You don't think I want the same thing think, Clover? To physically be there when you cry at night because I'm not here? To hug, kiss, and tell you everything will be okay?? Clover Porter, you're the only man I have ever loved and it hurts me to my core to see you like this," she whimpered.

"You don't know how this feel, Hat, you just don't," I said.

"Yes, I do know how you feel. You lost me and I lost you, trust me, I know your pain."

"Manhattan, even as a ghost you're still beautiful like the day I met you. You don't understand baby, I miss you so much, every day is hard without you. If I could change all of this, I swear I would in a heartbeat. You didn't deserve any of this and at the end of the day, it's still my fault," I attempted to fight back my tears, but I could no longer do that. Leaning against the wall naked, I started to cry.

"Baby, have a sit, please," she begged pointing to the empty spot next to her.

"Ard."

"It doesn't matter what anyone says Clover, I don't blame you. Deaux did what she did because of envy, not love. I was the woman she wanted to be, but Deaux could never be me."

"That doesn't make me feel better."

"Stop crying, Clover, you are a good person, you just made some wrong decisions. This is where you learn from your mistake and start to live a different life, okay, a life without me," she replied.

"How am I supposed to live without you, Manhattan, I love you," I asked.

"You don't have to leave without me, I always be in your heart and surrounding you, but you have to let me go. I want you to move on and me happy, you deserved to be loved again. In order for youse to move on, I can't come back, I have to let go as well."

"I don't want to move on!"

"Do it for me, please, I hate seeing you like this. Make someone happy the way you use to make me happy, but treat her right. She's going to be beautiful, smart, caring, and addicted to water ice. Her favorite spot with be Max's and she's going to love eating cheesesteak with you on Sundays," she laughed kissing my forehead.

"How do you know all that," I asked wiping my wet face.

"Because I know everything, just trust me on this one. You're going to love her, but please, treat her right. You're getting a second chance on love, but you don't have to rush into anything with her. Truly be her friend first and let her do the same, you're going to need a friend." She replied.

"Yea, whoever SHE is, but she'll never be you. They don't make you kind anymore, I don't mind admitting that to myself."

"I love you, Hat."

"I love you too."

Knock! Knock! Knock!

Reaching under the pillow, I grabbed my Glock Forty running to the door. I was paranoid like a mutherfucker, but also mad that Hat disappeared and we couldn't finish our conversation.

Slowly creeping to the window, I slightly peeked out of it to get a view of outside, but I couldn't see anything. Just a beautiful girl standing on my doorsteps. Maybe this was a set up, but if it was, I was leaving this bitch stankin' with no problem. Sorry, Hat.

"Who is it?" I asked from behind the close door.

"I'm sorry to bother you, but I caught a flat tire in front of your house. My cell phone just died and I need to call someone to help me. Can I use your phone, please, I don't have to come inside." she asked.

"Uhhh, yea, sure, just give me a second," tucking the gun in my bookshelf, I then ran to my drawer to grab a clean pair of dry clothes. Once I slipped them on, I ran back to the door to open it. The woman that should wet on my porch was just as beautiful as Hat with big cognac brown eyes. Her natural brown curly hair sat at her waist looking like spiral curls. Her beauty had me speechless, but it was this feeling she gave me. Like I knew her from somewhere, but I didn't have a clue who this broad was.

"Oh my God, thank you so much. I knocked on your neighbors door, but they ignored me."

"Yea, Mrs. and Mr. Jefferson are some joes." I laughed, handing her the phone.

"Too bad I had to find out this way, but I'm Laker Jenkins by the way," she answered.

"I'm Clover Porter, but everyone calls me Spitta," I replied.

" Clover, Uumm, aren't you that guy who girlfriend was killed like two months ago?"

"Yea and her name was Manhattan," I answered.

"Aww, I'm sorry for your loss, but did they ever find the killer," she asked.

"No, they didn't, but would you like to come in for a dry towel or a change of clothes? I know sitting in those wet clothes are uncomfortable," I chuckled.

"Yes, thank you so much. Once I get home, I'll wash, dry, and bring your clothes back to you, I pinky promise," she laughed walking in and closing the door. I couldn't believe I was letting my guard down, but something about this joint had me feeling mad comfortable already.

"You're good ma, keep them to remind yourself to always keep a spare tire and clothes in your car," I joked while walking to my room. I opened my dresser pulling out a pair of blue basketball shorts and a white t-shirt. Then I walked into the bathroom grabbing a big pink towel, but I quickly put it back to grab another one. It was Manhattan's favorite towel, she couldn't have that.

Reentering the living room, I handed Laker the clothes saying, "look, shorty, you can change in the laundry room." I pointed at the open door passed the kitchen. Nodding her hand and smiling, she walked to the laundry room closing the door. A few minutes later, she reentered the living room wearing my clothes with the towel wrapped around her hair.

"You are a life saver, Clover Porter." She laughed sitting next to me trying to make another call on my phone. I laughed also.

"It's all good, but the way you said my name is funny."

"Why, that's your name, right, or is it my southern accent?" She questioned.

"Naw, Manhattan always said Clover Porter when she said my name. Not Spitt, Clover, Spitta, or Clove, it had to be Clover Porter."

"That's funny, but cute, Manhattan must have been one hell of a woman." She said.

"Why do you say that?"

"The way you lit up when you spoke about her." She laughed.

"Yea, she really was, you had to be full of hate to not like her. Are you from here, you probably know her."
"I'm from McComb, Mississippi, but I moved here three years ago. I live in Germantown."

"Wow, you're far from home, but do you like the city of brotherly love."

"Hell yea, I love Philly way more than McComb. I'm still getting adjusted to the climate change, but it was the best decision I made," she laughed.

"What made you move here," I asked.

"I wanted a change, something new, you know? If I tell you how I chose Philadelphia you probably would laugh at me."

"Promise I won't, tell me," I stated.
"Wwwwelllllll, on four pieces of paper, I wrote four different cities to choose from. There were Philadelphia, Colorado, Georgia, and New Orleans and that's how I chose Philly," she shrugged her shoulders smiling and I laughed.

"Woowwww, I bet you kill it at the casino," I said still laughing.

"To be honest, I'm not the gambling type. Casinos do not get my hard-earning money at all."

"I feel you on that, shooting dice burn my pockets," I chuckled. I couldn't stop staring at Laker, she was too beautiful. Laker reminded me of an angel that fell from above, God had to be searching for her. This must be the girl Manhattan was talking about, she was perfect and breathtaking, just like her. Thank you, Manhattan, I will always love you.

The End.

Made in the USA
Columbia, SC
07 July 2020